WAR ZONE: MANHATTAN

Volodinsky pointed towards midtown Manhattan. "We could increase the destruction if you'd let us move the device towards the center of the island. Here we waste a third of the energy over the Hudson and East Rivers."

"No," Dubov quickly responded. "This site's been chosen for maximum psychological effect. The detonation's to be symbolic as well as physical. Five hundred thousand dead will be quite sufficient."

Gazing down South End Avenue at the apartment buildings stacked along Battery Place, Volodinsky sneered, "If it's so symbolic, Comrade, why not just blow up a few monuments in Washington?"

Impatiently, Dubov shook his head. "No, Doctor. It has been decided that there has to be a large number of civilian casualties. It's important to demonstrate we have the *will*, and the *means* to kill civilians." Looking out over lower Manhattan, he said, "Here, we have a large population and Wall Street. It's their showplace. Better to hit them here."

"Comrade Dubov, exactly what are our objectives?" asked Volodinsky.

"Easy, Doctor. It's best not to ask too many questions. Remember, curiosity killed the cat."

"But, to act like common terrorists?"

"Not terrorists," corrected Dubov. "What we do is an act of *war*."

THE
NOSTRADAMUS
PROPHECY

JOHN S. POWELL

LEISURE BOOKS NEW YORK CITY

A LEISURE BOOK®

December 1999

Published by

Dorchester Publishing Co., Inc.
276 Fifth Avenue
New York, NY 10001

ISBN 0-8439-4652-0

Printed in the United States of America.

ACKNOWLEDGMENTS

I thank my editor, G. Martha Hamblin, for her patience, encouragement, painstaking editing, and unrelenting attitude toward redundancies, errors, and lack of clarity. Her sharp eye for details, tireless fact checking, and timely suggestions have made this novel a much better book.

My appreciation goes to John Perlin and Dr. Beth Powell for their early critical readings of the first draft and their encouragement at a crucial stage. Also, to Mark and Maynard for their thoughtful analyses and recommendations. In addition, I am indebted to Geary Potter for her support and creative advice.

I am also grateful to the Perkins library and the Math & Physics library at Duke University for their excellent resources and helpful personnel. In addition, the following sources provided invaluable background information in my research for the novel: Both of Richard Rhodes's excellent, readable books, *The Making of the Atomic Bomb* (1986) and *Dark Sun: The Making of the Hydrogen Bomb* (1995); the US government publication, *The Effects of Nuclear Weapons* (1977); Michael Riordan's *The Day after Midnight* (1982); Kevin N. Lewis's article "The Prompt and Delayed Effects of Nuclear War," *Scientific American* (July, 1979); the Gale Research Company publication, *The Effects of Nuclear War* (1979); and all issues of *The Bulletin of the Atomic Scientists* for the past ten years for their continual monitoring of the global threat posed by the proliferation of nuclear weapons.

Some of the more important publications used for background on the workings of the intelligence services are Polamar and Allen's *Spy Book: The Encyclopedia of Espionage* (1997); Lee Lapin's *The Whole Spy Catalog* (1995); Mark Perry's *Eclipse* (1992); Bob Woodward's *Veil:*

The Secret Wars of the CIA 1981-1987 (1987); Philip Knightley's *The Second Oldest Profession: Spies and Spying in the Twentieth Century* (1986); Christopher Andrew's *For the President's Eyes Only* (1995); Samuel Katz's *Soldier Spies: Israeli Military Intelligence* (1992); *Jane's Security and Co-In Equipment*, Ian Hogg, editor (1992); Vladimir Kuzichkin's *Inside the KGB* (1990); and all issues for the last three years of the *Covert Action Quarterly*.

Last, but not least, I would like to acknowledge the following sources for information on Nostradamus and his prophecies: John Hogue's *Nostradamus & the Millennium* (1987) and his *Nostradamus: The New Revelations* (1994); Francis X. King's *Nostradamus: Prophecies Fulfilled and Predictions for the Millennium & Beyond* (1994); and Henry Roberts's *The Complete Prophecies of Nostradamus* (1982).

THE
NOSTRADAMUS
PROPHECY

Chapter 1

"*I—I've done it. The gate opener's turned off,*" whispered the soft, feminine voice into the micro-transmitter. "*He'll be here in ten minutes.*"

"This is Backfire-one. All units, check weapons," ordered the stocky leader of the elite *Spetsnaz* commando unit. Brushing fresh snowflakes from the cold eyepieces of the Zeiss binoculars, he scanned the gravel pathway leading up to the entrance of the two story, brick dacha. All was quiet. The harsh light from two 1,000-watt floodlamps glistened off the soft, dry snow clinging to the ornate, wrought iron gates.

"Disengage safeties. All units report."

"*Backfire-two, ready.*"

"*Backfire-three, in position.*"

The black Mercedes slowed to a crawl as it swung onto Statskevich Boulevard. Without turning, the driver tapped lightly on the glass partition separating him from the passenger's compartment.

General Nicolai Kuzov woke with a start. There already? He sat up, rubbing his tired eyes and loosening the black, army-issue tie. It had been a long, hard day. Endless reports, dozens of calls from a stream of mindless, meddling bureaucrats, *and* that visit from General Zakharov. His brow knitted into a frown. *Why the sudden interest by the Federal Security Service in how many warheads had been dismantled?* Zakharov couldn't suspect—there was no evidence. Tongues had wagged when Kuzov bought a new Mercedes, but that was over a month ago. Besides, what important Russian general didn't have a little private business on the side? No, it was a coincidence, nothing more. A personal visit from an old comrade.

He watched the familiar neighborhood glide by as the black, Chevy Suburban chase car carrying his security detail pulled ahead. In ten minutes he would be able to kick off these cheap military shoes, open a bottle of vintage Bordeaux and begin an evening of peek-and-snatch with little Olechka. He smiled as he thought of his new, buxom playmate. She was the perfect mistress. Twenty years old, blond, blue-eyed, and, above all, compliant. Better go easy on the wine, he chided himself, or he wouldn't last fifteen minutes. It wasn't that he was growing old. Fifty-three was still a good age, and the urge was still strong. It was just the constant, draining tension that always surrounded the disposal of nuclear warheads that sapped his energy.

The general settled back against the rich leather seats of the Mercedes. His nostrils flared with pleasure at the luxurious, new-car aroma. Reaching for a cigarette, he hesitated—smoke would only taint the delicate fragrance of the Algerian leather. He ran his hand lightly over the burled-walnut paneling, letting his fingers caress the swirls and texture. From now on, he would ride first class. No more freezing his butt off huddled in the back seat of a lumpy, rusting, government Zhiguli.

For a treat, he had brought along a bottle of 1987 Chateau Mouton-Rothschild and 200 grams of beluga caviar. His right arm tightened around the cold, silver ice bucket holding the caviar. Black market delicacies, they had cost a month's wages, but what didn't these days? Straight off a Ukrainian farm, Olechka was too country to appreciate such sophisticated pleasures, but he would teach her. He hoped she had remembered to bring the black leather restraining straps and that red satin halter, the one that made her breasts stick out like ski jumps.

He pulled a picture of his smiling mistress from the secret compartment in his wallet. She was lying on her back on white silk sheets, smiling seductively at the camera. He was lucky to have found such a passionate, responsive, unspoiled country girl. He preferred them young and simple, before they became jaded by the perversions of Moscow. Olechka was still warm and appreciative. He hoped she didn't become too secure and demanding—like the others.

The two strong shots of Stolichnaya vodka gulped down since leaving the office were starting to smooth out the jagged edges of the last few days. As head of security for the Twelfth Main Directorate it was his responsibility to provide protection for strategic nuclear warheads during transportation and storage. These last two weeks had been hell. Twelve hours on, twelve hours off. Nothing to eat but peasant food. The last take-down had included five SS-19 Stiletto missiles from ICBM silos in Aleysk and two SS-18 Satans from Uzhur. He drew the number *50* on the fogged window. Fifty warheads secured and transferred to their intermediate-staging bases. Not bad for a final effort. That was enough megatonnage to reduce Europe to radioactive rubble. He rubbed his hands together and reached for another Stoli miniature. With September's quota transferred and accounted for, it would be a month before the next batch was ready for disposal. By then, it would be someone else's headache.

The general's lips curled up in a smug, self-satisfied smile. In two weeks, he would be a *Novye Russkie*, one of Russia's new business elite. He could afford a fine home in London, Ireland, or perhaps Canada. No more making do with a vulgar, cheap, Moscow *cotedgi*. Some of his friends had dachas in Marbella on the Costa del Sol, but he preferred English-speaking countries. Good food, opera and plenty of willing, sensuous—but, what about Olechka? For a moment, he had almost forgotten her. Maybe he would take her along as his new personal secretary and tell Evgenia she was furnished and paid for by Moscow. That line just might work. Evgenia was dumb as a cow— she believed anything. But, it didn't matter. Evgenia had fallen too far into the bottle to care.

With his right index finger he scrawled *DM 7,500,000* beside the *50*. Just that day, confirmation had come in that the funds had been deposited into his numbered bank account in Liechtenstein. He had thought about using a Swiss bank but had decided against it. You couldn't trust those Swiss. They had been too damn eager to supply information to the Interior Ministry about his good friend, General Petrov. True, Petrov had been dealing in drugs, but why take a chance? No, Liechtenstein was better.

He underlined the figure. Seven and a half million deutsche marks.

All, invisible "black" money and all *un's*—untraceable, unaccounted for and untaxed. That would buy a lot of respect in his new life and a lot of Swiss chocolates for Olechka. He made a mental note to himself. Don't feed Olechka too many sweets. He didn't want her ballooning-up like Evgenia.

"*Slight delay ahead, Comrade General,*" crackled the voice over the car's radio. The driver of the chase car rolled down his window and waved for the Mercedes to stay back. "*The gates haven't opened.*"

"*Yadrena votsch,*" Kuzov grumbled. Another senseless delay. All because of those blasted cheap gate openers from Belarus. This was the third time this month they had jammed. He flipped on the car's intercom, "Dimitri, tell those lazy bastards to get out and open the gates by hand. I haven't got all night to—"

Whoomp! An explosion of blood and brains splattered the interior of the Mercedes' driver's compartment. A single, tungsten tipped 7.62mm round from a Dragunov sniper's rifle had sliced through the bullet-proof glass, shattering Dimitri's skull. The car lurched forward, slamming into the rear of the security vehicle.

Wham, Whomp, Whomp! Three .50in rounds from a Barrett 82A1 smashed into the Chevy chase car. The heavy 1,000-grain slugs pierced the engine block, slashing open fuel lines, flooding the vehicle's undercarriage with high-octane petrol. The car burst into flames, cremating the three wildly struggling bodyguards trapped inside. The guard who had stepped out to open the gates glowed like a human torch as burning gas engulfed his head and torso. Staggering three feet, he collapsed in slow motion, his arms stretched skyward in terminal supplication. The concussion from the exploding Chevy lifted the Mercedes off the pavement, hurling it back against a utility pole. Rivulets of burning fuel splashed over the hood, dripping onto the engine block.

A gray, unmarked van screeched to a halt beside the smoldering Mercedes. Six Spetsnaz commandos jumped out and began spraying layers of heavy foam over and under the car to keep the fire from reaching the fuel tank.

"Drag him out!" shouted the leader as flames began to lick up from under the hood.

The lock on the rear door was quickly drilled open and Kuzov was pulled out, bleeding and unconscious. Two commandos jerked a cotton sack over his head and dumped him roughly into the back of the waiting van. The Mercedes exploded in an orange ball of flame, rocking the van.

Inside the dacha, the lights blinked on.

"*We have him, Comrade Olechka. You will be rewarded for your cooperation.*"

"*Da,*" replied the calm voice as she reached for another chocolate bonbon.

OCTOBER 9: THE WHITE HOUSE

"Frankly, I don't give a rat's ass," declared Bruce Bastardi, pounding his fist on the finely polished, walnut conference table.

"Pardon?" replied Bryan Warner. This sophomoric outburst from the President's National Security Adviser surprised him. Such lack of control was out of place in a serious discussion about the veiled threats recently received from North Korea.

"Exactly *what* don't you understand, Mr. Warner?" Bastardi demanded, his voice dripping with spite. "As the CIA's Deputy Director of Operations, it's not your goddamned place to question what I say." Satisfied he had silenced Warner, Bastardi settled back in his leather judge's chair, his right eye twitching in agitation. He glanced irritably around his newly redecorated office, trying to regain his composure. It wasn't a corner office, but in Washington where proximity to the Oval Office defined the pecking order, his location on the first floor of the West Wing underscored his special influence with President Stephen J. Morehead.

Warner didn't reply. While he occasionally suffered fools, he never argued with them. Better to keep quiet than be dragged into a no-win shouting match.

The National Security Adviser's theatrics were an ominous sign of the personnel changes the White House had planned for the CIA. The Washington scuttlebutt—which had been carefully planted, nourished, then denied—said Oscar Shymanski was being groomed to take over as Director. Just last week the *Washington Post* had quoted a "reliable source" as stating that the President had approved a blueprint for, "cleaning out the Augean stables of deceit and mismanagement at Langley and bringing in new blood."

"I believe Mr. Warner was asking what the hell you meant by *your* statement that you don't care about Pyongyang's reaction," Stirling Phillips interjected coolly. As Chief Negotiator for the State Department's team handling the Geneva nuclear accord, Phillips was not intimidated by Bastardi's tantrum. A close personal friend of Senator Andrew Coffin, Chairman of the Senate's powerful Foreign Relations Committee, Phillips was politically immune to such threats.

"I'm sorry, Mr. Phillips," Bastardi apologized. It infuriated him that Warner and Phillips had been roommates at Annapolis. Their friendship was the only block to his having convinced Morehead to replace the DDO weeks ago. "My point is that North Korea doesn't have a choice. They either allow our inspectors to verify that their nuclear weapons program has been frozen, or we'll have Seoul stop work on those two 1,000-megawatt, light-water reactors."

"North Korea *always* has a choice," Phillips replied, pulling out a pack of Winston cigarettes and placing it beside one of the four No Smoking signs on the conference table. Lighting up, he continued, "What concerns me is the failure of the President's advisers to understand that simple fact." He had tried several times to convey to Morehead how destabilizing it would be to Kim Jong Il's government if construction of the $4 billion nuclear reactors were discontinued or canceled.

"Stirling, what's your worst case scenario?" Warner asked.

"It's bad, Bryan. Ever since Kim Il Sung died in '94, there's been a power vacuum in Pyongyang. Last week South Korean intelligence informed me there's a showdown brewing between Kim and some of the younger firebrands in the military. If work on those two reactors doesn't continue on schedule, Kim's going to lose face. If that happens—"

Warner finished the sentence, "A coup with an invasion of the South."

Phillips nodded. "That's the way I see it."

"That's not the Security Council's assessment at all," Bastardi declared, flapping his hand in front of his face to dispel the cigarette smoke. "They wouldn't dare attack Seoul. What concerns us are the reports that Pyongyang's been cheating on its nuclear weapons program." Turning to Warner, he added, "If the DO could do its job, we'd know what the hell's going on over there. We'd know if they've got four nuclear warheads and whether they're busting their little butts trying to crank out another five or six. But, no. Here we are with the world's *greatest* intelligence service, and we don't know jackshit."

Warner started to protest, "Mr. Bastardi, I can assure you that—"

"Christ, if we had to launch a peremptory strike on their nuclear facilities, we wouldn't know where to start."

Once again, Warner forced himself to keep his temper in check. Unfortunately, there was some truth to the accusation. North Korea had always been a hard target and the CIA didn't have a single asset in place who knew the location or workings of their nuclear weapons program. The end result was that a key part of the US's Asian policy was being dictated by a paranoid, cold war, Stalinistic regime in Pyongyang, stuck in a time warp dating back to the early 1950s.

"I can't put my finger on it," Phillips said, "but something big is in the wind. Things have gotten too quiet in Pyongyang. We're not getting the usual chatter."

"Think there's already been a coup?"

"Possibly. At our meeting in Berlin last week there was a whole new set of negotiators. Mostly young, gung-ho military types. They stated their position, then clammed up. No haggling, no counterproposals, no refusals, no nothing. Just glassy-eyed stares and vacant, fixed smiles."

"If those bastards try anything—" Bastardi said, clenching his fist.

Ignoring the bluster, Philips turned to Warner, "There's no telling what they'll do. Their rice bowls are empty, their stomachs are growling and the whole economy's in shambles. Combine that with a standing army almost as large as ours and it could be crunch time."

OCTOBER 10: MOSCOW

General Stepka Filip Zakharov leaned forward in his wheel chair and squinted through the grimy, one-way mirror overlooking room 273. As head of the Federal Security Service's Moscow branch, he was a familiar figure at the Lubyanka interrogation center. In the middle of the next room, strapped to a soiled gurney, lay the crumpled body of General Nicolai Kuzov.

"Doctor, how's the prisoner?" Zakharov asked as he reached for his ever-present oxygen mask. The stale cigarette odors, combined with the stench of body fluids and disinfectants, were beginning to irritate his lungs.

A look of concern crossed the face of the heavy-set nurse hovering by Zakharov's side. After fluffing the pillow behind his back, she made minor adjustments to the flow of oxygen. Built like a Vladivostok longshoreman, she kneaded the general's wasted, aching muscles with the sensitive touch of a professional safe-cracker.

"General, you must not exert yourself," admonished Doctor Babin, the psychiatrist overseeing the interrogation. He had decided it would be wise to show concern for a man powerful enough to treat a general from the Twelfth Main Directorate like a common criminal. Usually Babin looked forward to interrogations, but not this one. A sense of foreboding made his hands tremble.

"Don't bother with me, Doctor. Concern yourself with the prisoner," snapped Zakharov. The questioning was dragging out. It wouldn't be long before military intelligence—the *Glavnoe Razvedyvatel'noe Upravlenie*—started asking questions. When the conspirators discovered Kuzov was at Lubyanka, important government officials would demand the investigation be stopped.

"We conditioned the patient as fast as we could," Babin protested. A professional, he took pride in his work and good work could not be rushed. To get the patient to regress to the point of cooperation, there were drugs that had to be administered and psychological pressures that had to be applied. Babin always referred to the prisoners as "patients." It salved his conscience about using his medical skills to keep them alive, at least until the interrogations were finished.

"There, see *that*?" Babin announced, pointing to an erratic blip on the EEG monitor. "He's hallucinating now, completely disoriented. Doesn't know whether he's dead or alive." As additional, sharp, irregular waves jutted across the screen, he added, "The patient is in great pain."

The EKG monitor began beeping and flashing a red warning light. Babin muted the electrocardiograph, "The ordeal is taxing his heart. I must warn—er—advise you, Comrade General, his heartbeat is very irregular. If we continue, it could go into arrhythmia."

General Zakharov grabbed the intercom microphone. "Major Ivanov, come to the control room."

"Right away, Comrade General," answered the interrogator. The fastidiously dressed technician carefully removed his rubber gloves and apron, and wiped a few drops of spittle and blood from the collar of his starched shirt. Glancing at his reflection in the one-way mirror, he straightened his tie, then slid back the door and entered the darkened observation room. As the pupils of his eyes adjusted to the dim light, his thin, spare lips formed a perfunctory smile. He stuck out a delicate, sensitive hand, "Comrade General—"

Zakharov scowled and looked away.

The Major stiffened, then slowly pulled back his hand.

The General detested the slightly built Major with the tinted glasses and neatly trimmed beard. Although such people were necessary, he didn't consider them comrades and refused to show them the respect due regular soldiers. Had the conspirators struck first, it could just as easily have been him lying there naked, half-dead, stretched out on that filthy gurney. It would have made no difference to Ivanov.

"What has he told you?" Zakharov demanded.

The corners of the Major's mouth turned down. He had met these condescending, tin-pot soldiers before. They needed information but were too soft and weak to get it themselves. Still, they were dangerous, and it was better not to cross them. Turning, he peered through the mirror at the broken figure on the gurney. "For the past hour he's been babbling, muttering gibberish about Swiss chocolates and deutsche marks. Occasionally, there's some mention of warheads. That was his job, disposing of nuclear warheads."

"I know, I know," grumbled the General. "Specifics, Major, I need specifics."

Looking over his notes, Ivanov wiped a drop of urine from the plastic covered pad. He disliked messy notes, it was a sign of sloppy technique. "This morning, at 1015, he confirmed the warheads are thermonuclear and that the transfer has already taken place. Then, he mumbled something about 'Phoenicians, Phoenix.' I couldn't make it out. The computer room has it for analysis. It may be important—"

"Damn it, he's trying to hold out," General Zakharov muttered. By now the GRU's moles at Lubyanka would be calling their masters. "And the sponsor? Did he say who paid him?"

"He refuses—I'm not sure he knows. He did say the operation was brokered by a Russian syndicate, the Dolgochenskaya—"

"I don't care about the syndicate," growled Zakharov. "I want to know who financed the project, who's making the decisions. He must know. What about the money? What has he done with that?"

The Major shrugged, "I tried—but, he refuses."

"Let me talk to him," General Zakharov snapped, rising slowly and painfully from his wheelchair and shuffling towards the interrogation room. Turning to Babin he wagged a bony, index finger, "Doctor, don't let anything happen to our prisoner."

Babin glanced at the overhead monitors. The vital signs were deteriorating. Mustering courage, he said, "Comrade General, if the interrogation continues, I cannot—*cannot* be held responsible. He must rest. Please—an hour or two, then you—"

"We can't wait," General Zakharov declared. Sliding open the door and stepping into the interrogation room, he stood beside the prostrate figure. In a voice both pleading and demanding he said, "Nicolai, Nicolai, it's me, Stepka. Can you hear me?"

After a brief pause, the dark, sunken eyes blinked open. Gradually, they focused in recognition. A feeble, strained voice garbled, "Stepka, is that really you? Help me!"

Holding onto the railing of the gurney for support, Zakharov said, "Nicolai, I came here to help. But, I can't—unless you tell them the name of the state sponsor. It's not your fault. You've done your best. Who was it? Who paid you?"

"It–It was the Dolgochenskaya syndicate. They forced me to do it, Stepka. I didn't want to—"

"I understand, Nicolai. It was the others," Zakharov said, soothingly. "But, the syndicate was only the go-between. You said something about 'Phoenicians.' Did they furnish the money?" He waited for a reply. "Was it Iraq? Iran? Libya?"

The eyes closed, the lips moved, but there was no sound. After a pause, the mouth slowly, painfully formed words, "Stepka, I–I can't remember."

Zakharov moved closer, "Nicolai, the people who are doing these terrible things *know* there was a sponsor. Some country with lots of money. They won't stop until you tell them."

"Help—help me, Stepka."

Zakharov backed into the shadows at the far corner of the room. He could see the terrified eyes searching for him. After a brief wait he stepped back into the light. "Nicolai, I want to help. But how? If you don't give them the name, the pain will only increase. They have Olechka. Unless you talk—"

"No—not little Olechka!"

"Tell me and I'll save her. I promise you, as your friend."

Kuzov's eyes blinked. He tried to raise his left arm. It strained against the straps, then fell back.

The intercom crackled, "*Comrade General, the pulse is growing weaker.*"

Once again, the pale lips began to move. Zakharov leaned closer while Kuzov gathered his remaining strength. In a rasping whisper he told Zakharov what he wanted to know.

"Good. Now, tell me what you did with the money and I'll have them release you."

"I–I–" The body on the gurney stiffened, the eyes closed. Then, the body gradually relaxed. A gurgling noise bubbled up from the swollen lips as a rush of air broke free.

The door to the interrogation room slid open. "Comrade General, all monitors are flat!"

General Zakharov looked down at the still figure. There was a tranquil expression on the ashen face. It always amazed him how peaceful the dead appeared. He patted the bare, heavy-set shoulder. Three days ago Kuzov had it all. Now this. Zakharov shook his head. Fortune smiles, then betrays. Lady Luck is a whore.

OCTOBER 14: ATLANTIC CITY, NEW JERSEY

It was dark when the three men dressed in seamen's dungarees, denim shirts, and black wool sweaters stopped in front of The Golden Dragon Tattoo Parlor. The faded lettering at the top of the door read: 2604 Atlantic Avenue. A garish, neon Chinese dragon winked at the trio through an unwashed window. A cardboard placard promising "Traditional, New Wave and Custom Artistic Skin Illustrations with Hospital-type Sterilization" was taped to the glass panel. The tallest of the three knocked on the door.

Behind tightly drawn blinds, a fluorescent light flickered on. A low-pitched voice clattered over an intercom. "Yeah, whadda you want?"

"We're here for tattoos. We called earlier," said Alexander Dubov, in fluent American with a slight English accent.

"Did you bring da money?"

"Fifteen hundred, cash."

"Okay, okay, keep your shirt on." A rustling was heard, then a metallic, sliding *clunk* as two sets of deadbolts were released. "C'mon in," said the forty-seven-year-old tattooist. His sun-weathered skin was the texture and color of old parchment. An off-white T-shirt read, "Get Pricked by a Pro, Captain Z, Artist-in-residence. Irezumi Ink."

The tattooist's thin body was a walking billboard for his trade. Images of snakes and flowers ran up his arms and across his back. Drawings of dragons and anchors decorated his neck and the backs of his hands. Without ceremony he led them to the rear of his shop, past hundreds of designs pasted on the walls. Pointing to the sheets, he said, "If you likes any of dem flashes, I can do 'em all."

"No, we want custom work," said Dubov. "We have our own designs."

"Okay," muttered the tattooist. "No problem. I do good originals, best work on da Boardwalk." He looked up defensively, "I ain't no scratcher." Satisfied his artistic talent wasn't being challenged, he relaxed. "Half da money now and half when I'm done."

Dubov pulled six color photos from a large, manila envelope. He handed them to Captain Z. "Can you duplicate these? I want *exact* copies."

Examining the primitive details and occasionally shaking his head, the tattooist rasped, "I can do better then dat crap with my eyes closed. Dat's shit work, nothing but jailhouse tattoos. Must've been done by some amateur with a knife and fork."

"That's what I want."

"And you want temps?" Shaking his head at the waste, Captain Z snorted, "You sure you gonna pay me fifteen hundred bucks for dese cockamamies?"

"That's right, but they've got to last for at least three days.""

"Dey'll last two weeks if you takes care of 'em."

Dubov nodded and handed over seven hundred and fifty dollars.

Captain Z slowly counted the bills. Satisfied, he said, "Okay, it's your money. Kid's play. It'll take three, maybe four hours."

Tapping Dima on the shoulder, Dubov said, "You go first."

"*Da.*"

"You sounds like Russians," sneered the tattooist, showing huge gaps between tobacco stained teeth. Getting no response, he said, "Okay, take off your shirt."

Removing his sweater and denim shirt, Dima sat down in the cheap metal chair covered by a gray towel. He stared at the glistening row of needles lined up on the shelf in front of him.

Noticing Dima's expression, Captain Z said, "When you wants real tattoos, like a *real* man, come back and see me. Won't cost any more than dese fakes." Turning his attention to the photographs, he asked, "Which ones do you get?"

"These," responded Dubov, selecting two photos.

Captain Z examined the illustrations carefully. "Dose are some mean travel marks. Let's see. You wants dis one of a knife going through da neck, painted on da shoulders? Den, you want dis here one of a gangster with a machine gun painted on da chest?" Eyeing Dubov suspiciously, Captain Z said, "I seen dis kinda work before. Some Russian gangster was showing it off. Said he got it in da slammer. Claims all da convicts over dere got dem kinda marks."

"That's right," Dubov replied. "We're shooting a TV series in Brighton Beach. These two guys have bit parts as Russian gangsters."

"Yeah?" came the response. Captain Z had heard all sorts of lies, but he didn't care. For him it was just another job.

In an hour and a half the artist had finished with Dima. Leaning forward, he pulled the fluorescent light closer for a final inspection. Holding the photographs beside the illustrations he mumbled a satisfied, "Humph."

The copies were exact. Had Dubov not known they were merely painted on, he would have sworn they were the original tattoos.

"Next," said Captain Z crooking his finger at Petya. "Hop up to da throne. Let's see. You gets a—whadda you call dat thing?"

"Epaulet, it goes on the right shoulder."

"Yeah, epaulet, dat's it. And dis one, a skull with a dagger going through da eye and coming out da back?"

"The skull goes on his right forearm. Also, I want three cupolas across the shoulder blades with the numbers 19:28 at the end."

"Yeah, da Leviticus."

"Leviticus?"

"It's from da bible. You know da quote, 'Thou shall not make any cuttings in your flesh or tattoo any marks upon your body.' "

By 1:30 A.M. Captain Z had finished. "Good job," Dubov commented, pulling out his billfold. It was with regret that he nodded to Petya. Captain Z was an excellent artist.

"I can do body piercing—eyebrows, septums, ears, da head of your schlong, navels, whatever."

"Not today," Dubov said, removing seven, one-hundred dollar bills, two twenties and a ten.

"You can remove da temps by—"

Whup, whup, whup! Three slugs from Petya's silenced .38 Smith and Wesson slammed into the back of Captain Z's skull. The tattooist's head jerked forward, his shocked eyes staring into space. The body lurched forward, crashing into the autoclave, spurting blood over Dubov's face and sweater. The torso convulsed for thirty seconds, then stopped.

Dubov grabbed a hand towel from the back of the work bench and wiped the sticky, warm fluid from his clothes and skin. Waving the bloody rag at Dima he said, "Pull out some drawers and throw that junk on the floor. Make it look like a robbery."

Using alcohol, Petya wiped down the pistol, then tossed it into a corner trash can. Turning off the lights, the three men left the parlor, quietly closing the door behind them. Outside, the air was fresh and clean with a cool breeze blowing in from the ocean. Two blocks away, three blue-hairs, bused in from New York on the "Golden Age Special," huddled around a picnic table counting their losses from the rigged slots at Captain Nemo's Potluck Parlor.

Chapter 2

OCTOBER 15: CIA HEADQUARTERS, LANGLEY, VIRGINIA
The landing gear of the JetRanger helicopter struck the concrete landing pad with a jolt, sending a shock wave racing up Patrick Murphy's spine. The impact ripped the Compaq laptop from his grasp, sending it crashing into the fire extinguisher bolted immediately aft of the pilot's seat.

"Damn," muttered Murphy, catching his breath and collecting his thoughts. Bending over, he retrieved the broken remains. He hoped the hard drive hadn't been damaged.

Staring through the Plexiglas window at the driving rain, he shook his head. What should have been a routine landing procedure had turned into a white-knuckle, near-death experience. This was the third close call in less than a month.

Murphy checked his watch. 10:30P.M. What could be so rush-rush with Warner that would force the pilot to land in this slush? Bad enough to be jerked away, mid-putt, from his first real vacation in two years, but having to hustle back to Langley aboard the helicopter-from-hell was not a good sign.

"Sorry, sir" apologized the pilot, still frozen to the controls. It was clear he hadn't anticipated that last gust.

"It's okay," Murphy said sympathetically. "You did fine, it's just the weather." There was no need to blame the hapless pilot, he was stressed enough as it was. "Thanks for the ride."

Murphy braced himself. He could see the rain sweeping across the landing pad in sheets, big drops splattering the concrete. Grabbing the battered laptop, he took a firm grip on his new sunshine yellow, golf umbrella, and uttering a soft, "Geronimo," pushed open the helicopter door. Stepping into the downpour, he hit the umbrella's pop-up button. A sudden gust of wind slammed into the fabric, inverting his prized purchase into a walking stick with skirt.

A black staff car screeched to a halt ten feet outside the downdraft from the rotor blades. In a crouched position Murphy splashed over, grabbed the door handle, and gave it a hard tug. It was locked. He pounded on the roof with the umbrella handle.

The driver flipped the lock, reached over and pushed open the door. "Sorry, sir," he said with a sheepish grin.

Sorry, sir? That was the second, "sorry, sir," in less than five minutes. Murphy's day was not ending well.

It took three minutes to reach the entrance to the sprawling CIA headquarters complex. After surviving the scrutiny and smirks of the security guards, Murphy went to the men's room to dry off and survey the damage. It was hopeless.

Squishing his way down the corridor, he entered the elevator. Up two floors, he turned right, then sloshed over to an unmarked door. It was the office of Bryan Warner, head of the Directorate of Operations, the CIA's clandestine side of the house.

Murphy started to knock, but paused. A chill ran down his neck, radiating out both arms, causing his whole body to shudder. His grandmother, a believer in signs, had once told him that a sudden chill meant someone had just stepped on your grave. Standing there with his hand poised in mid-air like a statue, he muttered, "It's the damn rain." Gritting his teeth, he rapped twice, then entered.

Angela Ramirez, Warner's administrative assistant, glanced up from her desk, "Murphy, you're looking—how can I put it—*wet*. There's still room on the Ark—which animal group?"

"Yeah, real funny, a barrel of laughs," he responded half-heartedly. Catching a glimpse of his reflection in the glass partition behind Ramirez' desk, he grimaced.

"Wait a second, I'll buzz you in. Mr. Warner's been waiting." Placing her hand to the side of her mouth, she whispered, "Something's up. And, it's big."

The intercom light blinked, "*Is that Murphy?*"

Pointing towards the shattered umbrella, Ramirez said, "Hey, Mary–Mary Poppins. You may as well leave your transportation here."

Murphy's shoes squeaked the seven steps to the door labeled Private. Wet imprints on the carpet marked each step. After knocking, he entered.

The office was spacious, well-lit and Spartanly furnished. At the far end was a plain oak desk with a large leather chair. A rectangular conference table, surrounded by six, slatted hardback chairs, occupied the center of the room. Along the walls ran a series of bookshelves crammed with legal texts, international treatises, psychological studies and dictionaries in Russian, French, German, Spanish and Farsi. On the wall behind the desk was a framed Annapolis diploma, a citation for the Navy Cross and a series of five, plainly framed Vietnam-era photographs. In each picture, small groups of smiling, young naval and marine officers posed self-consciously for the camera. In the center photo, a beaming naval Lieutenant held the corner of a Viet Cong battle flag. It was Warner, circa 1972, a week before the ambush that air-vacced him to a hospital ship with a leg full of shrapnel. Holding the other end, dressed in camouflage combat fatigues, were Marine Second Lieutenants Laurence Clarke and Patrick Murphy.

Warner motioned Murphy to a seat. "Sorry for the inconvenience, the rain and all that. Better take off that wet jacket." Walking over to a closet, he withdrew three hand towels and a charcoal gray sweater, and tossed them over. "Haven't seen it rain this hard since the monsoons in 'Nam."

While Murphy removed his coat, Warner said, "Received a message this morning from a walk-in who looks like he may be a Russian insider. He's using Cairo as home base." Taking a seat at the conference table across from Murphy, he continued, "The source claims that several loose nuclear warheads are in unfriendly hands and headed this way."

Murphy's eyes widened. He was no longer tired or bothered by the damp clothes. "How good's the information?"

"Don't know," Warner replied, selecting a Cuban cigar from a mahogany humidor. "All we've got so far is a single, unconfirmed report. Is our source legitimate? Don't know. Are his bona fides solid?

Don't know. Are there really loose nukes headed this way? Probably not, but we're damn well going to check it out."

"Bottom line, Bryan, what's your best guess?"

"I've got a bad feeling about this one." He took a long puff on the cigar, then blew the smoke out in small circles. "Message was sent from Paris. Had a couple of references to code phrases known only to a handful of top level Russian muckety-mucks. Course, that doesn't prove anything, but, still—"

Murphy was struck by how tired Warner appeared. As Deputy Director of Operations, he had aged visibly in the two and a half years since taking over as head of the DO. The wrinkles and dark shadows around the eyes marked him as a prematurely old fifty-two.

Warner stood and walked to the window, "I want you to go to Cairo and check it out. You know Egypt and how the Soviet system used to function. I figure our source is probably a member of the old guard."

Murphy nodded. "You mentioned several nukes—"

"Message said five. But before we get into that, let's bring in Kathryn Mills. She's our FBI liaison." Warner flicked the switch on the intercom, "Ms. Ramirez, please send in Ms. Mills."

The door opened and a self-assured, thirty-two-year-old woman with a trim build, short blond hair, and smooth, suntanned skin strode in. She was dressed in L.L. Bean, late evening, office casual. Her clear eyes and quick stride evidenced a health food and exercise regimen Murphy had long since abandoned.

Jesus, thought Murphy as he stood up. She looked like she'd just stepped out of a granola bar commercial. Where did the Bureau find these Ken and Barbie doll people? Glancing at her small waist, he tried to suck in his own gut. There had been an inch of slippage since Christmas. He had meant to keep up his jogging routine, but the couch potato's law of physics—a body in motion tends to stay in motion, a body at rest tends to stay at rest—had interfered.

"Please call me Kat, with a 'K,'" she said, grasping Murphy's hand in a strong, confident handshake.

Murphy took a deep breath. She smelled soapsuds fresh. Probably just stepped out of a redwood hot tub after a half-hour workout on a StairMaster. He thought of his own image—matted hair, damp, disheveled clothes. She must *really* be impressed.

"Just call me Murphy, with an 'M,'" he said, in a weak attempt at humor. When she took her seat, he noticed there was no wedding ring on her left hand.

Warner parked his cigar in an ashtray. "We're fortunate to have Ms. Mills with us. Her credentials are top notch. In addition to FBI, she's a veteran of the DOE's Nuclear Emergency Search Team."

Murphy nodded. He was familiar with NEST's history. It had been founded in 1975, after the FBI received a demand from a would-be blackmailer to pony-up $200,000 or see Boston vaporized. The specialized organization of over 1,000 on-call volunteers, was the Department of Energy's response to an Executive order to build a strike force capable of chasing down and neutralizing hostile nuclear warheads on American soil. Murphy had visited their Pajarito site in Los Alamos and watched them construct dummy, homemade nuclear bombs using Radio Shack components. Their current logbook showed 110 threats to date, for which they had been mobilized thirty-one times. All had been false alarms—so far.

"Did you take part in Mirage Gold?" Murphy asked.

"Sure did," came the quick response. "Love those French Quarter beignets and that chicory coffee."

Warner looked up. "Mirage Gold? Don't believe I've heard of that one."

"It was a joint exercise in New Orleans between the Bureau and NEST," Kat replied. "Our objective was to locate three fictitious nuclear warheads hidden in the city by a terrorist group calling themselves the 'Patriots for National Unity.'"

Warner nodded, "Ms. Mills is also an expert on Russian crime syndicates. She spent two years with the Bureau's C-24 Russian Organized Crime unit in New York."

Staring at Kat with a mixture of admiration and envy, Murphy asked, "You figure the Russian syndicates are involved?" To be so young, her 201 personnel file was certainly crowded.

"Wouldn't be surprised," Kat answered. "Not much goes on in Russia that some *organizatsiya* doesn't control or have its hooks in. The whole country's one big thieves' world, or as they call it, *vorovskoi mir*. Right now, rumors are circulating that if the money's right, nuclear materials are available."

Kat's knowledge of the market for bomb grade nuclear products had been gained first hand. Last November, the Bureau sent her to Germany to check on a 5.6-gram cache of plutonium-239 the *Bundeskriminalamt* had found in an auto mechanic's garage. In December, she went to Prague to examine a six pound shipment of uranium-235 seized by Czech police. It had been hidden in a car occupied by a Russian, a Belarusian, and a Czech nuclear scientist. Most troubling to the Bureau were reports that the New York Russian syndicates were trolling for nuclear materials.

"Read where the FBI's opened an office in Moscow," said Murphy. It was still hard for him to adjust to the changes that had taken place since the break up of the USSR. He knew it was a case of an old dog and new tricks, but the thought of the Russian Federal Security Service and Interior Ministry sharing top-secret files with the FBI and CIA just didn't compute. "Sounds downright chummy."

"It is," replied Kat, with a mischievous grin.

Murphy turned to Warner. "Bryan, if nuclear warheads are headed this way, what's the drill? Who's going to be in charge of the investigation?"

"It'll have to be a combined effort. There won't be time for pissing contests. Until they reach the US, we'll be lead dog. Once they've crossed the border, the ball goes over to the Bureau and NEST.

"From what I've seen in Europe, the toughest problem is going to be establishing credibility," said Kat.

"How so?" asked Murphy.

"In Germany there were too many agencies, too many rumors and too much background noise. It was almost impossible to separate fact from fiction. Nobody seemed to know what was going on."

Murphy knew Kat wasn't exaggerating. Any search for nuclear warheads would involve the FBI, the CIA, the National Security Agency, the DOE's Nuclear Emergency Search Team, the National Reconnaissance Office, and the Defense Intelligence Agency, just to name six of the country's seventeen separate intelligence services. If Russia was thrown into the mix you could add the Federal Security Service, the Russian Interior Ministry, and Military Intelligence.

Warner reached across the table and handed Murphy and Kat briefing packets labeled *Top Secret.* "Inside is the message we received this morning. It was encrypted in the Evergreen code."

"The Evergreen?" asked Kat. "Isn't that highly restricted? I thought that was Eyes Only between the heads of the CIA-FBI and FSB-MVD."

"Exactly," replied Warner, impressed with Kat's knowledge of codes. "It's supposed to be limited to reports on missing nuclear materials. It indicates our source must be pretty high up."

Murphy and Kat opened their packets:

> To Bryan Warner, DDO, CIA:
> Kali has awakened. She has five children, one small, four large. She has been with us for more than 60 days. Her dance debut is scheduled for the US. The midwives are the Shaheeds of the Islamic Ummah. Send to Cairo your personal representative *with full authority.* Will not deal through Cairo Station. Reply to Paris, fax 38-347779. Must trade. Most urgent!
>
> Walnut

Warner stood and walked over to a chart hooked to an easel. "Let's examine what we've got." He wrote in big letters, *Kali has awakened.* "That's Evergreen for nuclear weapons are missing."

"Are we talking small, tactical warheads or something in the strategic, megaton range?" Murphy asked.

"One small, four large. I assume large means strategic—probably in the hundreds of kilotons. I hope not as big as a megaton. Maybe the small one's tactical. There's a breakdown of Russia's stockpile in your packet."

In the briefing material was a listing of the most recent data available on Russia's arsenal. Of 30,000 nuclear warheads still in existence, an estimated 11,750 were currently shown as operational. Of these, 7,250 were designated strategic offensive, with large nuclear payloads in various ICBMs, submarine launched missiles, and Russian Blackjack and Bear bombers. Twelve hundred were classified strategic defensive mounted in Gazelle and Gorgon anti-ballistic and Gammon and Grumble surface-to-air missiles. An additional 1,600 were land based non-strategic, housed in air force Backfire, Blinder, Badger, and Fencer fighters and bombers. Finally, there were 500 naval non-strategic warheads in submarine launched cruise missiles; 600 in their Backfire, Bear, Badger, and Blinder naval attack aircraft, and 500 torpedoes and depth bombs in various anti-submarine warfare weapons. The nuclear physics packages from the 18,250 non-operational, dismantled warheads were being stored as pits in leaky warehouses scattered throughout Russia. It was not a reassuring report.

Murphy ran his finger along the middle section of the message. "'She has been with us for more than 60 days. Her dance debut is scheduled for the US.'"

Warner frowned. "That's the troubling part. It's telling us the warheads disappeared over sixty days ago and will be used in the US."

"When you say 'used,' do you mean—"

"Used. That's right—detonated. At least that's the way I read it."

"Sixty days. They could already be here," Kat observed. "What's the Director's reaction?"

"Not much," Warner replied, lowering his eyes. "Vaughn wants to know more about the source before he gets too excited." Warner didn't care to admit it, but the message couldn't have come at a worse time for the Agency. Daniel Vaughn had been Director of the CIA for less than two months and was still in the early stages of his learning curve. A Pentagon analyst, he had been President Morehead's fifth choice for ringmaster of America's intelligence services. A Harvard Ph.D., Vaughn was more at home analyzing Star Wars' laser guidance systems than managing people. He had been pressured into accepting the position by his old friend, Senator Wayne Hawk, Chairman of the Senate Intelligence Committee. A Republican and critic of the Morehead Administration, Hawk had demanded someone he could trust as head of the country's intelligence function.

"Has anyone checked with the Russians to see if any warheads are missing?" asked Kat.

"We're in the process," replied Warner. "Oscar Shymanski, the Agency's new Executive Director, insists on personally handling that part of the investigation. Says he wants to be sure we don't rush in and make fools of ourselves."

All Murphy could do was roll his eyes. Shymanski was chief yes-man and water boy for Bruce Bastardi, the President's paranoid National Security Adviser. With a Democrat as President and a Republican Congress, Bastardi had shoehorned Shymanski into the intelligence system to serve as chief damage control officer for the Administration. It was his task to head off embarrassing investigations into White House policies and personnel.

Turning his attention back to the message, Murphy asked, "What's this reference to the Shaheeds of the Islamic Ummah? Are they terrorists?"

"Could be," replied Warner. "Translated it means 'Martyrs of the Islamic Community.'" Warner was wary of any organization with the term *martyr* in its title. "We put the name on the Interlink. Nothing so far." Turning to Kat, he asked, "Any leads at the Bureau?"

"Negative, sir. We're still checking with Interpol and a few other sources."

"Better enter *Shaheeds* into ECHELON's dictionaries," said Murphy. He had used NSA's world-wide snooping system before for locating hard-to-find terrorists. No transmission—e-mail, fax, telex, telephone—goes out or comes in anywhere in the world that isn't scanned by ECHELON's computers for an extensive list of keywords.

"'Will not deal through Cairo Station'? Is there a problem with security in Cairo?" Kat asked.

"Maybe our source doesn't think Cairo can handle the deal, or maybe he just wants special attention," Warner replied. He frowned as he realized he would now have to formally notify the FBI that Cairo Station's integrity was in question. Bringing in the Bureau's National Security Division to check on CIA personnel always bothered him.

"The message is signed, 'Walnut,'" observed Murphy.

"That was the code name for a Soviet walk-in whose case was bungled by a couple of CIA officers in the late 1980s. He knew the workings of the Soviet football. Your friend Friar was his case officer for a couple of months. He warned Walnut off when he suspected there was a mole in our Soviet Section. Good thing he did, or Walnut would've been at the top of Aldrich Ames's hit list."

"Who's Friar?" Kat asked.

"Name's Laurence Clarke," Murphy replied, with a grin. "He and I go back a long ways. We shared a cell together for four years as cadets at the Virginia Military Institute." Murphy walked over to the photo behind Warner's desk, the one with the young officers holding a VC flag. "Here we are in Vietnam, keeping the country safe for democracy. He's the six-foot-three, I'm the five-foot-ten."

Kat examined the photo, noting the young, hopeful faces.

"He was something of a legend here at the DO before taking early retirement," Warner said.

"A real cowboy, " Murphy said, approvingly. "Lives in North Carolina with his wife, Marcie. She was a CIA analyst for several years. Fact is, they met at Langley."

"Is he on retainer?" asked Kat.

Murphy laughed, "Yeah. But, only as an analyst. Marcie's got him on a short leash—no field work. His specialty was counterterrorism. This case would be right up his alley."

"How'd he get the name Friar?"

"I started calling him Friar Laurence after he laid a real doozy of a honey trap for Colonel Vlynskji, the KGB's *resident* agent in Athens. Friar got pictures of Vlynskji on top of the Matterhorn during one of the colonel's frequent ski trips to Switzerland. Unfortunately for the colonel, the Matterhorn was a transvestite who worked the train station at St. Moritz."

Kat smiled, "What's laying a honey trap got to do with the name Friar?"

"It's a play on Laurence. Remember Friar Laurence in *Romeo and Juliet*? He's the Franciscan monk who kept hatching elaborate schemes and dabbling with potions. Friar's favorite quote is the monk's, 'Virtue itself turns vice, when misapplied, / And vice sometime's by action dignified.'"

Kat nodded. She looked forward to meeting Friar.

Warner glanced at the clock on the wall. "That's about it for tonight. Ms. Mills has agreed to give you a detailed briefing on Russian syndicates at 0700 tomorrow morning. I've set it up for room B2701."

"7:00A.M.? Thanks, Kat," Murphy replied.

Placing his hand on Murphy's shoulder, Warner said, "There's an airline ticket in your packet. Your flight leaves Dulles for Cairo at 2030 hours tomorrow night. You're routed via Orly. A one-stop was the best we could do."

The intercom light on Warner's desk winked on. "Mr. Warner, I have a phone call from a Mr. Tovi Hersch with Mossad. He says it's urgent."

OCTOBER 15: MANTEO, NORTH CAROLINA

Dubov smoothed down the fake beard covering his face and casually surveyed the late evening crowd packed into the Bilgewater Room at the Rusty Dog Tavern. There would be plenty of eyewitnesses when the FBI made the rounds.

"Russian, I'sh wants anotha' one of them doggy-rums," mumbled Captain Tyrell Wentworth, skipper of the *Break of Dawn*. Wentworth, a Bilgewater regular, had drained the last dregs from his house special while trying to focus his blood-shot eyes on the auburn-haired coed sitting two tables away.

Dubov pushed his chair back, scraping the legs noisily over the wooden floor. Standing, he rapped an empty shot-glass on the table and bellowed, "Barkeep. Three more double Stoli vodkas and a Rusty Dog for the cap'n."

A couple of boozers at the next table glanced over at the four men and shook their heads. Good, thought Dubov.

"Who're them guys with Poot Wentworth?" Otis Clawson, captain of the *Lucky Lady*, quizzed the bartender.

It was early autumn and the Manteo waterfront was deserted except for a few locals and end-of-the-season holdovers packed into the Rusty Dog Tavern. The day's generous run of bluefish and pompano had the deepwater anglers in a jovial, partying mood. A steady stream of 110 proof Haitian rum, cheap house vodka, and no-name whiskey flowed from the bar's three over-worked spigots. Tonight was the final blow-off of the fishing year for most of the Rusty Dog's patrons. It was their last, desperate hurrah before returning to ordinary, boring, house-payment, car-pool lives.

The Rusty Dog was a Manteo tradition, the creative vision of a pair of corporately downsized, Vermont snowbirds who had flown south during the winter of '87, and stayed. It was famous for its faux-seaport decor and strong, cheap drinks. To provide the aesthetically correct maritime flair, the Vermonters had draped the Bilgewater Room with fishnets full of dried blow fish and glass buoys. The walls were decorated with dozens of replica-antique harpoons, imported by the gross from Sam Li Enterprises in Taiwan.

Over the bar loomed a large, stuffed dog with reddish brown fur. Whenever the house received an order for the Rusty Dog Special, the eyes of the taxidermic specimen would light up, its mouth gape open, and three sharp barks erupt from a hidden loudspeaker. As a finale, the mascot wagged its tail which was attached to the clapper of a ship's bell.

In addition to the alcohol, the act that brought the tourists in took place in a 155 gallon saltwater aquarium housing an octopus named Gus and a scalloped hammerhead shark called Molly. In their eternal search for food, Gus and Molly performed a deadly *pas de deux*. If Gus got careless and wound up as Molly's entree, it was happy hour for the rest of the night. The tavern averaged three replacements a month.

"It's showtime," Dubov whispered in Russian to his two companions. "Make it look good."

With a wink, the two husky Chechens jumped to their feet and began yelling and cursing each other, first in Russian, then in English. Thumping Dima on the chest with a powerful right fist, Petya knocked the drink from his hand, sending it crashing to the floor. The room fell silent. Growling in Russian, Petya and Dima began circling one another.

"What the hell's going on over there?" yelled the bartender, who wisely chose to stay safely behind the bar.

"Enough!" shouted Dubov, jumping between the two belligerents. "Sorry, everyone. It's a private matter. Too much vodka."

"If they don't calm down, I'll call the cops," blustered the bartender. "Who's gonna pay for that broken glass?"

Again, Dubov apologized. Holding up both hands, he explained to the crowd, "They're just sailors arguing over their tattoos. Each says his is the best."

"Whas them funny words they keeps saying?" inquired a soused local, perched precariously on a bar stool, elbows anchored securely to the mahogany bar.

"Russian," answered Dubov. "These fellows are Russian sailors from Murmansk. Their ship's up in Norfolk. They're just letting off some steam. They've been on board too long."

"Two hundred dollars!" shouted Petya.

"Three hundred!" yelled Dima.

"What'er they talkin' about now?" asked the barkeep.

Dubov grabbed Dima and Petya by the arms. "You want a vote? You sure?"

"*Da! Da*!" They declared in unison.

Dubov turned to the crowd, which had begun to form a semicircle around the three men. "I need some judges. Someone to decide which one has the best tattoos."

Eyeing Petya's scarred face and Dima's barrel chest and massive arms, the spectators backed away.

"All judges get two free drinks."

There were whistles of approval at this ground rule. The crowd shuffled closer.

Dubov signaled for Dima to remove his shirt. Bare-chested, the Chechen strutted around in a small circle, showing each judge the details of his tattoos.

"What's that one?" called a shrill voice from the back of the room.

"Which one? This one?" asked Dubov, pointing to the dagger tattooed on Dima's shoulder.

"Yeah, looks like it goes right through his neck."

Dubov leaned over and examined the tattoo. "Means he served hard time at the Kovrov labor camp in Siberia. The dagger's a sign he was a professional murderer, a hit man."

There was a low murmur from the crowd.

"What's that on his chest? Looks like a guy with a machine gun," asked a regular standing by the exit sign.

Dubov took Dima's arm and pulled him into the light. "Shows he was an enforcer in prison. He did the boss's dirty work."

Again a low rumble of awe rippled through the spectators.

"Can I join in?" giggled Crystal Hamilton, a legal secretary from Greenville. Crystal had just drained the last dregs of her second Rusty Dog and was floating in the twilight zone between euphoria and nausea. With whistled encouragement, she climbed precariously onto a chair and with both hands jerked up her pink, fleecy sweater. Hoots of appreciation greeted the large yellow rose tattooed on her braless, ample left breast. Weaving from the numbing effect of 110 proof rum, Crystal toppled backwards into the waiting arms of two admirers.

"How 'bout that one?" called a petite redhead, standing on her tiptoes. The redhead's disgusted boyfriend jerked her away as she leaned forward to touch the tattoo.

Petya flexed his muscles, rippling the painted tattoos on his biceps. The crowd applauded when they saw the skull and dagger on his left forearm and the epaulet on his right shoulder.

"The epaulet shows he was the underboss at a labor camp," explained Dubov.

"And that skull and dagger?" cooed a tall, bleached-blond.

"Means he likes skulls and daggers," replied Dubov, roaring with laughter.

The crowd stomped its approval.

"Any more tattoos?" asked Ray Jester, a life insurance salesman from Richmond who was visiting Manteo with his mistress.

Dubov directed Petya to roll up his pants legs.

The crowd leaned forward to inspect the three tattooed stars on each of his knees.

Dubov stepped back to let the spectators take a closer look. The FBI would want details. "The stars show he was the *pakhan*, or head convict. He kneeled to no one."

It was time to end the show. Holding his hand over Dima's head, Dubov asked, "Is he the winner?" The crowd applauded, whistled and stomped their feet.

"Or this one?" He held a hand over Petya. Again there was enthusiastic applause and dozens of mugs rapped on table tops. "I declare him the winner," Dubov said, holding up Petya's arm. The crowd threw dollar bills on the heads of the two contestants and began chanting, "Drinks, drinks, drinks."

Looking sullen and mumbling in Russian, Dima staggered to the bar to pay.

Dubov looked down at Captain Wentworth whose head was lying

on the table. "Leave him," he ordered Petya. "Tomorrow's his big day. He'll need all the rest he can get."

When they were outside, a light sea breeze blew the salty organic smell of ocean into their faces. The fun and games were over.

Chapter 3

The fading light from the setting sun tinged the sparse, cumulus clouds with brilliant oranges, shaded blues, and deep reds. The display from nature's palette stood in sharp contrast to the dull, architecturally dead, government buildings housing NOSIC, the US Navy's Ocean Surveillance Information Center. As the sun continued to fade, quartz security lights buzzed, then flickered on, illuminating rows of razor-wire encircling the compound.

Inside the heavily guarded buildings, high-IQ, techno-wizards played their deadly game of hide-and-seek with the world's silent services. Using real-time acoustical and optical data from a super-secret, worldwide, Integrated Undersea Surveillance System, these highly trained technicians function as the eyes and ears of the US Navy. In case of nuclear war, the nation's survival depends on the ability of these prodigies to rapidly locate, identify, and target enemy ballistic and fast-attack nuclear submarines. The equipment at their disposal is all state of the art. Their goal is to be able to locate any submarine, anywhere, anytime.

This evening, the individual in charge of the Western Atlantic Sector was Commander Allan E. Rhodes, Jr., a thirty-six-year-old MIT graduate from Lawton, Oklahoma. In high school, his dream had been to escape the cactus scrub of the Wichita Mountains and see the world, compliments of Uncle Sam. After joining the navy, it wasn't long before reality collided with fantasy. In fourteen years of active service, Rhodes had managed to serve only one short tour aboard ship and that had been as an ensign on a submarine tender. Now he viewed the world through the two-dimensional, electronic eyes of the Ocean Surveillance Information Center.

Tonight was Rhodes's tenth wedding anniversary and his wife Liz's thirty-fifth birthday. When he got off duty at 2200 hours he planned on taking her to the Hole in the Wall eatery in Old Town, Alexandria, where they featured what he liked best—a thick, twenty-two ounce, Omaha T-bone steak. Ten years. It was hard to believe they had been married a whole decade. Decade. He didn't like the sound of the word. It was too much like decay. He checked his watch, 1947 hours.

Rhodes stifled a yawn. The whole day had been boring. Earlier in the afternoon, an American Ohio-class boomer had cruised by, but that was about it. The only unusual activity had been the diesel-electric that had popped up on the screen six hours ago. Strange to have a diesel this close to shore. It was now off the North Carolina coast, due east of the Ocracoke light house, hugging the edge of the Continental shelf and moving in a north-northeasterly direction. It still hadn't been identified as to class and origin. Maybe he ought to check it out. That would give him something to do until he saw Liz.

Rhodes pressed 11 on the console. "Chief Koenraad? Commander Rhodes here." If anyone could identify that diesel, it was Senior Chief Petty Officer Clementius O. Koenraad.

"*Aye, aye, sir,*" came the immediate response.

Career navy right down to his navy-issue socks, Koenraad was something of a celebrity within the ranks of the superstitious technicians at NOSIC. Nicknamed "Dr. Udjat," it was rumored he had a supernatural sixth sense for tracking and identifying subs. The specialists in his section claimed he possessed the all-seeing power of the falcon headed Egyptian god, Horus. On the wall over his desk was a papyrus scroll with a black and red hieroglyph of a human eye, combined with the black feather markings of a falcon's eye. Under the hieroglyph was the dedication "To Dr. Udjat," followed by the ancient Egyptian incantation: *I am the all-seeing Eye of Horus, God of Slaughter, Mighty One, whose appearance strikes terror.*

To boost their own personal mojo, each technician kept taped to the top of his or her computer console the reverse side of a US dollar bill with the All Seeing Eye of the Great Seal, circled in red.

"How about it, Chief," Rhodes inquired. "Got a tag on that diesel?"

"*Can't say I have, sir. Been following her ever since she entered my sector. Just can't seem to get a make. She's been cruising along the Gulf Stream at nineteen knots for the last couple of hours. Triton says he needs more information.*" Triton was Koenraad's new, Cray supercomputer. He thought it especially appropriate that Cray had thought to name the computer after a Greek god of the sea.

"How about coming up to the control room. Let's see what we've got." It was unusual for Koenraad to admit he was stumped, especially with a slow moving diesel.

"*Aye, aye, sir.*"

In thirty seconds, Koenraad was standing beside Rhodes, a mug of molehill coffee cradled in his left hand. "Commander, the deck configurations on that sub are *way* off. My guess is it's got some kind of cargo or electronic gear bolted topside."

Strange, thought Rhodes. Why would a sub be carrying cargo? Maybe it was an experimental model out on field trials. Had Castro wrangled a fourth boat out of the Russians? And why was it running so close to the coast?

Koenraad examined the blip on the computer screen. "She's been running submerged ever since we picked her up. Probably getting an extra knot or two from the Gulf Stream. Length's sixty-seven to seventy-five meters. Width, about five to six meters. But, it's the height—nine meters, that's out of whack."

Rhodes shook his head while watching the screen. At last count, forty-three countries had subs. He couldn't understand why the superpowers would want to fill the ocean with potentially hostile subs. Even the US was getting into the act by producing German 209s for the Egyptians at Ingall's shipyard in Pascagoula, Louisiana.

Koenraad scrutinized the computer printout. "One thing's for sure, she's an advanced model. Quiet as a ghost. Probably has one of those new air-independent propulsion systems."

Rhodes grunted, "She could stay submerged for weeks with an AIP. We need a closer look. At least get an acoustical signature of her mechanicals for Triton's memory banks."

Lost in thought, Koenraad stared at the battery-acid swirling in the bottom of his coffee cup. "The more I study it, the more it looks like a Russian Kilo. Probably has every upgrade available. What about the Libyans and Iranians? Are all their Kilos accounted for?"

Rhodes jaw tightened. Even a remote possibility that an Iranian or Libyan sub might be prowling the US coast made him uneasy. "I'll call Norfolk for a chopper." He had been waiting for an excuse to use the new SH-3D Sea King assigned to NOSIC. It was fully equipped with an advanced ASQ-13B dunking sonar system and a new ASQ-81 magnetic anomaly detection device. "We'll have them drop a buoy."

"Aye, aye, sir."

In Russia, East meets West in the jagged peaks of the Caucasus. Here, in the southwestern corner of the country, between Dagestan in the east and Ingushetia in the west, lies the landlocked, ethnic warrior culture, once referred to by Boris Yeltsin as "the criminal state of Chechnya." For over two centuries, Moscow has tried, without success, to change the unique Islamic customs of the Chechens. In the mid-1800s the Czars' armies waged a futile forty year campaign to bring them to heel. During World War II, Joseph Stalin ordered his secret police to herd the entire Chechen population onto sealed railway boxcars for exile to Siberia. It was ethnic cleansing in its purest form. Of a total population of 450,000, one-third died during the exile. In 1957, Khrushchev acknowledged the failure of Stalin's policy of genocide through banishment and allowed the Chechens to return home to the Caucasus.

In 1991, as the old Soviet Union began to crumble, Jokhar M. Dudayev, ex-Soviet air force general and President of Chechnya, proclaimed Chechen independence. This encouraged Moscow to try once again to force the Chechens to assimilate or perish. It was a replay of the recommendation of Czar Nicholas I's civil administrator, Platon Zubov, who wrote in 1834, "The only way to deal with this ill-intentioned people is to destroy it to the last."

Unfortunately for Moscow, this latest attempt was no more successful than the first. Russia's underpaid, poorly trained troops were no match for the highly motivated Chechens. The Russian conscripts could not defeat the Chechen culture of no-surrender. Theirs is a way of life that glorifies warfare, preaches death before dishonor, exalts loyalty to one's family and friends, and holds only contempt for the enemy. During his exile in Siberia, Aleksandr Solzhenitsyn encountered the Chechens in Stalin's gulags and found them unlike anyone else. In *The Gulag Archipelago*, Solzhenitsyn wrote that the Chechens were the only ethnic group who refused to accept the *psychology* of submission. Confinement did not break their spirit. In the labor camps, everyone was afraid of them and they lived as they pleased.

It was into this warrior culture, which now numbers over two million, that Vakhid Khadji Sayid—or as the name listed on his forged passport read, Alexander Dubov—was born on 30 January 1958.

ATLANTIC OCEAN

Dubov held the small, portable NOAA radio receiver to his ear, "West winds ten to twelve knots, seas four to five feet, west wall of the Gulf Stream, fifty-three nautical miles from shore." He scowled at the mention of five foot waves.

Leaning over the railing of the swaying trawler, he retched into the dark, swirling foam. Foul smelling flecks of fish chowder splashed on the edge of the deck and toes of his shoes. Wiping his mouth with the sleeve of his slicker, he continued to heave into the waves. Trying to focus on the horizon, he searched for the line separating sea from sky. Unable to get his bearing, he forced himself to turn towards the bow when the *Break of Dawn* slammed into the next wave. The icy spray sent a chill down his back, but at least it washed the dreck from the matted hairs of his false beard.

Dubov was determined to stay out on the open deck rather than go inside the warm pilot house where Captain Tyrell Wentworth could watch him turn pale. It would be up to Petya to keep the captain sober. Besides, the stifling diesel fumes made him gag. He also didn't want Wentworth looking too closely at his features after being splashed by seawater. The false beard, the makeup over the scar were good, but might not withstand close scrutiny in the glare of the cabin lights. No, it was better to remain on deck where the air was fresh and he could suffer alone.

The time was 9:12P.M. It had been four hours and fifteen minutes since leaving the dock. They should be there by now. A half-full, waning moon slid into the open from behind a bank of clouds. Dubov spit into the ocean and swallowed hard. The swelling in his throat was beginning to subside.

"Reminds me of the Barents Sea," thundered a deep voice in Russian as a powerful hand clamped down on his shoulder.

Dubov jumped. He hadn't noticed Petya's approach. Recovering quickly, he asked, "Anything on the scope?"

"Not yet. I estimate we're still five, maybe ten kilometers from the rendezvous point."

"How's the captain?"

Petya smiled. "No alcohol. Better than last night," Holding his nose he added, "It stinks like a pigsty in there. You're better off out here. How much cargo do we collect?"

"Five containers. It's a special shipment." Although Dubov trusted Petya completely, he parceled out information only on a need-to-know basis. "Someday you'll bore your grandchildren with what you're doing for Chechnya tonight."

Petya was puzzled. Dubov had never before mentioned Chechnya when discussing business.

Dubov scanned the horizon with his binoculars. Still no flashing light. What if something had gone wrong? Turning back to Petya, he asked, "Is the mine ready?"

"*Da*. The shaft's been cleared and the generator's working." For the past two months the syndicate had been buzzing with rumors. Dubov had denied there was anything unusual going on, but Petya could tell. Unexplained messages had come in from Grozny. Important money, with no questions asked, had been used to buy expensive equipment and rent odd locations. Petya had been placed in charge of leasing the abandoned iron mine in western North Carolina. And, most curious, Dubov had warned him against telling anyone, even Dima.

"Good, better get back to the captain before those tattoos wash off, or he finds a bottle."

After Petya disappeared into the pilot house, Dubov mentally rehearsed the mission one last time. There was no room for error, the stakes were too high. He probed for weaknesses; problems were going to occur, they always did. He would just have to stay flexible. Two years planning, rehearsing, then more planning. Endless travel to Moscow, Grozny, Vladivostok, Kabul, Cairo, Berlin, making arrangements, recruiting, training.

The waiting had been the hardest part. Whenever his resolve flagged, he thought of Chechnya. Grozny pillaged, villages in ruins, the people ravaged. It would have to be rebuilt as it had been so often in the past. The new world-order had offered no help, they still considered Chechnya just another Russian province. The Ukraine, Georgia, Azerbaijan, had all received Western aid, but not Chechnya. The solution was obvious. Chechnya would have to find friends where it could. He shook his head. Grozny looked worse than Berlin at the end of World War II.

Two months ago the final go-ahead had been given by the Phoenix Committee. What they were about to do would rewrite the rules of warfare. The meaning of victory would have to be redefined. While Washington spent hundreds of billions on antiquated tactics and strategies, Phoenix would slip in unobserved and in the blink of an eye, it would be over. The old military mind-set of dealing with definable enemies and clear-cut borders was outdated. It was a lazy and fatal way of thinking. America's Maginot line of satellites, stealth bombers, and nuclear submarines was worthless.

Dubov reflected on the twisted trail that had led him to the pitching deck of the *Break of Dawn*. From running insurance scams in Chicago to supervising the Shali syndicate's entire US operations. Now this, and only forty-one years old. When it was over, his family would be respected. There would be monuments erected in Shali and Grozny. He would become a legend, his name spoken in hushed tones. A special statue, made of the finest marble, would be built to honor the memory of his mother, he would make certain of that.

Remembering the pain of his childhood, he wondered if this undertaking was all part of some grand, cosmic plan. The youngest in a Muslim family of six sons and two daughters, his earliest memories had been of deprivation and humiliation. Shasha, his mother, had died shortly after he was born. The shame had been too great and she had hanged herself. It wasn't her fault, only her destiny. Whenever Dubov had asked his father why, he would only shake his head and mumble *vot takiye dela*—what will be will be. It was not until he was ten that Dubov learned the sordid details from Grachev, the local butcher. During the May Day celebrations, nine months before he was born, his mother had been raped by a drunken Ukrainian army major. The major, stationed at the Second Army's infantry barracks just south of Grozny, had paid the ultimate price for his transgression. His castrated body, cut in half, was found four days later in a garbage dump at the camp's entrance. His penis had been stuffed down his throat and his testicles cut off and fed to the pigs. It was an effective warning to other Soviet troops to stay away from Chechen women.

As Dubov grew older, it was noted by the local gossips that he didn't resemble his brothers or sisters. What bothered him most was the rejection by his father. At age fourteen he was sent to live with his grandfather and grandmother in Grozny, where he was apprenticed to an expatriate, London gun-runner who was fond of slitting throats and quoting Shakespeare.

Dubov ran a finger over the makeup covering the three inch scar stretching from the right side of his forehead to the middle of his right cheek. It was scarcely noticeable now. A souvenir from a knife fight in Grozny that, at eighteen, had changed his life. Viktor, the youngest son of Grozny's police chief had made the mistake of calling him a bastard. When the fight was over it had taken four strong men to pull him off the body. At first, he thought he would be hanged. Instead, the incident made him a hero. Witnesses said it had been a fair fight and had been provoked. In the coffee houses of Grozny, it was no longer "Sayid, the young bastard from Shali," but "Sayid, the fighter, the warrior." He had become someone to be feared. On his next visit to Shali, he heard his name mentioned with respect. Young women wanted to be seen with him. Even his father started referring to him as "my strong willed son." The rumors about his parentage stopped.

Captain Tyrell Wentworth pushed open the door to the pilot house and reluctantly stuck his pudgy, unshaven face into the wind. His bulging eyes strained against the sea spray, searching for Dubov, the man he knew only as "Russian."

This was not the first night trip Wentworth had made for Russian. Over the past year and a half there had been three others. One for cocaine from the Colombian Cali cartel and two for hashish and heroine from Afghanistan. The pickups had been for submerged containers, jettisoned from freighters and private yachts. The boxes had been chained together and marked by sophisticated, low frequency buoys. Tonight was different, they were going to rendezvous with another boat. The change in procedure disturbed Wentworth.

On sighting Dubov, the captain called out, in a voice made hoarse from too many unfiltered cigarettes, "Russian, where the fuck's that other boat? I ain't seen nothin' yet. Maybe it h'aint coming." Ready to turn back, Wentworth had made up his mind. If there was no pickup, he would demand half payment. He wasn't going to let Russian push him around.

"Should be along anytime now," Dubov replied, scarcely able to hide his contempt for the constantly whining and complaining captain. There was no respecting a whimpering drunk who couldn't keep his boat from smelling like an Azerbaijani garbage scow. Still, Dubov managed to call Wentworth "Cap'n." It was a cheap price to pay for the power to manipulate.

"Contact," shouted Petya from inside the pilot house. A blinking green dot appeared in the upper left quadrant of the directional grid. "Twelve hundred meters, east-northeast, and closing."

"Got it," Dubov yelled, his eyes fixed on the horizon. In the distance he could make out the faint glimmer of a flashing light. Waving to Wentworth, he ordered, "Slow engines."

The *Break of Dawn* shuddered to a crawl as Wentworth pulled back on the throttle, nosing the bow in the direction of the contact. Reaching into a large, black satchel, Petya pulled out a portable signal gun and flashed, "Mars has risen."

As they approached the sleek silhouette lying low in the waves, the moon slid out from behind the clouds. Wentworth's jaw dropped open. "Sonofabitch, i-its a goddamned sub," he stuttered, his chest tightening. It was a bad sign. A sub could only mean trouble—big trouble. What was Russian up to?

Grabbing the handrail, Dubov worked his way forward. He shouted to Wentworth, "Bring her about and hold at 100 meters."

The sub flashed a reply, "T-h-e—h-o-u-r—o-f—j-u-d-g-m-e-n-t."

Dubov nodded to Petya, "Signal them to float the containers."

The sub answered, "Affirmative. Prepare to receive boarder."

As the trawler drew closer, Dubov could make out the shapes of five large, oblong containers, or pods, bolted to the sub's deck. One in front of the conning tower, four aft. The container in front of the conning tower measured one and a half meters in height and two and a half meters in length. The other four were two meters high and three and a half meters long. Crewmen in wet suits were unbolting the pods from the deck. A motorized rubber raft was lowered over the side of the sub and a lone figure climbed in. The small craft rapidly approached the trawler.

When the raft was fifteen meters away, a nylon rope was tossed over from the trawler. In the half-light of the moon, it was difficult for Dubov to make out the features of the boarder. "Shamikan?"

"Dubov?"

A hemp ladder with aluminum rungs was lowered over the side of the trawler and Shamikan scrambled aboard. Slightly built, with dark curly hair, his smooth complexion made him appear nineteen rather than the twenty-nine listed in Interpol's computers.

"How was the trip with our psychotic friends?" Dubov asked.

"I'm tired of rice and fish soup," Shamikan said, thumbing his nose at the sub.

Dubov chuckled. "And the cargo?" The warheads had been placed in double-hulled containers, the inner hulls housed the warheads, the outer shells, seawater. When the water was drained, the pods would float.

"They're drawing off the water now."

Dubov signaled for Petya to jump into the raft and hand up the three wooden boxes brought over by Shamikan. There was no time to waste. Discovery during this phase of the transfer would be disastrous. If that happened, the warheads would have to be sunk and the mission scrubbed. Once the containers were on board, the only option would be to blow up the trawler.

Petya quickly passed Shamikan two boxes of Semtec plastic explosives and a crate holding ten 5.45mm AKS-74 Kalashnikov submachine guns. Each container of Semtec held enough explosives to blast a hole in the ocean sixty meters wide and twenty meters deep.

A message flashed from the sub, "P-o-d-s—r-e-a-d-y—f-o-r—t-r-a-n-s-f-e-r—A-c-k-n-o-w-l-e-d-g-e—a-n-d—s-t-a-n-d-b-y."

Dubov was no longer cold and sweat soaked the armpits of his shirt. "Signal them to proceed with transfer."

The sub submerged ten meters, floating the pods free. After backing off 100 meters, it resurfaced. Six frogmen jumped into the frigid water and swam to the floating containers which were roped together.

"Okay, Cap'n," Dubov said, "bring in the cargo."

The *Break of Dawn* approached to within forty meters of the containers, before it was forced to back off by the ocean swells. The pods would have to be secured by cable and pulled individually to the boat, then winched aboard.

Wentworth was feeling better now. A warm glow radiated out from the center of his gut. While Petya had been preoccupied, the captain had stolen two quick swigs of grain alcohol from a bottle of antiseptic in the trawler's emergency medicine kit. His mind was made up. He would demand an extra $25,000 for making a pickup from a sub. God only knew what was inside those black containers.

Petya flipped the lever of the winch used for hauling in shrimp nets. All the experience he'd gained from the previous drug runs would be put to use tonight. Swinging the boom starboard, he spooled out the steel cable to Shamikan in the motorized raft. The cable was ferried to the waiting frogmen who attached it to the eyebolt on the first pod. Inflatable rubber bumpers were attached to the sides of the pod to keep it from crushing the trawler's hull. As the boat heaved and swayed, the first container was slowly pulled through the choppy seas until it was ten meters away. Just as they were preparing to winch it aboard, a six foot swell caught the trawler, forcing it to come about. The lurching motion almost pitched Dubov over the side. At the last second, he grabbed a shrimp net for support.

Pulling himself upright, Dubov glared at Wentworth. "Hold her steady, Cap'n."

"Goddammit, I'm doing the best I can," Wentworth grumbled, gunning the engine and heading the bow into an approaching swell.

Dubov peered over the railing at the container bobbing dangerously close to the trawler's waterline. He considered linking the pods together and towing them back to Wanchese, but that would be too slow and might attract attention. There was no alternative. They would have to be winched aboard and stowed in the hold.

"Okay, Cap'n. Try again," Dubov yelled.

Once again, Wentworth maneuvered the boat until the pod was ten meters off the starboard side. When Dubov raised his arm, Petya engaged the hoist. The boom creaked and groaned as the pod was lifted clear of the water. Another swell caught the boat, causing it to roll portside. The container slammed against the starboard railing, knocking out a section of wood. Pulling on the guide rope, Dubov managed to position the pod over the hold. Pushing forward on the lever, Petya slowly, carefully, lowered the container until it clunked into place.

The same procedure was followed for the remaining four pods. With the last container, Wentworth was so busy watching Petya operate the boom he lost his heading. A swell caught the boat port side, almost wrenching the guide rope from Dubov's hands. As soon as the container was safely in the hold, Dubov leaped into the pilot house. He could smell the alcohol. Grabbing the front of Wentworth's slicker with both hands, he pushed forward, slamming the captain against the back of the cabin.

"If you screw up just one of those containers—"

Wentworth's face went white.

Dubov released the captain, then made his way to the starboard side where he helped Shamikan climb back on board from the raft and secure the hold.

Waving at Dubov, Petya pointed towards the sub. They were frantically signaling.

Petya read the message aloud, "A-i-r-c-r-a-f-t—a-p-p-r-o-a-c-h-i-n-g— T-e-n—t-h-o-u-s-a-n-d—m-e-t-e-r-s—P-r-e-p-a-r-i-n-g—t-o—d-i-v-e."

Without waiting to retrieve their six frogmen, the sub slipped beneath the waves and disappeared.

Dubov whispered instructions to Shamikan, then opened the door to the pilot house. "Cap'n, pick up the swimmers and let's get out of here."

As the trawler approached the frogmen, Shamikan motioned for them to climb into the rubber dinghy. When they were in and alongside, Petya and Shamikan raised their submachine guns and efficiently, methodically, shredded the raft and frogmen. The tangled mass of rubber, neoprene, and bodies sank slowly beneath the waves.

"Let's get back to shore," Dubov shouted.

Wentworth needed no encouragement. Pushing the throttle forward, the engine rumbled to life as diesel fumes billowed from the stern.

Whup, whup, whup. Dubov could hear the helicopter blades before he could see the aircraft. It came in low and fast, skimming just above the water's surface, its powerful searchlight sweeping back and forth across the waves. Dubov motioned to Shamikan and Petya to hide under a tarp. When the searchlight picked up the bow of the *Break of Dawn*, the helicopter slowly circled the trawler, working its beam from bow to stern.

"Wave," Dubov commanded Wentworth, taking off his own watch cap and lifting it towards the aircraft. Wentworth managed a couple of feeble flutters with his right hand. After circling the boat twice the helicopter dipped its nose in a southeasterly direction and continued its search.

Dubov let out a low whistle. It had been close. Tapping Petya on the shoulder, he said, "See if you can find their frequency."

Placing the portable shortwave radio on auto-scan, Petya listened to the headset. Shaking his head, he said, "They must be using a special military wavelength."

Dubov watched the helicopter's running lights disappear into the night. Turning to Shamikan, he ordered, "Set the charges."

Shamikan opened the side panel of the wooden container with yellow stripes and clicked the dual initiator toggle switches to On. The battery whirred to life. Now all that would be required was simultaneous pressure on both red buttons.

No one spoke as the *Break of Dawn* rode the ocean swells towards Wanchese. The only sounds were the deep throbbing of the engine and the slapping of waves against the trawler's hull.

Chapter 4

OCTOBER 16: HILLSBOROUGH, NORTH CAROLINA: 10:15P.M.
Warner was running late. Friar unfolded the blue silk handkerchief
and withdrew the dogeared deck of tarot cards. Tapping the deck
lightly against his forehead, he asked, "What is the purpose of Warner's
visit?" Shuffling the cards three times, he spread them in a wide fan-
fold on the redwood picnic table. With his eyes closed, he reached
for the first card.

The *Nine of Swords*. An image of a weeping woman, her head held
inconsolably in her delicate hands. Sitting at the foot of a plainly
furnished bed, she had a quilt pulled up to her waist. It was a picture
of utter desolation and despair. Nine double-edged swords with in-
terlocking hilts, hovered menacingly over her head. He brushed a
dried oak leaf from the table and placed the card on it, faceup. The
Nine of Swords—a warning of deception and death.

As a birthday stunt for his forty-ninth, Marcie had hired Sister
Chaldean, a local Saponi Indian psychic, to perform a reading and
present Friar with a gilt-edged deck of Waite tarot cards. The deck
the psychic chose was special. It was the Kennedy deck from New
Orleans, reputed to have been used by Sister Rose in August 1963 to
predict the President's assassination. In her reading, Sister Chaldean
prophesied that Friar would soon become a teacher of war and student of the occult, especially the tarot.

Within a week of the reading Friar had been offered a position at
the University of North Carolina as guest lecturer in Southern military history. A month later he attended a seminar by Professor Alfredo

Fontanese on the effects of the tarot and palmistry in shaping Southern culture. By August, he knew the history of the cards well enough to write an article for *The North Carolina Historical Review* entitled, "The Influence of the Tarot on early Nineteenth Century North Carolina Society."

Much to Marcie's dismay, Friar occasionally consulted the cards to answer personal questions. She teased him that if the neighbors saw Brother Laurence dabbling in the occult they would question whether he was sporting a full deck. But, one of the pleasures of no longer working for the CIA was the freedom to walk the fringes.

While Friar waited on the patio for Warner, he ran his hand lightly over the deck until it was drawn to a second card. Slowly pulling it out, he turned it over. *The Tower*, a Major Arcana card. It showed a crumbling medieval battlement, struck by lightning and set ablaze. Two frightened figures plunged headlong from the ramparts onto the rocks below. He placed the card on the table beside the *Nine of Swords*. Another ill omen—destruction and punishment, forecasting the ruin of the House of Life.

He drew a third. *The King of Pentacles*. Friar grimaced at the image of the morose king, frowning as he stared at the pentagram in the orb resting on his knee. It was a portent of corruption in high office, of danger from a stubborn, vengeful person in a position of great power. Who could that be? Certainly not Warner.

Friar collected the cards, wrapping them in their silk handkerchief and returned them to the mahogany storage container. Enough playtime. He would try again tomorrow. Better not mention the cards to Marcie. It wasn't that she was a believer, but still—

Leaning back in his new cypress chaise longue, he stared at the night sky. In the pitch black, he could faintly make out the shapes of several oak and maple leaves drifting down, one by one, in slow, lazy spirals. Autumn was his favorite time of the year. It meant pumpkin pie and cool weather. He followed a lone leaf as it floated to earth, gently landing on the compost heap. That was it, he reflected. In the end there's only compost. Tomorrow he would begin raking.

Friar thought of how little he missed the CIA. He had made the right choice, leaving before he became part of the problem. During his tenure, the US had won the cold war. Now, with the old Soviet

Union only a footnote in history, there would be a transition during which the intelligence function would have to be redefined. It would be painful, maybe even terminal for the Agency.

The past fourteen months in Hillsborough with Marcie had been memorable, not so much for what had happened, but for what had *not* happened. No frantic calls in the middle of the night, no congressional hearings headed by pompous bureaucrats, posturing and pandering to a jaded press. Instead, it had been one of those rare, plus years when the grass grew on schedule and he felt younger in October than he had in January. Ah—Marcie. Try as he might, he couldn't understand why a level-headed woman like her, would leave a well-paying job as a shrink-analyst with the Agency to marry a neurotic like him. Now, how had that last evaluation phrased it? "A pronounced neurotic, with psychotic tendencies?"

"Laurence," Marcie called from the kitchen. "Warner phoned from his car. He's running fifteen minutes late."

Marcie was one of the few people who called him Laurence. Marcie, his mother, and one or two college classmates. He liked that.

Friar took another sip of wine. Why such an impromptu, late night visit from Warner? It wasn't like him to come calling this close to the witching hour. Whatever he wanted, Friar would run it by Marcie for approval. As part of his transition therapy she had allowed him to freelance occasional consulting assignments with the Agency, but *no* field work. Masquerading as an expert at Langley helped him keep tabs on Murphy and a dwindling number of the old guard, but that was about it. There wasn't any adrenaline rush from sitting in front of a computer screen and reading someone else's field report.

Since he had met Marcie, life had become idyllic, maybe too much so. He wondered what price would be extracted by the yin, when least expected. There would come a reckoning, there always had. He remembered the early years with Joanie, when he was young and all things were possible. He dimly recalled the smiling face of Kevin, who had just turned three. When the images hovered too far beyond the fringes of memory, he would drag out the old photographs. But, that only brought back the pain—the drunken driver, the head-on collision. At least it had been quick and they hadn't lingered. The beach had never been the same, although he still made an annual pilgrimage to Wilmington to drop a bouquet of forget-me-nots off the bridge at Harbor Island. No, his yang had definitely gotten ahead of itself. The yin was there, crouching in the shadows.

"Bryan's here," Marcie said, ushering Warner onto the patio.

"Hi, Friar. Sorry I'm late," Warner said, trying to sound as chipper as possible. "I know how you retirees are. Cookies and vanilla ice cream by nine. Tucked in and fast asleep by ten."

Friar smiled, "It's the life, Bryan. So, how was your day?"

"Okay, I guess. The way I see it, any day you're not subpoenaed by Congress, blown up by a car bomb, or told you have a terminal disease, it's a good day."

"Don't you think it's about time you left Langley?" Marcie asked. "There's a whole 'nother existence outside the Beltway."

"Marcie's had a fun day," said Friar. "She was chairperson for Hog Day here in Hillsborough."

Warner arched an eyebrow, "Hog Day?"

Friar chuckled, "It's part of the good life. Hog Olympics, hog hollerin' contest, porcine beauty pageant, and, above all, barbecue."

"Laurence oughta know," Marcie said. "He ate enough pig meat to grow bristles."

Warner was pleased to see them adjusting so well to Hillsborough. It gave him hope for the time when he emptied his desk—he wished he hadn't come.

Sensing Warner's unease, Friar picked up a Manhattan glass from a tray on the table. "The usual? Black Jack with a hint of Martini and Rossi?"

"Make it a double," Warner pleaded, removing his coat and tie and unbuttoning his collar. "To tell the truth, I may be joining you *real* soon. I've got the hounds-of-hell baying at my heels."

"Sounds ominous."

"It's the Administration. They're making noises about reinventing the Agency."

"Like I said, ominous."

"Did Murphy get back okay?" Marcie asked. "He sure left Pinehurst in a hurry. All his note said was 'Off to Langley, duty calls.' "

"That's part of the reason I'm here." Warner paused, reluctant to spoil the pleasant mood. "He left for Cairo a couple of hours ago. His trip's tied in with what I came to see Friar about."

Friar handed Warner his drink, frowning as he remembered the Tarot cards. "Slow down there, Bryan. Don't forget, I've gone private."

Warner sipped his Manhattan, feeling guilty about accepting hospitality under the guise of friendship, only to sneak in a field assignment. He knew how Marcie felt about Friar going operational. "It's a special op. Got your name written all over it. There's a little travel involved, but nothing major." Noticing Marcie's crossed arms, he attempted to explain, "Frankly, Friar's the only one who can handle it."

"Thanks for the compliment," Friar replied, "but I don't flatter myself by thinking I'm irreplaceable. The cemetery's full of people who thought they were."

Warner parked his drink on the corner of the table. "Concerns important information on several nuclear warheads reported missing, maybe headed this way."

Friar winced—*loose nukes*. He had wondered how long it would be before he heard someone from the Agency uttering those words. Thirty-six thousand nuclear warheads rattling around in the world's arsenals and security deteriorating. It was only a matter of time before some terrorist decided to lift the lid of Pandora's nuclear box. Just yesterday he had read an editorial in *The Bulletin of the Atomic Scientists* that said the hands of the Doomsday Clock had been *advanced* two minutes. Now it stood at fourteen minutes until midnight. The *Bulletin's* Board of Directors had decided the world had grown more dangerous, not less, since the breakup of the old Soviet Union. At least the USSR had maintained its weapons under tight security. Now it was Nuclear Economics 101. The rising demand curve had finally intersected the lowered supply curve.

"Rumor or confirmed?" Friar asked.

Marcie quietly closed the lid on the grill and sat down beside Friar. For the first time since their marriage, she was afraid—for Friar, and for herself.

"Strictly rumor so far," Warner replied. "Received a message from an Iraqi source that has me worried. This contact goes back in history, back to your time. He's going to require special handling." Noticing the skeptical look on Marcie's face, he said, "I'm sorry, but there's no one else."

Warner wasn't exaggerating. The recent scorched-earth policy against the clandestine services by a hostile administration had taken its toll. Financially ruinous lawsuits, Congressional witch hunts, and constant media harassment had forced most of the gifted and talented to simply hand in their notices and go private. Working for the DO was no longer a smart career choice. The CIA had even resorted to running "Your rewards will be great" ads in publications as diverse as the *Wall Street Journal* and *Ebony*. Friar had cut out several and posted them on the refrigerator door. "What kind of recruit reads the *Wall Street Journal*?" he had asked.

"You don't have *anyone*?" Marcie asked, shaking her head. She knew there were times when Laurence missed the excitement of field work and didn't want him tempted.

"Not for this job."

"Sounds like he's setting you up, dear," Marcie said.

Squeezing her hand, Friar said, "Bryan, just suppose I said yes. What kind of support would I get? Who's going to back me up? I've got no idea what passes for legal these days."

Dodging the question, Warner replied, "That's why I need you. You know how the game's played and how to get results." He couldn't give a better answer because there was none.

"Murphy said the Company has a new Executive Director, a real piece of work."

"Yeah. Oscar Shymanski. He's Bruce Bastardi's protégé and my new boss. This is the first time I've ever had to report to the Executive Director's position. I use to go straight to the top."

"I take it, by protégé you mean ass-kisser?" Friar said bluntly.

Warner smiled weakly, "It was a forced appointment. The Director had to cut a deal and Shymanski was part of the price." Warner had been present when Vaughn got the call from President Morehead. It was power politics, plain and simple.

Warner was ready to set the hook. "There's something I haven't told you. The Iraqi requested you by name."

"By name?" Friar was surprised. Who out there still remembered him? Most of his contacts had been purged by Hussein.

"He chose an interesting route for delivering his message. Sent it to us through a friend of yours at Mossad—Tovi Hersch. You remember Tovi. Used to be known as—" Warner drained the few remaining drops of his Manhattan. "What was it? Rainman? No, it was Sand—Sand–something or other."

"Sandman," answered Friar.

"Yeah. That's it. Sandman. He's been a player at Mossad for quite a while. Didn't you two work together on a couple of projects back in the eighties?"

"I remember Tovi," Friar nodded. Only too well. In September 1985 when Friar was stationed in Baghdad, the Sandman had come close to sprinkling slumber-dust in his eyes—permanently. In those days, Friar lived dog-years. Every year in Iraq was equivalent to seven back in the States. The problem was, you never knew the game, theirs or yours. His run-in with Hersch had been over the US's and Israel's screwed up Mideast policies during the Iraq-Iran war. Israel was secretly backing Iran, while the US beat the drums for Iraq—or so Friar thought. Part of his job had been to pass along tidbits of intelligence to Hussein's *Al Mukhabarat*. When one of Friar's sources tumbled onto a plan by Israel to supply Khomeini's forces with American-made TOW anti-tank missiles, he dutifully informed Major Kareem Mukhtar, his Iraqi counterpart. No one bothered informing Friar that the operation had "Made in the USA" stamped all over it. The swap was part of a convoluted plot by the National Security Council to supply American made TOW missiles to Tehran in exchange for Iranian influence in gaining the release of thirty-nine American hostages held in Beirut by the Islamic Jihad. The whole operation had been staged and run by operatives from the NSC. Hell, the National Security Council wasn't even supposed to have operational capabilities.

Friar recalled how, in July 1985, he learned from Mukhtar that an Iranian hit squad had been nosing around his apartment. One step ahead of the body bag, he was only two blocks away when his living room disappeared in a ball of flame. Savama operatives from Iran's foreign intelligence had planted four ounces of Semtec in his telephone. Overly eager, they had mistaken the answering machine for his voice and had triggered the explosives prematurely. It was only later that rumors of the Sandman's involvement filtered into Cairo Station. When the reports were sufficiently verified, Kit Watson, the Station Chief, quietly passed word to Mossad that there would be retaliation if Friar were harmed. It would be the Old Testament eye for an eye variety.

Afterwards, Friar worked closely with Tovi on several assignments. The Baghdad incident was never mentioned, but they both knew it was there. The only acknowledgment Friar ever received was a one liter bottle of Remy Martin, V.S.O.P., Fine Champagne Cognac, on the first anniversary of the apartment bombing. A note was attached, "Sorry for Baghdad. Wrong place, wrong time, wrong person." Over the years they had developed a mutual respect for each other, but they never forgot they worked for different masters with different agendas.

Warner pulled his lounge chair closer to Friar's, "The Sandman flew all the way over from Tel Aviv to deliver the message. Said to tell you it was payback time for one of your cooperative ventures. He said you'd know which one."

"Okay, what's the message?"

"It's from General Kareem Mukhtar."

"Mukhtar? I thought he was dead." Friar had heard by the grapevine that Mukhtar was killed in '93 when several Tomahawk cruise missiles from the *Peterson* and the *Chancellorsville* leveled the headquarters of Iraq's Intelligence Service in Baghdad.

"True, we had crossed him off the list, but he resurfaced last spring. According to Hersch, the message from Mukhtar was hand delivered to a Mossad operative in Beirut by an Israeli army major kidnapped last year by Hamas."

Warner handed Friar a folded, number 10 envelope. Inside was a single sheet of yellow, lined paper. On it was handwritten:

> To Laurence Clarke:
> Sending you warning as promised. Have information of great importance of nuclear threat to the United States. Identity of terrorists is Shaheeds of Islamic Ummah. Will meet you at Devil's Throat,

> 24 October. Come alone. Fax confirmation to 4146-7224 Frankfurt.
>
> Mukhtar

Now Friar understood why Tovi had said it was payback time. In October 1986, in appreciation for a favorable report to Langley on Mossad's new spirit of cooperation, Tovi had told him of a planned Savama raid to kidnap Mukhtar's wife, Jamila, and their only child, Zafir. The grab was to have taken place at a medical clinic in Basel, Switzerland, where Zafir was undergoing treatment for hemophilia.

In a business where information is power, the Sandman's intelligence was worth its weight in gold. Friar quickly passed the warning along to Mukhtar, who, as expected, was most appreciative. He invited Friar to his home on the outskirts of Baghdad and thanked him profusely. He promised that if the chance ever came to reciprocate, he would contact him.

Friar handed the note to Marcie. While she read it, he asked, "What's the reference to the 'Shaheeds of the Islamic Ummah'?"

"I'm not sure. At least not yet. But that's the tie-in with Murphy's mission I mentioned earlier. He's on his way to Cairo to meet a different source who connects the Shaheeds with nuclear warheads headed this way." Pointing to the paper in Marcie's hand, Warner asked, "What's his reference to 'Devil's Throat'?"

"It's a neutral meeting place Mukhtar and I agreed to in '86. We've both been there before. It's called *Garganta del Diablo*, and it's one of a series of falls on the Rio Iguaçu at a point where Brazil, Argentina, and Paraguay intersect."

"Why go so far?"

"It's safe for Mukhtar. He won't be noticed at Iguaçu. There's a local population of over 30,000 Arabs within a five mile radius of the Falls. You've got both Sunni and Shiite mixed together. The Hezbollah has logistics bases at Foz do Iguaçu in Brazil and at Cuidad del Este in Paraguay. Hamas is there also. It's a real hotbed for terrorist activity in South America."

"Think Mukhtar's acting on his own?" Warner asked, aware that any contact with Iraq was suspect.

"Probably. He owes me one."

"Laurence hasn't agreed to go," Marcie interjected.

Warner felt awkward. He didn't want to get caught between Friar and Marcie. "All I need is a quick look-see. Find out what Mukhtar's got, then back home. I'd go myself if I thought he'd deal with me."

"Well, Laurence?" Marcie asked.

Putting his arm around her shoulders, he said, "We can decide later." He wanted to give her the freedom to say no in private. He had promised no field work and he meant it.

"Okay, later" she said softly. Her heart sank. She knew she would have to let him go. Laurence, being Laurence, would consider it his duty to help Warner. It was part of his personal code of honor, his sense of loyalty. She had no illusions he would ever change, nor did she really want him to.

"Could be nothing," Friar said. "A quick trip to Argentina, a *bife de chorizo* at Las Nazarenas, a little side trip to the Falls to make reservations for our second honeymoon, then back home for another helping of barbecue."

"Think about it for a couple of days," Warner suggested.

"We'll let you know by noon tomorrow," Marcie replied.

Laurence looked into her eyes and understood. Turning to Warner he said, "Bryan, if it's yes, I'll need backup."

"Name it."

"I want Marcie on the project with full clearance and access to all the Agency's resources." He didn't mention it, but he also wanted to know she would be safe.

"No problem," Warner answered without hesitation. He welcomed Marcie's help. She would make a good liaison with other intelligence services since, unlike Friar, she could get along with anyone.

"I'll need a diplomatic passport. I don't want any hassle with government officials in Argentina or Brazil."

Warner nodded, "Anything else?"

"Joe Don Bordeaux. See if you can find Joe Don. I'd like him down there with me." Friar knew he would need someone watching his back and keeping the rear door open while he concentrated on Mukhtar. It had been over two years since he had heard from Joe Don. The last report had him on the Colombian-Mexican cocaine circuit working as a freelancer for the DEA. An ex-Vietnam Black

Beret, with a chunk of shrapnel in his left shoulder and a Silver Star in his desk drawer, Joe Don was the one person Friar trusted in the field.

"I'll put out an inquiry," Warner replied. "If it's a go, how about you and Marcie meeting me at Bosworth House in Williamsburg at noon on the nineteenth."

"Okay by me."

"There's a short fuse on this one," Warner reminded them. "By tomorrow, I should have a report from Murphy on his Cairo source."

Friar placed his wine glass on the edge of the picnic table, "Bryan, one more thing. I like to do things my way. When I get to Buenos Aires, I don't want to have to check in at the embassy or work with CIA personnel I don't know." It had been a long time since he had seen Mukhtar and there was no telling what kind of baggage he would be dragging to Iguaçu with him, especially after Desert Storm. There were no ground rules for meeting an Iraqi intelligence general in the middle of no man's land to discuss nuclear terrorism and he didn't want his hands tied.

Warner smiled. He was glad to see Friar hadn't lost his edge. If nuclear warheads were involved, they both understood that the ends justified the means, as long as the means weren't too messy.

"It's your call," Warner assured him. "Of course, I can't put anything in writing these days. But, if there's trouble, I'll be there to back you up."

Friar nodded, "Just wanted to make sure we were both singing from the same hymnal. You know me, 'Better to be judged by twelve than carried by six.' "

Marcie tried to keep her voice from breaking when she asked Warner if he wanted another drink. Turning, she walked quickly to the kitchen so Laurence couldn't see the tear forming in the corner of her eye.

OCTOBER 17: WANCHESE, NORTH CAROLINA: 2:30A.M.

The *Break of Dawn* idled up to the dilapidated dock on the eastern outskirts of Wanchese. The 1930s cypress structure, formerly part of the Grandy Brothers' fish house, was located in a remote section of Croatan Sound, well away from prying eyes.

All was quiet. A slight breeze rustled the leaves of the willow oaks crowding the water line along the windward side of the island. Wentworth cut back the Morse throttle, slowing the boat to a drift. In the distance, a light blinked on while a dog barked indifferently.

Had anyone noticed, they would have dismissed it as Poot Wentworth coming in drunk as usual. The old alligator hides and cottonmouth moccasin skins tacked to the unpainted walls of the boat shed helped reinforce his carefully cultivated image as the waterfront's town character. The profile of an unpredictable loner helped provide good cover for his sporadic smuggling activities.

The dock was a ramshackle affair with twelve barnacle encrusted pilings driven into the soft, silty mud of Croatan Sound. On top of the pilings was a platform of warped planks haphazardly nailed together. At the end of the walkway, a large wooden boat shed, remnant of grander days during Prohibition when boatloads of Scotch and rum were smuggled in from Bermuda, helped screen Wentworth's movements.

As they pulled alongside the dock, Dubov scanned the shadows with a pair of night-vision binoculars. If there had been a leak, they would be drifting into a trap with no chance of escape. The half-moon slipped out from behind a bank of clouds, flooding the area with pale light. Dubov stood on the bow and listened. There were no unusual sounds.

While Wentworth was busy mooring the boat to the dock, Dubov motioned Shamikan over. Screwing a suppressor onto the muzzle of a Kalashnikov, he pointed towards Wentworth. "If he tries to escape, shoot him."

Shamikan nodded and moved behind the captain.

Watching the tree line and buildings for movement, Dubov signaled Petya to go ashore for a quick reconnaissance. With cat-like grace, Petya jumped over the railing onto the rickety dock and disappeared into the shadows. Five minutes later he flashed an all-clear.

Dubov breathed a sigh of relief. In a low voice he said, "Okay, Cap'n, take her in."

The trawler's engine rumbled to life. Relaxing for the first time since the trip began, Dubov reached into the pocket of his slicker and pulled out a crumpled pack of Camel filter-tip cigarettes. Tapping out the first of the day, he lit up, inhaling a long, deep stream of soothing nicotine. He had promised himself to kick the habit when the mission was over, but for now, he needed the diversion.

Wentworth pushed forward on the throttle, slowly maneuvering the trawler into the ship channel. The poor lighting made judging distances difficult. Phantom obstacles loomed in his path.

"Problems?" growled Dubov as the trawler bumped a piling.

"It's the goddamned dark," Wentworth blurted out. "I can't see nothin' without my lights."

Dubov signaled Petya to flip on the lights inside the boat shed. "That'll have to do."

Slowly, painstakingly, Wentworth backed the *Break of Dawn* into the boat house. As the stern approached the loading platform, his sweaty hand slipped, opening the throttle a little too much. The boat lurched backward, striking the platform with a resounding thud. Wentworth cringed. Ten seconds passed—no response. With his shoulders still hunched, he peeked in Dubov's direction. Russian was standing on the loading platform, looking at him and smiling.

"Good job, Cap'n," Dubov forced himself to say. Waving to Shamikan, he gestured for him to start unloading the cargo.

Wentworth's fear of Russian now switched to manic elation. After all, it was his boat and they couldn't operate without it. A sly grin stole across his face. After this trip, he would anonymously check with the Drug Enforcement Agency on reward money. If enough was offered—as much as two hundred thousand—he would turn Russian in. He would trade testimony for cash, *and immunity*. The DEA would have to offer immunity, or there was no deal. It would serve Russian right, ordering the captain of a Wanchese trawler around like a common deck hand.

After securing the boat, Dubov pulled Petya aside. "Go get Dima and have him bring up the big truck. Make it quick. We've got to be out of here by sunrise."

"What about the cargo?"

"Shamikan and I can handle it. Remember, I want Dima's truck loaded and parked before the Shaheeds get here."

Petya nodded, climbed into the new, dark blue Ford delivery van with "Tischler Appliance Co." painted on the side and drove away.

It took Dubov, Wentworth, and Shamikan over an hour to winch the five, dull-black aluminum containers out of the boat's hold, hose them down with fresh water and place them on the loading platform. Drained of seawater the four larger pods weighed 1,400 pounds each and the smaller one, 950 pounds. Fastened to the side of the smaller container was a bright yellow, aluminum plate labeled "1."

"That's it," Dubov announced, pointing to the smaller pod. Working rapidly with a 1¾ inch lug wrench, Shamikan removed the bolts holding the top half of the container in place. Attaching a cable to the eyebolt they lifted off the top half of the shell. Inside was a second, rectangular, baby blue, plastic container with "# 1, GE Refrigerator Model 704E," stenciled on its side. Using the overhead crane, they lifted the refrigerator from its outer shell and placed it upright on the loading platform.

"Refrigerator?" exclaimed Wentworth when he saw the markings. "Don't that beat all." It was obvious, Russian was bringing in high quality drugs in household appliances. Probably pure heroin. The DEA would pay a fortune for that information.

Dubov examined the four larger pods. Placing his hand on the one stenciled "5," he ordered, "Let's take the top off." The procedure was repeated, only this time, inside the outer aluminum shell was a large, pale brown plastic container marked "# 5, G.E. Commercial Freezer A23."

Fifteen minutes later Dima arrived driving an unmarked tan, Ford rental truck with a twenty-four-foot bed. He parked the vehicle in the trees behind the shed.

Dubov walked over to Wentworth. "Cap'n, you've done enough for now. Take a break. Shamikan, go get the cap'n a drink." Slapping Wentworth on the back, he said, "You've earned it."

Wentworth beamed.

When Shamikan returned with a pint of Myers rum, Wentworth grabbed it, unscrewed the cap and took a long swig. "Thanks, Russian. That's damn good nerve tonic." Shamikan escorted the captain into the small, wooden building that served as his office and closed the door.

When Wentworth was out of sight, Dima backed the large truck into the loading shed. Raising the truck's rear door, he used a Komatsu forklift to unload three large, light green freezer containers from the bed of the truck and place them on the loading platform. They were identical to the pale brown plastic box removed from pod five. Next, he loaded the unopened pods—two, three, and four—into the truck. Working quickly, he piled the four empty shell halves from pods one and five in with the unopened pods. When he had finished, Dima returned the truck to the rear of the shed.

All that remained on the loading platform were the three light green decoy freezers, the pale brown plastic container holding the freezer from pod five, and the smaller, baby blue container labeled Refrigerator.

In the distance, Dubov could see the headlights of the Shaheeds' trucks approaching. The schedule was tight, but holding.

Chapter 5

OCTOBER 17: WANCHESE: 5:15A.M.

The lights from Petya's delivery van flickered in and out of the gray Spanish moss draping the water oaks lining Baumtown Road. The vehicle slowed to a crawl as it turned onto the shell-covered driveway leading up to Wentworth's loading shed. In the passenger seat sat a wiry, silent, thirty-six-year-old Arab with pitch black hair and a full Islamic beard. A beaklike nose—slanted to the side by a blow from a Russian Army major's boot in Afghanistan—protruded from the quizzical, elfish face.

At three minute intervals, four fourteen-foot-bed Ryder rental trucks lumbered in behind the van, parking beside the shed.

"Hashim!" Dubov shouted, waving to the figure slouched low in the delivery van.

The van door creaked open and the slightly built man slowly climbed down, eyes darting left and right, searching for signs of a trap. Satisfied, but keeping his right hand resting lightly on the butt of a 9mm Steyr pistol, Hashim stepped out of the shadows and approached Dubov. "And how was the pickup?" he asked in Russian. He was careful not to address Dubov by name. It irritated him the Chechen had not been as cautious. "Are we on schedule?" He spoke with the calm voice of someone accustomed to early morning rendezvous.

"We're running late. But the cargo's ready to be loaded." Dubov admired Hashim's icy reserve. It had been this coolness under pressure that had convinced Dubov to select him in the first place. There was no room for emotion in what had to be done.

"Then Allah has been kind," Hashim answered, invoking the name of a deity in whom he no longer believed.

A full fourteen inches taller than Hashim, Dubov looked down into the cold, passive, predatory eyes and wondered what passions kindled the pathological hatred that marred his soul. Rumors said his father, a leader of the Islamic Alliance, had been betrayed by the Americans in Pakistan. The planners in Grozny had cautioned Dubov against using the professional terrorist, but he had insisted.

The background files on Hashim were skimpy. Some said he was Iraqi, others, that he spoke Farsi with an Egyptian accent; still others, that he was definitely Pakistani. What was known for certain was that in 1985 he had been in Cairo where he fell under the Messianic influence of the Sunni zealot, Sheikh Tahir Abdel-Jabbar. It was Abdel-Jabbar who had issued the *fatwa* against the communists that had convinced the impressionable Hashim to go to Afghanistan to take part in the anti-Russian jihad.

For a time, Hashim had served the CIA as liaison with the mujahedeen at Jalalabad. When the Russians withdrew in 1989, and the puppet government in Kabul collapsed in 1992, he had stayed behind with the Nostalgic Jihadis. It was during this period that he developed his rabid dislike for all things American. By late 1992, the flame of religious fervor had burned out and been replaced by a smoldering obsession to destroy the Great Satan.

In the four Ryder trucks were the ground troops for phase one. Each vehicle carried two carefully selected members from the newly formed Shaheeds of the Islamic Ummah. The Shaheeds were a militant splinter group of ex-Afghan jihadis recruited by Sheikh Gamal Jibril from the much larger Party of Martyrs, which had been run out of Egypt as a terrorist organization in late 1998. After entering the United States on a visa obtained in Kuwait, the Sheikh had wasted no time in declaring a new fatwa against the Unholy Trinity—the United States, Israel and Egypt.

The driver of the first truck was Nahid Azzam, a native Moroccan who had served the jihad for three years in Afghanistan. He had been wounded twice and still walked with a limp. William Jones-El, a black Muslim from Queens, drove the second vehicle. He was an

Afghan vet who had functioned for the mujahedeen as medic and truck driver. The third driver was Manuel Menendez, a Puerto Rican who had lost the left side of his jaw and three fingers on his right hand to a mine while fighting for the mujahedeen in the outskirts of Kabul. The fourth truck was driven by Hadi Aseraf al-Riyami, a veteran of the radical Muslim rebel movement in the Philippines.

Each driver was accompanied by a younger, trainee-martyr whose responsibility was to ensure the destruction of the cargo if something went wrong. To accomplish this, he was expected to stay with the container and detonate the attached explosives by hand. Such a mission required the services of a special type of brainwashed devotee.

Hashim had been in charge of selecting and training the martyrs. The techniques used were the field tested procedures perfected by Hamas. The selection process began when twelve of the most likely candidates were led into a New Jersey cemetery at night. The recruits were told to lie down in empty graves in groups of three. The graves were covered with a heavy black cloth and sprinkled with dirt. If the volunteer could stay buried for twenty minutes, he passed the first test. Next, eight of the bravest novices were instructed to lie in individual graves and told to recite passages from the Koran. From these, the six who showed the least fear were selected and led into the wilderness where they spent three days and nights, alone, reading and reciting passages from the Koran. From this group, the final four were chosen.

The payoff for martyrdom was substantial, if only promissory. Sheikh Jibril assured the volunteers that if they were called to heaven in the name of the cause, they would be declared true martyrs. As martyrs they would go straight to paradise where they would sit next to God. For all eternity, they, and seventy of their chosen relatives and friends, would enjoy permanent bliss and dine on never ending rivers of golden honey. As an added bonus, they were each promised seventy-two virgin brides to help while away the boredom of the everlasting.

Dubov took Hashim aside, "Are the drivers ready?"

"They've been instructed. The facilities in Chicago, Dallas, San Francisco, and New York are prepared."

Dubov grabbed Hashim's arm, "You didn't mention New Orleans."

"It's okay," Hashim assured him. "There was a problem with the Guidry brothers. They demanded an extra five thousand dollars. By the time the truck gets there, the place will be ready."

"Good," Dubov said, releasing his grip. "Shamikan will go with the New Orleans shipment. What have you told your drivers about the cargo?"

"They think the crates contain plastic explosives. That is sufficient."

Dubov nodded. "Let's get moving. Your van gets loaded first."

Hashim backed the delivery van into the shed. Using the forklift, Dima carefully loaded the vehicle with the baby blue plastic crate labeled, GE Refrigerator, Model 704E.

Dubov tapped Petya on the shoulder, "Go get Wentworth and Shamikan. I want the captain here for the next part."

After relieving himself in the bushes, Wentworth stumbled up to Dubov. Reeking of rum, he muttered, "Shay, Russian. You wants to see me? Are you ready to pay?"

"In a minute, Cap'n. First, I need help loading these containers."

"Whersch them big metal boxes?" Wentworth asked, swaying unsteadily on his feet.

"They've been put away. The real cargo is in these plastic containers." Looking into Wentworth's glazed eyes, Dubov worried that he had given the Captain too much to drink. It was important he see, and remember.

As the Ryder truck for New Orleans backed up to the loading dock, Dubov called to Dima, "Put the brown container marked number five on this one."

One by one the remaining three Ryder trucks were driven into the shed and loaded with the light green plastic containers labeled "GE Commercial Freezer A23."

When the last truck was ready, Dubov walked over to Hashim. In a low voice and in Russian, he said, "Your warhead will be the first. It's scheduled to be detonated at the third call for prayer on the thirty-first. Tell no one." Looking at Hashim's diminutive size, he said, "I could send someone with you to help unload."

"The fewer who know where I'm going, the better."

It was 6:45 A.M. The eastern horizon was beginning to glow a light orange. "If you leave now, you should be in downtown Manhattan by 4:30 this afternoon. Good luck."

"As Allah wills it," Hashim replied, swinging his light frame behind the steering wheel of the delivery van.

Dubov watched in silence as the van's taillights disappeared into the early morning mist. He regretted not being able to share *all* the details of the operation with Hashim. The complexity of the plan would have appealed to him. It was strange, Dubov thought, how the wheel of life turns. Fifteen years ago he and Hashim had been enemies in Afghanistan. Both Muslims, they would have ripped out each other's throats without blinking an eye. Now, they were allies. A phantom pain wracked his left shoulder. He rubbed his hand over the old scar and wondered if Hashim had fired the rocket that had sent him to the hospital. Dubov shook his head. The role assigned to Hashim was unfortunate.

Returning to the loading platform, Dubov called Wentworth over. Patting him on the back, he said, "Let's go to your office. I have your payment." Turning to Petya, he said "Get the briefcase and the cap'n's special present."

"Follow me," Wentworth beamed, staggering towards the gray, clapboard shack that served as his home and office. He had decided against turning Russian in for a reward—unless the DEA offered at least three hundred thousand.

When Petya joined them in the shack, he handed Dubov a leather briefcase and a quart of rum.

Dubov waved the rum at Wentworth. "Cap'n, here's a man-sized drink and a briefcase full of appreciation. Take it, it's all yours."

Wentworth grinned broadly. It was Myers, his favorite. His eyes grew misty at Dubov's thoughtfulness. Unscrewing the cap, he poured himself a water glass full of the dark liquid. In his haste, he failed to notice that the plastic seal was missing. Raising the glass to his mouth, he hesitated—

Dubov held his breath. Had he seen?

The captain grinned and thoughtfully wiped the smudged rim of the glass with the greasy sleeve of his denim shirt, "You first, Russian, my good friend."

Dubov exhaled, "Thanks, Cap'n, but I've got a long way to go today."

"In that case, bottom's up," Wentworth exclaimed, drinking the rum down straight. When the last drop had disappeared, he lowered the glass and gazed warmly in Dubov's direction. As the 100 proof alcohol coursed through his system, he carefully lifted the leather briefcase and lovingly placed it on a sheet of plywood balanced on two sawhorses. Flipping both latches at once, he raised the lid and looked down at the neat stacks of crisp, hundred dollar bills.

As he counted the stacks, his vision began to blur and the tip of his nose started to tingle. Wiping his eyes with his hand, he tried to focus on the money. Swooning to the left, he knocked the briefcase off the makeshift table. Beads of sweat popped out on his forehead. He shouldn't have sloshed down that whole glass of rum. Lurching forward, he clutched at the plywood table. Losing his balance, he crashed to the floor.

"Is he dead?" Petya asked, kicking Wentworth's leg with the toe of his boot.

"No, only passed out," replied Dubov, leaning over and examining the pupils of Wentworth's eyes. He hadn't planned on the captain drinking so much Veronal. "He'll be out at least eight to ten hours. Let's turn him over on his stomach. I don't want him choking on vomit."

Dubov pried a wad of bills from Wentworth's grip and placed them back in the briefcase. Tweaking the Captain's fleshy jowls, he said, "Remember your lines well."

ORLY AIRPORT, PARIS

Murphy's head snapped back with a jolt. His eyes blinked open. Where was he? Oh yeah, Orly airport. Shifting his weight from his right hip to his left, he tried to find a bearable comfort-zone on the hard, contoured plastic seat. Multiple time zone travel, with only snatches of micro-sleep, always upset his biorhythms. In *Health Now* he had read an article that blamed ozone poisoning for giving passengers the blahs, but he figured it was the lack of sleep. He had tried all the gimmicks—melatonin, eating light, yoga exercises—nothing seemed to work.

Lately, life had become one long series of spine-crunching seats in nameless, pastel-colored, passenger lounges. The only things that ever changed were the languages in the ads for the duty-free stores. He shifted his weight again.

Unable to rest, he decided to pass the time engaging in his favorite airport sport, people watching, preferably female people. Orly was a real crossroads, full of all sorts of shapes, colors, and sizes. Three seats down, two screaming boys with olive complexions, dark eyes and black curly hair, tussled over a miniature car. Murphy guessed they were eight or nine. Glancing at their mother—five-foot-two, a hundred and five pounds—he judged they could be older. He always had trouble telling ages when the parents were small. They were babbling a bastardized French. Probably Algerian, maybe Haitian. He checked the clock—9:34A.M. Ninety minutes of dwell time until his flight. If he was lucky, the plane would only be half full.

Stretching his left leg to ease a cramp, he continued to scan the passenger lounge for interesting women. On reaching Cairo he planned on taking a nice long soak in a hot tub, sipping some first class hooch and crashing for twelve hours straight. The overnight from Dulles had been cold, noisy, and packed. At least the Company's bean counters had okayed a business class ticket. Even then, he had been kept awake by a gaggle of Georgetown students who had managed to party their way across the Atlantic. He remembered when he was that age, when travel was exciting, but that had been several lifetimes ago.

After loosening his tie, he removed his jacket. The armpits felt clammy from perspiration. Then he remembered—the nightmare. There he was, standing in the cabin of a plane, beside a silver canister with a red cross plastered on its side. The gauge on top of the canister started slowly ticking down to 0. He tried to move, but his arms and legs were frozen. Blurred instructions in Arabic and Russian were written on the side of the canister. While he watched, the object morphed into a shiny, oblong nuclear bomb. Trying to yell to warn the crew, his mouth moved, but no sound came out. When the hand on the gage reached 0, the blond flight attendant turned and in a friendly voice said, "Have a nice day."

It was the second time in less than twenty-four hours he had been haunted by the same dream. It was all so vivid. The black hand on the gauge, the good-natured face of the flight attendant, the smell of cordite. Cordite? He remembered the sharp smell of cordite from Vietnam. He wondered if a nuclear explosion smelled of cordite.

Trying to cheer himself up, he decided to concentrate on something pleasant. The purchase of a new sports car when he returned home. Four days of R and R in Paris on the flip side of the Cairo trip. Nothing worked. Standing and stretching he spotted the neon liquor and tobacco signs at the duty-free store. Time for a walkabout.

In the men's room, Murphy bent over the stainless steel sink and splashed cold water on his face. As he dried his cheeks and forehead with a paper towel, he stared at the tired, bloodshot eyes glaring back from the mirror. It had finally happened, he looked as bad as his passport photo.

Leaving the men's room, he strolled over to the den of bad habits, the duty-free store. He decided to treat himself to a box of Cuban cigars and a couple of liters of good booze. In the refrigerator against the far wall were the *Habana*s. Although the current Cuban cigars were no longer the world-class stogies of the fifties and sixties, the fact they were still illegal in the US made them desirable. After a few minutes of comparison shopping, he selected a box of Partagas El Presidentes. He would buy a box for Warner on the way back home.

Keeping an eye on the time, he meandered through the premium liquor section. Reading the labels, he settled for a bottle of Luksusowa vodka, and a liter of Johnny Walker, black. In Cairo, the good stuff was hard to find and cost a fortune.

Next, he wandered over to the newsstand. A book titled *Nostradamus: Prophecies for the Millennium* caught his eye. He picked up a copy and thumbed through the pages. Good, there were lots of color photos and diagrams.

Murphy wondered if Friar still remembered his obsession with Nostradamus when both were first classmen at VMI. It had been Murphy, the English major-romanticist, a believer in prophecies, and Friar, the chemist-pragmatist who had chided his roommate for monumental gullibility. But, dabbling in the mumbo-jumbo like some thirteenth century soothsayer had been fun, a welcome diversion from the boredom of military life. Twice Murphy had visited the Library of Congress to read translations of *De Daemonibus* and the *Kabbalah*. He had loved it all, the secret incantations, the esoteric symbols.

As a senior project, he had written a paper on the interpretation of Quatrains 67 and 97, in Century 10. After a limited amount of research he had divined that the quatrains announced the end of the world in 3797. Friar had not been amused. Murphy had even purchased a brass bowl at a flea market in Lexington for a trial run at water gazing, but Vietnam had interfered. Now, it was Friar who was playing with the tarot. Murphy chuckled as he planned how to present the Nostradamus book to Friar as a Christmas present, along with a shiny new brass bowl and a deck of tarot cards.

Leaving the newsstand he headed back to the passenger lounge. Noticing a coffee trolley, he stopped for a large cappuccino. He was feeling better. The walk had started the blood circulating and the book on Nostradamus had brought back pleasant memories.

While waiting for the caffeine to kick in, he sat down and resumed his people watching. A pair of young, bronzed starlets with blond hair and hourglass figures wiggled by, their tight miniskirts bulging in all the right places. Probably Scandinavian, most likely Danish. Occupation? Movie star wannabes on their way home from an Italian or French film festival. Married? Definitely not—they laughed too much.

Next, he noticed a tired, Asian woman with the thousand yard stare. She was standing in a corner of the lounge, her back propped against a support column. Balanced on her left hip was a sleeping infant, while tugging on her skirt was an active, two-year-old boy. Sticking out of the mother's mouth was the baby's pacifier. Murphy pegged her as a housewife from Hong Kong, on her way to New York to meet her overworked, underpaid husband.

Shifting his gaze, he noticed a striking woman with glossy, shoulder length chestnut hair, sitting directly across the aisle facing him. When their eyes met, she blushed and quickly turned away. Unless he was mistaken, she had been watching him. He noted the finely sculpted features, the classic chin, the full mouth. Age? Thirty to thirty-two. She swept a stray hair from her forehead with a delicate gesture. Good, he thought, no wedding ring. She was dressed in a camel-colored cashmere sweater, coordinated with a plaid wool skirt. On her lap was a Burberry raincoat. Definitely English, he concluded. Nice full-bodied figure, with well proportioned legs. Murphy preferred the voluptuous, Rubenesque look to the thin, heroin-chic so popular with fashion models. Occupation? Probably owns a dress shop in London. She's returning home from a shopping trip to Paris and maybe a tryst with her Italian lover.

Next, his eyes focused on a small, dark-haired girl playing with a well-worn Raggedy Ann doll. She reminded him of Sarah, his daughter, when she was that age. He had bought her a Raggedy Ann at Harrods. A wave of regret engulfed him. On assignment in England, he had missed her sixth birthday. The doll had been shipped by overnight express, but it wasn't the same as his being there. Now Sarah was twenty-six with a daughter of her own. A single parent forced to juggle a career with raising a child. He could never think of Sarah without reminding himself of what a failure he had been as a parent.

At first he had blamed Sue. She would never accompany him on any of his overseas tours. By the time the Agency agreed to an extended stateside assignment, the locks of the apartment in Alexandria had been changed. Twelve years of marriage, and they were complete strangers. For Sarah's sake, he had gone through the motions— two marriage counselors, an attempt at reconciliation, but it was too late. The fire had burned out and all that remained were ashes of the might-have-beens.

He never figured out what went wrong. When Sue's mother died shortly after their tenth anniversary, she had become obsessed with aging. He first noticed it when the mirrors started disappearing from the house. After work, he would come home to find her sitting alone in the dark, rubbing youth cream on her face, arms, and legs. Her doctor had recommended psychiatric evaluation, but she had refused. As her phobia grew worse, Murphy began finding excuses to stay away. He started seeing other women.

When the divorce was final, Sue turned to the bottle full-time. Murphy tried to gain custody of Sarah, but the court turned him down, citing his constant travel and philandering. When Sue finally achieved her alcoholic shortcut to oblivion, Sarah came to live with him in Alexandria. Murphy tried to re-establish a meaningful relationship, but there was too much distance between them. He sensed she blamed him for Sue's death.

Murphy promised himself that when he left the Agency and moved to Chapel Hill in six months he would make it up to Sarah and little Kimberly. Maybe he would have better luck with Kim.

"TWA flight 12 to Cairo, now boarding, gate seven."

Murphy reached in his briefcase and removed his ticket and passport. He held them side by side. Last year he had checked in at Athens with a passport that didn't match the name on his ticket. That little stunt had almost landed him in detention.

Standing in line, he examined the ticket and passport one last time. Both read, Patrick A. Murphy. He liked traveling under his own name on a diplomatic passport. It got him special treatment and kept the local gendarmes off his back. The airport officials in Egypt were especially nosy and meddlesome.

"Next," called the bright, young ticket agent with the peaches and cream complexion. "Passport, please." She spoke perfect English with a slight Parisian accent. With one glance she had tagged Murphy as American. How could these airline personnel always tell? He felt as if he were traveling with a neon sign dangling from his neck flashing, "American spy." He handed Bright Eyes the ticket and passport.

Examining the documents, she checked her computer screen. "Mr. Murphy, your wife is already on board. Your ticket has been upgraded to first class. Your new seat is 4A."

Wife? Sue's been dead for over ten years. Murphy started to correct the smiling agent, but hesitated. Maybe, if he was lucky, he could wrangle a first class seat out of the foul-up. Then he could get some sleep.

BOONE, NORTH CAROLINA

A tinge of homesickness settled over Dima as the truck lumbered through the Blue Ridge Mountains, into the outskirts of Boone. The craggy outcroppings of granite and the changing fall colors reminded him of his home in Goy-chu. Turning off US Highway 421 onto NC 105, he wondered if there was much bear hunting in these mountains. Gearing the truck down for a stop light, he thought of his father, who hunted black bear in the Caucasus for a living. He would feel right at home in these—

Whomp. The sudden impact made the truck lurch forward, narrowly missing a gray-haired woman pushing a shopping cart full of groceries across the street. In the sideview mirror, Dima could see the steam hissing from the crumpled radiator of a bright yellow, Nissan 300ZX.

"What happened?" Dubov grunted, jolted awake by the sound of shattering glass and twisting metal.

"*Glupetz*," Dima shouted, shaking his fist at the reflection of the sports car in the mirror. "Some idiot rammed us from behind." Pulling the truck to the side of the road, he reached to switch off the engine.

Grabbing Dima's arm, Dubov said, "Keep the motor running. It could be a trap."

Climbing down from the truck's cab, Dubov quickly glanced around. He loosened his jacket to free the handle of the Glock automatic hidden in the belt holster in the small of his back. Walking to the rear of the truck, he examined the slightly dented bumper, then stepped over to the sports car. Inside were two teenagers dressed in Appalachian State University sweatshirts. Much too young for FBI or CIA, he decided. The hood, radiator, and headlights were smashed. On the Nissan's twisted plastic bumper was a sticker with the outline of a skull and mushroom cloud with the words, "Just one nuclear blast can ruin your whole day."

A policeman who had been drinking coffee across the street at Wendy's came running up. Waving to Dubov, he said, "I saw the whole thing. Wait right here."

The officer walked over to the sports car, and peered in at the two dazed young men slouched in the front seats. Rapping on the driver's window he asked, "Sir, could I please see your driver's license and registration?"

The odor of beer drifted from the car when the window was rolled down. In a daze, the driver fumbled through his billfold, but was unable to locate his license.

Disgusted, the policeman stepped back and in his most authoritative voice demanded, "Sir, would you please step out of the vehicle?" It irritated him having to call these over-privileged students "sir."

He secretly enjoyed writing DUI tickets for the frat-brats with the flashy sports cars and unlimited expense accounts. This would be the tenth this week.

When the door of the Nissan creaked open, a half-empty beer can thudded to the ground, spewing suds on the officer's carefully polished shoes. On the floorboard, behind the driver's seat, rattled the empty remnants of two six-packs.

Dubov approached the policeman. Noting his name tag, he said, "Officer Clapp, it really didn't hurt my truck. We're in a hurry. Mind if I drop by the station tomorrow morning to fill out the papers?"

"No, sir," came the instant reply. Pulling himself up to his full five-foot-six inch, 165 pound frame, Officer Clapp declared, "State law says you got to make an *immediate* report when there's injury or property damage exceeding five hundred dollars. Looks to me like this here Nissan's pretty well banged up and them boys just might be hurt."

Dubov looked at his watch. 1:34P.M. Shaking his head, he backed away. The less Officer Clapp noticed about the truck, the better. If he became too inquisitive—

Forty-five minutes later, after taking names and license numbers, making measurements of skid marks, and filling out the accident report in minute detail, officer Clapp waved them on.

It was 3:45P.M. by the time the truck reached the foot of Yellow Mountain.

"There's the turnoff," Petya said, pointing to a black, rusting mailbox half-hidden by two rhododendron bushes. "On the right, 100 meters."

Dima swung the fourteen-wheeler onto the narrow dirt road and shifted into low. The engine groaned as the truck began the laborious climb up the steep road to the Cranberry Iron Works, half a mile away.

"What's the altitude of the mine?" Dubov asked.

"The entrance is 1,100 meters above sea level. The mine runs back horizontally into the mountain for about a kilometer and a half. Several slopes off the main shaft go down a hundred meters or so. They're all flooded with water."

"Excellent," replied Dubov. "And the condition of the main shaft?"

"The roof's caved in at several places. There's a major collapse 115 meters back in. We cleared most of it and cut a path 400 meters to the seventh slope."

When the truck reached the crumbling entrance gate leading to the mine, Dubov could see several old buildings clinging to the side of the mountain like relics from a Western ghost town. The structures consisted of a series of dilapidated, wooden framed buildings with vines and trees growing through broken floor boards and roofs. Remnants of brick chimneys rose from the two largest, weathered structures while rusting tin covered the roof of the main building. At the northern and southern ends of the property, tailings of spent iron ore were piled in thirty foot heaps. A narrow, gravel road led past the buildings to the mine entrance, which was framed with sagging wooden beams, shored up by timber jacks.

With Petya's guidance, Dima gingerly backed the truck up to the entrance. After the truck was parked, Petya started a gasoline generator, which provided electricity to a string of 100-watt bulbs leading deep into the interior of the main shaft. Inside the mine, the air was thick with the smell of musty earth, bat guano, and cobwebs.

It took the men ninety minutes to unload the truck. With the forklift, they put pod number three in the main room of the largest of the wooden structures. The remaining two unopened pods were placed twenty meters inside the mine. They would move them to their final storage positions after Dr. Volodinsky had finished his work.

"Howdy, neighbor," boomed a loud voice.

Dubov jumped, startled by the intrusion. Turning towards the sound, he saw two figures dressed in coveralls, standing at the mine entrance, thirty feet away.

"Y'all must be the new renters," the larger of the two said, walking toward Dubov and extending a weatherworn hand. "I'm Big Ed Hazelwood, this here's my sixteen-year-old boy, Little Ed."

"What can I do for you?" Dubov asked, taking Big Ed firmly by the arm and leading him back outside the mine. Think, he told himself—what had they seen?

"Read in last week's *Avery County Journal* how someone was planning on renting this here mine. Said they was gonna convert it into one of them tourist attractions."

Tugging on Big Ed's shirt sleeve, Little Ed said, "Pa, I bet it's gonna be an ore mining outfit where tourists pan for gold and gems. The kind like they got over at Spruce Pine."

"Is that so?" Big Ed asked, scratching his chin.

"We're thinking about it," Dubov replied, guiding the two men towards the gate. "But, it'll be at least next spring before—"

"What's all them funny looking things over there?" Big Ed asked, pointing to the four empty pod halves lying on the ground beside the truck.

"Containers for safety equipment," replied Dubov. "There are a lot of cave-ins inside the mine." Spotting a dusty, silver GMC pickup parked immediately outside the gate entrance, he walked the two men to their vehicle. Forcing a wide, friendly, down-home smile, he said, "Look, we're busy unloading generators, checking wiring, removing rocks. I'll give you a tour later, when the mine's not so dangerous. Why don't you give me your telephone number?"

Big Ed gazed at Dubov, "You fellars from up North?"

"Chicago," replied Dubov.

"Thought so," Big Ed replied, nodding to Little Ed. "I kin always tell. You sure got a funny accent. Me and Little Ed live down the road you just come up. Second house on the right. We work at Finlay's General Mercantile, over in Minneapolis. The store don't need both of us after October." Big Ed extended his hand a second time, "Don't forgit, last name's Hazlewood. Big Ed Hazlewood. Phone number's 733-1400. I sure would like to find out what you got planned. Maybe you can give Little Ed a job for the winter. He's a real hard worker."

"I'll let you know," Dubov replied, opening the door of the pickup and holding it until Big Ed climbed in.

When Dubov returned to the mine, Petya was waiting. "Should we go take care of them? We could wrap their bodies in chains and dump them down one of the flooded slopes."

"No. Might attract too much attention. I know where they live."

ORLY AIRPORT

The on-board flight attendant examined Murphy's ticket. With a wave of her hand she directed him to the left, towards first class. Entering the land of overindulgence and special privilege, he strained to catch a glimpse of the passenger seated in 4B. With his recent bad luck it was sure to be a ninety-year-old granny who had mistakenly switched the wrong ticket. Standing on his tiptoes, he peered over the head rests. Counting the rows from front to back—1B, 2B, 3B, 4B—he saw *her*—the London dress shop owner. His pulse jumped. For the first time in months, the gods of fortune were smiling on him.

Murphy nervously tapped his boarding pass against the palm of his hand while he waited for the passenger in row seven to wrestle a large carry-on into the overhead bin. So, the dress shop owner *had* been staring at him in the passenger lounge. What was the connection? Warner and a couple of CIA personnel were the only ones who were supposed to know which flight he was on. Was she CIA? FBI? Without taking his eyes off his seatmate, he walked the few remaining steps to row four. Self-consciously clearing his throat, he waited for her to acknowledge his presence.

Looking up, she stammered in fluent English, "Mr. M-Murphy, I-I hope this seat is satisfactory." She extended her hand.

Murphy took it, not knowing what to expect. It was soft and delicate—and trembling. Embarrassed, he held on for a second, then reluctantly let go.

Reaching over, she removed her Burberry coat from his seat.

A middle-aged flight attendant with Tammy Faye makeup and a fixed, face-lift smile, approached, "Care for a drink?"

A warm, fuzzy feeling settled over Murphy as he eased down into the plush, leather seat. "Champagne, please." Looking at his companion, who had diverted her eyes, he added, "For both of us."

Murphy sat back, closed his eyes and breathed deeply. He was afraid to ask questions and break the spell. The faint scent of Chanel Number 22 tickled his nose. While reveling in his good fortune, he felt a nudge on his arm. When he opened his eyes, his mystery companion handed him a copy of the TWA flight magazine. A handwritten note was paper clipped inside:

Mr. Patrick A. Murphy,

We are pleased you responded so quickly to our message. My name is Natasha Romanov. I am the daughter of General Stepka Filip Zakharov whom you are going to Cairo to meet. My father is seeking asylum for himself and his family in exchange for information of great importance to your government. Please do not ask questions until we are safely in Cairo.

When we arrive at the terminal, gather your bags and escort me through customs. I assume you are traveling on a diplomatic passport. I have a standard American passport listing me as your wife. A car and driver will be waiting.

If you agree, please nod.

Murphy re-read the note, turned and nodded. On the bottom he jotted, "When we get to Cairo, I have to check in by telephone with my friends. They are expecting me."

Natasha's face knotted into a frown. Taking the note, she scribbled, "Your Cairo Station has been compromised by Russian military intelligence."

Murphy's eyes widened—Cairo Station penetrated by the GRU? Out of the corner of his eye he could see the tension in her unlined, unwrinkled face. If she was really the daughter of a Russian general, why undertake such a dangerous trip? For all Murphy knew, *she* could be GRU.

Leaning towards her, he said in a low voice, "It's just a routine call." If Russian intelligence had wormed its way into Cairo Station, the less he told them over the phone, the better. He glanced at her left hand, which still held the note. If she was to pose as his wife, she would need a wedding ring. Holding up his ring finger, he touched it. "Ring?"

She looked puzzled, then jotted, "Single, widow."

Murphy smiled. She had misunderstood, but had given him the answer he most wanted to hear.

When the flight attendant arrived with the champagne, she handed a glass to Natasha, then Murphy. "First time? In Cairo?"

"Yes," Murphy replied, taking Natasha by the hand. "It's *our* first time." He had been to *Um al Dunyaù*—Mother of the World—dozens of times, but never with anyone like Natasha. On previous trips, Cairo had seemed dusty, crowded, noisy, and hostile. Now, he was actually looking forward to landing. It only took two sips of champagne and a glance at Natasha to silence the warning bells going off in the rational, left side of his brain.

MANHATTAN: 4:49P.M.

Hashim backed the Ford delivery van up to the loading platform at the North Tower of the Skyview Plaza apartment complex. The entrance to the Holland tunnel had been stacked with traffic, but downtown Manhattan was unusually quiet. Watching his reflection in the rear view mirror, he zipped up the denim coveralls embroidered with "Fakhir" on the left breast pocket and "Tischler Appliance Co." on the back. It took ten minutes to locate the building superintendent and arrange for the delivery of the refrigerator to apartment 2807.

"Okay, Faker, that's gonna cost you 250 bucks," Quincy Totten declared. "Sometin' that heavy's gonna take two men." Pointing a yellowed, tobacco-stained finger at an illegible sheet of paper tacked to the wall, he said, "See that? Two men—$250. Union scale. No exceptions." Watching Hashim closely, the gaunt, middle-aged man, with crowded teeth, added, "Gonna hafta be cash money. Quincy Totten don't take no checks."

"Okay," Hashim grumbled, irritated at Totten's curt manner and condescending tone. It was obvious the price had been hiked an extra hundred when he saw Hashim was Arab. Handing the building super a wad of tens, Hashim said, "I'm going up with the refrigerator to make sure you don't damage it."

Totten nodded, then sauntered off to find his helper.

After twenty minutes of grunting, sweating, and cursing, the oversized container, strapped to a creaking hand truck, was rolled into place in the apartment.

"Dat was some heavy mutha-fucka. What kinda refrigerator you got there?" asked Alphonse Sapp, Totten's beefy, stoop-shouldered union helper. "Want we should uncrate it?"

"No," Hashim replied. "Just leave it. The owner doesn't want it touched."

"Dat's fine with me," Sapp said, throwing up his scarred hands. "I ain't never seen no plastic container like dat. Have you, Quincy?"

"Nope. Can't say I ever did," Totten responded, examining the strange, baby blue plastic crate. Slowly counting out seven of the ten-dollar bills, he handed them to Sapp. "Here's your half."

When Hashim returned to his van he took one last look at the Skyview Plaza. He hoped both Totten and Sapp would be working at the apartment complex at noon on the thirty-first, when his father's death would be avenged.

Chapter 6

OCTOBER 17: CAIRO

The five and a half hour flight from Paris to Cairo was all too short. Murphy desperately wanted more time with Natasha, a chance to ask *real* questions. She had limited their conversation to the idle chit-chat that frequently passes for dialogue between spouses. He hoped her apparent lack of interest was part of an act, an effort to avoid unwanted attention from nosy passengers. To keep his fantasy alive, he allowed himself to project a deeper, hidden meaning to their non-conversation.

Thirty minutes prior to landing, while Murphy was trying to determine how to clear customs with a new wife in tow, Natasha handed him her American passport. Inside the cover, below a rather severe photo, was printed, Natasha R. Murphy. Any doubt he had about the efficiency of General Zakharov's organization vanished when he saw the home address: 1341 Glenview Ave., Alexandria, Virginia. *His* address. He thumbed through the worn pages. There were dozens of stamps from Heathrow, Miami, Orly, Rome, Moscow. It was a masterpiece of forgery, a real testament to the cobbler's trade.

Clearing customs was a breeze. When Murphy showed his diplomatic passport, the supervisor rushed over and personally escorted them into the main terminal.

With a firm grip on their handbags, and pushing the luggage trolley ahead like a plow, Murphy and Natasha threaded their way through the usual gauntlet of taxi shills. "Taxi, sir? Taxi, madam? See the pyramids, half price. Ride a camel? Best guide in Cairo. Cheap."

On spotting Natasha, a heavy-set Arab, dressed in an off-white cotton shirt, khaki pants, and checkered red-and-white headdress, worked his way through the crowd. "*Ahlan wa-sahlan,* Miss Natasha. Your car is waiting."

"Thank you, Ahmed," she replied, handing him her bags.

After making the obligatory phone call to Cairo Station to let them know he had arrived, but carefully avoiding any mention of the purpose of his mission, Murphy joined Natasha at the curb. The clash of car horns and shouts of street peddlers was exactly as he remembered from his previous visits. Had he not been so fatigued and preoccupied with Natasha, he might have noticed a pair of intense eyes watching their every move.

"Carry your bag, sir?" asked a stumpy, thickset figure, dressed in the grimy, flowing galabia of a street peddler. A soiled fez was perched on the top of his greasy head. Crowding up to Murphy, the peddler grabbed for the bag of duty free cigars and liquor temporarily parked beside Murphy's feet.

"Back off," Murphy growled, jerking the plastic handle from the peddler's grip.

From across the street, Ahmed yelled in Arabic and shook a muscular fist at the intruder, who quickly melted into the crowd. Hastily ushering Murphy and Natasha into a 1990 red Toyota Land Cruiser, Ahmed quickly slammed the doors shut. "That man up to no good," he mumbled as he switched on the ignition and swung the heavy vehicle into the flow of traffic headed southwest.

From behind a donkey cart loaded with straw, the street peddler watched the Land Cruiser disappear down Salah Salem Avenue. Lifting the corner of his robe, he pulled a cellular phone from the back pocket of his dark brown military pants. "They've left the airport," he said in Russian.

As the Toyota rumbled over the uneven pavement, Natasha looked out the window and sighed. It was as if some great weight had suddenly been lifted from her shoulders. Turning to Murphy, she said, "We can talk now. Ahmed is one of us. He can be trusted."

"Where are we headed?" Murphy asked, pleased at the softening of her voice.

"To the City of the Dead. My father is waiting there. He would've been at the airport to meet us, but he's not feeling well." Lowering her eyes, she said, "He's dying from emphysema."

"Sorry," Murphy responded, genuinely concerned with anything that might upset her. Changing the subject, he said, "You speak excellent English."

"Thank you," she replied. "I attended Reading University in England for four years. That's where I met my husband, Sergei. We lived in London from 1993 until 1996."

Murphy's face fell at the mention of the word, husband, "But, I thought—"

"He was murdered last year. Shot to death at the Moscow airport in broad daylight by Russian gangsters who–who demanded—" Her voice trailed off. The memory was too painful to continue. She took a handkerchief from her purse and dabbed her eyes.

"I'm sorry," Murphy said, wanting to reach over and take her in his arms. Batting zero in the small talk department he decided to wait until after their meeting with the general before asking further questions.

In twenty minutes they reached the northeastern entrance to the City of the Dead. The City, a funerary complex of marble and concrete tombs, stretches for more than three and a half miles along Cairo's eastern edge. In addition to serving as a cemetery, for over three centuries the extensive graveyard has provided shelter to Cairo's homeless who live in and among the mausoleums and crypts. A no man's land on the fringe of Egyptian society, the back streets and burial chambers are home to Cairo's drug dealers, criminals, militants, and spies.

During his last Egyptian tour ten years ago, Murphy spent several weekends browsing the City's historic, Mamluk funerary structures. The history and culture of the Mamluk sultans, who ruled Egypt from 1250 until the Turks took over in 1517, fascinated him. Of particular interest was their unusual form of government. It was a meritocracy that required Mamluk sultans to prove they had once been slaves in order to hold high office. When a sultan died his wealth and power was returned to the ruling amirs for redistribution. To provide minimal support for their families after their demise, the Mamluk Sultans built elaborate tombs in the City of the Dead. Family members were allowed small stipends by the amirs for taking care of the crypts.

On entering the gate, Ahmed turned left, and drove past the Khanqah of Barquq, a funerary complex containing two of Cairo's tallest minarets. At the third concrete corner post, capped by a small onion-shaped dome, the Land Cruiser turned right, then slowly made its way down a narrow, gravel path. Pulling up to the entrance of a large, stucco mausoleum, Ahmed climbed out and signaled for Murphy and Natasha to follow. He led them to a heavy metal door painted white to blend in with the stucco. Murphy noticed the lens of a security camera protruding from the top of the door frame. Ahmed knocked twice, once, then twice.

The door creaked open. A Russian guard, with a neck the size of a tree trunk, squinted at Ahmed, then stepped out into the glaring sunlight. He was dressed in a nondescript, olive drab uniform. In his left arm he cradled a Kalashnikov AKS-47. Nodding to Ahmed, he patted Murphy down for weapons. Without speaking he motioned with his head for them to enter.

"Natasha," a weak but commanding voice called from the far side of the room.

"Father!" she replied, rushing over to the gaunt, frail figure seated in a chrome plated wheelchair. "You look tired."

"I'm fine, now that you're here," replied General Zakharov.

The inside of the mausoleum was cool and smelled of earth. The thick concrete walls and high ceiling helped keep out the stifling afternoon heat. A coat of white plaster made the single room, illuminated by two bare 75-watt bulbs, appear much larger than it was. A heavy wooden table, surrounded by three folding metal chairs, was situated in the center of the room. On the table were three Wedgewood cups and saucers, and a sterling silver tea service.

General Zakharov, an old fifty-nine, peered out at the world through dark brown eyes, set off by a pair of bushy, gray eyebrows. The collar of his starched white shirt hung loosely around his neck. A long narrow face, with high, sunken cheekbones, evidenced his losing battle with emphysema.

Still holding the general's hand, Natasha said, "Father, this is Mr. Patrick Murphy."

"Ah, Mr. Murphy. I'm pleased you're here," the general wheezed, his thin lips twisting into a crooked smile.

Murphy reached over and shook the general's hand. He was surprised at the strength of the grip, but there was no warmth in the fingers.

"I hope you don't mind if I remain seated. My health hasn't been good. Too many of your excellent Virginia cigarettes. My doctor tells me the alveoli in my lungs are as black as the sins on my soul."

"You'll get better, Father," Natasha assured him, "as soon as we get to America."

The general gazed at Murphy, "I understand there are specialists in the US who treat this disease. Good doctors at Johns Hopkins and Duke Universities." The general spoke perfect English, a byproduct of ten years in London as resident director of the KGB's English network.

"Quite a few," Murphy responded, not knowing if there were any at all. He had been in the game so long it was easier to lie than tell the truth. He would ask Warner to check around. A reference to the right doctor or hospital might make a good bargaining chip.

"Yalena, some Black Russian tea," demanded the general.

Out of the corner of his eye, Zakharov noticed Murphy examining the bottom of his saucer. "Don't worry, Mr. Murphy. It's Wedgewood. A gift from Kim Philby, one of England's finest." Philby, the Third Man in the Cambridge Communist Spy Ring, had reported to the general while Zakharov was in Beirut in 1960 and 1961. There was a twinkle in the general's eye as he glanced at Natasha. He had never been a good communist. He had always been too fond of life's little, expensive luxuries.

Zakharov waved to Ahmed, "Take Fabiyan outside and stand guard. We don't want to be disturbed." He dropped four cubes of sugar into his teacup, then turned to Murphy, "I hope you won't think me rude, but we must proceed with business. I tire easily and time is short."

"I understand," Murphy replied, eager to begin. The jet lag was beginning to weigh on his eyelids and he knew that if he closed them for even a moment, he might fall asleep.

"Good. I'm gratified Mr. Warner sent someone of your caliber to discuss my proposition. We have quite a dossier on you." Pausing, he said, "I was assigned to the Russian embassy in Cairo as trade attaché when you were here in 1978. I doubt you remember me, my cover name was Polevanofsky."

Murphy blanched—Polevanofsky—he knew that name well. His nickname at the Agency had been "Ivan the Terrible." In March 1978, Ivan had been responsible for the brutal torture and murder of a CIA officer. It was said to have been in retaliation for the slaying of a KGB agent by a rogue CIA operative caught up in a drug deal gone bad. Murphy glanced at Natasha. How could she possibly be related to Ivan?

The general settled back in his wheel chair and sipped his tea, satisfied Murphy remembered. It was important that Murphy not misjudge and think him weak because of his poor health. "First, some background on me so you can decide for yourself the validity of my information." Zakharov shifted in his wheelchair. It made him uncomfortable talking about himself. "I have been a member of the KGB and its successor organizations for over thirty years. In 1991, the KGB got trapped in the midst of a power struggle—so ridiculous for an intelligence service to get involved in politics." The muscles in Zakharov's jaw twitched, "General Kryuchkov, who was head of the Commissariat, made the mistake of leading the attempted coup against Gorbachev. As punishment, the KGB was technically dissolved."

The general frowned as he examined the backs of his hands, rubbing at the dark brown age spots. "I remember that day well. August the eighteenth. Hot as the cinders of hell. The crowds outside chanting, 'Down with the KGB. Death to the cowards.' They toppled Dzerzhinsky's statue and smashed it to pieces. Inside, we were guzzling vodka and shredding documents as fast as we could. Some were even praying. Can you imagine, Mr. Murphy—KGB on their knees praying? It was a comical sight. We thought it was over."

The general looked wistfully at Natasha as he remembered the glory days of the old Soviet Union. He gently patted her hand. "Fortunately for us, it wasn't long before the new order decided they needed our services. I was transferred to the Ministry of Security. Again, in 1993, the Ministry of Security was too slow defending Yeltsin in the October putsch. So, we were reorganized again. Since

1991, the KGB has been renamed *eight* times. Our current title is FSB—Federal Security Service. Like they say, the more things change, the more they stay the same."

Hoping to keep the general's attention from drifting, Murphy said, "Your message mentioned missing warheads."

Zakharov hesitated, "Before we get into that, there are three conditions." Raising a bony index finger, he said, "First, my family and I are to be granted immediate and unconditional asylum in the United States. There will be *no* negotiations on this point."

Murphy nodded. That would be no problem. He would personally guarantee Natasha was taken care of.

"Second, that $10 million be deposited into my private bank account in Switzerland."

Murphy swallowed hard. He could never recall Washington having paid even half that much for information. It would take weeks to get approval for a sum that large—if ever. The amounts paid for leads to the World Trade Center and Oklahoma Federal building bombings had only been in the $2 million range. The reward for information leading to the arrest of Mir Aimal Kansi, the Pakistani shooter at the main gate at Langley, was $3.5 million.

Noting Murphy's reaction, the general said, "I can assure you, the information I have is inexpensive at a hundred—a thousand times that figure." Waving his hand, Zakharov said, "But enough about money. My third requirement is that *no* attempt be made to obtain information from me, or my family, on matters not concerning the warheads." His eyes narrowed, "I am no traitor. I offer this information as a service to Russia, not the United States. Do you understand?"

"I understand, but I'll have to obtain approval from Washington before—"

"Yes, yes, I know, I know," interrupted the general, irritated at being delayed by details. "Now, let's talk about the warheads."

"Please," Murphy replied.

The general leaned back, "When the Soviet Union collapsed in the late 1980s it created a power vacuum. To fill the void, a new *nomenklatura* was created in Moscow. An oligarchy of Kremlin elite made up of powerful bankers, ex-KGB, and countless *mafiya* syndicates. The politicians are only figureheads. For the right *blat*, anything is available. The situation is intolerable."

In her briefing, Kat Mills had told Murphy that Interpol estimated that as many as 400 Russian banks, 150 state-owned enterprises, 35,000 businesses, and 50 stock exchanges were directly controlled by the Russian mafiya.

"What about the military?" asked Murphy.

"Especially the military," growled the general, "along with its toady GRU. Modern Russia is a Potemkin village where democracy is an illusion. The laws are a joke." His voice grew harsh, "To cross the privileged few is to sign your own death warrant."

"As you have done?"

"As I have done," Zakharov reluctantly admitted. "I have well-connected friends in the FSB, and the government, but they are powerless against the *organizatsiya* that stole the warheads. Important members of the government and the Army are involved." He was clearly worried. Two years ago, Dimitri Kholodov, a reporter for the newspaper *Moskovsky Komsomolyets*, had been murdered for investigating illegal arms sales by officers of the Western Army Group. Kholodov had provided information to the FSB in a futile attempt to gain protection. The killing had been done in the open, with a suitcase bomb, as a warning to others not to look too closely into the business affairs of the Western Army Group.

"You mentioned warheads," Murphy said. "I assume you mean complete systems, not just weapons-grade U-238 or deactivated pits." It was no secret Russia was having difficulty accounting for over 1,300 tons of bomb grade uranium and 17,000 nuclear pits scattered throughout its poorly guarded facilities. But, these materials would be difficult to assemble into working bombs, especially thermonuclear warheads.

The general replied, "Mr. Murphy, I will tell you this. Two months ago one small and four large strategic nuclear warheads disappeared from storage depots in Russia. They were delivered to agents of a foreign power extremely hostile to the US. I have learned that this country intends to detonate one or more of these weapons somewhere in the continental US within the next thirty days."

The certainty of the general's statement startled Murphy. He shifted uneasily in his chair. "You have proof?"

Zakharov looked Murphy in the eyes. "The purchase was made from top ranking officers in the military, men with important commands." It sickened him that several had been his friends. "Four of these traitors have been identified and questioned. We have confessions."

"Who else is involved?"

The general paused and reached for his oxygen mask. After a few deep breaths, he said, "The transaction was brokered by a Russian syndicate. One of the names given to us is that of the Dolgochenskaya crime organization. It has operations in Moscow, Frankfurt, and New York. However, we have been unable to confirm this. There are reports other syndicates, possibly a Chechen and a Vladisvostok organization, are involved."

"Anyone else?" asked Murphy.

"There is a militant Islamic sect calling themselves the 'Shaheeds of the Islamic Ummah,' that appears to be part of the organization. But, beware of disinformation, Mr. Murphy. With so many groups, there may be wolves disguised as sheep and sheep pretending to be wolves."

Murphy nodded. "You mentioned a foreign power?"

"A long time enemy of the US." A half-smile crossed Zakharov's face. "Would you care to guess how they paid for the warheads?"

"I have no idea," Murphy replied. He didn't want the general to know how poorly informed the CIA was on what was happening.

Zakharov threw his head back and laughed, "With counterfeit American hundred dollar bills. Fake money, Mr. Murphy. The whole transaction was financed with worthless pieces of paper."

Murphy blinked, "Are you sure?"

The general was amused at Murphy's surprise. "The buyer is a poor country with very little hard currency. But, they are excellent craftsmen, and have modern printing presses hidden in caves. Their engraving is almost perfect. They even have access to the same paper used by your Bureau of Engraving. Do you know what their biggest problem was?"

"They couldn't change the serial numbers?"

The general grinned and shook his head. "Producing different serial numbers is child's play. No, Mr. Murphy, their biggest problem was duplicating the *poor* quality of your hundred dollar bills. They had to lower their standards to print 'real' American money."

"How much did the warheads cost?"

"One hundred million dollars each. We tried to trace the flow of funds, but the syndicates control too many banks. We did find out about General Nicolai Kuzov. Counterfeit bills were deposited into his private account at Bank Leueshaft in Liechtenstein. Fortunately for us, we have connections at Leueshaft."

"And you know who the state sponsor is?" Murphy asked, hoping to catch the general off guard.

Zakharov chuckled, "It will surprise you. However, to learn that, you will have to wait until my three conditions are met. Tell Mr. Warner this—the four largest warheads are from a single SS-18 Satan intercontinental ballistic missile withdrawn from service in Silo 224B at Dombaroskiy six months ago. Two have yields of 550 kilotons each and two are in the 750-kiloton range.

Good God, thought Murphy. Just one of those would reduce Washington to a pile of rubble.

"Tell Mr.–Mr. Warner—" Doubling over in pain, the general began coughing uncontrollably.

Yalena quickly and expertly strapped the hard vinyl oxygen mask over his nose and mouth. Jerking the plastic tip from a hypodermic needle, she injected a muscle relaxant into the wrinkled skin on his left forearm. Closing his eyes, he gasped several times, sucking in large gulps of air. Slowly, his breathing returned to normal.

Natasha placed her hand on her father's shoulder, "You must rest. You are overexerting yourself."

The general gently waved her away.

Yalena placed a stethoscope to his chest and listened closely. Turning to Natasha, she whispered in Russian, "He'll be all right. Give him a few minutes to recover. This happens frequently."

CHARLESTON, SOUTH CAROLINA

The linen envelope with the golden crest, addressed to David Ellsworth Pellingham III, Esquire, arrived at Hampton House, 84 Queen Street, with all the fanfare of an overdue telephone bill. It was unceremoniously crammed through the brass mail slot along with the usual circulars, magazine notices, and credit card solicitations.

By the time Pellingham arrived home, it was already dark. He was exhausted. The afternoon had been a waste. Four hours of petty bickering with the Charleston zoning commission over the placement of a MacDonald's restaurant on the fringe of the historic district. Exhaling slowly, he closed the door. Time for a double Jack Daniels on the rocks with some bitters and a splash of branch water.

Glancing at the pile of mail lying in a heap on the highly polished, oak floor, he separated the jumble with the toe of his expensive, Allen Edmonds tassel loafer. The corner of an oversized envelope caught his attention. Catching his breath, he thought—maybe, just maybe. With trembling hands he bent over and picked up the nine-by-twelve inch envelope. His mouth went dry as he ran his fingers over the engraved name—*The Society of the Cincinnati*. Reading the address label, printed in bold, old English script, he spoke the words out loud, "David Ellsworth Pellingham III, Esquire."

"The Society of the Cincinnati." He mouthed the words slowly, luxuriating in the sound. The corners of his mouth turned up in a boyish, ego-satisfying grin. His shameless politicking and ass-kissing had paid off. He had gotten an invitation—*the* invitation.

He thought of waiting for Eloise before opening the envelope. She had been in Wilmington visiting her mother and would be home any minute. He wanted to impress her. It would be great to—his heart sank with a thud. *What if it was a rejection?* The mere possibility temporarily paralyzed him. Dropping the envelope on the mahogany hall stand, he stood back and stared at it as if it were a snake. No. It couldn't be a rejection. A rejection would have come in a small, ugly, little number ten envelope—if they even bothered notifying the poor unfortunates who were turned down. He glanced around to make certain no one was watching. He would have to open it in private, just to make certain.

Retrieving the envelope, he walked into his paneled study, locked the door, and drew the blinds. Taking a brass letter opener from the reading desk, he carefully slit the end flap. If it was a rejection, he wouldn't tell Eloise. It would be months before she found out. That would give him enough time to prepare an excuse for not having been selected. As his confidence returned, he slowly slid the invitation out a quarter of an inch. Squinting at the letterhead, he saw the colored engraving of an eagle, the Society's emblem designed by Pierre L'Enfant. Tugging harder, he could see the gold medallion of an eagle's body with a garland wreath halo, attached to a dark blue ribbon. It could only mean one thing. *He was in.*

Collapsing into a leather chair, he wiped the perspiration from his brow. It was the realization of a life's dream. He reflected back on his childhood days as the oldest son of a convicted embezzler. The family dishonor, the strain on his consumptive mother, the struggle through college on scholarship money, the meals of peanut butter and bread. He cringed as he remembered sixty hour work-weeks waiting tables, fixing broken water pipes, hauling out garbage from that dilapidated old boarding house. Now this—membership in the prestigious Cincinnati. His mother would have been so proud.

He pulled out his grandfather's pocket watch, the one his mother had given him when he graduated from Duke Law School. Inscribed on the back was the quote: "Boys of iron must pass through the fires of adversity to be forged into men of steel."

It had taken years for the genealogist to locate the proper ancestor. The Society was absolute in its requirement that only direct male descendants of Revolutionary War officers were eligible for membership. It was a great-great-great grandfather on his grandmother's maternal side who had finally been certified. A Lieutenant Rufus Isiah Ellsworth who had served with the South Carolina Militia at the Battle of Eutaw Springs. Family lore had whispered that Lieutenant Ellsworth was a drunk and womanizer, but such details were unimportant now.

Pellingham held the invitation at arm's length. It was magnificent. He would have it framed and give it to Eloise for Christmas. He read the cover letter. The induction ceremony was to be held at noon, October thirty-first, at the historic Fraunces Tavern, 54 Pearl Street, in lower Manhattan. He was familiar with Fraunces Tavern. It was the site of George Washington's famous farewell address to his officers in 1783.

He couldn't wait to tell Eloise. October thirty-first—Halloween. Too bad she was eight and a half months pregnant. She would have to miss the induction ceremony. Grabbing a pen, he started scribbling a list of names on a notepad. The first was Atlee, his eight-year-old daughter. Watching the ceremony would certainly be more educational than spending another school day at the Charleston Harbor Day Academy. He would make the occasion a real memorable affair. Dinner at the Four Seasons, a play on Broadway. Heck, he would even invite Eloise's younger sister, Marcie, and her husband, Laurence Clarke, to the ceremony. They would be impressed.

Pellingham placed the invitation back in its envelope. There was just enough time to put a bottle of Dom Perignon on ice before Eloise got home. Being pregnant, she couldn't drink a whole glass, but she could toast the Cincinnati.

CAIRO

General Zakharov signaled Yalena to remove the oxygen mask. He was noticeably weaker, but the color had returned to his cheeks.

Natasha sat quietly by her father's side, stroking his hair.

"You see, Mr. Murphy, how my daughter concerns herself too much with my health?"

Yalena adjusted the pillow behind Zakharov's back and handed him a tattered, leather notebook. Balancing a pair of gold, wire-rimmed spectacles on the bridge of his nose, he glanced down at a page of indecipherable scribbles. "Where was I?"

"You had just mentioned four missing warheads from a single SS-18 Satan missile." Murphy admired Zakharov's determination to continue, but he had not forgotten he was dealing with Ivan the Terrible.

"Oh, yes. I remember." The general closed the book and gazed at the ceiling. There was no need for notes, he knew the details by heart. "The missile was one of two Satans taken from Uzhur and sent to Glazov for storage. As you probably know, the SS-18 Satan is what is commonly called a MIRV, or multiple independently targetable re-entry vehicle. In the nose cone of each missile are five 550-kiloton and five 750-kiloton warheads." The general coughed, clearing his throat.

"Go on," Murphy encouraged.

"While the missiles were in transit, security for their safety shifted to the Twelfth Main Directorate of the General Staff. It was when they reached Glazov that four of the warheads inside the nose cone of one of the SS-18s vanished. They were replaced with exact replicas, complete in detail down to the actual serial numbers. Fifteen days ago, the SS-18s were shipped to Uruzan for disassembly. When they arrived, the Ministry of Atomic Energy began separating the warheads into their component parts. It was at this point the theft was discovered and my department was called in. We moved fast enough to catch several of the traitors." He hesitated, "But, when you clean out a nest of vipers you must catch them all, or the ones left behind can destroy you."

"What about the fifth warhead, the small one?" asked Murphy.

The general shook his head, "That was the strangest part of the purchase. The buyers were quite specific. They wanted a compact 100-kiloton warhead from an SS-NX-24 cruise missile."

"The size of one of those is what, about that of a suitcase?"

"A large suitcase," answered Zakharov. "The nuclear payload measures half a meter in diameter, is one and a third meters in length and weighs only 115 kilos. Had the buyers not insisted on such a small warhead, their activities would have gone undetected."

"A pocket nuke," Murphy murmured. In the world of nuclear warheads, bigger was no longer better. The multi-megaton behemoths of the seventies and eighties were rapidly being replaced by warheads with less kilotonnage. The rule of thumb stated that as accuracy doubled, the kilotonnage required to achieve assured destruction could be reduced by a factor of eight.

The general continued, "Since there were no 100-kiloton cruise missiles being dismantled, the warhead had to be stolen from an operational unit. The organizatsiya decided to bribe an admiral for a warhead from a Delta II submarine at the base in Yagel'naya. That was a mistake. Admiral Golyanov panicked when he heard I wanted to talk to him." Zakharov chuckled, "All I wanted was to question him about the source of heroin being sold on the docks at Yagel'naya."

"You mentioned an Islamic group."

Zakharov reached for the oxygen mask and took several deep breaths. He watched Natasha while she helped Yalena adjust the flow of oxygen. He had ordered her to stay in Paris, but of course, being his daughter, she had disobeyed. He nodded approvingly—she had his stubbornness. Removing the mask and turning back to Murphy, the general said, "I'm not sure how the militants fit in. There are reports they control the warheads. But, why would the sponsor place them in charge?" The general shrugged, "Regardless of whose finger is on the trigger, a large American city has been marked for destruction."

Murphy could feel the perspiration forming in the palms of his hands. "Do you know which city?" He immediately thought of Sarah in Atlanta. He had to make certain she wasn't in danger.

"All in good time, Mr. Murphy."

"What about the built-in safeguards? Can they be bypassed?"

"I've been informed by the man you know as Walnut, that the permissive action links for the older, larger warheads are easily circumvented by someone with minimal knowledge. The smaller, newer one has a more sophisticated security system."

"Who's Walnut?" Murphy asked, remembering that Zakharov's original message had been signed, "Walnut."

"He's a friend of mine. One who shares the same disillusionment with the new Russia. Walnut is very concerned about the current collapse of Russia's nuclear security systems. When I mentioned I was contacting the CIA he asked that I pass along a warning. A senior nuclear scientist, Dr. Fredek A. Volodinsky, has disappeared. This physicist helped design the protocol for arming the Satan warheads and knows the code for bypassing the permissive action links."

Murphy jotted Volodinsky's name on his notepad. "Where are the warheads now?"

"We traced them to Vladivostok where they disappeared five weeks ago. We checked the list of ships in port at the time. No leads. We even checked the records of the airlines and transport planes at the airport. Nothing. The warheads simply vanished."

"Vladivostok? That's completely across the continent on the Sea of Japan."

The general's eyes flashed, "Ah, but Vladivostok is key to answering the riddle of who the state sponsor is. At first we thought the organizatsiya was just trying to avoid the Geiger-Müller meters and radiometric gates at the European airports, docks, and border checkpoints. Now we know better. The warheads were hauled to Vladivostok for a reason."

"But why Vladivostok?" Murphy repeated. The general was dangling a clue, but what was it? Vladivostok wasn't Russia's only deep water port so why cart the warheads that far? Murphy tried to clear his mind, but fatigue was setting in.

The general touched his nose with his right forefinger. "To find that out will cost you $10 million."

"One more question. Why pick Cairo for our meeting?"

"For safety, Mr. Murphy. The local head of the FSB owes me a personal favor." Zakharov scowled, "Last year, I saved his son, Cheslav, from being gutted like a pig and dumped in the Volga. Four *Uruk* enforcers from Kazakhstan were searching for him. Cheslav was a bad boy, a very bad boy. He lost over twenty kilos of the Kazak's heroin to an undercover operation run by my department. I also have Egyptian friends in Cairo who owe me blood debts. It was they who provided me with the details about the Shaheeds."

"Does the GRU know you're here?"

"I'm not sure. I told my office I was taking a holiday in Italy. Since then, I've received a warning that military intelligence has put out inquiries. False reports have begun to circulate in Moscow that I'm involved with smuggling drugs and pose a security threat. I hope you realize what that means."

Murphy understood only too well. If the GRU found the general, they would dispose of him—and Natasha—and Murphy. Now, like the general, he knew too much.

Zakharov tossed his head, "Terrorism is a fool's game. The organizatsiya has gone too far. Too many important people know and are involved. They will stop at nothing to silence me." The general motioned to Yalena. He was out of breath and could go no further.

"I'll send this informaiton to Mr. Warner at once."

"Thank you again for coming to Cairo," the general said, his voice reduced to a hoarse rasp. "Remember, your local station is not secure. The GRU has turned one of your officers. Also, I hope you don't mind that Natasha stays with you. It will be more efficient that way."

Murphy knew what he meant by efficient. Natasha was to act as watchdog to make certain he didn't betray them. He wondered what her orders were? How far would she go if he didn't cooperate? Was she capable of murder? He was too tired to care. Looking at her gentle hands and kind face, he couldn't imagine her holding a gun. "I welcome her company," he said, casting a hopeful smile in her direction.

Returning the smile, she looked down, then blushed.

The strain of the trip now settled over Murphy like a fog, pulling at his shoulders, legs, and arms. His eyes burned and his joints ached. A dull pain radiated out from the back of his neck, across the top of his skull, deep into his sinuses. He had lost the power to concentrate. Whenever he closed his eyes, hallucinations crowded out his thoughts.

Murphy's exhaustion did not escape Natasha's notice. She kissed her father on the forehead, then took Murphy by the arm and led him out of the mausoleum. "I've arranged a place for us to stay." When he asked where, she waved off the question and simply patted his arm. He offered no resistance.

As the Land Cruiser bounced through Cairo's noisy streets, Murphy closed his eyes. He awoke to Natasha's gentle prodding.

"Murphy, we're here," she said, stepping from the vehicle and taking him by the hand. Murphy looked up. They were in front of the Mena House Oberoi, near the Giza pyramids.

Without speaking she led him into the foyer of the nineteenth century palace. They walked quickly over the polished marble floors, past the engraved brass fixtures, and ornately carved *mashrabiyya* screens, straight to the elevator.

On the sixth floor, Murphy obediently followed her into suite 604. It was a spacious combination of rooms decorated with overstuffed couches and solid rattan furniture covered in orange and brown, earth-toned cushions. At the far end of the living room was a kitchen with a well-stocked bar. On the right, a doorway led into a large bedroom with a king-sized bed and balcony overlooking Cheop's pyramid. He wondered if Natasha would be staying nearby. He was surprised when she directed the porter to place her bags, and his, on the cedar chest at the foot of the bed.

The thought of staying with Natasha energized him. The last ounce of adrenaline surged through his system, recharging his exhausted blood cells. Following Natasha into the living room, he settled onto a plush couch. An ice bucket containing a bottle of Mumm's Cordon Rouge was at his elbow.

"Excuse me while I freshen up," Natasha said, disappearing into the master bath.

Murphy popped the cork and poured two glasses. He leaned back and watched the setting sun as it touched the palm trees lining the desert. At last, his luck had changed.

In ten minutes, Natasha returned wearing a pink, silk negligee. Her sleek hair cascaded over her shoulders, and the last, golden rays of sun reflected off the soft smoothness of her skin. The bodice of the negligee was cinched tight to reveal the full, sensuous shape of her torso. Murphy was smiling, his eyes closed, his head resting on the arm of the couch. He was fast asleep.

Chapter 7

"What does it mean, Comrade Dubov? 'I *heart* New York'?" inquired the short, corpulent man stuffed like a Ukrainian sausage into a gray, ill-fitting polyester suit. His head wagged from side to side as he squinted at the red heart on the billboard across the Westside Expressway. On top of his head was a bald spot circled half-way around by a halo of thick, kinky black hair. A pair of thick pebble-specked glasses tottered precariously on the bridge of his stubby, bulbous nose. Dr. Danya Motka Boyra, thirty-eight, Latvian by birth and a former lab manager of the isotope separation facility at the Arzamas-16 warhead design and assembly plant, spoke in Russian, the common language of the three men standing on the tar roof of the Skyview Plaza apartment complex. From their thirty-fourth floor vantage point they had an open, unobstructed view of lower Manhattan, the Hudson River, Brooklyn Heights, and Jersey City. It was important to have a clear line of sight if the effects of the blast and heat waves were to be maximized.

"It means 'I *love* New York,'" replied Dubov with a smile. "The heart stands for love." The pudgy Latvian's childish fascination with even the simplest pleasures amused the Chechen who found such unbounded enthusiasm refreshing and slightly contagious.

"Oh, that's good, very good," chuckled Boyra, his double chin bouncing up and down. "I *love* New York." His pale, nut-brown eyes darted back and forth, scouting the horizon for more billboards. A frown creased his face as his stomach began to rumble. "Comrade

Dubov, when do we eat? I'm starving."

"Shortly, Dr. Boyra, shortly. When we're finished here."

Grinning impishly, Boyra thought of the double portion of lobster thermidor he would order that evening at the American Harvest restaurant. And, a big boat of thick, mornay sauce with a side dish of drawn butter. "*Kashu maslom ne isportish.*"

"You're right, Comrade, a person can't be *too* spoiled."

As a security measure Dubov had arranged for the two physicists to share a suite at the World Trade Center's exclusive Vista Hilton International. The hotel was within easy walking distance of the Skyview Plaza and by restricting them to the World Trade Center's 5-acre mall, the danger of their being mugged or becoming lost was minimized. To encourage them not to venture too far, he had authorized unlimited room service and meals in the hotel's American Harvest and Greenhouse Bar restaurants. They could order lobster, steak, champagne, whatever they wanted. The expense was immaterial. At noon, October thirty-first, the bill would be canceled.

Looking out over the lower Manhattan landscape, Dubov asked, "Dr. Volodinsky, what's your opinion of our location?"

The slight, underweight physicist scanned the mixture of glass, concrete, and steel in a slow, deliberate manner. "It will be adequate," came the measured reply. A stone-faced, humorless, disciplinarian, Dr. Fredek A. Volodinsky was irritated that Dubov tolerated, even encouraged Boyra's stupid jokes and childish antics. A man of careful personal habits and precise, economic thought, Volodinsky was annoyed at having to share living quarters with a slovenly, unorganized peasant like Boyra.

Volodinsky's cold, slate-gray eyes followed Boyra as he gleefully bobbed around, clapping his hands and jabbing his fat fingers at the Statue of Liberty. What a buffoon. Had Dubov only allowed him to use one of the older, larger warheads, there would have been no need to bring the Latvian clown along at all. Now, Volodinsky, a former Satan Development team leader at the prestigious I.V. Kurchatov Institute, was expected to treat this intellectual midget as an equal?

It especially annoyed Volodinsky that Boyra was the only one who knew the *complete* firing sequence for the newer, smaller 100-kiloton unit. Dubov had specifically ordered them to share all information, but Boyra was keeping some of the details to himself. Most of the code for bypassing the warhead's built-in safeguards had been explained, but Boyra had not mentioned the protocol for circumventing the gravitational-force sensing device. Volodinsky knew Boyra kept the complete arming sequence in his laptop computer. If only he could find the password.

"Are you listening, Comrade?" Dubov asked, snapping his fingers in front of Volodinsky's face. "Is the tower high enough?" Dubov gestured towards the sturdy metal frame anchored to the roof by heavy bolts. Seven meters high, it was topped by a wooden platform measuring three meters by two meters. A square, gray, metal box the size of a refrigerator was fixed to the platform.

Volodinsky's face turned red, embarrassed at being caught daydreaming. That was the type of behavior one would expect from Boyra. "Er, uh—it's a good height, Comrade. Every meter we can elevate the device, the better. What's in the box now?"

"Fake air pollution monitors, just to occupy space. We can make the switch on the thirtieth." Constructing the tower had been easy. Dubov had bribed Quincy Totten, the building superintendent, to overlook the required building permit. Totten had been told the tower was part of an international ozone monitoring program being conducted by the UN.

Scanning lower Manhattan with a pair of binoculars, Dubov asked, "Dr. Volodinsky, would you go over the sequence of events following detonation?" Although he had been briefed on the general effects of the explosion, he found it difficult to envision the full magnitude of destruction by looking at photos and listening to dry statistics.

The physicist walked unhurriedly around the roof, studying the skyline. He jotted down measurements of the various sized structures, their distances from the tower, and the composition of materials. At sixty-five, his mind was still razor-sharp and his photographic memory had faded only slightly. While circling the roof, he was careful not to scuff his meticulously polished shoes on the soot covered bricks at the base of the retaining wall. It was no secret that a person's character can be determined by the condition of his shoes. He noted with satisfaction that Boyra's dirt-brown oxfords looked as if they had been run over by a Manhattan garbage truck.

"It will be dramatic, Comrade," Volodinsky declared, drawing the words out slowly. He was secretly thrilled to be part of such a momentous experiment. The results would be studied by the scientific community and military strategists for the next hundred years. The increase in knowledge would be priceless. New York would replace Hiroshima and Nagasaki as *the* primary source for information on the effects of radiation and other nuclear phenomena on a major city and its inhabitants. Those pompous bureaucrats at the I.V. Kurchatov Institute who had declared him redundant would come begging for him to speak.

"Details, Doctor. Details," demanded Dubov.

Volodinsky bristled at the demeaning manner in which Dubov addressed him. Removing an ivory comb from the pocket of his suit coat, he calmly smoothed down a few strands of windblown hair. "Comparing the damage from a conventional, chemical warhead with that of a nuclear bomb is like comparing the game of checkers with chess. With standard trinitrotoluene, you merely have the blast wave—*boom!*" He gestured dismissively in the direction of the World Trade Center. "Some heat, a little fire, but mostly just the shock front. With TNT you achieve a death rate of only 10 percent."

"*Only* 10 percent?" Dubov asked. He remembered the destruction to his unit in Afghanistan from the mujahedeens' rockets and mortars. There was nothing insignificant about *that* 10 percent.

"Correct. No more than 10 percent of those injured by the explosion will die as a result." Volodinsky drew a deep breath, "Now, with a nuclear explosion, you are not so dependent on the blast wave. Lethal damage is generated by five different phenomena. It's like a game of chess. More complicated, interesting, and productive."

"And the death rate?"

Volodinsky's eyes lighted up. That was the best part. "You get a kill rate of *54 percent*. Fifty-four out of every hundred casualties will die. That was the rate realized at Hiroshima and Nagasaki."

Dubov peered at the tall, silent buildings dotting the lower Manhattan skyline. They now looked like massive tombstones.

Volodinsky continued, "There are an infinite number of lethal effects which are cross-dependent. What they will be and how they will modify the overall damage, we have no way of predicting." Maybe he would write a series of books on the subject. They would be best sellers. Offers for important faculty positions from prestigious universities would pour in from all over the world.

"No way of predicting, Doctor? Surely there are computer models."

Volodinsky's mouth dropped open. *His* word on nuclear physics, challenged by an untutored criminal? This would never have happened in the old days when he had been one of the elite chocolate eaters at the Institute. Wasted. All those years of dedicated work on top secret projects at Chelyabinsk-70. Now he was reduced to having his word questioned by a common mafiya goon.

Fighting to control his emotions, Volodinsky bravely stuck out his chin and brushed an imaginary piece of lint from his lapel. "If you knew *anything* about physics, Comrade Dubov, anything at all, you would know that the damage from radiation and heat will depend on unknown factors. There's air temperature, humidity, composition of the target, and a thousand other variables." It was difficult to keep his voice from quivering.

Sensing Volodinsky's vulnerability, Boyra interjected, "If you will re-count the major effects, Doctor, I think you'll find there are more than five."

"Five, only five," Volodinsky shot back, annoyed at the intrusion. Holding up his right hand, he counted them off on his slender, meticulously manicured fingers. "First, there's the initial nuclear radiation. Then the electromagnetic pulse. Next, the heat and light wave. Fourth, the blast wave with its trailing winds. Fifth, and *last*"—he scowled at Boyra—"fallout, or long term radiation."

Listening to the recitation, Dubov was more convinced than ever that the Phoenix Committee's ambitious plan would work. The American public would be devastated. The wheels of government would grind to a halt.

Adjusting his tie so the Windsor knot was precisely centered over the top button of his starched shirt collar, Volodinsky resumed his explanation. "As you can see, Comrade Dubov, the results from the 100-kiloton device will be infinitely more destructive than anything you could possibly obtain from a simple chemical warhead. At the

Kurchatov Institute we estimated that a nuclear detonation produces casualties 6,500 times more efficiently than a chemical explosion."

"There is a *sixth* effect," Boyra insisted, impatiently tapping his chubby fingers on the third rung of the metal tower. "There is certain to be a *firestorm*." Peering out over the Manhattan landscape, he said, "Yes, definitely. Everything's in place." A red food stain showed on the cuff of his wrinkled shirt as he pointed towards the tall buildings on the horizon. "All that's needed is a fuel loading capacity of 8 pounds per square foot. We certainly have that. No doubt, no doubt. And, a firestorm will substantially increase the amount of collateral damage." He meant "casualties" but couldn't bring himself to talk about deaths. It depressed him to think real people—men and women he had met on the streets and in the restaurants—might be hurt. He preferred to picture the destruction only in terms of damage to buildings and other inanimate objects.

"There's no guarantee of a firestorm," huffed Volodinsky.

"There was a firestorm at Hiroshima," Boyra reminded him. "And, the buildings there weren't nearly as concentrated as these. Look for yourself." He motioned towards Wall Street. "All those structures, so close together. Gas lines, flammable interiors, millions of kilos of loose paper. No firestorm? Ha! *Analyyzator*." He muttered the word under his breath, but loud enough for Volodinsky to hear.

Volodinsky's body stiffened at the insult. No one had ever called him a "toady ass-licker" to his face.

Dubov quickly stepped between the two feuding physicists, "Please, Doctors. We're supposed to be working together. Dr. Volodinsky, from where we're standing, how far will the destruction reach?"

Boyra scowled at Volodinsky. "The firestorm's more important than your stupid electromagnetic pulse. That EMP crap's nothing but hog swill."

Volodinsky's thin lips curled into a sneer. Turning his back on Boyra, he said, "Not counting the firestorm, the lethal area will extend to the point where the overpressure reaches 5 psi."

"What do you mean by 'lethal area'?"

"That's the circular area within which the total number of survivors equals the total number of fatalities outside the circle."

Dubov cupped his hands over his ears. "Slow down—please." He was finding it difficult to follow the technical jargon. "And, 'over-pressure'?"

"That's pressure measured in pounds per square inch above standard atmospheric pressure. At sea level, the standard atmospheric pressure is 14.7 pounds per square inch. Any sudden change above or below that amount can be devastating. A jump of only half a psi can shatter glass."

"And if we have a firestorm?"

"With a firestorm, 90 percent of the people will die within the area where the overpressure reaches 3 to 4 psi. The whole site becomes one large inferno. Temperatures will exceed 1,000 degrees Celsius—hot enough to melt metal and glass." Glancing at Boyra, he continued, "At that temperature, all organic matter, no matter how *thick* and *fat*, will spontaneously combust. People inside buildings will suffocate from lack of oxygen."

Dubov frowned. The talk of burning brought back the nightmares of Afghanistan. "How long will it last?"

"Until all the combustible material is consumed," replied Boyra. Pointing proudly to his imitation Rolex, purchased that morning from a street vendor, he said, "In Hiroshima it lasted six hours."

Dubov peered at lower Manhattan through his binoculars. In his mind's eye he could already see the fire and smoke billowing from the crumbling buildings. "Comrade Volodinsky, go over the sequence of events one more time—slowly."

Volodinsky climbed up six rungs on the ladder attached to the metal tower. The added height gave him a 360 degree view of the horizon. Making a sweeping gesture with his right arm, he said, "Within six seconds after detonation, everything you see for a distance of 2,100 meters will be destroyed. First, the initial radiation of gamma rays and neutrons shoots out in a circle. The radiation will measure a lethal 500 rem as far as 1,700 meters."

Noting a puzzled look on Dubov's face, Volodinsky explained, "Rem. Roentgen equivalent man. To determine the rem you simply multiply the rad, radiation-absorbed-dose, by the rbe, radiation-biological-effectiveness. At 500 rem, 50 percent of those exposed will die." He was pleased to see Dubov was having difficulty following the technical explanation.

"I understand," replied Dubov. Such terms as overpressure, psi, rem, and initial radiation meant little. It was enough to know they were lethal. "So, you expect radiation to be a major source of casualties?"

"Not at first," Volodinsky answered, almost apologetically. "The main destruction will come from the heat and blast waves. These two phenomena kill quicker and at greater distances than the initial radiation. Also, the taller buildings will tend to block the radiation from reaching the smaller structures in their shadows."

"Don't forget the fallout, and the firestorm," reminded Boyra.

"I haven't *forgotten*, Comrade," Volodinsky replied testily. Turning back to Dubov, he continued, "There will eventually be a significant number of causalities from hard radiation emitted by the fallout. But, that will take hours, even days."

"And the firestorm," chided Boyra.

"Yes, yes, your damn firestorm—if it ever develops. But, the heat and blast waves will cause the most damage."

"When do they occur?" asked Dubov.

"At the instant of detonation the explosion will create a fireball which will send out a tremendous heat wave. With a 100 kiloton warhead the heat wave will last three and a half seconds, enough to fry anyone caught in the open within 4,000 meters. With a conventional bomb, the maximum temperature reached is approximately 5,000 degrees Celsius. With a nuclear warhead, you get temperatures at the point of explosion ranging in the tens of *millions* of degrees Celsius. There are no earthly equivalents. That's as hot as it gets at the center of the sun."

"You mentioned buildings. How much protection will they provide?"

"It depends on their distance from ground zero. Even reinforced concrete can't withstand the heat from the fireball which will reach a radius of 575 meters." Holding onto the metal tower with his left arm, Volodinsky twirled the dial on a small plastic nuclear bomb effects disk. "From where we're standing, anyone not in a reinforced building within 2,000 meters will be incinerated. Beyond 2,000 meters, any kind of structure will offer some protection from the heat wave."

"You said the blast wave is the most destructive part of the explosion."

"That's correct. There's a common misperception that radiation and heat produce most of the damage, but that's not true. The major destroyer is the blast wave with its trailing winds. The shock front will strike with a crushing force of at least 5 psi for as far as 2,100 meters from the point of detonation."

"And, the people inside buildings?"

"Not much protection. If the blast wave doesn't crush the building, it simply surrounds the structure and roars in through broken windows and doors, pulverizing everything inside. Ceilings, floors, furniture, and bodies are all smashed up and dumped into the streets. There's very little escaping the blast wave."

Dubov peered in the direction of City Hall, trying to get a feel for distances. "From where we're standing, how far does 2,100 meters extend?"

"You'll have to ask Comrade Boyra, he has the map," Volodinsky replied.

Looking down at Boyra's bald head, Volodinsky watched while he unfolded the street map of Manhattan. What bothered him most about the Latvian was his disgusting habit of chasing after those disease-infested, fifty dollar prostitutes frequenting the back alleys and strip joints near the hotel. It was no excuse that the thirty-eight-year-old, recently divorced, sybarite "only wanted to have fun." Hadn't he ever heard of syphilis, herpes, gonorrhea, AIDS? Volodinsky, who had recently become impotent, snorted with disgust as he pictured Boyra, stomach flopping over his belt, panting at the silicone excesses of the lap-dancers at the *Pussy's Tale* and *Bottoms Up* strip clubs. It hadn't been difficult learning where Boyra spent his off hours. Volodinsky kept finding those trashy matchbooks with their crude pictures every time he rifled the pockets of Boyra's jackets.

Volodinsky thought of Ekaterina, his wife. Only thirty-two, it wouldn't be long before she started looking elsewhere. He had tried all the aphrodisiacs—yohimbine, melatonin, bethanechol chloride——none of them worked. At first he thought his impotence was psychological, but his urologist, Dr. Federov, had assured him it was due to the vascular damage caused by diabetes and the recent onset of arteriosclerosis. As a test, he had let the doctor inject twenty-five micrograms of alprostadil into the side of his penis. The resulting erection lasted four hours, but was wasted. By the time he reached the apartment, Ekaterina was out shopping and he had to rush back to the emergency room for the antidote. The doctor had warned him that cutting off the flow of oxygen for longer than four hours threatened permanent damage. Dr. Federov suggested a penile implant or the use of a vacuum pump, but Ekaterina had said no. After this New York business was over, he would check on those two new wonder drugs, Sildenafil and Phentolamine. A recent report said 80 percent of the subjects using them had achieved erections. That would be his special anniversary surprise for Ekaterina.

Volodinsky wondered if he should tell Dubov about Boyra's late night excursions. The orders had been explicit—do not leave the hotel after dark. Dubov wouldn't find his little Latvian so funny if he knew about those side trips. Volodinsky shook his head. He was no informer. Besides, even he liked to slip out to Lincoln Center for opera or take in an occasional concert at Carnegie Hall.

Boyra flattened the map on the retaining wall and showed it to Dubov. There was a circle drawn at 2,100 meters and one at 4,000 meters. The 2,100 contour stretched from West Houston Street in the north to Rutgers Street in the east. It included sections of SoHo, Little Italy and Chinatown. The line curved around Cadman Plaza in Brooklyn and Governors Island in the south, and as far west as Henderson Street in New Jersey.

Volodinsky climbed down from his perch on the metal tower for a better view of the map. "Some of the buildings at the edge of the 2,100 meter perimeter will only be slightly damaged. The taller structures in front will shadow them from most of the radiation and heat. But, when the blast wave and drag forces arrive—"

"How much damage will the Financial District suffer?" asked Dubov.

After a few calculations, Volodinsky replied, "Wall Street will be blown back into the history books. It will cease to exist." It pleased him to think of Wall Street and the financial district being destroyed. He blamed the American capitalists for the downfall of the old Soviet system and ruining his way of life.

"What about the New York Stock Exchange?"

Volodinsky measured the distance on the map with a meter stick. "It's 640 meters from here—the overpressure from the blast wave will measure 50 psi, followed by winds of 1,930 kilometers per hour. There will be nothing left."

"And the American Stock exchange?"

"That's at 86 Trinity Place, 340 meters from ground zero. The overpressure will be a crushing 180 psi, the heat wave, a carbonizing 1,200 calories per square centimeter. It will be totally engulfed by the fireball. Nothing but pulverized, radioactive dust."

"The World Trade Center?"

Volodinsky looked across the roof at the Twin Towers. "It's 400, maybe 430 meters away. At that range, the structures will simply disappear."

"The United Nation's building? It's important to leave our calling card."

Volodinsky squinted at the map as a slight breeze rustled the edges. "That's on the East River between Forty-second and Forty-sixth Streets, about 5,500 meters from here. The shock front will measure .9 psi. That's sufficient to break windows and knock them around a bit. Anyone standing outside will be scorched by second degree burns."

Dubov now understood the full power of the small 275 pound thermonuclear warhead resting peacefully only four floors below. "How many fatalities can we expect?"

"It depends," Volodinsky responded. Unlike Boyra, he enjoyed discussing casualty figures. Numbers killed and wounded was a convenient gauge for measuring success. It was the ultimate determinant of effectiveness, a way of justifying his life's work. "I estimate, overall—provided we include people cut by flying glass—we can expect a total of between 850,000 to 950,000 casualties. Of those, 54 percent, or roughly 459,000 to 513,000 will die. If you factor in a firestorm and the fallout, maybe as many as 1,000,000 to 1,250,000 casualties. Wouldn't you agree, Comrade Boyra?"

"People killed? I don't know about that," Boyra replied, turning his head so he wouldn't have to look Dubov in the eye.

Dubov let out a low whistle. "That's a lot of people." A lot of Americans. In ten days, Washington would be transformed into Pandemonium, the capitol of Hell. Dubov could see the politicians now, live on CNN, hiding in their safety bunkers, posturing for the cameras, vowing swift justice and revenge. They wouldn't know what had hit them or why.

Volodinsky pointed towards midtown Manhattan, "We could increase the destruction if you'd let us move the device towards the center of the island. Here we waste a third of the energy over the Hudson and East Rivers."

"No," Dubov quickly responded. "This site's been chosen for maximum psychological effect. The detonation's to be symbolic as well as physical. Five hundred thousand dead will be quite sufficient."

Gazing down South End Avenue at the apartment buildings stacked along Battery Place, Volodinsky sneered, "If it's so symbolic, Comrade, why not just blow up a few monuments in Washington?"

Impatiently, Dubov shook his head, "No, Doctor. It has been decided that there has to be a large number of civilian casualties. It's important to demonstrate we have the *will*, and the *means* to kill civilians." Looking out over lower Manhattan, he said, "Here we have a large population and Wall Street. It's their showplace. Better to hit them here."

"But isn't there some other way?" asked Boyra who had grown fond of the food and entertainment in New York.

"I'm afraid not, Dr. Boyra. It's the same point the Americans made when they dropped the first two atomic bombs on Japan. They could have used demonstration bombs on strictly military targets, but the impact would have been muted. By choosing Hiroshima and Nagasaki for Little Boy and Fat Man, they convinced the Japanese government—and the Soviet Union—that they had the *will* to use nuclear bombs on civilians. It was an effective demonstration that ended the war."

"Comrade Dubov, exactly what are our objectives?" asked Volodinsky.

"Easy, Doctor. It's best not to ask too many questions. Remember, curiosity killed the cat."

"But, to act like common terrorists?"

"Not terrorists," corrected Dubov. "What we do is an act of *war*. We are soldiers, not terrorists. This will be the first war, fought and won with the detonation of a single nuclear weapon. Comparatively speaking, the causalities will be extremely light."

"Comrades, I have a name for our project," Boyra exclaimed, jumping up and down. Without waiting for a reply he blurted out, "We can call it our Manhattan Project."

"Manhattan Project?" hissed Volodinsky.

"That's right," announced Boyra proudly. "The Americans called the development of their first atomic bomb the Manhattan Project. We have our own experiment. Maybe we should call it our, 'Lower Manhattan Project.'" He laughed so hard, tears streamed down his face.

Dubov smiled at the Latvian's little joke. "Good, Comrade Boyra. That's very clever. Now let's get back to business. Dr. Volodinsky, will the explosion reach the Statue of Liberty?"

Volodinsky studied the map, then twirled the dial of his nuclear bomb effects disk. "The torch is 3,355 meters away. We have direct line of sight—nothing to block the heat or blast waves. The shock front will strike with an overpressure of approximately 4 psi. Drag force winds of 225 kilometers per hour should be sufficient to destroy any interior not made of metal. If the weather's clear, and we have good visibility, the heat reaching the statue will be between 12 and 14 calories per square centimeter and will last for three and a half seconds. Yes, Comrade, the statue will be destroyed."

"You mentioned an electromagnetic pulse?"

"It's a brief, powerful surge of electrical energy. Tens of thousands of volts of energy released in a fraction of a second. The EMP will knock out all of the computers, transmission antennae, telephone systems, and power grids in lower Manhattan. The communications network within the Financial District will be obliterated."

"Anything else?" Dubov inquired.

"Black rain," added Boyra, angling for the last word. "There will definitely be black rain. The explosion's going to cause an uptake of water from the Hudson River that will mingle with the radioactive debris, falling back to earth as black rain. That's what happened at Hiroshima."

Looking at his watch, Dubov decided he had heard enough. "It's time to go downstairs and check on our device."

"Comrade Dubov, let's eat," Boyra pleaded. Swinging his arms, he said, "We can go to the Windows on the World. It's at the top of the World Trade Center. I'll treat. I've never been there before." His face lit up, "I like my steaks rare. In twelve days, everything's going to be cooked well-done."

WILLIAMSBURG, VIRGINIA

Friar and Marcie splurged and spent the night in the honeymoon suite at the Williamsburg Inn. No TV, just a bottle of Charles Krug chenin blanc, room service filet mignon, and each other. It was their first anniversary and they didn't want the pending trip to Iguaçu to spoil the event. For brunch, they took a quiet corner table in the Regency Room and ordered the "Down-East Special." It was a high calorie pig-out which included Colonial peanut soup with sippets, Smithfield country ham, farmhouse scrambled eggs, homemade buttermilk biscuits, Virginia apple butter, damson preserves, cheese grits, and a large boat of sawmill gravy.

With an hour and twenty minutes left until their meeting with Warner, they loaded their bags into Marcie's Camry, left it parked in the Inn's lot, and strolled over to the Duke of Gloucester Street, or DOG Street as it's known to the locals. As a reminder to Warner that they were only working as contract temps, Friar dressed casually in a pair of tan chinos and a light blue, button-down shirt. Marcie wore a loden green fisherman's sweater over a chamois knit shirt, and plain wool slacks.

Walking past the Magazine and Guardhouse, they stopped at Raleigh Tavern for a mug of hot apple cider. Sitting on one of the wooden benches, they sipped the spicy brew and held hands like teenagers.

The buzzing of Friar's wristwatch broke the spell. "Almost time to meet Bryan. Guess we'd better head on over. Wouldn't want to be fired, first day on the job."

Marcie tried to smile, but her thoughts were miles away, back to their honeymoon a year ago in Montana's Bob Marshall Wilderness. Gazing at the old Capitol building at the end of DOG Street, she couldn't remember the trees ever having looked so beautiful—the yellow sweetgum and poplar, the rust-orange oak, the flaming-red maples. Feeling a chill, she reached over and took Friar's arm, draping it across her shoulders.

Pulling her close, he said, "Marcie, I want you to know, that if anything happens—"

She squeezed his hand, but said nothing.

They arrived at Bosworth House on York Street at 11:50AM. The building, located on the edge of the historic district, was a small, two-story, white weatherboard structure. It had eight windows with handblown glass panes, each protected by a pair of large, functional, black wooden shutters. The roof was covered with gray cypress shingles. At each end of the building was an exterior chimney constructed of red, handmade clay bricks. The safe house was a reproduction of the eighteenth century dwelling of Colonel Josiah Bosworth, commander of a company of Virginia light infantry at Yorktown.

Instead of going in, they pushed open the gate and strolled along the red brick path leading to the garden at the back of the house. They walked past the carefully pruned boxwood hedges, to the white, cast iron bench in front of the 600 square foot reliance building.

"Laurence, this house is much too nice for government use. Let's buy it some day and live in Williamsburg." She had often spoken to him about her dream of retiring to a small colonial house near the restored area of Williamsburg.

"You've got it," he replied.

At 11:55A.M., they entered the house through a side door opening directly into the kitchen.

Precisely at noon, Warner arrived. "Glad to have you on board. Happy anniversary."

"Thanks," Friar replied. "Any word from Murphy?"

Warner nodded, "A report came in at 10:15A.M. Let's sit down, I'm beat." It took fifteen minutes for Warner to brief them on what Murphy had learned from General Zakharov.

"If the warheads left Russia over a month ago, they could be here by now," Friar observed.

"The clock's ticking."

"Of course, it could be a hoax," said Marcie. Based on her experience at Langley, she knew how often rumors of rampaging terrorists had turned out to be nothing more than the unfounded exaggerations of overactive imaginations. "When's Murphy going to bring the general here for questioning?"

Warner patted his eyes with a damp cloth. "Slight snag there. Zakharov's demanding $10 million before he comes over. Director Vaughn said he would have to be carrying the warheads in his suitcase to get that kind of money."

"It's pocket change if he's right," Friar said.

"Yeah, I know, but that's way too much for unconfirmed information. I'm hoping he gets reasonable."

"Once he's here, he's lost his bargaining position."

"We've got an ace up our sleeve. Word from Moscow is the GRU wants to talk to him." Warner made a slashing motion across his throat with his hand. "Zakharov knows what that means."

"Has Moscow acknowledged that any warheads are missing?" Marcie asked.

"Shymanski put out an inquiry. The Russians claim their inventory is accounted for. We even contacted *Gosatomnadzor*, their safeguard agency for nuclear materials. They're all parroting the same old line—everything's fine, their security system's foolproof."

"Which means only a fool would believe them," said Friar.

Warner nodded, "It's pretty clear they're sandbagging us."

"What about the Federal Security Service where the General worked?"

"We asked them point blank if they knew anything. The answer was no, but they seemed real concerned we inquired. According to them, Zakharov is supposed to be on holiday in Italy." Warner shifted uneasily in his chair. "I'm afraid I've got some bad news. My time at the Agency is up."

"What do you mean, *up*?" asked Friar.

"Vaughn called me in yesterday afternoon for a little chat. It was about the difficulties facing the Agency and the need to restructure. He explained that the Administration wants a more sensitive image at the DO. Claims the public needs to see new faces and an improved, more responsible culture."

"When?" asked Friar, his voice indignant and sympathetic.

"Effective November first. Vaughn assured me it's nothing personal. He says he tried to prevent it, or at least delay the move until the first of the year." Warner knew it was Bastardi's revenge for the way Stirling Phillips had dressed him down at the October ninth meeting on North Korea.

"But why so sudden?" asked Marcie.

"It's part of the Administration's effort to overhaul the intelligence services. They won't rest until everyone's politically correct."

"They're going to ruin human intelligence," Friar said. He frowned as he remembered Murphy telling him about the communiqué from Vaughn's office. It was an all-ships-at-sea warning the DO's case officers to take special care when contacting potential sources who might be guilty of human rights violations. "Les Aspin had it right. To find out what's going on in the whorehouse, you don't ask Mother Teresa."

"And it's budget time," Marcie observed. She had read about the battle brewing between the White House and Congress over how the $26.6 billion dollar intelligence budget was to be divvied up. Ten billion dollars was earmarked for the military, $3 billion for the CIA, $4 billion for National Security Agency, $6 billion for the NRO, and the rest split up among the others.

Warner shrugged, "I guess it goes with the territory." It wasn't so much his termination that upset him, but the Pollyannish insistence by the White House that the use of "dirty" human sources be discontinued.

"What happens now?" Marcie asked. "I guess this scrubs Laurence's mission."

"No!" Warner said, his eyes flashing. "We've got to find out what General Mukhtar has to say." Looking at Friar, he said, "Promise me you'll see this thing through."

Friar had never seen Warner so upset. He couldn't refuse. To back out now would be to join the political hacks twisting the knife in his back. "Okay, Bryan, I'll go. But don't forget, when I get back—"

"I agree. You've done your part."

"What about Joe Don?"

"We finally located him. He'll be at Langley for a briefing on the twenty-first. One more item. Tovi Hersch plans on meeting us here tomorrow for about an hour. He wants to ask you some questions.

Mossad seems very concerned."

"Anything I need to know?"

"He didn't say." Taking Friar by the arm, Warner said, "Why don't you and Marcie make the Williamsburg Inn your headquarters until this is over"

"Fine by me," Friar replied, with a quick wink at Marcie. "Do I just send the tab to the Agency?"

"Send it to me. I'll put it through." It was Warner's anniversary gift.

Chapter 8

CAIRO

While Murphy waited for Warner's reply, he was free to luxuriate with Natasha in their own private garden of earthly delights. It was nirvana—the shared, intimate, erotic pleasures, the rebirth of hope and love—all coming at a time in life when he was emotionally drained and least expected it. Natasha, his earth goddess, was the primal life force who awoke feelings he had thought long dead.

Through Natasha's eyes, he was seeing Cairo for the first time. The dusty, grimy, noisy metropolis had been magically transformed into Ali Baba's land of Arabian Nights. And Natasha? She was his Scheherazade. Murphy reveled in his re-awakened senses. There were colors he had never seen—the burnt ocher of the pyramids, the brilliant whites of the painted buildings, the deep blues of the Nile. There were sensuous aromas he had never smelled—exotic spices, water hyacinths, jacaranda, Persian lilacs.

Their first day together was spent doing the little touristy things he had sworn he would never do. They rode a camel to the pyramids of Cheops, Cheophren, and Mycerinus. They visited the Pharaonic ruins at Saqqara and toured the Coptic church of Abu-Serga. At the Papyrus Institute, Murphy purchased a replica cartoon painting of the Satirical Papyrus showing a cat herding geese, with a lion and antelope seated at a table playing *senet*. He had the Institute inscribe Natasha's and his cartouches, side by side in the lower right hand corner. At dusk they retired to a small, sandalwood table in a corner of the Nile Casino Cafe where they watched the sun set over the head of the Sphinx. Sipping dark Turkish coffee, they held hands and listened to the haunting chants of the muezzins calling the faithful to prayer.

On the second morning, they rose before dawn and rented two thoroughbred horses for the short ride through the darkened desert to the Giza pyramids. They arrived just as the first rays of sunlight streaked across the horizon, painting the top of Cheops in a golden glow. As light flooded the valley, the undulating Nile mists made Cairo appear to be floating on a light blue sea. For a moment they were suspended in time, just the two of them, standing together on the edge of eternity.

That afternoon they visited the Khan al-Khalili, the ancient bazaar, built in 1382. Known throughout the Mideast as "The Khan," the marketplace was a profusion of men dressed in full length galabias and women conservatively attired in Islamic *hijab*s, *magneh* headdresses, and chadors. Murphy led Natasha leisurely through a labyrinth of dusty, narrow streets crowded with fortunetellers promising—for a small fee—to share the secrets of the cosmos. There were con-artists offering "authentic" pieces of Pharaonic temples and dealers hawking handcrafted woodwork, rugs, and copperware. Along El Badestane Street they dallied over the wares of the antique sellers.

Reaching al-Mu'izz li-Din-Allah, the Street of the Gold Sellers, they entered a small doorway under a worn, wooden plaque that read, Nassar Bros. After three cups of Turkish coffee and an appropriate amount of haggling, Murphy commissioned two identical cartouches with Natasha's hieroglyphs on the front and his on the reverse.

Just before sunset they had Ahmed drive them to Zamalek Island where Murphy bartered with a smiling, toothless boatman for an evening cruise along the Nile in an ancient, wooden felucca. The small, sturdy sailboat, with its single sail rigged to a creaking mast, was one of the thousands still plying the river much as they had done since the days of the first Pharaoh, Menes, in 3100 BC.

Before boarding the felucca, Natasha surprised Murphy with a wicker picnic basket of *mollokhiyya* soup and lamb cutlets from the Mena House. As the sun faded and the mists rose, they floated the Nile, sharing sips of vintage French wine and watching the moon begin its journey across the clear, desert sky.

"Thank you for taking me in," Murphy whispered.

"Thank you for letting me."

The next day they returned to the Khan for the finished cartouches. Murphy attached Natasha's to a gold chain and slipped it around her neck. Strolling over to Fishawi's cafe on Hussein Square, they stopped for Turkish coffee and sweet rolls. At Natasha's insistence they ordered a *sheesha* and took turns puffing on the water pipe and blowing smoke in each other's faces.

Afterwards, they visited the al-Azhar mosque. Built in AD 972, it houses the al-Azhar University, the oldest school of learning in the world. Walking through Hussein Square, Murphy said, "Chances are whoever heads the Shaheeds has contacts here. We may want to check it out."

That evening they attended the 7:00P.M. performance of Verdi's *Aida* at the Cairo Opera House. For a late dinner they returned to the Mena House and dined on shrimp curry and chicken *Jalfrazi* in The Moghul Room. Later, to keep their cultural yin and yang in balance, they visited the Alaa el Din at the Sheraton for a 1:00A.M. belly dancing act featuring Fifi Hasna, the "Oriental Jezebel."

OCTOBER 20

Next morning, while lounging on the patio and enjoying a leisurely breakfast of bean cakes with eggs, *beleh* dates, and *gibna beida* cheese, Murphy's pager began to beep. Stepping inside the suite, he flipped on the DatoCom encryption processor. The message light blinked green. His heart sank—it was from Warner. After reading the transmission, he slowly walked back out onto the patio. "It's time to set up a meeting with your father. I have a reply." The magic idyll was over.

The traffic was heavy, but it only took forty-five minutes to reach the entrance to the Museum of Egyptian Antiquities. As usual, Ahmed treated the drive down Gaysh Street as an Olympic racing event. Weaving in and out of a steady stream of vintage taxis, he crossed over to Abdul Aziz Street, then brought the Land Cruiser to a halt at the north end of Midan Tahrir.

Murphy glanced at his watch. There was enough time to grab a quick cup of Nescafe from a sidewalk trolley. While they waited, he studied the faces of the tourists and locals milling around the museum's entrance. With a trained eye, he searched for the telltale signs of someone paying too much attention to their movements. But if there was a knife hidden in a draped sleeve or a gun tucked under a loaf of *aysh fransawi*, he knew he would never see it coming.

At five minutes before noon, they slipped into a side entrance marked Staff Only. The museum was familiar ground to Murphy. On previous tours, he had used it dozens of times to rendezvous with skittish sources. The cavernous building, packed with hundreds of visitors and over 120,000 Pharaonic artifacts, made it easy to arrive and depart unnoticed.

Inside, they were met by a young Museum guard with smooth, olive-complexioned skin. He was neatly dressed in a pressed, military uniform and sported a large, well-groomed handlebar mustache. Eyeing them warily, he checked their profiles against descriptions jotted down on a King Tut, souvenir postcard. Satisfied, he escorted them to Room 52, the off limits Mummy Room which has been closed to the public since 1981. This was Murphy's first glimpse at the shriveled remains of the great Pharaoh-gods. He was pleased to be able to share the experience with Natasha.

Taking Natasha by the hand, he led her past the prune-faced body of Amenophis III and the well preserved, bald Seti I. The reality of these corpses, stripped of their regal finery and protective wraps, waiting out eternity in hermetically sealed showcases, was something of a letdown. Stopping in front of the crumbling remains of Ramses the Great, Master Builder of Thebes, Karnak, Luxor, and Abu Simbel, he wiped a layer of dust from the glass face plate. Leaning over, he scrutinized the leathery face of the Son of Ra, beloved of Amun; King of Upper and Lower Egypt, Strong in Right; the Golden Horus, and beloved of Ma'at. It was hard to envision this wasted five foot, eight inch frame, with its sunken eyes, skinny neck, hollow cheeks, pencil thin arms, beaklike nose, and tufts of orange hair, as the Terror of the Hittites and ruler of the fabled Nineteenth Egyptian Dynasty.

"It's spooky," murmured Natasha, holding tightly to Murphy's arm. "It's like creeping around in a graveyard."

There was a loud rap on the door. General Zakharov entered, dressed in a pair of slate blue trousers and a cream colored, long-sleeved cotton shirt. Appearing rested, he was no longer confined to a wheelchair but was walking with the assistance of Yalena, who guided him to the nearest seat. They were trailed by a husky Russian body-guard, dressed in the military brown of an Egyptian soldier and carrying an AKS-74 Kalashnikov.

"Well, Mr. Murphy. Have you enjoyed your Cairo vacation?" Winking at Natasha, the general said, "My daughter tells me you two have taken in the sights."

"Sh—she's a good guide," Murphy answered, glancing at a shyly smiling Natasha.

Waving a fragile hand towards the row of mummy showcases, Zakharov said, "I hope you weren't inconvenienced by our change in venue. It's an old habit of mine—never meeting twice in the same place." Motioning for the bodyguard to leave, he asked, "What news from your Mr. Warner?"

Murphy hesitated, "He's having trouble getting approval for the $10 million you requested. He can offer a total of $5 million with a $2 million down payment. The balance payable when you reach the US—*and* the warheads have been located." Murphy was uncomfortable haggling with the general like a rug peddler in the Khan.

Zakharov grimaced, "I'm afraid Mr. Warner doesn't understand the value of my information."

"It's not that," Murphy assured him. "It's just that he's been unable to confirm that nuclear warheads are actually headed towards the US. If there was only more time—"

"There is *no* more time," snapped the general. "Tell your Mr. Warner that if he waits much longer, it will be too late."

Gesturing for Natasha to follow, the general shuffled to the far corner of the room, stopping beside a dusty shelf of alabaster canopic urns containing the mummified internal organs of the Pharaohs. After a heated, ten minute exchange, he returned. "My daughter tells me I can trust you. As you know, I am not the trusting type." He reached for Natasha's hand. "But, for the sake of my family, I am forced to accept your terms. Have your organization deposit the money into my account at Bonhote & Cie in Neuchatel, Switzerland. When that is done, we can talk."

Murphy hesitated, "There's one more condition. Mr. Warner needs additional proof. Moscow denies any warheads are missing."

"Moscow *denies*?" scoffed the general, his voice strained with emotion. Seized by a coughing fit, he frantically beckoned for Yalena to bring the oxygen tank. After a few quick gulps, he reached over and removed a sheet of paper from his briefcase. Handing it to Murphy, he said, "Here are the serial numbers for the warheads. But, of course, Moscow will deny these also." Waving his hand in the air, he said, "Send them anyway. At least it will make the traitors lose sleep."

"I'll transmit them at once."

"Also, have Mr. Warner check my statements with Major Igor Ivanov at the Moscow branch of the Federal Security Service. He conducted the interrogation of General Nicholai Kuzov." Zakharov realized he was signing the major's death warrant, but he never liked Ivanov anyway.

"Yes, sir."

"Oh, and tell Mr. Warner that as soon my bank notifies me the $2 million has been deposited, I will tell him *where* the first warhead will be used."

The certainty in the general's voice sent a chill down Murphy's back. He was more convinced than ever that Zakharov was telling the truth. Reviewing his notes, he said, "General, at our last meeting you said a warhead would be used within thirty days. Do you have a precise date?"

"No, but it could be as soon as two to three weeks."

"Watch carefully," Murphy said, as he began typing a message into his notebook computer. Using public key cryptography, he was encoding instructions to his own private banker at LaRoche & Cie in Basel, Switzerland. With the computer's built-in modem, he could safely transmit the message over the hotel's phone lines.

"What're you doing?" Natasha asked, looking over his shoulder.

"It's a message to my Swiss gnome."

"Switzerland? A secret account? Murphy, you'll get in trouble."

Murphy grinned and kept typing. "Later, I'll take you to meet the bank manager. Right now, only one other person knows I have it. "

"Who?" Natasha demanded, suddenly jealous.

"No, nothing like that," he said, pulling her so close he could feel the heat of her body. "*His* name is Friar Clarke." He couldn't wait for Friar and Marcie to meet Natasha.

"Oh," she said, pursing her lips. "I'm sorry. I shouldn't pry." She regretted her feelings were so obvious. It would be better to keep him guessing, but she knew it was useless—she cared too much.

"Friar's the only one I can trust to keep quiet and deliver the money to my daughter, Sarah, if anything happens to me."

Natasha looked away. She didn't want to hear about Sarah. Not yet anyway. The thought of sharing Murphy with anyone, even his own daughter, upset her. Changing the subject, she asked, "What are you instructing your banker to do?"

"I don't have much. Only $85,000. That'll give us a good down payment on a house." Murphy knew it wasn't a lot to show for a lifetime of work, but it was all he was able to conceal from Sue's divorce lawyer. That Shylock, with his Gucci loafers and Armani briefcase, always suspected Murphy was hiding assets, but he couldn't prove it.

"Us, Murphy? You said, 'It'll give *us* a good down payment.' "

"Us," he repeated. "You and me, as soon as we're married." It was a lousy way to propose, but he would do better when they reached the States.

Natasha hugged Murphy around the neck, almost knocking the laptop to the floor. She didn't know whether to laugh or cry. She hadn't dared hope that he would actually marry her.

Murphy kept typing. "Natasha, your father said a warhead was scheduled to be detonated within a month?"

"Yes. Maybe as soon as a couple of weeks. Why?"

"I'm instructing my broker to short the US stock market."

"What does that mean—short the market?"

"Can't miss. If a nuclear bomb goes off, the stock market's going to drop like a lead balloon—40 to 60 percent minimum. Hell, maybe as much as 75 percent. Even if they find the warheads before they explode, the scare factor's going to kick the bejesus out of the averages."

"I know nothing of those things," Natasha replied, draping her arms around his neck. Now she could make plans.

"It's a sure bet," Murphy replied, trying to convince himself. At least it was worth the gamble. By buying deep, out-of-the-money XMI January puts, he would have plenty of time to sell the position if nothing happened. As soon as the warheads were discovered, he would liquidate. If a nuclear explosion did occur, he could net six, maybe seven hundred thousand dollars when the market collapsed. He would advise Friar to do the same when he got back to the States.

"It's your money," Natasha said. For the first time since Sergei was killed, she felt hopeful for the future. Moving to the US was going to be an exciting adventure. She couldn't wait to tell her father.

WILLIAMSBURG

A drenching rain, pushed along by strong gusts, lowered the wind chill to a nasal-dripping thirty-three degrees. At 2:00P.M. sharp, Bryan Warner stepped briskly through the front entrance of Bosworth House. Using both hands, he pulled the wood-paneled door shut, giving an extra tug until he heard the heavy, solid brass latch click into place. Scraping his muddy shoes on the welcome mat, he inadvertently shorted the electronic motion detector.

Once again, Marcie and Friar had arrived ahead of him. They were in the kitchen, brewing a fresh pot of coffee. The aroma from the ground beans gave the sterile safe house a homey, lived-in smell. "Ready for your afternoon jolt?" Friar asked. He was pleased to see Warner looking rested.

"Please, just half a cup."

"Only half?" asked Friar, who remembered Warner as an eight-cup-a-day guzzler.

"It's the caffeine. It aggravates my hypoglycemia. Blurred vision, the sweats, dizziness, the works."

"Your age is showing," Friar chided.

"There's always decaf," Marcie added.

"Decaf? That's like taking a shower with your raincoat on," Friar said.

Warner eased down on a bar stool beside Marcie. "How are the honeymooners?"

"Catching up, Bryan. Catching up. What about Murphy?"

Warner's face darkened, "His report came in at 0930 this morning. The Russian general's given us what he claims are the serial numbers for the warheads."

"Do they check out?"

"We sent them to Moscow, but it was a waste of time. Same old bureaucratic stone wall. Zakharov suggested we confirm his story with a Major Ivanov at the FSB."

"And?"

Warner shook his head. "The head of the FSB said the major was killed in a car crash on the Ring Road last Thursday night. Official report states the accident occurred when his 1987 Lada struck a concrete bridge support and burst into flames. He was on his way back to his office after a meeting with General Sazonov."

"Sazonov? Isn't he Chief of the Third Directorate?" asked Friar.

"One and the same."

"That's military counterintelligence," Friar observed. Ivanov dead. It was a bad sign when the FSB couldn't even protect its own people. It meant whoever was searching for General Zakharov held the power cards in Moscow.

"Does Shymanski know about this?" Friar asked.

"We tried to bypass him," Warner replied. "But he's got his own set of snitches. Problem is, he believes the Russians and doesn't know when to keep his mouth shut."

"He's a goddamned virgin," Friar replied caustically. "Bryan, when are you going to bring Murphy in?"

Placing his coffee cup on the countertop, Warner said, "I can't wait any longer. It's getting too dangerous. As soon as I leave here, I'm going to give him twenty-four hours to head back, general or no general."

"What about the $10 million?" Marcie asked.

"Zakharov's come off that figure. The asking price is down to $5 million with a $2 million deposit. He says as soon as he gets the $2 million, he'll come over and tell us *where* the first warhead is scheduled to be detonated."

Friar didn't like the sound of Warner's last statement. Why would terrorists set off a nuclear warhead without warning? It didn't make sense. Holding the US hostage for a hefty ransom made sense. Coercion and threats made sense. But detonating a warhead just for the hell of it?

"Is the $2 million a can-do?" Marcie asked. She knew how slowly the Agency's wheels moved when it came to parting with money.

Warner uttered a dry laugh, "Yes and no. Shymanski has decided it would be *illegal* to pay Zakharov for information. He's issued a directive forbidding the Directorate of Operations from paying the general a cent without checking with him first."

"Illegal? What's wrong with that cretin?" Friar asked.

"He calls it his Guatemalan Initiative. Claims a background report shows Zakharov is guilty of human rights violations. Shymanski also believes Moscow's lies that the general's tied in with the Turkish heroin trade."

"Of course the general's dirty," Friar said, shaking his head. "He's Ivan the Terrible for Christ's sake. Did you check with Vaughn?"

"The Director's too new to know how to handle it. He suggested I run it by Legal Affairs before doing anything."

"There's not enough time for that," Friar huffed. "You're not going to let that horse's ass send Murphy home in a body bag are you?"

"No way," Warner said. "Like I said, I'm ordering him in."

"What about the general?" asked Marcie.

After a moment's hesitation, Warner confided, "Don't worry, no nuclear warhead's going to be smuggled into the US on my watch. I set it up with Jan Frazier in Administration to make the transfer. She's using slush funds Shymanski doesn't even know exist. By now, the $2 million should already be in the general's Swiss bank account."

"Is there anything we can do to help?" Marcie asked, aware Warner was putting his pension on the line by going around Shymanski.

"Not at the moment." Warner didn't want Friar and Marcie implicated if his plan backfired. "The important thing is to find out what Mukhtar knows."

Friar didn't reply. He was worried about Murphy. "If Shymanski does anything to harm Murphy—"

"I was hoping Vaughn would back us up," Warner said. "Guess he's afraid if he cries 'wolf' this early in his administration he'll lose credibility."

"Has he thought how bad he's going to look if he keeps quiet and nukes *do* show up?" Marcie asked. "Remember, the bottom line to the wolf saga was that there really was a big bad wolf out there. And this one has real nasty fangs."

"Marcie's right," Friar grunted. "Bryan, any idea how you're going to fit in at the Agency after the thirty-first?" He hoped his question wasn't out of line, but he needed to know.

"Haven't got a clue. Guess I'll just have to take it one step at a time. Anything else before I go get Hersch? He's waiting at Christiana Campbell's Tavern and eager to talk."

In fifteen minutes, Warner was back, followed by a slightly built man with a receding hairline and closely cropped, silver-blond hair. He stood five-feet-five and gazed impishly at the world from a narrow, puckish face. The bronzed wrinkles were souvenirs from fifty-two years of exposure to the relentless Mideastern sun. With an everyman face, he could, and frequently did pass for Russian, English, French, German or American. Fluent in five languages, he possessed a photographic memory that was selective and precise.

Tovi Hersch, a k a the Sandman, was born in the port city of Haifa to Sonia, an Austrian-Jew, and Wolfgang, a German-Jew. Wolfgang, who had immigrated to Palestine in 1938, fought against the Third Reich as a commander of the Haganah's fabled German Platoon. The older of a set of fraternal twins, Tovi inherited his father's Aryan looks and his mother's steel-trap intellect.

When he was fourteen Tovi entered the Haifa Military Academy. Graduating with honors at eighteen, he immediately enlisted in Israel's Defense Forces. In 1968, he won the Courage Medal for exceptional bravery in a commando raid on a Palestinian stronghold at Karameh, Jordan. The action left a metal plate the size of a silver dollar in the lower, right quadrant of his skull, forcing him to abandon his dreams of a military career. In 1970, he volunteered for and was accepted by the Institute for Espionage and Special Tasks, better known by the acronym, Mossad.

"Friar!" Tovi exclaimed, grabbing his hand with a powerful grip that belied the Sandman's diminutive stature. "You don't look a day older than the last time I saw you. When was it—in '89 in Tel Aviv— or was it '90?"

Friar smiled, "Tel Aviv? No, actually, it was Cairo—October 15, 1990, at Scoozi's. Remember? That small Lebanese restaurant on al-Masaha Square in Giza. You ordered the house special, the Chicken Scoozi and I had the Lebanese *fatta*."

Friar was amused at the little mind games Tovi like to play. Getting dates, places and names wrong to test the other person's power of observation and recall. To prepare himself, he had made a habit of jotting down items of minutia after each meeting. It disarmed Tovi to think someone might remember events better than he.

Friar patted the wallet in his back pocket, "I believe I paid for the last round of drinks. Two double Hennesey V.S.O.P.s."

Tovi grinned, his pale blue eyes flashing, "I'm flattered you recall our meeting so well. But, Scoozi's doesn't serve alcohol and, it was *I* who paid for the dinners."

They both broke into laughter. After an introduction to Marcie and ten minutes of reminiscing over old battles and old scars, Tovi said, "I don't mind telling you there was a great deal of interest at Mossad in that message from General Mukhtar."

"Mukhtar chose an interesting way of delivering it," Friar replied, pleased to have Mossad's attention. He considered Israel's intelligence services, warts and all, to be the finest in the world, especially when it came to gathering human intelligence from hard, Mideast targets like Iraq. He admired their no-nonsense approach in dealing with terrorists, and their freedom to use extreme measures when necessary. He knew that for Israel, good intelligence and swift retaliation was not an option, but a condition for survival.

In addition to Mossad, Friar had great respect for Shin Bet, Israel's less flamboyant internal security and counterterrorist force. But, the service for which he had the highest regard was A'man—military intelligence—with its 7,000 highly trained infiltrators, moles, assassins, and analysts. Of special interest was A'man's Collections Department, with its Arabic speaking HATZAV, or Open Sources Unit.

Judging from the expressions on Warner's and Friar's faces, Tovi could tell they were not inclined to let him indulge in a fishing expedition. Protocol dictated that if he wanted information, he would have to be the first to share something of value. "Of course, the author of your message intended for us to read it—which we did.

Then, we had to ask ourselves, why? What was the real purpose of this message?"

The Sandman paused to evaluate Friar's and Warner's reactions. Satisfied the transmission wasn't a hoax or a byproduct of some convoluted CIA plot, he continued, "We wondered—is this communication a personal one from a volunteer or part of some half-baked scheme hatched up by Baghdad Central? The unusual way it was delivered, the reference to a terrorist group calling themselves the Shaheeds."

For the next fifteen minutes, Warner, Friar, Marcie, and Tovi discussed Mukhtar's message. The Sandman watched as Warner strained to get him to fill in the blanks. Warner's indecision told him all he needed to know. The CIA was groping in the dark. They didn't have a clue who the Shaheeds were or how Mukhtar fit in. The US's Mideast HUMINT resources were junk grade and they all knew it. Washington had placed its intelligence bet on electronic eavesdropping and expensive satellites circling the globe, and this was the payoff. To find out what was going on inside the lice-infested head of a Mideast terrorist, you had to crawl into the gutter with him. Only Mossad, Shin Bet and A'man were willing to do that. Tovi wanted Warner to fully appreciate how much the Agency needed Israel's help and the information it could supply from its unwashed assets.

Sensing Tovi was holding back, Friar tried a different approach. "I'm surprised Mossad can't identify a few ragtag militants. With all your resources, I expected more."

Tovi smiled at Friar's feeble attempt to goad him into divulging what he knew. Still, it was time to move on. "When we read Mukhtar's note, we sent out emergency inquiries to Shin Bet and A'man for background information on the Shaheeds." His face knitted into a frown, "This morning at 0230 hours, I received a report from A'man. One of their assets working for HATZAV in Baghdad identified the Shaheeds as a small, militant group of Sunnites recently recruiting in Basra. Best we can tell, it's a splinter group from the Party of Martyrs Mubarak kicked out of Cairo last year."

This was exactly the kind of information Friar had been hoping for. "Are they still active in Iraq?"

"No." Tovi hesitated. He was being candid, maybe too much so, but he would have to chance it. "These aren't your average fanatics. Their propaganda calls for the total destruction of the Great Satan, Israel, and the infidel Mubarak of Egypt. Rumor has it they're planning something *big*. It's reported they've moved their headquarters to the US."

The Sandman was dancing on hot coals. Too much information about the Shaheeds' US organization would only confirm the current extent of Mossad's American operations. Ever since the Pollard scandal in 1985, Mossad had been ordered to maintain a low profile in its intelligence gathering activities inside the US. Pollard, an American civilian Naval intelligence analyst, had been arrested and found guilty of spying against America for the Star of David. No one in Tel Aviv wanted another flap that might harm Israel's special relationship with the US or place in jeopardy the $3 billion it received annually from Washington. In 1991, eyebrows had been raised when Mossad informed the CIA and FBI about a summit meeting of militant Islamics on the outskirts of Washington. The powwow, sponsored by a covert branch of Hamas calling itself the Association for Mideastern Understanding and Research, was the largest gathering of militant Islamics ever held in the US. It amazed Tovi that neither the CIA nor the FBI were even aware the conference had taken place. Sometimes, he just shook his head at America's death wish.

After a brief pause, Tovi decided to confront Warner and Friar head-on. "There are rumors in Baghdad the Shaheeds have acquired control of a strategic-sized Islamic bomb."

Friar raised an eyebrow. During his tenure in the Mideast he had often heard reports of the more radical sheiks preaching the call for an Islamic bomb. It was supposed to be a nuclear device controlled collectively by the Muslim community to be used for waging holy war against the infidels.

Tovi studied Warner's face for confirmation. It was obvious he knew more than he was admitting. "Mossad's *very* concerned. We've run across this kind of talk before, but the quality and intensity of the chatter has us looking under our beds."

"Any hints of Iraqi sponsorship?" queried Warner.

"None so far, but it can't be ruled out."

"What about Iran?" Friar remembered the vice-president of Iran calling for an Islamic bomb in 1992.

"Nope. There's no evidence they're involved either."

"And you say the bomb is *strategic*?" Warner asked, continuing to pump for information.

"Those are the rumors. An advanced hydrogen-fusion device. It's Mossad's conclusion that if it's thermonuclear, it must be Russian."

Warner was impressed with how precisely Mossad's analysis fit with the information supplied by Zakharov. "What's Israel's national interest in this?"

"Frankly, we would consider any nuclear warhead in the hands of militant Islamics an immediate threat to our security."

"Even if the target is the US?" asked Friar.

"Absolutely," declared Tovi. It wasn't hard to imagine how such a weapon could be used to drive a wedge between Washington and Tel Aviv.

"Has Mossad considered the options?" Warner asked.

The expression on the Sandman's face grew dark, "The *only* option is to locate the warhead and launch a preemptive strike."

Friar nodded, "It's my guess we're dealing with a very sophisticated organization. There's more here than just a disorganized bunch of Islamic radicals running around with towels on their heads chanting 'Allah is Great.'"

"I agree," said Tovi.

"What's Israel's commitment?" asked Warner.

"I've been authorized by the Knesset to offer the CIA and FBI the full cooperation of all Israeli intelligence services. I am to serve as liaison. It would please me if Friar were my contact."

Warner was glad to have such unqualified support. Unfortunately, with Bastardi advising the President, he couldn't expect the same from the US services. Glancing at Friar and Marcie he replied, "Agreed. If Friar's willing. He can fill you in on the details of what we know. Unfortunately, the situation is even more dangerous than you've outlined."

Friar made eye contact with Marcie. This expansion of their involvement was precisely what she had feared. They were slowly being dragged in for the duration.

"One other item," Tovi stated. "A report from A'man's collections department has identified a Russian nuclear physicist who's disappeared. His name is Dr. Danya Boyra."

"What's so special about him?" asked Friar.

"For the last couple of years A'man has been running periodic ads on the Internet trolling for Russian nuclear scientists willing to hire-out for top dollar. Ads have been entered from personal computers in Cairo, Frankfurt, and Toronto."

"So?"

"Two months ago they advertised for someone familiar with the firing sequence and codes for Russia's newest nuclear weapons. Boyra answered from a computer in Moscow. He claimed to know all about the permissive action links for the smaller thermonuclear warheads and how to circumvent them. When A'man tried to follow up with a visit, he was gone."

"Any idea where?" asked Warner.

"We sent a team around to his apartment in Moscow. Neighbors said he had left to visit a cousin in the US."

Chapter 9

"Two 9mm Glock 19s, with Warp-3 suppressors," Friar said, checking over the barely legible notes scrawled in a pocket calendar. "Don't let them talk you into substituting silencers. I want suppressors." Time was short, and Marcie had agreed to shop Friar's and Joe Don's want list to the Agency's armament section.

"Silencers—suppressors, what's the difference?" she asked, intent on understanding the instructions.

"A silencer slows the bullet down below the speed of sound. A suppressor only muffles the noise of the muzzle blast. It's a trade-off—sound for stopping power."

Scratching his chin, Joe Don weighed the pros and cons of the different handguns. "Marcie, how 'bout getting me a couple of revolvers. A .357 Ruger GP-100 with whatever type of suppressor they recommend, and a backup Colt .44 Magnum Anaconda."

"Joe Don, when're you gonna smarten up and switch to the Glock," Friar teased the tall, strapping Cajun. "Fully loaded, it weighs less than two pounds. Hell, you hardly know you're carrying it."

Joe Don chuckled softly, "No, Hoss. Had me an automatic once. Jammed when my ass was in a crack. Just about buried this 'ole coonass. Nope, I'll let you office types play with those little plastic toys. They remind me too much of the Roy Roger's cap gun I had when I was a pup."

"It's *not* plastic," Friar replied. "The working parts are all metal." Joe Don smiled and went back to ticking off the items on his check sheet. "Let's see. I'll be carrying my ordnance in with me on the cargo plane. You're toting your's in as diplomatic luggage, right?"

Friar nodded. "I'm catching the American Airlines red-eye out of Miami to BA. From Buenos Aires I take Aerolineas to the airport at Foz do Iguaçu. I'll attract less attention by going in commercial."

Turning to Marcie, Friar said, "Tell armaments you want the Glocks modified to the New York trigger standard. Also, have them throw in a box of 9mm, 147-grain Silvertip hollowpoints and a box of 9mm Glazer-fragmentation rounds." Friar was very choosy when it came to his ammunition. It was basic physics—weight of projectile times velocity equals transferred energy. He especially liked the 90 percent kill ratio obtained with a direct body hit from a fragmentation round. Three hundred thirty subprojectiles exploding into the target's soft tissues gave him what he considered the necessary edge.

"Marcie, would you have 'em kick in a couple boxes each of hollow points and frags for me?" Joe Don added. "Also, a Heckler & Koch MP5K-PDW submachine gun with suppressor. Get the new model, the one chambered for the .40in Smith & Wesson cartridge. And, one last thing. A Heckler PSG-1 sniper rifle with a couple boxes of .308in Winchester Match ammo."

"Have we overlooked anything?" Friar asked.

"Don't believe so, Hoss," Joe Don replied, in a slow, back-bayou drawl. "Tomorrow, I fly that old DC-3 to the Aeroporto Internacional on the Brazilian side of the river. Make it look like a routine smuggling job by toting in some kitchen and electronic hardware, maybe a few cases of cigarettes, and a couple of VCRs, stuff like that. On October 23, you check into the Hotel Internacional on the Argentinean side. At 1730 hours I meet you on that little island, San—something or other. You know, the one in the middle of the river below the falls. The following A.M., you hook up with your contact. Thirty minutes later, we're back on the yellow brick road, neat and clean."

"The island's called San Martin."

"Yeah, that's it, San Martin."

Marcie lowered her clipboard. "Joe Don, I've got a personal question. Do you mind?"

"Shoot, little honey."

"Why are you still in this business? Haven't you ever wanted to get out?"

"You mean, have a real life?" A shadow crossed his face as he made a half-hearted attempt to laugh off her question. Resting his broad shoulders against the cinder block wall, he said, "I guess it's like this. I've tried to put money aside. Ever since I got my first pay check I thought how nice it would be to some day own a small ranch near Jackson Hole, out in Wyoming. At night, when I dream, I'm sitting on the front porch looking out over my spread. The snowcapped peaks of the Tetons are in the background. There's a big pasture with white fences and a hundred Black Angus just milling around, getting fat." His eyes lit up, "In the afternoon, I go trout fishing on the Snake River. Net a couple of ten pound browns and a large rainbow. Then, the alarm clock goes off, and I'm staring at four dirty walls in some backwater South American town, going undercover for the DEA." Reaching in his back pocket, he pulled out a crumpled, folded envelope. "Here's a notice from my wife's lawyer telling me I'm behind on alimony and child support. I guess I'm just not meant to go through life eating filet mignon and drinking Jack Daniels. I'm lucky if I can afford hamburgers and beer at the end of the month."

"What's up?" Friar asked, closing the door to Warner's office. He was breathing hard after having rushed over from his meeting with Joe Don and Marcie. "The pager said extremely urgent."

"He's done it now," Warner said, disgustedly.

"Who's done what?"

Unable to sit, Warner paced back and forth in front of his desk. "Shymanski, that's who. He's placed Murphy and the mission in jeopardy."

"How?"

"Dabbling in operations. I just found out that two days ago he sent the serial numbers for the missing warheads to a General Trofimoff in Moscow. He requested they be verified."

"Trofimoff? Isn't he—"

"GRU? Damn right. He's head of Russia's Defense Council. Jack Trainor, chief of our Moscow Station, saw the inquiry. He thought it so unusual he gave me a call."

"And?"

Throwing his hands in the air, Warner said, "Now the GRU knows for certain we're running an operation in Cairo to bring the general over. Trofimoff played Shymanski like a five dollar fiddle. Asked him if these were the same serial numbers being passed around by an impostor claiming to be General Zakharov."

"Looks bad," Friar said, sitting down in the nearest chair. If the conspirators were already fabricating a cover story that meant they expected Zakharov to disappear.

Warner nodded. "Shymanski fell for it hook, line, and sinker. Trofimoff told him the real Zakharov had just returned from holiday in Italy. Even offered to let him speak to the general. Trofimoff claimed any intelligence about missing warheads was bogus and assured Shymanski the serial numbers were phony."

"If that's their line, they must think they can get Zakharov before he leaves Cairo." Friar had a deep respect for the efficiency of the GRU. They were secretive and deadly and, unlike the old KGB, had not come to an accommodation with the West.

Warner reached into the humidor on his desk labeled "Stress Management," and pulled out a Cuban cigar. "That damn Shymanski. Right after he blabbed to Trofimoff, he contacted Cairo Station to warn them about the impostor posing as the general. Of course Cairo station didn't have a clue what he was talking about."

"No one except the GRU's mole."

"That was two days ago. I checked with Tony Fabrizio at Intelligence. NSA confirmed that communications between Army headquarters in Moscow and Cairo went berserk right after Shymanski's call. All sorts of references to Zakharov were picked up. An hour ago, I sent Murphy a direct order to grab the general and get out."

"The GRU's going to be watching the airports."

"I thought of that. The USS Kearsarge is in the Mediterranean just south of Cyprus. They're sending over a Super Stallion to pick them up. I've cleared it with the Egyptians. We can land the helicopter on their military runway."

Friar grimaced, "Hope Murphy's going to be okay. He's always had the luck of the Irish."

OCTOBER 22: CAIRO

The blood drained from Murphy's face as he read Warner's message. Racing into the next room he found Natasha leisurely setting the table for a full English breakfast of poached eggs, ham, toast, and orange marmalade. Her terry cloth robe hung invitingly open, revealing the soft, warm curves of her body.

Holding his forefinger to his lips, he signaled her not to say a word. Grabbing a pen and notepad he wrote, "Contact your father at once. Important message from Warner. Be careful, the room may be bugged." If the GRU already knew about them—he recalled that overly curious bellhop, the one who kept glancing around while the check was being signed. When was that? Yesterday. It was yesterday morning, at breakfast. Using the remote control, he switched on the television and turned up the volume.

"What's wrong?" Natasha jotted on the pad. Her face was tense, her eyes wide and alert. She could read the danger in Murphy's expression.

The phone rang. Natasha looked at Murphy. He nodded. She picked up the receiver and switched on the encryption system. Suddenly, her face went ashen. Forgetting Murphy's advice, she spoke rapidly in Russian.

Turning to Murphy, she whispered, "There's been an attempt on father's life. He says we must leave the hotel at once. Ahmed, our driver, was working for the GRU."

"Was the general hurt?"

Holding her hand over the receiver, she replied, "No. The armored limousine saved his life. Ahmed was killed and two other attackers wounded. One of father's bodyguards was shot."

Murphy's mind was racing. He took the receiver from Natasha and set it down. Taking her by the arm he led her into the bathroom and turned on all the faucets. "Tell your father to meet us at hangar eleven at Cairo's military airport in one hour."

"Murphy, he—"

Gently covering her mouth with his hand, Murphy whispered, "An American military helicopter will meet us there. We'll have a Marine escort to the ship." Squeezing her hand, he added, "I love you."

Natasha peered deeply into his eyes and the fear melted from her face. Speaking rapidly, she said, "Father wants to tell you where the first detonation will take place and who the sponsor is. He says it's important you know, in case—in case he doesn't—doesn't—" She hid her face in her hands.

Murphy ran back into the living room and grabbed the phone. This was the information he had come to get. They might be overheard, but he had to take the risk. Both men spoke quickly. When they had finished, Murphy hung up. He would send Warner a full report from the *Kearsarge*. There wasn't time now, every second's delay increased the risk. Snatching a marble ash tray from the writing table he smashed the telephone encryption system. Dragging the twisted remains into the bathroom, he threw the jumbled wires and computer cards into the tub full of water.

The room telephone rang again. Murphy raced back into the bedroom, grabbing Natasha's arm just in time. "Don't answer it," he whispered. He scrawled on his pad, "We've got to leave. Change into street clothes and take only what you can carry."

Breathing hard, Natasha asked in Russian, then English, "What about my dresses, my suitcases—"

"Leave them," he replied. "You can get all new things in the US."

Four minutes later, there was a loud knock on the hall door. A gruff voice called out, "Message for Mr. Murphy, Mr. Patrick Murphy."

Murphy stood stock-still. The room wasn't registered in his name—no one knew he was there—no one but Ahmed. With his right hand, he withdrew the 9mm Steyr pistol from its holster and quietly racked back the slide. He could fire through the door if he had to. Slinging a backpack over his shoulder, he motioned for Natasha to follow. Silently sliding open the balcony door, he stepped onto the patio. Touching Natasha lightly on the shoulder, he pointed towards the fire escape ladder connected to the balcony. Leading the way, he climbed onto the metal structure and instead of going down, went up. At the next landing, he stepped over the railing, onto the balcony of suite 704. Sliding open the door, he went inside, pulling Natasha in after him.

"I've been renting this room as backup," he said, pleased he hadn't been caught napping.

Below, they could hear wood splintering as the door to suite 604 came crashing in. The muffled sounds of voices and curses in Russian and Arabic drifted up through the floor. They could hear furniture being shoved aside and the clumping of heavy footsteps moving from room to room. The voices grew louder as the balcony door was yanked open and two heavyset figures lumbered to the railing and peered down. A black BMW with heavily tinted windows, screeched to a halt six floors below. The intruders gestured wildly, yelling down in Russian. One of the figures, with a narrow-brimmed hat pulled down over his coal black hair, clamored onto the fire escape ladder and started down. Sparks flew from the steel taps on his heavy, army-issue boots.

Natasha listened carefully. "They're shouting that we've escaped. They're going crazy trying to find us."

Locking the balcony door and gently resting his hand on Natasha's trembling shoulder, Murphy said, "Don't worry, we're safe—for now." Winking at her, he asked, "Are you ready for some playacting?"

"Playacting?" She cocked her head, "Murphy, this is no time for games."

Taking her by the hand, he led her into the bedroom and closed the door. "Natasha, please take off your dress."

"Not now," she protested. "We've got to get to the airport to meet father."

Murphy hugged her and laughed, "It's not that kind of game." Glancing regretfully at the bed, he opened the closet door. Inside was an aluminum, foldup wheel chair, a black canvas suitcase and a large, brown paper shopping bag with rope handles. Unzipping the suitcase, he pulled out a carefully folded, white nurse's uniform. Shaking it out, he held it against Natasha's torso. "You get to play Florence Nightingale. I hope this fits."

"Murphy, how did you get these things?"

"An Egyptian contact from the old days. I kept him from dying from the measles during an epidemic in the late eighties."

Murphy dumped the contents of the shopping bag on the bed. Inside was a gray wig, a loden green Bavarian hunting hat, and a rumpled, charcoal gray tweed suit. While Natasha put on the nurse's outfit, Murphy put on the tweed suit. Walking into the bathroom, he placed a towel around his shoulders and began dusting his face with talcum powder. After achieving the desired shade of age and decay he pulled on the wig.

Looking at her image in the mirror, Natasha scowled. "This dress is too big. You don't think I'm *fat* do you?"

He stuck his head in the bedroom and motioned for her to turn around. The outfit was stiff with starch and bulged in all the wrong places, making her look slightly frumpy. "You're perfect just the way you are. Don't worry about the outfit. It's part of the disguise. I don't want you attracting too much attention in the lobby."

On seeing Murphy's makeup, Natasha laughed, "You look just like my grandfather."

Murphy was glad his appearance amused her. "We'll wait twenty minutes, then go out through the lobby. They won't be expecting us to leave that way. Call the bell captain and order an airport limousine." Remembering that Natasha had once taught German, he added, "Speak to them in German. Tell them you're nurse Dietsel. Say the limo is for Herr Hans Brücher in suite 704."

While Natasha placed the call, Murphy opened the suitcase and pulled out a flat, cardboard box. Inside was a Heckler & Koch submachine gun, wrapped in a yellow and green plaid lap robe. Inserting a thirty-round clip, he laid the weapon on the bed.

Watching the time, he sat down at the writing table and from his backpack pulled out page 93, torn from his book on Nostradamus. With a red pen he circled the paragraph labeled Century VI, Quatrain 97. On a piece of hotel stationery he wrote:

> Concierge:
> Please fax this message to 919-732-4400 in the US:
> Dear Cindy, Research confirmed. Quatrain 97 in
> sixth century is valid. For sponsors, look to the
> Normans. Repeat, Normans.
> Cousin Clyde

> There is a US $100 bill in this envelope for your
> trouble. There is also a check made payable to cash

for $200. This check will clear for payment if the fax reaches the US within 24 hours. Thank you.

When he had finished, he folded the note and placed it in an envelope along with the money and check. The check was written on his Agency account under the name, "Jerome Pending."

The phone rang. Natasha answered, *"Yah."* She listened for ten seconds, *"Danke,"* then hung up. "Murphy, the limousine's here."

"It's show time, my little Mata Hari," he said, tweaking her nose. He was surprised how calm he felt. A short trip to the airport and he and Natasha would be on their way to a new life together in the US. A feeling of nostalgia for the Mena House, and for Cairo, swept over him. These past few days had been the happiest of his life.

Climbing into the wheelchair, he nodded, "Let's move Herr Brücher's butt out of here." Chambering a round in the Hockler, he placed the weapon on his lap. The solid weight of the cold steel felt reassuring. He pulled the lap robe up to his waist. No need for a silencer—too bulky. If they were forced to shoot their way out, the noise would be an advantage. "When we get to the lobby, please hand this envelope to the concierge."

"What is it?" Natasha asked, turning the sealed envelope over in her hand.

"A riddle for a friend."

"Father!" Natasha called, as the airport limo pulled up to the entrance of hangar eleven. She could see the general sitting in the back of the beige Mercedes, parked inside the hangar.

A seven blade, sixteen ton CH-53E Super Stallion helicopter stood on the tarmac, its rotors turning. The aircraft was surrounded by six marines, decked out in full battle gear. A marine captain, dressed in desert camouflage, jogged over.

"Patrick Murphy," he called. "I'm looking for Patrick Murphy."

Murphy stepped out of the limousine, removed the wig and started brushing talcum powder from his clothes. "I'm Patrick Murphy."

The captain compared Murphy to a copy of a faxed photo. "Delta blues, sir."

"Stray dog," Murphy replied.

"Affirmative, sir. I'm Captain Pardue. We have orders to lift off as soon as you and a General Zakharov are on board. Can you identify the general, sir?"

"Follow me." As Murphy led the captain to the Mercedes, he began to relax. A former leatherneck, it gave him a secure feeling to be in the care of a squad of aggressive, kick-ass US Marines.

Captain Pardue and a marine medic escorted Zakharov to the waiting helicopter. The general's oxygen tanks and suitcases were quickly shoved aboard.

"*Nyet, nyet,*" a shrill voice shouted from a small group still huddled beside the Mercedes.

Murphy could see Natasha in the middle, hands in the air, arguing in Russian. He rushed over, "What's wrong?"

"It's Yalena. She says she's not going with us. She wants to return to Moscow. She's afraid something bad will happen to her family if she defects."

"Leave her," Murphy said, gently but firmly pulling Natasha toward the helicopter. "There's a medic on board the chopper. Your father's going to be fine."

As Natasha climbed up the aluminum ladder, she looked over her shoulder at Yalena, who was weeping. "I don't understand. She cared so much for father."

"Don't worry. She can join him later."

The helicopter's three 4,380-shp turboshaft motors roared to life as Captain Pardue swiftly pulled in his perimeter guard. When they were safely on board, the helicopter lifted off and began a slow circle over the airport.

As the Super Stallion lumbered up and over the pyramids Murphy took Natasha's hand. "Look, you can see Cheops and the Sphinx."

Natasha watched as a panoramic view of Cairo filled the Plexiglas window, "Think we'll ever come back?"

"Whenever you want."

Natasha glanced at her father who was resting peacefully on the webbing that served as a seat. He gave a weak wave and smiled.

"Oh, no!" Natasha gasped, covering her mouth with her hand.

"What's wrong?" Murphy asked, seeing the fear in her eyes.

"Over there," she said, pointing to the medic who was adjusting the flow of oxygen. "There are *three* canisters!"

Murphy nodded reassuringly, "There's plenty of oxygen. We can get more on the ship."

"But father only travels with *two*!"

Murphy's heart stopped as he saw the third canister. It was his nightmare. The silver tank with the red cross painted on its side. The dial began to move.

"Natasha." Murphy said, pulling her gently towards him and wrapping both arms around her warm body. He could smell the scent of Persian lilacs. Looking into her face, he kissed her softly on the forehead. "Just you and me. Forever."

She smiled, holding on tightly. Her eyes locked with his. "Forev—"

The southern face of Cheops glowed a fiery red from the reflected light of the explosion.

HILLSBOROUGH

Two rings—a fax. Marcie ignored the machine as it whirred to life. Probably just another sign up for the Julia Estelle Women's Society. That would be the second this week. It would have to wait until Laurence returned from Iguaçu and life was back to normal. Right now she was too busy helping him pack.

On her next pass by the living room she almost bumped into the now silent fax machine. She could see the corner of a sheet of paper protruding from the out tray. Glancing at the salutation, she read, "Dear Cindy:—" Wrong person. Good, now she could just toss it in the trash. Taking the paper she noticed the point of origin—Cairo. *"Laurence!"*

Friar held the paper to the light.

> Dear Cindy: Research confirmed. Quatrain 97 in sixth century is valid. For sponsors, look to the Normans. Repeat, Normans. Cousin Clyde.

"It's from Murphy." A Dear Cindy could only mean trouble.

"Is he in danger?" asked Marcie.

"I'm afraid so." Even Murphy wouldn't clown around with a Dear Cindy. Noting the choppiness of the message and its short length, it was obvious Murphy had been in one hell of a rush when he wrote it.

The phone rang. It was Warner. He tried to break the news as gently as possible, but it struck home with the impact of a baseball bat to the gut. Murphy was dead. Blown up, along with the general and his daughter, in a helicopter over Cairo. News of the explosion was being shown on CNN. The media was reporting it as a training mishap.

Friar's voice was hard and cold, "Was it the GRU?"

"Probably, but it could've been any of a number of groups."

"Just before you called, we received a fax from Murphy. Haven't figured it out yet. It's some kind of homemade code."

There was a moment of silence at Warner's end. *"That fax could be important. I haven't received anything from him for the past twenty-four hours. He was probably waiting until he got to the* Kearsarge *before filing his report."*

"We'll work on it and let you know," Friar said, and slowly hung up the phone. Images of Murphy flashed before his eyes—remembrances of a friend whose Irish luck had run out.

"Sorry," Marcie said, placing her hand on his arm. "The fax can wait."

"No, let's do it now," Friar replied, eager to have something to do to help keep the dark thoughts at bay.

Marcie nodded. She would talk with him later about Murphy, when he was ready. Taking the fax from the writing table she reread the message.

"Quatrain? That's a poem with four lines," she said out loud. "Think he was referring to a poem?"

"Not likely. Murphy wasn't the poetic type." Examining the fax, Friar repeated, "*Quatrain* 97 in the sixth *century.*" There was something familiar about that combination. "Quatrains—centuries? Marcie, you're the analyst, what's the connection?"

"Well, in code 101 at Camp Peary they mentioned the use of quatrains and centuries by Nostradamus. He used them for enciphering his prophecies back in the sixteenth century. As I recall, he was using them to keep one step ahead of the Inquisition."

Friar snapped his fingers. "That's it. Murphy and his damned

Nostradamus mumbo-jumbo." Now Friar remembered. Nostradamus had written nine volumes of predictions containing one hundred prophecies each. The volumes were called *centuries*, the prophecies, *quatrains*.

In twenty-five minutes, Marcie was back from the Hillsborough library with a world atlas and a copy of Banain Kincaid's *The Nostradamus Prophecies*. On page 211 was Century VI, Quatrain 97:

> *The sky will burn at five and forty degrees,*
> *Fire approaches the great new city,*
> *In an instant a great flame bursts forth,*
> *When they want proof they will look to the Normans.*

"Okay, what've we got?" Friar asked, while scribbling the first three lines on the chalkboard he used to rehearse his lectures.

"Here's Kincaid's interpretation: 'A destructive fire, possibly a nuclear explosion, will strike a large city in the new world located near the forty-fifth parallel.' He goes on to list several American cities that fit the bill: Portland, Oregon; Minneapolis; Chicago; Detroit; New York."

Marcie opened the atlas to a map of the US and traced the arc cutting across the continent at 45°. "Minneapolis and Portland are the only two of any size sitting right on the forty-fifth parallel. New York's at 41° and Chicago's at 41.5°.

Friar examined the map, then reread the fax. In bold strokes, he wrote New York on the chalkboard. "If I were a terrorist, I'd target New York."

Marcie nodded. "I'm inclined to agree. Of course, it's only a guess. What about, *When they want proof they will look to the Normans*? It must be important. Murphy even repeats '*Normans.*'"

Friar wrote the phrase on the chalkboard. "Looks like he was trying to tell us who's responsible for the warheads, and it's not that Islamic group."

"France? Whenever I see Normans I think of the French. Or, he could've been telling us the French know *who* the sponsor is."

Friar studied the wording. "We'll have to work on that part. How about checking with French Intelligence while I'm in Iguaçu. I'll give Warner a call and let him know we think the where might be New York."

LANGLEY

Warner lifted the lid on the brass trimmed humidor and offered Friar one of his three remaining, carefully hoarded H. Upmann cigars. Each was wrapped in a thin, cedar sheath and was stored in a sturdy, aluminum cylinder. He hoped Friar would take the hint and smuggle in a box of Cubans when he returned from Argentina. "All set for Iguaçu?"

Much to Warner's relief, Friar declined the cigar. He didn't want to smell like a tobacco barn during his last few minutes with Marcie. "Yep. I should be there by this time tomorrow.

"So, you're convinced New York's the target?" Warner was going to bypass Shymanski on this one. He would take it straight to Director Vaughn.

"That's the way Marcie and I read it. If the terrorists want maximum impact, they're going to place the warhead in Manhattan."

"Any idea *where* in Manhattan?"

"My guess is downtown, in the financial area. You remember the World Trade Center bombing in 1993, and the Sacco and Vanzetti affair in 1920?"

"Sacco and Vanzetti. Weren't they the anarchists who tried to blow up Wall Street."

"They're the ones. They set off a horse-drawn wagon full of dynamite near the Morgan Guarantee building. Killed thirty-some and wounded another four to five hundred. That wagon was the car bomb of its day."

"You think our group's going to use a car bomb?"

"Wouldn't be too difficult. All they'd have to do is park a van or station wagon on the street or in a garage, then *boom*."

Warner shifted in his chair. "I've got a special favor to ask before you leave for Argentina."

Friar frowned. He had promised Marcie he would take her to dinner at the Bombay Club before heading out to National airport.

Sensing Friar's hesitation, Warner said, "We've got a local informer who claims nuclear warheads are being smuggled into the country. Could be an important confirmation."

"When and where?" Friar knew it was useless to argue. Besides, it might provide important background information for his meeting with Mukhtar. Marcie would understand. She always did.

"All you've got to do is meet him for dinner at the Willard Room over on Pennsylvania Avenue. The get-together's set for 1900 hours. Shouldn't take but an hour or so."

"How was the contact made?"

"Two days ago, we put out an inquiry on the Intelink for information on the Shaheeds."

Although he was computer-challenged, Friar was familiar with the Intelink. It was the Agency's own version of the Internet, used by the country's numerous intelligence services to keep in touch with each other on a real-time basis. It was ideal for shotgun inquiries.

Warner continued, "This morning I received a call from Jason Dorn, who's FBI and head of the Counterterrorism Center. Seems he was contacted by the informer a couple of days ago. The source mentioned a group calling themselves 'The Islamic Martyrs.' It's not 'Shaheeds,' but it's close enough."

"You mean it's been *two* days and the CTC hasn't done a damn thing?" Friar had met Dorn three years before on a routine investigation of an Iranian terrorist cell suspected in the World Trade Center bombing. Based on his first and only meeting, he was not impressed.

"It wasn't until Dorn read my inquiry that he became concerned. The CTC gets dozens of calls a month from sources claiming to have leads on terrorist groups."

Friar nodded, "What's the informer's asking price?"

"Dorn said he wants $500,000 to even discuss it. Says he can back up his claims with proof."

"So, you want me to baby-sit Dorn while he evaluates the source?"

"That's about it. Wouldn't hurt to have a second opinion."

"Why the Willard Room?"

"It was the informer's choice. In fact, he insisted on the Willard."

"Do we have a name?"

"He calls himself Dubov. Alexander Dubov."

Chapter 10

OCTOBER 22: WASHINGTON, DC

It was 6:55P.M. when Dubov handed the keys of the rented executive-gray Lexus SC400 to the ponytailed parking valet who came bounding out of the entrance of the Willard Inter-Continental Hotel. Stepping into the hotel lobby, Dubov checked the overhead clock. Good, right on time. First impressions were always important, and he wanted to be seen as a punctual, dependable person who could be trusted on even the smallest detail. After all, the success of his plan depended on establishing credibility with the FBI.

Dubov paused at the entrance to the Willard Room and examined his reflection in the expensive glass panels inlaid in the heavy mahogany door. Carefully adjusting the burgundy, Italian silk tie, he thought, *Image. Perception and image.* Shakespeare was right—apparel does oft proclaim the man. He wondered how good an actor he would make when face-to-face with the FBI. What were the proper mannerisms for an informer? He shrugged. Too late to worry about that now. It would all have to be done right on the first take, there would be no dress rehearsals.

"Mr. Dorn's table," Dubov said in a confident voice to the suave, silver haired maitre d' hovering protectively over the reservation list. As his eyes adjusted to the subdued light, Dubov glanced around. The décor was turn-of-the-century, red-velvet Edwardian elegance that oozed epicurean charm and reeked of purchased influence. The pleasing, yeasty aroma of freshly baked bread drifted into his nose—the sign of a first-rate kitchen. In the background he could hear the clink of cocktail glasses mixed with the chatter of unlimited expense accounts closing under-the-table deals with smiling, compliant public servants. He had chosen well.

After a two minute wait, Dubov was escorted to a private booth in the back of the main dining room. Inside the richly paneled cubicle sat Dorn and Friar.

Dorn rose and extended his hand, "Mr. Dubov? I'm Jason Dorn."

"Pleased to meet you," Dubov answered, studying Friar out of the corner of his eye.

Stepping aside, Dorn motioned towards Friar. "Hope you don't mind that I've brought along Mr. Clark to hear your proposal."

Dubov looked Friar up and down. "Are you FBI also?"

Friar smiled, "No, just an adviser."

While the three men settled into the plush, leather covered seats, Friar studied Dubov's face—the strong jawline, the old scar, the intense, brown eyes. He was impressed with the placid expression. It was unusual for an informer to be so relaxed at the first meeting. "Interesting choice of restaurants, Mr. Dubov. Do you come here often?"

"First time actually. It was recommended by an old comrade. He said it's a popular place for seeking money from Washington." Holding his hand beside his mouth, Dubov said, "The small amount I'm asking is nothing compared to what changes hands here everyday." Running a finger along the expensive, hand-blocked wallpaper he shook his head. "If only walls could talk."

With a practiced eye, Friar observed Dubov while he prattled on. There was something odd—something out of place about this informer. The profile being portrayed so artfully didn't fit that of a typical snitch. There was too much confidence. "You speak excellent English, Mr. Dubov. If I were a betting man, I'd wager—the Caucasus—with several years spent in England?"

Dubov tensed, *who was this adviser?* Gradually, his facial muscles relaxed, "Thank you. Actually I'm from Chechnya. Or rather, what's left of Grozny. You are also correct about the English part. I studied English Literature at the University of Swansea, in Wales." It was important to establish his Chechen roots to help build credibility and explain motive.

"Mind if I ask what business you're in?"

Dubov hesitated, *so, you're the one in charge.* "Let's just say I am a facilitator and consultant. I represent my associates in the US. I also help American businessmen cope with the bureaucracy in Russia." Lowering his voice, he said, "Russia can be a very dangerous place if you don't understand the rules."

"So I've heard."

Dubov nodded, "You sit down to play poker. Someone in a leather jacket deals you two cards. The game has been switched to blackjack and you lose. What can you do? Who can you complain to?" Touching his forefinger to his nose, he said, "We help make arrangements for our clients. In Russia, you must have the right *krysha.*"

"So, you're in the protection racket?"

"Please, Mr. Clarke. We prefer to think of it as providing security. A form of corporate insurance against certain problems."

A tall, athletically built man in an ill fitting table-captain's uniform approached the booth and in an uncertain voice began reciting the list of daily specials. Friar cringed at the mangled mispronunciation of *soufflé de homard.* The least Dorn could have done was pick an agent who spoke rudimentary menu-French.

After struggling through the list, the captain blushed, turned on his heels and disappeared into the kitchen.

Dubov smiled at the little charade. Turning to Dorn, he said, "I think I'll have the smoked Norwegian salmon as an appetizer and the lobster with truffles for an entree." Placing the oversized, satin bound menu on the table, he asked, "Does the government's budget permit a wine selection?"

Dorn squirmed at the "market price" notation beside the lobster. The bill would be outrageous. How was he going to justify a huge dinner tab to Josephine Winesap in accounting? She was certain to red-flag it for audit. He could hear her clucking now. A steak and potatoes type, he always prided himself on keeping expenditures within Bureau allowances. As far as informers were concerned, a Big Mac and Coke was about it—*never* a sit-down at the Willard. Changing the subject he said, "I believe you have information—"

Leaning forward, Dubov asked, "Has the $500,000 been approved?"

"I—I'm afraid we'll have to know a good deal more before we can— that's a lot of money."

Dubov cocked an eyebrow, "Lot of money? Not for what I know."

Running his hand down the wine list, Friar asked, "Since you're having lobster, would a 1994 Clos du Bois chardonnay be acceptable?"

"Actually, I was hoping for French, not Californian. Perhaps a '92 Latour Puligny-Montrachet?" Dubov hesitated, Friar was staring. Turning back to Dorn he asked, "And, what more do you need to know?"

"We need actual proof that nuclear warheads are involved."

Dubov braced himself. This was the critical stage. Too many details without being paid and it would look suspicious. Too little, and they would think he was bluffing. "I can tell you this. Five warheads are already inside the US. I have a friend who has seen them." He sat back and waited for the full impact of his statement.

Friar was impressed by the conviction in Dubov's voice. How did this informer know so much? More important—was it true? One thing for certain, Dubov's statement should provide Warner with the confirmation needed to get the wheels turning. "Proof, Mr. Dubov, give us some real proof."

Dubov could tell he had struck a nerve. Speaking slowly and deliberately he said, "There are three groups involved. A terrorist cell calling themselves the Islamic Martyrs, a large Russian crime syndicate and a foreign country who plans you great harm." Taking a sip of water, he said, "You get the names of each organization after the $500,000 has been wired to my bank account at Rahn & Bodmer in Zurich."

"You've already given us one name," Friar said.

Dubov chuckled, "You mean the Islamic Martyrs? Terrorist groups change names as often as they change clothes. For $500,000, I'll give you the name of the person in charge. I can also tell you how and where they brought them in." Noting the questioning expression on Dorn's face, Dubov said, "You can be assured these fanatics didn't smuggle the warheads into the US just to test your border controls."

Dubov knew more about US border controls than he cared to admit. Nine months earlier, he had personally tested the Canadian-

US border crossing at Prescott, Ontario. Driving a pickup loaded with 1,000 pounds of uraninite, he had triggered a Geiger alarm in the control booth at the customs check point. It was after that test the Phoenix Committee decided to bring the warheads in by submarine.

Dorn scribbled a few words in a small notebook. "It will take time to get approval. I'll need at least a week or two."

Dubov scowled, "No, Mr. Dorn. You don't have a week or two."

Friar mulled over Dubov's comment. *Not two weeks?* For what? "Can you tell us *how* you got this information?"

Dubov laughed, "What kind of an informer would I be if I gave away my sources?"

Friar snorted, "You expect us to waste our time chasing shadows just because you've dreamed up some cock-and-bull story about nuclear warheads? Come on, Mr. Dubov, give us something tangible."

Dubov smiled at Friar's attempt to rush him. "All five are thermonuclear, strategic warheads from Russia's stockpile. Four are large, one is small. When I'm paid, you get the details."

Friar sat back in his seat and studied Dubov closely. The informer's story checked out with Murphy's report. Without consulting Dorn he announced, "Okay, Mr. Dubov. Half the money now, the rest when you've given us the information." There was no time to wait while the request wound its way through channels at the FBI. Warner would have to find the money in one of the DO's rainy-day accounts. "Call Mr. Dorn at his office tomorrow morning and give him your wiring instructions. Let's meet again in four days."

"Agreed," Dubov replied, surprised Friar had consented so easily. Relaxing, he pulled a silver cigarette case from his inside coat pocket and removed a Camel filter-tip.

Dorn shook his head in amazement. Friar, on his own authority, had promised this unknown informer $500,000. The Bureau would never have permitted that.

"Mind if I smoke?" Dubov asked. Without waiting for a reply he reached for the book of matches resting in the pewter ash tray and lit up.

Friar watched the Chechen slip the matchbook into his pocket.

Inhaling deeply, Dubov savored the calming nicotine. He glanced at Dorn with disdain. In Chechnya an informer would be arrested and interrogated—and, he would confess.

The rest of the meal was devoted to small talk about the deterioration of the economy in Russia since the collapse of the old USSR, and the conditions of the slate mines in northern Wales where Dubov had worked between semesters at the University of Swansea. Dorn joined in the conversation where he could. At 8:45 P.M. Dubov excused himself and left.

When Dubov was out of sight, Friar signaled the table captain. "Any problems?"

"No, sir. We got the pictures and saved all the drinking glasses and silverware."

"Good." Turning to Dorn, he said, "Jason, have the Bureau run a DNA profile on our informer. The saliva from his water glass should be sufficient. Also, get as many prints as possible. That name "Dubov" has got to be an alias. Check with Interpol and put out an inquiry on our informer over the Intelink."

"Why don't we just take him in for questioning?"

Friar shook his head, "Better not crowd him. He's a professional and would only clam up." Friar reviewed the evening's events. He had the distinct feeling the Chechen wanted them to know what was going on.

"Thanks for the meal," Friar said, as the table captain brought Dorn the check. Glancing at his watch, he rose and headed for the lobby. Marcie would be waiting to drive him to the American terminal at National. At least they would have a few minutes together. He'd call Warner from Miami.

OCTOBER 23: IGUAÇU FALLS, ARGENTINA

Friar opened the drapes and gazed at the cataracts from the balcony of his suite at the Hotel Internacional. In the distance he could see the mist rising from the massive *Garganta del Diablo*. A mile away, the falls looked deceptively peaceful and benign. Sixty feet higher and four times wider than Niagara Falls, the 275 cataracts of Iguaçu stretch for an impressive two miles along the river marking the border between Brazil and Argentina. He planned to bring Marcie here next year for their second anniversary.

Checking his watch—4:25P.M.—he reached in his luggage and withdrew the pistol. It was time to meet Joe Don on San Martin Island. Leaving his bags piled at the foot of the bed, he removed a clip of 9mm ammunition from his briefcase. Everything was in place—fragmentation rounds alternating with hollow-points. Ramming the clip into the Glock's handle, he slid the pistol into the belt holster in the small of his back.

Five minutes later, he was strolling down the narrow, gravel path leading to the bottom of Twin Brothers Falls. Thick, tropical vegetation crowded both sides of the switchbacks. As he approached the river, the roar from the crashing water intensified until it drowned out all other sounds. Rounding the last corner, he was greeted by a cool mist of fresh water washing over him in waves. Standing at the base of the *Saltos Dos Hermanas*, his whole body shook from the force of 450,000 gallons of water per second, plunging 270 feet onto the rocks below. He wished Marcie were here to share the moment. She would call it the cosmic dance of Shiva. In the fading afternoon sun, a double rainbow arched across the undulating mist. It was a good luck sign from Marcie.

A quarter of a mile downriver he caught the water taxi for the short hop over to the *Isla Grande San Martin*. The island was an oblong strip of land in the middle of the Rio Iguaçu, flanked on the right by the *Saltos San Martin* and *Adan y Eva* and on the left by the *Tres Mosqueteros*. He could see Joe Don standing in the center of a clearing, clutching an Audubon field guide and looking into the mist with a pair of binoculars. Joe Don appeared to be following a pair of nesting black martins as they swirled in and out of the spray at the base of Adam and Eve Falls. When Friar approached, Joe Don nodded, lowered his field guide, and started walking towards the falls.

"Any problems?" Friar asked.

"Not really. There are a helluva lot more Arabs around now than there were back in '92. Other than that, no changes I can see." Joe Don pretended to jot a notation in his birdwatcher's log. "Any idea when and where you're going to meet Mukhtar? I want to do a reconnaissance."

"There was a message from the general when I checked into the hotel. He's scheduled the get-together for 0930 on the platform at the end of the Nandu walkway. That's the one leading out to the top of *Garganta del Diablo*."

"You mean that long-ass wooden walkway over on the Argentine side?"

"Yep. Trails out into the river for about a mile."

"Could be a set-up, Hoss," Joe Don warned. Unfolding a waterproof map, he ran his finger along the jungle trail leading to the *Paseo A La Garganta*.

"Nothing I can do about it now," Friar replied. "It's Mukhtar's show. I don't even know how to reach him. It's gonna be up to you to cover my back."

Joe Don wiped the mist from the front lenses of his binoculars, then studied the vegetation along the Argentine bank. "Don't like it. Not one damn bit. You're gonna stick out like a vegetarian at a wienie roast on that platform. A sniper could pick you off from any one of those small islands along the walkway. He wouldn't even need a scope."

It had crossed Friar's mind he didn't have much current information on Mukhtar. For all he knew, the person—or persons—waiting at the end of the walkway might not be Mukhtar at all. But, why? Who would go to all that trouble? Instinct told him to hunker down and keep out of sight, but he had been forced to register at the hotel under his own name in case Mukhtar wanted to reach him with any last minute instructions.

"Okay, Hoss, it's your little red wagon. Anything goes wrong, give me a shout." Joe Don examined the map, "Tomorrow morning, early, I'm gonna set up on one of these small islands where the walkway juts to the left. You can reach me anytime after 0730 on that communications gizmo in your life vest. The frequency's preset. If push comes to shove, just hop in the river, and I'll pick you up."

Friar watched the muddy water tumbling onto the jagged rocks at the bottom of Adam and Eve Falls. "No way I'm going to jump into that soup. The current's going to be strong as hell around the platform." When he checked into the hotel earlier that day, the desk clerk had told him the spring rains had come early, doubling the river's normal volume.

"Hey, don't worry, Hoss," Joe Don said. "Found me a brand new

Zodiac inflatable with a forty-five horsepower Merc over in Puerto Stroessner. You wouldn't believe the stuff they've got for sale over there. Some guy was even trying to buy a Stinger."

"A Stinger?" Friar had heard there were still dozens of the ground-to-air missiles leftover from Afghanistan. The CIA had tried to soak up the excess supply, but hadn't been able to account for more than a couple of hundred.

"As soon as your chitchat with Mukhtar's over, I'll swing by in the Zodiac, pick you off that platform, then chug on upriver to Brazil. It's a short hop from there to the airport."

"Piece of cake?"

"Piece of cake, Hoss."

The fresh dorado, caught that morning in the Parana river and grilled over mesquite charcoal was served in a meunière sauce with basmati rice. The meat was moist and flaky, just the way Friar liked it. Ignoring the sommelier's "white wine with fish" suggestion, he ordered a half-bottle of 1978 Malbec from the Navarro vineyards in Mendoza. The rich, red Malbec blended well with the delicate texture of the dorado. When the last drop of wine was drained from his glass, he scribbled his name and room number on the check, rose, glanced around at the other twelve tables, then left the dining room. He had halfway expected to see Mukhtar, but there were no familiar faces. On his way past the front desk he checked for messages.

"Sí, señor," the desk clerk responded, reaching a soft, stubby hand under the counter. "A short, older gentleman with white hair brought this by for you late this afternoon."

It was a miniature bottle of Remy Martin cognac with a sealed envelope tied to its neck. Stepping away from the desk, Friar opened the envelope. Inside was a note, "Friar, keep your eyes open. A'man has picked up communications from Iraq's *Estikhabarat* concerning Mukhtar's visit to Iguaçu. Looks like trouble." It was signed, "S."

The hair on the back of Friar's neck bristled—*Estikhabarat*—military intelligence. What the hell did they want? Mukhtar was *Al Mukhabarat*—general intelligence—or, at least he used to be. And what was the Sandman doing in Iguaçu? Friar casually walked around the lobby to clear his head and see if he was being watched. There was nothing suspicious. An elderly pair of what looked like European tourists were sitting in the TV room, sipping coffee and watching a grainy rerun of Gunsmoke, dubbed in Spanish. Friar moved closer. They were speaking fluent German.

Leaving the lobby, he walked quickly to the elevator, got in and pushed the button for the third floor. No one seemed to notice. When the elevator stopped, he stepped out, then glanced up and down the corridor. There was no movement. Unbuttoning his jacket, he strolled to his room. The Do Not Disturb sign still dangled from the door knob, just as he had left it. Running his hand along the top of the door, he felt for the matchstick wedged in place before leaving for dinner. *Gone.* Someone had paid him a visit.

Slipping the Glock out of its holster, he silently chambered a fragmentation round, then crouched to the right of the door frame. He knocked lightly, then waited. Silence. Shifting the pistol to his left hand, he reached over and inserted the heavy brass room key into the lock. Turning it as quietly as possible, he heard the *click* of the bolt falling into place. Still, no response. After a ten second delay, he twisted the knob and lightly pushed the door open with his foot. Counting to five, he rushed into the dark room, keeping low against the right wall. Pausing, he listened for unusual sounds. The only noise came from his own heavy breathing. Staying low, he worked his way forward to the light switch beside the kitchenette, then flicked it on. Seeing nothing out of place, he eased up to a standing position.

Everything seemed to be in order. Whoever had been there was gone. Holding the pistol close to his chest, he checked the adjoining bedroom and bath. The bedroom was darker than he remembered. Only one bulb was working in the overhead light. Glancing at the bed, he noticed the corner of the bedspread was turned down and a piece of chocolate lay on the pillow. Holstering the gun, he chuckled at his antics. It had only been the maid. Tovi's note had made him jumpy.

Trying to relax, he walked back into the sitting room, to the TV where he had placed the hollowed out Spanish/English dictionary. The miniature video camera with its infrared motion detector had been activated. Checking the tape, he noticed that eight minutes and ten seconds had been used. At least the gadget worked, but a travelogue of the hotel maid walking back and forth wasn't worth saving. Before erasing it, he decided to view the tape to make certain a second person hadn't entered before or after the maid. Eight minutes was a rather long time for simply turning down the bed.

Watching the small screen he saw a heavyset maid enter the suite carrying a laundry bag full of what looked like towels. She walked over to the reading desk and slowly, methodically rummaged through the papers lying on top. Probably scrounging for something to steal. He watched as she left the desk and went into the bedroom. Closing the door, she stayed there for five minutes and ten seconds. "Goofing off," he muttered to himself. Then she re-entered the sitting room, carrying an empty laundry bag and a tray of chocolates. After looking around, she belched loudly, then left.

Something about the last scene bothered him. He re-ran it, verbalizing her actions as he watched. "She's coming back into the sitting room. Now, she's stopped. Looking around—belching. Now she's heading towards the door with the empty laundry bag."

"That's it," he said to himself. The laundry bag. It was *empty*. If she had left clean towels in the bathroom, it should've been full of used ones.

Reaching for the phone, he dialed "0."

"*El gerente. Sí?*"

"This is room 307. I'm calling about the evening maid service."

"*Lo siento, Señor. The evening maid, she not show up for work. You want new towels? I send.*"

"No. No, thanks," Friar replied, returning the phone to its cradle. Retracing his steps, he walked back into the bedroom, then into the bathroom. The bath and hand towels used just before dinner had not been replaced. Returning to the bedroom, he pulled the chain to the reading light beside the bed. It didn't work. "Damn bulb," he grumbled.

A slight movement in the bedcovers caught his attention. Midway down, the bedspread appeared to rise and fall, ever so slightly. It must be the poor lighting. No—there it was again. This time, definitely a movement. He wondered if a rat might be trapped under the covers. With his right hand, he drew his pistol. Pointing the barrel towards the slowly shifting form, he reached for the corner of the bed spread. Grabbing an edge, he threw it back.

His blood froze. Staring at him, in all it's venomous fury, was the fierce, lance-shaped head of a thick bodied, five foot snake. There was no mistaking the dark triangular pattern on its back—the shape of its head. It was a fer-de-lance. Furious at being strapped to the bed, the serpent lunged forward, needle sharp fangs slashing out, droplets of venom flying through the air. Friar recoiled, his body slamming against the bedroom wall—knocking the gun from his grip.

Unable to escape the leather restraining strap tied around its tail, the viper quickly slithered back under the disheveled bedcovers. Only a long, dark head stuck out, tongue darting forward, measuring the distance to its tormentor-prey, its savage eyes following Friar's every move.

Gradually, the heaving in his chest subsided. Moving back into the sitting room, he eased down on the couch. Emptying the contents of the Sandman's miniature into a glass, he sipped the cognac. The sting in his throat helped clear his thoughts. After the adrenaline rush had slowed, he returned to the bedroom.

Unscrewing the good bulb from the ceiling fixture, he turned on the fluorescent lights in the bathroom, then drew the door closed until there was only a shaft of light streaking into the bedroom. Carefully avoiding the bed, he threw a pillow, a blanket and some clothes into the darkest corner of the room. Finally, he placed a straight-backed, wicker chair in the walk-in closet and sat down facing the bedroom. Screwing the suppressor onto the muzzle of his pistol, he pulled the closet door until it was almost closed, then opened the slats of the top half. It wouldn't be long before the maid returned to check her handiwork.

An hour and a half later, as his head began to nod, he heard a light rapping on the front door of the suite. Then silence. Again—this time louder—the sharp sound of knuckles against wood. A few seconds later, there was the metallic sound of a key turning in the heavy lock. Straining, Friar could hear the faint swish as the front door passed over the carpet. Another swish, then a light *click*. The floor in the living room creaked as heavy footsteps approached the bedroom.

Peering through the wooden slats, Friar could make out a stocky form, dressed in a maid's uniform, entering the bedroom. The bright, narrow beam from a flashlight swept across the bed then focused on the pile of rumpled clothes in the corner. Stalking around the bed, the intruder gingerly approached, prodding the heap of clothes with a long, slender object.

Grasping his pistol with both hands, Friar kicked open the closet door. "Freeze, you sonofabitch!" The door swung open, hitting the door stop at the bottom of the wall, then bounced back, striking the end of the suppressor, deflecting his aim.

The maid paused just long enough to determine Friar's location, then lunged. The blade of the machete came crashing down, splintering the slats, crunching to a stop on the heavy, brass tie rack, inches above Friar's head. With a deep, guttural grunt, the attacker jerked the machete out of the shattered wood and raised it again, this time slowly and deliberately. The face of the intruder leaned forward, peering uncertainly in the direction of the dark closet.

Friar could smell the stench of garlic and hear the labored breathing. Without waiting, he rammed the barrel of his pistol against the closet door and pulled the trigger. A flash of light filled the bedroom as the fragmentation round slammed into the wood, bursting into tiny projectiles. The intruder howled in pain as several small pieces of lead found their mark. Without pausing, Friar fired a second round through the closet door, this one a hollow-point and better aimed. The mushrooming lead plowed into the intruder's upper chest with a hollow *thud*. Keeping low, Friar kicked open the door, stepped into the room, and fired a fragmentation round directly into his attacker's gut. The impact lifted the body off the floor, knocking the machete from the maid's grip, throwing the intruder backwards across the bed.

As the attacker's body struck the mattress, a dark, lance-shaped head darted out from under the covers. Long, needle-sharp fangs disappeared into the exposed, throbbing carotid artery. The snake jerked its head back and forth, squeezing venom into the hot, rushing flow of arterial blood.

Friar grabbed the machete from the floor, sprang across the bed and slashed off the snake's head with a single stroke. The jaw and neck muscles of the severed head continued to contract, driving the venom deeper into the throat of the dying assassin. Blood from the wriggling, headless snake's body spurted in all directions, spraying Friar's face and hands.

The struggle was over as quickly as it had began. "Stupid," Friar muttered to himself, jumping off the bed. "You stupid jerk. You could've gotten yourself killed. Should've shot the bastard straight off." His whole body was shaking. No assassin would've gotten within five feet ten years ago.

Friar screwed the bulb back into the ceiling light and flipped on the switch. With the tip of the machete he gingerly prodded the limp body sprawled across the bed. The corpse lay on its back, fresh blood oozing from the gaping holes in its chest and gut. The eyes were half-open, staring blankly at the ceiling. The maid's wig had fallen off, revealing a head full of black, curly hair. Friar looked closer. The man weighed 200 to 210 pounds, and was forty-three to forty-five-years-old. The ashen facial features were those of an Arab. Underneath the ill-fitting checkered dress was a pair of dirty jeans. Friar rifled the pockets for identification—empty. A mixture of blood and urine soaked his fingers.

The telephone rang. Friar walked into the sitting room, still shaking. Wiping the blood from his face and hands onto his shirt, he picked up the receiver.

"*Senõr, is everything all right?*" It was the front desk. "*There were noises—loud noises.*"

"It was a rat," Friar replied, trying to keep his voice under control. "I had to kill a rat. It's okay now."

After the night clerk hung up, Friar walked over to the couch and lay down. Totally exhausted, he reached for the phone and dialed the operator. "This is room 307. Please give me a wake-up call at 8:00A.M. Understand? Wake-up call at eight in the morning."

"*Si, Senõr. 8:00A.M.*"

Resting his head on the couch's soft armrest, he closed his eyes. In a couple of minutes he would get up and wash off the blood.

Chapter 11

The loud ringing startled Friar. Still groggy, he reached for the phone.

"*Buenos días, Mr. Clarke,*" said a cheery, feminine voice. "*This is your eight o'clock wake-up call. Would you care for a continental breakfast?*"

Friar pushed the illumination button on his watch. 8:00A.M. Impossible. He had just dozed off. Gradually, the reality of time and place came into focus. Sitting up, he grimaced from the pain of a class-4 headache. His right hand felt tight—dried blood.

"*Mr. Clarke? Are you there?*"

"Please," he managed to squeak, his mouth dry, his voice hoarse. Licking his lips, he cringed—salt. There was snake blood on his lips. "Orange juice, toast, with a *large* pot of coffee." Hanging up, he got to his feet. There was no time to waste.

Opening the bedroom door, he reluctantly walked in. The body was lying faceup in the jumble of covers, the head of the fer-de-lance still attached to the gray tissues of his neck. The humid, overpowering, putrid smell of blood, sweat, and excrement made him gag. Holding a towel to his nose, he threw the corner of a sheet over the corpse's head.

Heading for the bathroom, he stripped off his blood spattered clothes as he went. Once inside, he closed the door and turned on the shower. Taking a bar of soap and bottle of shampoo, he stepped into the stall and rotated the dial to medium-hot. Lathering down, he stood there. The cleansing, refreshing, absolving water splashed over his body, washing away the flakes of blood from his face, hair, hands—but, not his mind. Watching the rust red rivulets swirl down the drain, he tried to piece together what had happened. Who had sent the assassin? Was it Mukhtar? He thought of Marcie. It wouldn't be good to tell her about the attack, at least not for awhile.

Drying off, Friar walked back into the bedroom. The rancid smell still stung his nose, but the shower had done the trick. He felt better, even invigorated. Rummaging through his limited luggage, he selected a set of clean, casual clothes, a dark green nylon jacket and a pair of sturdy, walking shoes. When he went to meet Mukhtar, he would have to abandon his suitcase and the rest of his blood-soaked clothes. Carrying the clean garments into the sitting room, he pulled the bedroom door shut and opened the windows, letting in a stream of cool, refreshing morning air. After the meeting, he would phone Argentine intelligence and brief them on the attack. Maybe they could help identify the body.

Friar strode briskly along the path leading to the Nandu walkway. The bright sunlight filtering through the trees and the caffeine shock from four cups of strong Brazilian coffee had burned away the mental fog. He was wide awake and eager to meet Mukhtar.

Along the path, the fragrances of orchids, bromeliads, and wildflowers drifted out of the jungle. In places, the heavy vegetation formed an overhead canopy, causing the heavy mist to condense and drip on his head and clothes. To his right, a pair of large, purple, iridescent morpho butterflies flopped lazily among the flowers. Crossing the crests of *Bejaruna* and *Bosseti* Falls, he could see, off to his left, two long rainbows arching over the Rio Iguaçu. More good luck signs from Marcie. Overhead, a toucan, with an oversized orange and black beak jutting out from a too-small face, swooped down and settled in a tree twenty yards away.

The sound of churning water increased as he approached the *Paseo a La Garganta*. Reaching the last clearing before the walkway, he stopped, and pulled out a pair of 10x binoculars, which he used to scan the small islands to his left. Joe Don was tucked away on one of them. It was time for a communications check. Flipping on the mike of the miniature transmitter fitted to his kevlar life vest, he placed the pea-sized receiver in his left ear.

"Joe Don, can you read me? It's 9:15 and I'm five minutes from the walkway."

"*Loud and clear, Hoss,*" came the reply. "*I was wondering where you were. Thought I might have to come looking. I'm on the last island on the left, right where the footbridge doglegs to the platform. I've got a clear field of fire. There are two guards standing at the entrance to the walk-way. Someone's already on the platform. If it ain't your boy, let me know, and I'll take him out. Good luck.*"

"Roger."

It took Friar five minutes to convince the two, thickset guards—who spoke no English—that he was indeed Laurence Clarke. From their bull necks, handlebar mustaches, mismatched civilian clothes, and casual arrogance he could tell they were Iraqi *Al Mukhabarat.* While they jabbered Farsi into half-hidden lapel microphones he overheard them mentioning Mukhtar's name. After wagging their heads and chattering to each other, they had Friar stand between them while they patted him down for weapons. Finding his pistol, they jerked up the back of his jacket and yanked it from its holster. Reluctantly, he let them keep it.

Finally, they motioned for him to proceed. Stepping quickly onto the sturdy wooden structure that snaked out into the shallow depths of the Rio Iguaçu, he headed towards the falls. In the distance, the footbridge disappeared into a thicket of trees leading to the platform overlooking the Devil's Throat. It took him fifteen minutes to reach the last turn. It was reassuring to know that Joe Don was nearby, hidden in the dense undergrowth. Rounding the corner he saw a lone, five-foot-six figure standing on the platform at the crest of the falls. It was difficult to tell, but the stance, the head full of hair, the hawklike nose—it was Mukhtar. The general was dressed in a light brown business suit and was watching Friar's every move through a pair of binoculars.

"Laurence! Laurence Clarke!" Mukhtar yelled, trying to make himself heard above the roar of the water. A frail man of sixty-two, his face had the gaunt, sad look of a person who had experienced too much suffering and had witnessed too many summary executions. With labored steps he moved towards Friar.

"Kareem!" Friar replied, racing forward.

After embracing, Mukhtar stepped back and looked Friar over. "Allah has been gracious to you my friend. You have only gotten younger."

"And, Father Time has added dignity to your years," Friar replied. He was shocked at how much Mukhtar had aged. Had he not been expecting to see him, he would not have recognized the general.

"You are too kind," Mukhtar said. "But, I have grown old since we last met. I have been cursed with having to live in interesting times." Mukhtar hesitated, "I often regret what has happened. Our two countries, once good friends, now enemies. But, it will not be this way forever."

Friar nodded. He had great respect for the Iraqi people and was pained by the suffering caused by the sanctions. "I'm glad you're safe. And, Jamila, how is she? And your son Zafia?"

Mukhtar beamed. "Jamila is fine. She pleases me more each day—" He stopped and gazed down at the brown, swirling water. "But, poor Zafia—he is with Allah. It was the hemophilia. The sanctions—we could not get the Factor VIII protein needed to make his blood clot."

"I'm sorry," Friar said. If only he had known, he might have been able to help. Taking the general by the arm he said, "I have to warn you. You may be in danger. Last night someone tried to kill me."

Mukhtar's head jerked up. "Who was it? A car tried to run me down this morning. Fortunately, my bodyguards saw it coming."

"I searched the assassin's body for identification. There was none. But he was definitely Arab. I have also received information that your military intelligence—"

"Uday," Mukhtar muttered. "Uday, Saddam's son is behind this. He thinks I am a traitor." He glanced over his shoulder at the empty walkway. "We must make this meeting brief." Moving closer, he said, "Two months ago I learned that a militant Islamic sect calling themselves the Shaheeds of the Islamic Ummah was recruiting in Basra. They were seeking volunteers for a terrorist act of gigantic proportion against the US."

"Does Uday know about this?"

"I have tried to keep the information secret from military intelligence. Uday would prevent me from talking to you. But I think he suspects—if he finds out I have spoken to you—" Mukhtar put his forefinger to his head and cocked his thumb. "Saddam has become very paranoid. He sees enemies everywhere. There are executions each week. Uday would delight in denouncing me and having me shot."

"Is Uday in control?"

Mukhtar shook his head. "No. My department reports directly to Saddam. Uday does not dare confront his father, but when Saddam is not around?" Mukhtar rolled his eyes skyward. "Some day, Uday will go to far and try to eliminate Saddam."

"If you want to defect, Kareem, I can arrange it."

"It's too late. I am dying of prostate cancer. Anyway, I am *al-Ibrahimis* and it would bring shame to my clan."

"Is there anything I can do?"

Mukhtar nodded, "I love my country and do not want to see it destroyed. If these Shaheed fanatics succeed, I fear the US will blame Iraq. You must believe me when I say my government has had *nothing* to do with these radicals."

Friar looked deep into Mukhtar's eyes, "Not even Uday's *Estikhabarat*?"

"Not even them. Laurence, I swear to you on the memory of my dead son, Iraq has taken *no* part." Leaning against the railing of the observation platform for support, Mukhtar said, "Our informants tell us the radicals talk of unleashing the Islamic Bomb against the Great Satan. Do you know what that means?"

"A nuclear attack against the US."

"Exactly. They seek only to destroy and will stop at nothing. Can you imagine the response from Washington if an American city is bombed? Uday does not understand how dangerous it would be for Iraq if such a thing happened."

Friar nodded.

"I have reason to believe the militants control five warheads. If this is true, Israel will feel threatened. They will have to become involved."

"What else can you tell me about the Shaheeds?"

Visibly worried, Mukhtar scanned the walkway with his binoculars. Satisfied, he turned back to Friar, "The terrorist doing the recruiting in Baghdad is an Iraqi from Safwan. He was born Abdul Sharif Ben Farran. Now, he is a freelance terrorist who goes by the alias, Hashim."

"Where is he now?"

Mukhtar handed Friar an envelope. "Here is a recent picture taken six months ago when he applied for a passport in Baghdad. At the moment, he's somewhere in the US with the Shaheeds. They're operating out of a mosque in Jersey City. My organization has penetrated their organization. We have an agent inside."

Friar opened the envelope and studied the photo. When he returned to Washington, he would have Dorn put out an APB and pick him up. "Anything else?"

Mukhtar nodded. "The attack is scheduled to take place on the thirty-first of October."

Seven days away. "Are you certain?"

"Our agent was one of the drivers with the Shaheeds when they took delivery of the warheads. He overheard the leader of the Russians tell Hashim a bomb would be detonated at the third call to prayer on the thirty-first. They didn't know our man understood Russian."

Friar couldn't believe his good luck. This was the confirmation Warner needed.

Mukhtar continued, "The warheads were smuggled into the US over a week ago. They were delivered by—"

"*Heads-up, Hoss,*" the earphone crackled. "*You've got visitors.*"

Friar turned abruptly and looked down the walkway. There was no one in sight.

"What's wrong?" Mukhtar asked.

"Someone's coming."

"*The two guards are down,*" Joe Don reported. "*Three men toting Kalashnikovs are running along the ramp towards you.*"

The thunderous roar of the falls had prevented the sounds of gunfire from reaching the platform. Holding the lapel mike close to his mouth, Friar asked, "Okay. What's the plan?"

"*I can take these three out from here,*" Joe Don said calmly. "*They'll be within range in a couple of minutes. Then I'll boat over and pick you up.*"

"Roger."

Kneeling, Friar motioned for Mukhtar to get down. Reaching for his pistol, he cursed softly as he felt the empty holster. Lying flat on the platform, he and Mukhtar held their breaths and waited. The only sound came from the rumbling of the falls.

One minute and ten seconds later, three hulking figures rounded the bend in the walkway. They were a hundred and fifty yards away. One by one they lurched sideways, as if struck by some giant fist, and plunged over the guard rail into the swift current.

"*Three down. Four more starting out. Okay, Hoss. Get ready to move.*"

From the edge of the island immediately next to the bend in the footbridge, Friar saw Joe Don emerge from the bush, pushing the Zodiac into the river. Hopping in, he revved-up the motor.

Friar patted Mukhtar's shoulder and pointed towards the fast approaching Zodiac. "That's for us."

When Joe Don was 100 yards away Friar stood and gestured for the general to prepare to climb over the rail.

As Mukhtar rose unsteadily to his feet, there were muffled sounds of wood splintering as small patches of platform began to disintegrate. Friar watched the little puffs of flying sawdust as they worked their way across the floor towards them.

"Gunfire!" Friar shouted. He wanted to duck, but didn't know which way to turn. Frantically searching the walkway and the shorelines of the nearby islands for the source of the bullets, he saw nothing unusual. No muzzle flashes, no smoke. Where were the shots coming from?

In slow motion, Mukhtar threw up his hands as the base of his neck and shoulder exploded in a mass of blood and bone. Without saying a word, he pitched forward and rolled gently over the railing, toppling into the muddy, rushing water.

Friar grabbed for his jacket but was too late. Face down in the murky water, Mukhtar's body drifted towards the mouth of Devil's Throat Falls.

"*Out front—up high!*" Joe Don's voice screamed over the ear piece.

Turning and looking up, Friar could see a bright blue and white helicopter rising out of the mist above the falls. It was a Bell JetRanger, the same kind used by the Hotel Cataratas for sightseeing, only this one was different. Instead of a side window full of smiling tourist faces, there was the ugly muzzle of a light machine gun pointing directly at him.

Without waiting, Friar crammed the photo of Hashim inside his jacket and jumped into the river, grabbing one of the pilings to keep from being swept away. Working his way, hand over hand, under the walkway, he pulled himself clear of the rapidly disappearing observation platform. Struggling to keep from being pulled under, he yanked on the lanyard. Instantly, the kevlar floatation vest filled with carbon dioxide.

"*Hold on, Hoss, I'm gonna try to get a bead on that bastard.*"

"Go back to the island, Joe Don," Friar ordered. "He's got you outgunned."

"*Too late now, he's spotted me. Get ready. I'm coming in.*"

The helicopter rose and dipped its nose towards the wildly maneuvering Zodiac, then began to circle for position.

Swhoosh! A slender trail of fire rose from the Argentine river bank, heading straight for the side door of the helicopter. The heat from the exploding aircraft warmed the knuckles of Friar's hands as he grasped the boards of the walkway.

"*Whoo-whee!*" Joe Don shouted. "*Did you see that sonofabitch light up?*"

"What happened?" Friar yelled.

Joe Don was laughing and waving his arms. "*It was a goddamned Stinger, Hoss. Somebody burned that motha's ass with a goddamned Stinger.*"

By the time they reached the cargo plane at the Foz do Iguaçu airport in Brazil, the plane's engines were warmed up and ready to fly. A mechanic sitting on a tow truck called out, "Mr. Clarke?"

"I'm Clarke." Friar responded, wondering who knew he was there.

"A fellow left this for you ten minutes ago. He said you might be needing it." He handed Friar a one liter bottle of Remy Martin, V.S.O.P. Fine Champagne cognac. A note was tied to the neck. "Friar: You owe me for one slightly used Stinger. You dog-paddle well. S."

OCTOBER 25: WILLIAMSBURG

"For sponsors, look to the Normans, repeat, Normans." Marcie went over the phrase again and again, as if repetition might help solve the riddle. Murphy's cryptic notation glared back at her from the green chalkboard at Bosworth House. With Friar looking on, she underlined *sponsors*, then *Normans*. Walking over to where he was sitting, she took his hand and placed it on her waist. She had wanted him to rest after his ordeal in Iguaçu, but he had insisted on taking another look at Murphy's message.

"Normans," Friar said, trying to shake off the weariness and maintain his concentration. "That could be a roundabout reference to any of those Islamic groups trying to kick France's butt. The Algerian Armed Islamic Group, the Islamic Salvation Front." He watched Marcie as she stood in front of him, facing the chalkboard. He hadn't told her much about Iguaçu, only that Mukhtar had been killed and the date the bomb was scheduled to be detonated. The rest could wait.

"Don't think so," Marcie declared. "If either of those organizations had a nuclear warhead, they'd put it in Paris, not here."

"By the way, what did the SDECE have to say?"

"I checked with a Colonel Dumas at the General Directorate of External Security in Paris. No leads. Of course, they've only had forty-eight hours to work on it." Keeping her eyes centered on the chalkboard, she stepped back into the sunlight. The heat felt good on her neck and shoulders.

"How about their other services?"

"Dumas said he'd run it by the *Direction du Renseignements Militaires* and the *Direction de la Surveillance du Territoire*. He promised to let me know if anything turned up."

Friar repeated, *"Look to the Normans.* Maybe Murphy was referring to some country with political ties to France." The French had certainly cozied up to Iran over their $2 billion oil deal with the French Total Group.

With a damp cloth Marcie erased *Normans*, replacing it with *French*. "Look to the *French*." After a moment's reflection, she said, "Seems to me he was referring directly to France, not to some hanger-on or also-ran."

"Lets face it," Friar declared, tilting his head back and closing his eyes. "It's a damned hodgepodge. Murphy thought he'd be here for the grand unveiling."

Marcie studied the chalkboard. Her analytical mind told her she was missing something obvious. They were looking through the message, not at it. Erasing everything, she wrote in the single word *Normans*. "That's got to be the key. I think he expected us to know what he meant by that."

"You can take it from here," Friar said. "I'm through thinking for awhile." He stood and stretched. Bone-deadening fatigue had begun to set in.

Marcie nodded sympathetically, "I've contacted Professor Rushford Rowlson at William and Mary. He's an expert on Nostradamus. I couldn't give him many details over the phone, but he assured me he'll have something for us in the next couple of days."

"Why not now? It's already the twenty-fifth."

"It's his security clearance. The FBI has a file on him a foot thick. They claim he was active in the anti-Vietnam war movement back in the late sixties. They estimate it'll be the twenty-seventh before they can give him a limited clearance."

Friar shook his head. It was a world turned upside down. The CIA and FBI could talk to the Russians about missing warheads, but he and Marcie couldn't discuss it with an American college professor.

Marcie walked over to Friar and took him by the arm, "You'd better get some rest before Warner gets here." She led him to the bed in the back room and forced him to lie down. "When you get up, there's something we need to discuss."

Friar rose up on his elbow, "Tell me now. You know I don't like surprises."

Marcie immediately regretted having mentioned it. "Well, I didn't want to bother you so soon after your trip, but we've got a family problem."

"A family problem?"

"Yesterday we received an invitation from Eloise to attend Ellsworth's induction into the Society of the Cincinnati."

Friar relaxed. It had been six months since they had visited Marcie's sister and the "Colonel" at their home in Charleston. "Hey, that's no problem. Let's get a room at the Mills House and make it a real vacation. Don't let Eloise talk you into staying at the mansion. I don't want to have to stay up all night listening to the Colonel's bullshit about how successful he is."

Marcie sat on the edge of the bed, "But, there *is* a problem. The induction's not going to be held in Charleston. Its scheduled for Fraunces Tavern in lower Manhattan at noon on October 31."

Warner was pleased Friar's trip to Iguaçu had been so productive. Now they had an important confirmation and the when, but there were still gaps and time was running out. Handing Friar a large mug of cappuccino sprinkled with cinnamon, he said, "I've got good news and bad news."

"Good news first," Friar pleaded.

"I found the $500,000 for your informant. The first half has already been wired into his account in Zurich. The balance is waiting your approval."

"Fantastic," Friar replied, relieved he wouldn't have to work the request through FBI channels. "I've got another meeting with him tonight." So far, Friar had more questions about Dubov than answers. "Was Dorn able to get a profile on his background?"

Warner nodded, "It's limited. He belongs to a Chechen syndicate that's been operating in the US for the past five years. He's been questioned twice, but no arrests. Once, four years ago for shipping stolen cars to Russia. Again, two years ago, for international bank fraud. The Bureau says Dubov is an alias, but they don't know his real name. They sent his picture and prints to Interpol and their Moscow office, but so far, nothing."

"I was afraid of that."

"Now for the bad news. Your request for a wiretap of the Shaheed's headquarters in Jersey City has been turned down."

"Goddammit, Bryan! What the hell's going on? Those clowns are hiding five nuclear warheads in the US and we can't get a simple wiretap?"

"Easy, Friar," Warner cautioned. "You've got to remember, we're talking surveillance inside the US. That's an FBI function and they're telling us it's a no-go. Dorn took the request to the Foreign Intelligence Surveillance Act Court and it was rejected. Shymanski didn't help by recommending against it."

Friar fumed in silence as he thought of Shymanski and what his meddling had cost Murphy. Now his bumbling was interfering with the search and creating delays. Friar had hoped Dubov's and Mukhtar's information would be enough to set off alarm bells all over Washington, but, so far, it was business as usual.

"Okay, Bryan. What about MEGAHUT? Can they take care of it?" Four years back, Friar had worked with the supersecret FBI-NSA unit on a special wiretap of a Brooklyn apartment belonging to Libya's UN undersecretary. Headquartered in midtown Manhattan, MEGAHUT's specialty was running black bag jobs on national security risks. "If Manhattan gets nuked, it's going to be their dipsticks that get scorched. Maybe if we give them a little advanced notice, they'll be appreciative and help us with a wiretap."

Warner shook his head, apologetic for not being able to accommodate Friar's request. Bending rules to that extent was not part of his personal code. "I'm sorry, but we've got to keep it legit. Dorn tells me the Bureau needs more than hearsay from a Russian mafiya informer and dead Iraqi General before he can get approval for an investigation. The FBI can't even clip newspaper articles on the Shaheeds until an investigation has been authorized."

"That's damned unbelievable," Friar replied, the stress from his Iguaçu trip boiling to the surface. "What's gotta happen before the Bureau starts taking names and kicking ass?"

"It's not their fault," Warner replied. "The law says they have to have *overwhelming* evidence the Shaheeds, as an organization, are involved in criminal activities. Right now, the Shaheeds are protected because of their religious status."

"So, bottom line, you're telling me that Murphy's death—Mukhtar's death—don't mean a thing. A bunch of ragtag militants are sitting on five nuclear warheads, and we're not supposed to upset them?"

Warner hung his head, "Unfortunately, our hands are tied. We simply need more evidence."

"What about Hashim?" Friar asked. "What's the FBI going to do about him?"

"Same story," Warner sighed. "The FBI needs hard evidence he's done something wrong. As it is, we can't even prove the warheads exist. Until there's something concrete—"

Friar arched an eyebrow, "Both Murphy and Mukhtar tell us the warheads are here. Their stories are confirmed by a mafiya informer, and we're tied up in knots over the civil rights of a terrorist? Am I missing something?"

"Sorry, but that's the way it works."

Friar placed his hand on Warner's shoulder. "Bryan, you've known me for what—twenty–twenty-five years? I can't play by these Mickey Mouse rules. With something like this, I only know one way and that's to go in and get it done. I think it's time Marcie and I headed back down to Hillsborough."

Exhaling slowly Warner said, "Friar, I need your help. You're the only one I can trust. I don't like what's going on any more than you do. I'm forming a special operations group—task force Red Bravo. Vaughn's given me early release as DDO to head it up. You've got to stay and be part of it. I'm depending on you."

Friar grumbled under his breath, but he couldn't let Warner down. In addition, he had some unfinished business with those responsible for Murphy's death. "How's it going to be structured? CIA? FBI?"

"Quasi-independent. Theoretically we report to Justice. That gives us operational authority inside the US. The task force has been assigned on paper to the Center for Counterterrorism, but I'll liaise directly with Vaughn at Langley."

"I'll check with Marcie."

Chapter 12

Friar popped four aspirin tablets into his mouth, washing them down with a swig of Perrier. He wanted a double Manhattan, but a double anything, combined with his lack of sleep, would be all it took to turn his lights out. It had been a long day. Closing his eyes, he breathed in the pleasant, citric aroma of crêpes suzette being prepared in a gleaming, copper sauté pan, ten feet away.

Seated with him around the linen-covered table at the Watergate Hotel's five-star Jean-Louis restaurant were an ill-at-ease Jason Dorn, and a confident Alexander Dubov.

Dorn grimaced at the a la carte prices on the hand printed menu. More fodder for Josephine Winesap's personal vendetta against wasteful spending by Bureau personnel. Just as he had predicted, the bill from the Willard had been scheduled for audit. Winesap would swoop down like a vulture if he dared turn in another three hundred and forty dollar tab.

"I believe I'll have the *prix fixe*," Dubov said. "Perhaps the *moules marinère* with *crème brûlée* for dessert."

Pretending to study the menu, Friar followed the Chechen's twists and turns out of the corner of his eye. He wondered if Dubov knew about Iguaçu. In front of Dubov's plate was a small, silver colored, satin-covered box of matches with "Jean-Louis" stamped in gold colored foil. It had been a rush job, but the Directorate of Technology had finished it that morning. The homing microtransmitter was state-of-the-art, complete with a long-life, lithium-ion battery. The only limitation was its half-mile range.

Friar closed his menu, placing it on his plate. "Not to be impolite and rush the conversation, Mr. Dubov, but I believe you have something for us?"

"What would you like to know first?" Dubov asked, impressed that the transfer of the $250,000 had gone so smoothly. With a wink, he said, "Perhaps I should have asked for more."

Friar's nostrils flared. He was tired and in no mood for games. "At our last meeting, you promised names, dates."

Dubov leisurely examined the wine list. After selecting a 1987 Château Greysac, Cru Grand Bourgeois, he turned to Friar, "During the evening of October 16, five warheads were delivered by submarine to a shrimp trawler off the coast of North Carolina."

Friar looked up. How did this informer know such critical information? "Go on."

"The name of the trawler is *Break of Dawn*. It was captained by Tyrell Wentworth. The warheads were smuggled ashore in Wanchese, North Carolina, where they were loaded into trucks and driven to their destinations. There are two 750-kiloton warheads, two in the 550-kiloton range, and one 100-kiloton device from a Russian naval cruise missile."

Friar was sitting on the edge of his seat, taking notes. He hadn't expected such details. "We'll check it out."

"By all means," Dubov replied. "And don't forget to wire the remaining $250,000 into my account." Dubov watched as Friar continued to scribble names and numbers on a notepad. "What's the matter, Mr. Clarke? Are your recording devices not working?"

Friar looked at the Chechen and for the first time that evening, smiled. He didn't care what Dubov's motives were, as long as the information was correct. Now Warner would have all the concrete evidence he needed to get the FBI to kick-start an investigation. Six days left, there was still time.

"You said you knew the name and location of the person controlling the warheads," Dorn asserted.

"He's an Iraqi terrorist calling himself Hashim. He's registered at the Imperial Plaza Hotel in Jersey City in room 1523 under the name, Shah Ibrahim. The hotel is owned by the Dolgochenskaya syndicate, which is working with the militants."

"What about the when and where?" Friar asked, trying to cross-check Mukhtar's information with Murphy's message.

"I'm afraid I don't know the answers to that," Dubov replied. "I can try to find out for an additional million."

"When can you have it?"

"Two, maybe three days. Give me three days."

"You've got it." If the information on Wentworth panned out, Friar was certain Warner would have no problem finding another million. "If you'll just give me a number where I can reach—"

Dubov crossed his hands, "No, Mr. Clarke, I'll contact you."

"State sponsor, you promised us the name of the state sponsor," Dorn reminded him.

"The country that provided the Shaheeds with the funds to purchase the warheads is Iraq." Dubov glanced at Friar who had stopped writing.

"Iraq?"

Dubov shifted uneasily in his seat. "That's what my sources tell me."

"What's your proof?"

"We followed the money trail. In Moscow we learned that a large amount of cash was seeking nuclear warheads. Of course, our organization would never traffic in such materials."

"Of course not," Friar retorted.

"We heard rumors the Dolgochenskaya clan was brokering the deal." Dubov shrugged, "Those scum have no scruples. We decided it would be profitable for us to investigate and pass the information along to your government."

"Where's the Iraqi connection?"

"We traced the flow of money to its origin. The funds came from eight separate Iraqi accounts located in banks in Liechtenstein, the Bahamas, and the Cayman Islands."

"I thought all Iraqi funds in those countries were frozen," responded Dorn.

Dubov shook his head, "These particular accounts operate under the cover of several South African mining businesses. Over the course of two months, the Iraqis transferred a total of 500 million US dollars to unlisted bank depositories belonging to various Russian military and government officials."

"You're positive the money came from Iraq?" Friar asked.

"Absolutely certain," exclaimed Dubov. "It also explains why you will not receive any cooperation in tracing the warheads from certain top ranking Russian officials."

"Can you provide a paper trail?"

Dubov reached over and took the satin-covered box of matches from the crystal ashtray. After using one of the gold-tipped wooden matches to light his cigarette, he slipped the box into his pocket. "I can ask my associates, but it will take weeks to get such records."

"Smoking's not good for you," Friar cautioned. "It'll be your death."

OCTOBER 26: WILLIAMSBURG: 7:45A.M.

With a nod of approval, Tovi Hersch surveyed the layout of his operations center at the Robert Graves House. Fronting on Duke of Gloucester Street, the small, five room house was located in the heart of the Williamsburg historic district, only a block from the King's Arms Tavern. There were front and rear entrances permitting visitors to come and go at all hours, unnoticed.

Hearing a loud knock at the front door, Tovi flicked on the monitor hooked to a video camera jerry-rigged over the door sill. The shimmy was gone, the picture was sharp and clear. It was Friar.

"Fancy setup," Friar quipped, sitting down in a high-backed, overstuffed chair and inspecting the expensive Williamsburg furniture pushed into a corner. "Washington's going to have to cut back on its aid to Tel Aviv."

"The rooms are barely adequate," sniffed Tovi, with a twinkle in his eye. "Besides, we're going to have to redecorate. Have some *dulce de leche*." He handed Friar a plate of toast with a crock of gooey, caramel colored paste parked on the side. The sweet, Argentine delicacy had the thick, sticky consistency of axle grease. "I'm afraid I developed a weakness for this gunk while I was down in Iguaçu."

"Thanks for saving me from a permanent out-of-body experience," Friar said, unsure of how to show his appreciation. "Were the bad guys Iraqi military intelligence?"

"That's Mossad's theory. It's their guess Uday's thugs were trying to prevent Mukhtar from selling out. They probably thought he was giving you information on their biological and chemical weapons program." Rubbing his elbows and neck, Tovi said, "I've never seen so damn many mosquitoes. One foot off the path and they bled you dry. You'd have to have a blood transfusion to stay in that jungle for more than an hour."

"It's ironic," Friar observed. "Mukhtar, killed by his own people while trying to save his country." When it was over, he planned on looking up Jamila and filling her in on the details. It would ease her pain to know Kareem was not a traitor.

"To tell the truth, we were having trouble telling the players apart on that platform. When we saw muzzle flashes coming from the helicopter's side door, we figured it was time to make our move." Tovi munched into a second piece of toast. "That Stinger's one helluva piece of ordnance. I can see why the Russians had so much trouble with it in Afghanistan. Was it worth it? Iguaçu, I mean?"

Friar nodded, "Yeah. Mukhtar filled in an important gap."

"Well?"

"Turns out he had someone on the inside with the Shaheeds. According to him, the terrorists plan to detonate a warhead on October 31, at the third call to prayer."

"Umph," Tovi grunted. That was sooner than expected. "Did he say where?"

"He was killed before I could ask, but I think it's going to be New York. He wanted me to know, and to pass word to Mossad, that Iraq is not involved."

Removing the No Smoking sign from the top of the writing desk and placing it face down in a drawer, Tovi pulled a meerschaum pipe from his jacket pocket and slowly filled the bowl from an old, battered tin of Prince Albert. "What we've got here is definitely a ticking bomb."

"I agree."

"The situation's starting to look pretty nasty." Tovi lit the pipe and took a couple of puffs. "Mossad has authorized me to use *extraordinary* means to locate the warheads. Do you know what that means?"

Friar nodded. He understood only too well it meant whatever

Tovi wanted it to mean. During the next few weeks they would learn more about each other's operations than was healthy. In a business where a country's interests dominate personal friendships, you did what was necessary. Sometimes that meant betraying a friend, but it was a two way street. It was no secret that logged into the US Defense Department's Integrated Data Base were the target coordinates for Israel's leading cities, towns, and, especially the launching pads of its Jericho missiles. If Tel Aviv's interests ever came into conflict with those of the US? There were no guarantees.

"Good," said Tovi. This was not the time for illusions or cumbersome morals. "You mentioned New York. Where in New York do you think they'll put it?"

"My guess is the financial district."

"Not midtown? Closer to the UN building?"

"Nope. If I'm right, they'll go straight for the financial district. Wall Street's too good a target to pass up."

"I concur," Tovi replied. "Hit the Twin Towers and World Trade Center. Destroy the New York and American stock exchanges." He paused, "We have certain intelligence that pinpoints lower Manhattan as the target." He didn't want to have to explain why he was so convinced it would be downtown Manhattan. It wouldn't do to let Friar know that Mossad had located Dr. Danya Boyra at the Vista Hilton International Hotel. Plans had been made and there was no need to involve him.

"Special request," Tovi muttered, tamping down the tobacco in his pipe. He wasn't sure how to put it. He didn't want Friar to think Mossad was placing Israel's interests ahead of those of the US. "I've got a list of twelve people Tel Aviv wants out of New York before any explosion. They're called the Twelve Apostles. They're *very* important to Israel in one way or another. Any problem?"

"Nope," Friar responded without hesitation. This was a decision he would make on his own. There was no need to pass it up the line where it could be countermanded by Shymanski or his master, Bastardi. He wondered if there was anyone he needed to warn. Apart from Marcie's brother-in-law, his list was a blank. Then an idea hit him. "Are any of your Apostles connected with big Wall Street firms?"

"Could be, why?"

"I have a return favor to ask." It was a special request, one for Murphy.

By the time Friar had finished outlining his plan, the Sandman was laughing so hard, pipe ashes were cascading onto the floor. "I'll see what I can do." He was no longer worried about Friar.

Friar next explained about Hashim and the difficulty in getting the FBI to launch an investigation.

"Don't let them pick him up," Tovi warned.

The comment surprised Friar. Hashim was their best link to the New York warhead.

"If he's taken into custody, the FBI will read him his rights, he'll demand to see his lawyer—"

Friar grimaced, "It may be too late."

WANCHESE: 2:31 P.M.

By the time the pontoons of Friar's helicopter splashed down in the silky-calm waters of Croatan sound, Kat Mills had finished her initial interrogation of Tyrell Wentworth. The shock of finding himself caught in the cross hairs of a sweep by a ten member FBI SWAT team, had rattled the captain into babbling answers as fast as questions could be thrown at him.

Meeting Friar at the dock, Kat stepped forward to shake hands. As she did so, the toe of her right shoe struck the tip of a warped board, sending her sprawling into his arms. Blushing, she sputtered an apology while he helped her back to her feet.

After an awkward pause, she confirmed that Wentworth had admitted smuggling in five large containers ten days earlier. It was just as Dubov had said. During questioning, the captain kept insisting it was a drug deal, but that was to be expected. Kat had not corrected him. She had also persuaded Dorn to give them an additional two hours to interrogate Wentworth before shipping him off to Washington for processing.

Friar was impressed. It was obvious Kat appreciated the value of good intelligence. A less savvy agent would have done the Miranda bit and hustled Wentworth to headquarters where a legal shark in a double-breasted Ermenegildo Zegna suit would have shut him up. Of course, the captain couldn't be prosecuted now, but that was immaterial. He was only a bit player whose information was a wasting asset and had to be taken while still of use. After a formal arraignment, they would file a motion requesting immunity in exchange for information, but that would take days, maybe weeks.

"Did the captain identify Hashim?" Friar asked.

"Affirmative. He pulled Hashim's picture out of a stack of photos two inches deep. According to Wentworth, Hashim was in charge of the truck drivers. He says he overheard the leader calling him by name."

"That was careless."

Kat nodded. "Wentworth claims Hashim drove a load of drugs to New York. He saw him studying a map of Manhattan just before he drove off in a van."

"Who else was in on the deal?"

"There were two Russian mafiya types who went with the trawler to collect the warheads. Another Russian joined them from the sub."

"Any names?"

"Not really. Wentworth called the leader, 'Russian.' Not very original. He said the other two mutts only spoke to each other in a foreign language, presumably Russian. Claims he couldn't understand their names."

"We need descriptions and profiles. When you get the captain to Washington, have one of your computer sketch artists work with him on faces."

"That reminds me. Wentworth said two of the Russians had fancy tattoos. Full beards and fancy tattoos. He said the bartender at the Rusty Dog Tavern in Manteo can back him up."

"The Rusty Dog Tavern?"

"That's his story. The night before the pickup, they went to the Rusty Dog and got plastered. According to Wentworth, the Russians put on quite a show, ripping off their shirts and strutting around like a couple of peacocks."

Strange, thought Friar. Why would anyone smuggling in nuclear warheads pull a stunt like that? "Kat, how about checking it out."

"Can do." Tilting her head towards the shed, she asked, "Care to see where they unloaded the warheads?" Glancing at Friar, she thought, *Murphy was right*. She did like the self-assured, trim, six-foot-three, ex-CIA-cowboy with the high forehead and streak of gray at the temples.

Inside the shed, a temporary array of fluorescent lights was strung along the walls and ceiling. Two teams from the FBI's Materials Analysis Unit were scouring every inch of the structure, looking for evidence. One team dusted for fingerprints. The other vacuumed the dust and debris, collecting small samples of fibers and hair for lab analysis. In the water, a frogman was sweeping the floor of the sound with an underwater Geiger counter.

Watching the frogman bob up and down, Friar leaned over and tapped his back. "Any traces of radioactivity?"

"No, sir. I've checked every piece of junk on the bottom, but nothing so far."

Friar turned to Kat, "Did Wentworth say how the warheads were housed?"

"He claims the 'drugs' were packed in double-hulled containers with the outer shell made of aluminum, and the inner container a rectangular, plastic box. They removed a couple of the outer shells and he got a good look inside. The larger one held a container labeled 'commercial freezer' and the smaller one was stenciled 'GE refrigerator.'"

Not bad, Friar thought. Disguising the warheads as household appliances. It would be almost impossible for NEST and the FBI to check every refrigerator and freezer recently moved on the east coast. "Let's go talk to the captain."

They left the shed and walked the short distance to the small, weathered, wooden structure that served as Wentworth's office. On entering, Friar noticed trash piled haphazardly on the concrete floor. In the far corner were two wooden fish crates used as garbage bins. One box was crammed with empty junk-food containers, the other held discarded beer cans and liquor bottles. Wentworth sat in the middle of the room, on a creaky aluminum lawn chair pushed up against a sheet of plywood balanced on two sawhorses. His head was buried in his hands.

A question popped into Friar's mind, *Why had professional terrorists left such a talkative witness alive?* They were certain to have realized he would cave in under intense interrogation. Friar swung his leg over a small wooden barrel that doubled as a chair, and pulled himself within inches of Wentworth's runny nose and puffy, blood-shot eyes. "Captain, you said there were four Russians involved. Can you give me a description?"

"Done told that woman," Wentworth grumbled, gesturing feebly towards Kat. His body smelled of caked-on sweat and his breath reeked of alcohol. "Them Russian sonafabitches never paid me. Slipped me a mickey, then stole my money."

"We're going to catch them," Friar said, sympathetically, "but, we need your help. What kind of clothes were they wearing? Did they drink? Smoke?"

Wentworth grunted, "Yeah. The big one did, the one who called hisself Russian. He smoked a lot."

"Pipe? Cigars? Cigarettes?"

"Cigarettes. Lots of cigarettes."

"What kind?"

"Don't know. They's some butts of his over in that ash can." Wentworth motioned towards an old Maxwell House coffee can on the corner of the sheet of plywood that served as his desk.

"This can?" Friar asked, holding up a quart sized container half-full of toothpicks, candy wrappers, tobacco ashes, and cigarette butts.

"Yeah, that's the one."

Friar carefully emptied the contents into a clear plastic bag and marked it as evidence.

Wentworth raised his head, "I wanna see my lawyer! You can't make me say nothing. I know my rights."

"Easy, Captain, easy," Friar cautioned. Looking him squarely in the eyes, he said, "We're here to protect you. Maybe you haven't figured it out yet, but those drug dealers want you *dead*. They've put out a contract for ten thousand dollars to whoever brings in your head."

Wentworth's face drooped and his mouth dropped open. "They're trying to kill me?"

"That's right. We busted the shipment of heroin they sent to New York. They're blaming you. They think you ratted them out." Friar moved the barrel even closer. "You help us, we'll keep you alive. Tell us all you know about smuggling in those drugs."

For the next hour and a half Friar quizzed Wentworth on the number of trucks, make, contents, description of the drivers, timing of departure, anything that might provide clues to the location of the warheads. The captain confirmed that the four large freezers were loaded onto identical Ryder rental trucks. That indicated to Friar that Hashim's van was carrying the refrigerator with the 100-kiloton warhead. Again, the question nagged him, *why was Wentworth still alive?*

At the end of the interrogation, Friar motioned for Kat to follow him outside. When they were alone, he began, "Ah,—Kat?"

"Yes?" she answered, aware from the tone of his voice that something was bothering him. Was it personal? Did he have a complaint about the way she had handled the investigation? It hurt her ego to think he might not approve.

"Time's running out. We've only got five days left."

"I know," she replied, listening carefully to his words, trying to decipher their meaning.

How could he convey what he had to tell her without actually saying it? He decided on the direct approach. "It would be best if the FBI didn't pick Hashim up." Getting no response, he tried again, "That terrorist is the best lead we have on where the New York warhead is hidden. If he's arrested, he'll *never* talk. He's not a pushover like Wentworth."

Kat nodded. What was he trying to tell her? Over his shoulder she could see the marshes across the sound. At another time, the dock, the fishing boats, the Spanish moss hanging from the water oaks would be so beautiful.

"That is—er—Hashim won't talk to *us*," Friar continued. He couldn't tell her that the Sandman and Mossad were frantically trying to locate the terrorist. That a special team had been flown in from Tel Aviv to conduct the interrogation. He couldn't explain that keeping Hashim out of the clutches of the FBI might be their only hope. Maybe, if he knew her better—but, it wouldn't be fair to ask her to jeopardize her career—at least, not yet.

Kat was relieved Friar wasn't upset with her work. Watching him wrestle with an explanation, she decided to go along, no questions asked. She was a team player and trusted his decisions. "I'll do everything I can to keep him on the streets."

Friar breathed an audible sigh of relief. "Thanks, Kat. And those rental trucks. Wentworth said there were four, plus that van. Have your people check with Ryder to see what they can dig up. It may be helpful to question Wentworth under hypnosis. He may know more than he thinks."

"Can do."

"And, one more thing—"

"Yes?" She moved closer.

"I need a rush DNA analysis on the saliva from each of those cigarette butts in that coffee can. We might find a match from the Bureau's database. If anything unusual comes up, let me know. And, please, just between the two of us, okay?"

"Roger," she responded. Strange, she thought, how eager she was to please him.

OCTOBER 27: WILLIAMSBURG

"Grab a seat, anywhere you can," Professor Rowlson said, directing Marcie and Friar to two straight-backed chairs piled high with books, papers, and magazines. "Just throw that junk on the floor."

To reach the chairs, they had to thread their way between boxes of publications, notebooks, and correspondence stacked haphazardly on the dusty, hardwood floor. The college's cleaning service had long ago given up any attempts to tidy up the "crypt." Along the walls of the brightly lit, well-worn office were bookcases crammed with European history books, texts on French literature, and stacks of old issues of *The New Yorker*, *National Geographic*, and *Foreign Affairs*. On top of a dark green filing cabinet propped against the wall, was a dusty plaque that read, "Professor Rushford A. Rowlson, Archambault Chair of Classical French History, College of William and Mary."

Marcie carefully removed a pile of student exams from one of the wooden chairs and placed them on the corner of the computer table that served as Rowlson's work area. His regular desk was buried beneath reams of printouts and student essays.

Marcie extended her hand, "Professor, thanks for seeing us on such short notice."

"No, no. Please call me Russ," replied the sixty-three-year-old scholar-bon vivant-author-lecturer and noted Nostradamian. His ruddy complexion contrasted sharply with the shock of thick white hair crowning the top of his head. "Makes me feel like an old Heidleberg *Gelehrte* when someone calls me Professor."

Marcie smiled. "Ah–Russ, as I mentioned over the phone, we're having trouble interpreting a message from a friend who used Nostradamus' Quatrain 97, Century VI, as part of his communication."

"Yep, your friend must have quite a sense of humor. Trying to use a Nostradamus quatrain to convey information is like using a horoscope to see what's on television."

"It was a sophomoric attempt at code," Friar offered by way of explanation. Actually, it was a game, a Murphy game. Friar could just picture him, scribbling away, scheming on how to unveil the true meaning over a dinner of grilled salmon and chilled chardonnay.

"Nostradamus would have liked that," responded Rowlson, chuckling and leaning back in his chair. "He was a great believer in obtuse codes. Encrypted prophecies, that's what his quatrains were. He meant them to be confusing—and they still are. Whether he possessed true powers of prophecy or was just a clever charlatan remains open for debate."

"Russ, is there an accepted interpretation for Quatrain 97?" asked Friar.

"I guess you could say yes and no," Rowlson said, fidgeting with a small, carbon encrusted briar pipe. "Q 97, C 6 is one of his more interesting four liners. A popular explanation is that it's a warning of a nuclear attack against New York."

"So, you think New York is the 'new city' in line two?"

"That's certainly Hogue's interpretation. Anytime you see the word *new* in one of his quatrains, it's probably a reference to what was then called the New World. However, some European experts claim that 'great new city' refers to Geneva, Bucharest, Belgrade, Rome, even Paris. Belgrade is the only European city of any size that sits immediately on the forty-fifth parallel. Still, other Nostradamus buffs contend that the 'five and forty degrees' is an astronomical designation, or a measurement of elevation rather than latitude."

"So, we're looking at a Rorschach, ink-blot type of explanation," remarked Marcie. She smiled at the numerous holes burned in Rowlson's charcoal brown cardigan by stray tobacco ashes.

"Exactly. With these prophecies, you tend to see what you want, or expect to see. Jumbling up the predictions was part of the old fox's plan for obscuring their real meanings. He claimed the quatrains could only be understood in hindsight, that it was dangerous for the public to know too much about the future. Personally, I find that explanation rather disingenuous. Looks to me like he was just making excuses for not being able to predict on cue." Rowlson paused and walked over to a large world globe. "Nostradamus may have just been piddling in the royals' punch bowl. He liked to play the part of court magician, feeding the high and mighty with his own brand of warmed-over intellectual excreta as a form of entertainment. It's amazing how gullible people can be."

"You're not a believer?" asked Friar.

"I'm of two minds," replied Rowlson, twirling the globe. "My logical left brain tells me it's all horse-puckey, that no one can forecast what's going to happen tomorrow, or the next day. Not even Nostradamus. But, the gray cells in the romantic right side of my head want to believe in the ability of certain prophets to part the veils of time and glimpse the future. Growing up I was told, by people who claimed to know, that astrology prophesied the birth of Jesus. On top of that, the book of Revelation in the New Testament is full of predictions—the rise of the Anti-Christ—the coming battle of Armageddon. It would be a dull, boring world if there weren't a little mysticism and juju out there somewhere to spice up the daily grunt-and-grind."

"What about Nostradamus' prediction that Henry II would be killed in a joust?" asked Marcie, who had done her homework. "There you have a documented prophecy followed by the actual event."

"He got good press on that one," Rowlson admitted. Digging through a pile of periodicals on his desk, he located the January issue of *Smithsonian*, and handed it to her. "On page 45 is an article I wrote which mentions Quatrain 35, Century I. The more I think about what happened to poor old Henry, the more convinced I am the prophecy was a hoax. It's pretty obvious to me now that Catherine de Medici orchestrated the jousting accident as a way of getting rid of an unwanted husband. She was up to her royal bustier in palace intrigue. My guess is she fed Nostradamus and a fellow seer named Luc Gauric, just enough information to permit them to foretell Henry's demise during the next tournament. That way, when the tip of Montgomery's lance pierced and shattered Henry's helmet—'eyes in a cage of gold'—it looked to the church and court like Henry's death was an act of God. Who could blame the poor, grieving widow?"

"Who was Montgomery?" asked Friar.

"A thirty-three-year-old stud brought in by Catherine to make sure Henry lost. As commander of the King's Scottish guards, he was in his prime and an expert at jousting. Unfortunately, he knew too much. When Catherine became Queen, she had him executed. But the prophecy did give Nostradamus' career a boost. Within a couple of years, he wound up a rich man protected by the most powerful woman in Europe. Catherine had to intervene several times to keep him off the Inquisition's rack."

"What was the Inquisition's interest in Nostradamus?" asked Marcie.

Rowlson laughed, "He was a very naughty boy. He liked to dabble in the occult which was considered *interdit* by the Catholic church."

Marcie put her arm around Friar. "Laurence here is a junior practitioner of the arts. The rack might do him some good."

"White magic only," Friar reminded her.

"Yes. I read your article on the influence of the tarot in early North Carolina society," Rowlson said, holding aloft a copy of the most recent issue of *North Carolina Historical Review*. "It was very interesting."

"Did Nostradamus ever practice the black arts?" asked Marcie.

"Not that was proven. He did own some forbidden texts. One was a book on Assyrian magic, *De Mysteriis Aegyptiorum*, which included the black magic text, *De Daemonibus* by Psellus. He also admitted to possessing copies of the *Keys of Solomon* and the *Kabbalah*. Later he claimed to have burned these, along with an understandable set of his prophecies."

"How did he conjure up his visions?" Friar asked.

"By using a combination of flame and water gazing. The rituals were patterned after the ones used by the Greek Delphic prophetess,

Branchus. All you need is a brass tripod, a brass bowl, some oil, a little water, and a good imagination."

Rowlson reached over to a hot water kettle balanced precariously on the corner of his work table. "Tea?" Without waiting for an answer, he flipped the switch. "Let's consider how Nostradamus encoded his visions. It might give us some insight into your friend's message." Glancing at his notes, he said, "We know that Nostradamus liked to use anagrams, synecdoches, ellipsis—"

"Whoa," Friar said, holding up his hand. "You've lost me."

"Sorry. An anagram is a scrambled word or phrase. For example, the use of the word *rapis* to mean *Paris*. Nostradamus liked anagrams, but there don't seem to be any in this particular quatrain."

"Okay, got that one."

"A synecdoche is a reference to a part when you mean the whole. Example—his use of the term *great new city*. Here we assume he meant New York in the New World, but he could have just as easily been referring to any city in the great New World, or the Americas as a whole. A synecdoche can also be a reference to the whole when you mean a part. An example would be the use of the word Normans to mean a small group of Frenchmen, or a specific town in France."

"So our friend might have been telling us that a French terrorist group, or cell holds the answer?" inquired Marcie.

"That's correct. If he followed Nostradamus' line of reasoning."

"What about an ellipsis?" asked Friar.

An ellipsis is the omission of a word or phrase which is understood. Take the last line of the quatrain—*Quand on voudra des Normans faire preuve*—'When they want proof they will look to the Normans.' Omitted could be the statement, 'because the Normans are known supporters of the Iranians, or the Libyans, or the Iraqis, or whoever.' "

"What do *you* think Nostradamus meant by Normans?" asked Friar.

Removing his tortoise-shell glasses and wiping them with the end of his tie, Rowlson replied, "It's my guess he was saying to be careful whom you blame. When you want to know who was responsible, you'll have to consider the Normans."

"Then, Normans is the key," observed Marcie.

"It appears so. But Normans can mean a lot of things. It could stand for Norsemen, or Scandinavians."

"It doesn't necessarily refer to the French?"

"That's right. *Norman* is a Middle English word derived from the Old French, *Normant,* which itself is a derivative of the Old Norse *northr* for north and *mathr* for man. What you wind up with is North-man. It could refer to anyone considered to be a North-man. North European, North American, North Russian, North Asian—"

"North Asian?" asked Friar.

"Yup. A single North Asian country or an alliance of North Asian countries would fit the bill." At that moment, the Professor's desk alarm began to buzz. "Oops. Got to go. Important faculty meeting in five minutes."

Friar glanced at Marcie and nodded. Rising to his feet, he said, "Thanks, Professor. You've been a big help."

"And, please, don't forget," added Rowlson, "It's not what Nostradamus meant by this quatrain that counts, but what your friend *thought* he meant. If you can locate the reference book he used in preparing the message, it'll probably give you the answer. Each author interprets the quatrains a little differently. Find that book and you'll be able to read your friend's mind."

"Thanks again," Friar said, pumping the Professor's hand.

In the warmth and fading rays of a golden Indian summer afternoon sun, Friar grabbed Marcie and gave her a hug.

"Laurence!" she exclaimed, surprised at the sudden display of affection.

"Marcie, I've got a pretty good idea who the sponsor is, but we need more information. Check with Personal Effects at the Agency and see if Murphy left the Nostradamus book at his hotel in Cairo. He was in a rush when he left, so I doubt he took it with him."

Chapter 13

Boyra hesitated, wiping his sweaty palms on the sleeves of his new polyester, checkered blazer. The mixture of apprehension and lust made his heart beat fast. With a shaking hand he reached for the gleaming, chrome-plated doorknob of The Pussy's Tale Exotica Club. Pushing open the forbidding door, he peered into the threatening, beckoning, erotic darkness. Grinning nervously, he breathed in the welcome, familiar odor of stale beer, cathouse perfume, and unfettered greed.

"Howdy, handsome," cooed Desiree D'Alberta, the peroxided owner, operator, procurer, and chief shill of the Pussy's Tale. Swaying from side to side with the practiced grace of a New Delhi snake charmer, she draped a flabby arm around Boyra's shoulder, "I saved your favorite table. I knew you'd come."

This evening was not the first time the freely perspiring physicist had visited the lap-dancing Mecca bordering the financial district. In fact, he was a regular.

Glancing around the room at her girls hustling drinks and grinding out lap-dances, Desiree added, "You're just in time. The featured act's about to begin."

Boyra sheepishly nodded and slipped the maitre d' of carnal flesh a crumpled twenty dollar bill. Tonight he had been promised a real headliner, a fresh, young, blond *artiste*, all the way from California, just for him.

Taking his chubby hand, Desiree led him to the back of the dimly lit room. On a small, plastic topped-table, beside a list of overpriced drinks, was a generic VIP Reservation card. From here he had an unobstructed view of the elevated stage with its gleaming, well rubbed, brass pole.

Placing her hand beside Boyra's ear, Desiree leaned over and whispered in a husky, moist voice smelling of nicotine and gin, "You're gonna *love* Angel. She's six-feet-four and was last year's winner of the Miss Nude Malibu Beach Hard Body Contest."

Boyra beamed expectantly. As soon as he had placed his drink order for two watered-down gin and tonics, Desiree signaled the band to begin. It wasn't much of a band, just two washed-up, hooked-on-crack musicians, too strung out to hold regular union jobs. While the house lights dimmed, Desiree thought of Angel, the strange, new dancer who claimed to be from Los Angeles. D'Alberta had never seen anyone so determined to perform for a specific john. That over-sized cunt had even bribed her five hundred bucks to set it up. It was probably some kind of a divorce trap. Why else would Miss Nude Beach waste her time grinding her young butt off in a dump like this. But, what the hell—five hundred bucks was five hundred bucks. For that kind of dough, she would set up the Pope. Glancing at Boyra, she thought—that fat little fuck must really be some ladies' man.

When the room was dark, an out-of-sync drum roll announced the beginning of the Dance of Seven Veils. Slowly, seductively, Angel stepped out from the shadows onto center stage. Twin spotlights focused their harsh reality on her tall, firm form, wrapped in seven layers of clothing.

Boyra's eyes bulged as he watched her twirl and glide over the pitted, red linoleum stage while the second musician scratched out an abortive version of the "Meditation" solo from Massenet's *Thäis* on his pawnshop violin. Boyra's head moved back and forth in time with the music as he followed Miss Hard Body, circling the stage, rising on her tiptoes, then falling gracefully to the floor, each time leaving behind a veil. He counted them—four—five—six. Finally, she was down to the last piece of cloth, a sheer, light blue, transparent fabric. Holding his breath, he watched as she lowered herself onto the linoleum, one last time. After an artistic pause, she rose, slowly, majestically, casting aside the final veil. The spotlights brightened to show every inch of her trim, nude torso. Around her waist dangled a delicate gold chain, anchored by a small ankh pendant. Her long, golden hair cascaded invitingly over her smooth, round breasts. Desiree had not exaggerated. Angel was indeed an erotic Amazon.

Boyra stood and clapped enthusiastically. The grace, the form, the tits. It had been exceptional and very educational. The way she moved, the artistic interpretation of the classic dance of the veils. He regretted not having asked for a front row seat. It would have made it easier to see that small yellow and orange butterfly tattooed over her left nipple. What class. Volodinsky was a fool, wasting his time at Lincoln Center. Opera was nothing compared to this.

Tonight was the second time this week Boyra had eluded his keeper to visit the Pussy's Tale. Conveniently located just three blocks from the Vista Hilton, it had become his place of solace and retreat. Here he could escape Volodinsky's constant nattering and complaining, and indulge his appreciation for the more corporeal pleasures of life. It had been especially easy tonight since Dr. Dour Aesthete was attending a performance of *Madame Butterfly* at Lincoln Center and wouldn't be back until midnight.

While waiting for Angel to dress and return to the main room, Boyra checked his pocket for the carefully hoarded wad of ten dollar bills. He couldn't believe his luck. Desiree had assured him that Angel wanted to lap-dance just for him. At the Pussy's Tale, with its flexible rules, lap-dancing was a hands-on sport. The only house rule ever enforced was the one requiring customers to keep their flies zipped, at least in the main room. For the generous and adventuresome, there was always a cubicle in the back.

The Pussy's Tale was the entrepreneurial inspiration of Desiree D'Alberta, born forty-six years ago in a grimy Brooklyn walk-up, as Hulda Klingfelter. Starting her career at sixteen as a dime-a-dance marathoner at the Pleasuredome in Times Square, it didn't take her long to graduate to escorting out-of-towners to the orgies at Plato's Retreat. Winding up in the back alleys of Broadway, banging drunks for five bucks a bong, was not her idea of how to spend the golden years of retirement. By the time Plato's closed, she had saved enough tax-free cash to open her own club. The Pussy's Tale was capitalism in its purest form. The customers, ranging from the foot soldiers in the trench coats to the drop-ins from the UN's foreign trade delegations, furnished the demand. The dancers, recruited off the streets and from the city's drug-rehab programs, furnished the supply. It was a business of short careers and rapidly depreciating assets.

"Want some company?" Angel asked, as she shyly approached Boyra's table.

He could smell the perfume, expensive, French perfume, the kind sold at duty-free stores for eighty dollars an ounce.

"Did you like my act? Would you like me to dance for you?"

"*D-Da*," Boyra stammered, nodding his head excitedly. "I, I very much like your company." He folded two ten dollar bills, reached over with trembling fingers and tucked them into her halter.

She patted his hand, then slowly, in time to the recorded strains of Joe Cocker's "A Woman Loves a Man," began to lap-dance. Moving to within a foot of the heavily breathing Boyra, she rotated her hips in a gently swaying motion that encouraged her loose fitting clothes to drape open, revealing the smoothness of her skin and the hourglass outline of her torso. Leaning forward, she allowed him to feel the heat from her body and smell the freshness of her skin.

With his breath now coming in short gasps, Boyra reached up and tucked another ten dollar bill in her halter, letting his fingers linger as long as possible. She wasn't like the others, the hardened regulars who ground out dances like they were sleepwalking and smelled of cheap house wine, disinfectant-perfumes, and cigarettes.

"Mind if I sit on your lap?" she asked innocently.

"*Da, da*," he exclaimed, bobbing his head up and down.

With long, sensuous fingers, Angel placed his quaking knees together, then, facing him, slowly lowered herself until she hovered inches above his lap. Swaying from side to side, she rubbed the inside of her thighs over the tops of his legs. "And this?" she asked, tugging on her lace halter.

With a fumbling hand, he tucked another bill in the top of her silk shorts, his fingers sliding down the inside of her leg. She nodded, then unbuttoned the halter, letting it drop to the floor. "Would you like to touch?" she purred.

Audibly panting, he placed another ten dollars in her shorts.

Taking his left hand, she held it against her firm, shapely breast. "And these?" she asked coyly, pointing to her silk shorts.

Another two bills were quickly wedged into the waist as he let his fingers rub up against the softness of her tight, slim abdomen.

Slowly, she unsnapped the Velcro fasteners and lifted the material away. Taking his hand she guided it lightly along her inner thigh. She moved her hips back and forth, softly caressing his fingers.

"The stalls," he pleaded, pointing to the private booths at the rear of the room. "Let's go to the stalls! I have lots of money."

"We need more privacy," she whispered in his ear. "We don't want to be disturbed. Are you staying close by? At a hotel? I could meet you there."

"*Da*–yes," he blurted. "Three blocks away, at the Vista Hilton. Room 1249."

"Shhh," she cautioned, holding a slender finger to her lips and looking around to make certain no one was listening. "It's our little secret."

Boyra could hardly breathe. This tall goddess wanted to go to *his* room. If he hurried, he would have plenty of time before that asshole Volodinsky got back. Volodinsky, what a loser. He would be furious. Probably call up Dubov and cry. Boyra didn't care, they needed him. He let his eyes wander over Angel's body one last time. It was going to be worth whatever it cost.

"You leave first. I'll follow," she promised. "I'll be there in thirty minutes. Order a bottle of champagne, I love champagne."

There was a light rapping on the door. Boyra stood on his tiptoes and peered through the peephole. Angel was in the corridor, her flowing blond hair backlighted by the lamp across the hall. He admired the proud way she held her head, just like Marilyn Monroe in the nude poster tacked over the iron framed bed in his Moscow apartment. He couldn't believe he would soon be making love to this vision. No one at home would believe it. He wondered if she would pose for a Polaroid picture in the nude. He would place it in a silver frame beside the poster of Marilyn. Maybe, for an extra hundred—only special friends would be allowed to look at it and touch it.

Angel knocked again, this time louder. Hurriedly unhooking the security chain, Boyra opened the door. She was wearing a short, dark purple, silk skirt and a cream-colored blouse under a tan raincoat. Hung over her shoulder was the strap of a large, pearl-colored, leather, overnight case.

"I–I have the champagne ready," he stuttered, beckoning for her to enter. "It's expensive, French champagne. If you don't like it, I can order another kind." As she passed him, he could smell the perfume. He liked the way it blended with the fragrance of her body.

"Can I take your bag?" he asked, reaching for the overnight case.

"No. It stays with me," she snapped. Realizing she had overreacted, she softened her voice, "I don't want to bother you, my handsome little man." Eleven inches taller than Boyra, she bent over and kissed the top of his head, gently rubbing her breasts against his cheek. Surveying the room, Angel casually removed her coat and undid the top three buttons of her blouse. "Why don't we sit down and have some champagne? I want to get to know you better."

Boyra rubbed his hands together. She wanted to know about him. She really cared.

Angel settled into an overstuffed couch facing the picture window while Boyra fumbled with the champagne bottle. The lights from Jersey City shimmered in the distance. Crossing her legs, she edged up her miniskirt.

"You have someone staying with you?" she asked, pointing to two empty coffee cups resting on the end table beside the TV.

"Y–Yes, a roommate, but–but he's a man," Boyra said, popping the cork and spewing champagne over the coffee table.

"Is he here now?" Angel inquired, tickling Boyra behind the ear while he filled two glasses. "Is he important like you?"

"No!" came the instant reply. "He's my personal assistant. No one that matters, just a cockroach," Boyra chuckled, raising his two hands to the top of his head and wiggling his forefingers like antennae. He smiled at the thought of Volodinsky walking in and seeing them together. "I sent him away so we could be alone. He didn't want to go, but I insisted." He thumped his chest with a pudgy fist. "After all, I'm the boss."

"And what do you do for a living, my lover man?" Angel moved closer, snuggling against his shoulder while sipping champagne. She placed her right hand on his knee, gradually walking her fingers up the inside of his leg. "Are you a big international business tycoon? You sound Russian. I love Russian men. They are *so* strong."

"I'm an important nuclear scientist," Boyra confided, placing his arm around Angel's shoulder. Looking down her blouse, he could see the outline of the yellow and orange butterfly tattoo.

"And are there any other nuclear scientists here helping you?" She ran her fingers along his crotch.

"No. I–I'm the only one." In a hushed tone he said, "It's a secret project. Just me and my junior assistant. But he's a peasant, nothing but a farmer. *Ni bogu svechka ni chyortu kocherga.*"

"What does that mean?"

"That he's *neither a candle to God nor a rod to the devil.*"

"I don't understand," Angel replied, kicking off her shoes and unbuttoning her blouse all the way. She was not wearing a bra.

Boyra laughed, "It means he's useless, a born loser. I only brought him along to please his mother. She's my housemaid in Moscow." Boyra grinned broadly, "In Moscow they call him the *Eunuch.* He can't get it up." Taking the end of his tie, he held it aloft, then let it fall limp. He rolled on his side with laughter. Volodinsky would go crazy.

Patting Boyra's crotch Angel teased, "I see you're no eunuch." Standing up, she kissed the top of his head again, leaving a second smear of lipstick on his bald spot. "Let's not waste time talking about your helper. Get the bedroom ready while I slip into something comfortable." As she walked slowly towards the bathroom she pulled off her blouse, letting it fall to the floor. She could feel his eyes following her. Turning, so that her profile was outlined against the sitting room wall, she said, "Turn the lights down low. That makes it more mysterious and sexy."

As soon as Angel had disappeared into the bathroom, Boyra grabbed the champagne bucket and raced into the bedroom. Quickly undressing, he tossed his clothes into a corner of the closet, then carefully unfolded and put on the pair of pale yellow, cotton pajamas his mother had given him as a going away present. He removed a liter of peppermint Scope from the top drawer of his dresser and took a huge swig. Sloshing the refreshing liquid around inside his mouth, he sucked it between his teeth, then swallowed. Next, he splashed several drops of Don Juan Pheromone cologne on his face and under his arms. Giggling, he reread the label, "Contains andros-terone, *guaranteed* to unleash the animal urges in your woman."

After dimming the lights he stepped back to survey the room. It was almost ready. Pulling open the top drawer of the dresser, he took out an unopened box of twelve rainbow colored, ribbed, Amazon Warrior condoms. Ripping open the box, he removed one and placed it on the night stand. Before returning the box to the dresser he removed two more and put them in his pajama pocket—just in case. From behind the dresser he retrieved a plastic bag from the Total Man Shop. Inside was a four ounce tube of strawberry flavored Yolanda Erection Gel and a five ounce bottle of Wild Man, Motion Lotion. These, he strategically placed under his pillow.

Standing up, he suddenly felt lightheaded. The excitement was too much. Easing down on the corner of the bed, he wiped his sweat-ing palms on the bedspread. After a moment's rest, he pulled back the covers and climbed in. Removing his thick glasses, he placed them on the night stand and reached for the condom.

"Ready?" Angel called from the bathroom.

"Here I am," he replied, trying to control his heaving chest. Her shyness showed how young and innocent she was. This was prob-ably her first time—as a professional. He promised himself to be gentle and understanding.

"I hope you like it," she said, stepping out of the bathroom and standing silhouetted against the light. She was wearing a sheer, light peach, baby doll negligee which stopped ten inches above her knees. The top was opened loosely.

Even without his glasses, Boyra could see the smooth curves of her body through the transparent fabric. He closed his eyes and strained to capture the whole sensual experience. This image, burned into his brain, would have to last a lifetime. Raising his hands to his face, he peeked through his fingers as she glided gracefully towards him. When she was beside the bed he reached over and pulled down the covers. "Want some cham—"

Thud! Thud! Thud! Three quick rounds from the silenced .22 caliber revolver ripped into Boyra's chest. At three feet, she couldn't miss. With a groan, his body slumped back against the headboard. Instantly sick, Angel turned away—the look in those eyes—the surprise—the incomprehension. Large splotches of blood began to stain the fabric around the three neat holes in his new pajamas. Boyra's body lay propped against the headboard, convulsing spasmodically. He moaned softly.

Not dead? She jerked back around, staring in horror at the thick red liquid spreading down the front of his torso. Leaning forward, she retched on the bedspread. Wiping her mouth with her arm, she grabbed a pillow and held it in front of his face. *Whomp, Whomp.* She squeezed off two more rounds. *Wouldn't he ever stop moving?*

Her instructor had told her to fire the last two shots directly into his eyes, but she couldn't. She was a drug addict, not a cold-blooded killer.

Swooning to the side, she fought to keep her balance. Stumbling into the bathroom, she knocked over the champagne bucket. Moving quickly, she removed the blond wig and negligee, then scrubbed her face, arms and hands with hot soapy water. After stuffing her old clothes into the overnight case, she put on a conservative pants suit. Shielding her face from the nightmare on the bed, she ran into the sitting room, searching for the champagne glass. With a handtowel, she carefully wiped off the lipstick and fingerprints. Using a handkerchief, she turned the doorknob and stepped into the hall.

On reaching the hotel mezzanine, Angel removed the Out of Order sign and entered the second phone booth on the right, next to the ladies room. With shaking hands she dialed the number written in pencil and marked through in red on the wall over the coin slot.

"Fran's take out," the Sandman answered.

"This is Bunnie." Her voice breaking from emotion and relief, she murmured, "It's–it's done."

"Was he alone?" came the cold, calm response.

"He has a roommate. A Russian helper called the Eunuch. The roommate's not a scientist, just an assistant." Leaning against the wall of the phone booth, she said, "There are no other scientists on the project."

"Good. There's a package waiting for you at the Golden Goose

Cafe at 711 West Washington Street. Ask the maitre d' for David. Tell David you are Bunnie. Do not say anything else or ask questions. Give him your key. When your key fits the lock, David will give you a package containing money and drugs. Immediately turn and leave. Take a taxi to La Guardia airport. Your ticket to San Diego is in the package. Do you understand?"

"Yes."

"Good. Did you leave the gun?"

"No, I—I forgot," she stammered, and began to cry softly. Fumbling with her purse she searched for the small envelope of soothing white powder. Thank God it was still there. As soon as she got off the phone, she would slip into the restroom and calm her nerves.

"Control yourself," came the icy reply. "Drop the gun in the nearest waste receptacle. Do not, I repeat, *do not* take it with you to the airport."

The Sandman never liked working with drug addicts. They were immature and unreliable, but he had no choice. He only hoped she hadn't botched the job. If necessary, she was expendable. At least she didn't know about the Mossad connection. She had been told they were drug dealers.

OCTOBER 28: LANGLEY: 10:30A.M.

"I stake my reputation on it," Shymanski exclaimed, his face flushed. He was furious at Warner for having gone over his head, straight to Director Vaughn. If he tolerated such insubordination, he would look weak and ineffectual to Bastardi. "That report about nuclear warheads being smuggled into the US is nothing but a bunch of hogwash." Exhausted and frustrated, he sat back and folded his arms, waiting for Bastardi to come to his defense.

The seating arrangement for the five men gathered around the oblong, oak conference table in Vaughn's office had been carefully orchestrated by Friar. Warner sat directly across from Bastardi while Friar sat opposite the flustered Shymanski. Friar wanted a chance to study in detail the meddler who had been so instrumental in bringing about Murphy's death. Vaughn was at the head of the table.

Out of the corner of his eye, Friar watched Bastardi shift uncomfortably in his chair. It was clear he didn't like meeting at Langley. It was too far from his own power base in the West Wing of the White House.

"I have to agree with Oscar," declared Bastardi, taking great pains to ignore Friar. He had not forgotten what happened three years ago when Friar had testified before the House National Security subcommittee that certain members of Morehead's inner circle were using arms shipments to the Mideast to solicit illegal contributions for Morehead's re-election campaign. Bastardi had almost lost his job over that brouhaha.

Centering his gaze on Warner, Bastardi continued, "I see no evidence whatsoever that hostile nuclear warheads have entered the US. What I do see is an alcoholic shrimp boat captain rambling on about a shipment of drugs. Hell, that's no big deal. Drugs come into the country every day." Casting a glance at Shymanski, he snickered, "That drunk's got the CIA running around like a barnyard full of Chicken Littles chanting, 'the nukes are coming—the sky's falling.'"

Warner tried to control his anger as Shymanski and Bastardi rattled on. With only three days left, he knew that nothing short of a declaration of a national emergency by President Morehead could possibly succeed at locating the warheads.

Bastardi leaned back, "There's going to be *no* emergency meeting of the Security Council, *no* evacuation of New York, and *no* bothering the President about these unconfirmed rumors." To underscore his point, he placed his pen back in his shirt pocket and slammed his notebook shut.

"So, you're going to ignore the evidence and do nothing," Warner said.

Casually examining his fingernails, Bastardi replied, "Evidence? What evidence? Oscar tells me you have no satellite photos, no communication intercepts, and no credible witnesses. All you've got is a hysterical report from a dead Iraqi general, some horseshit about drugs, and a shakedown attempt by a no-name Chechen informer. Do you know how many such warnings the FBI gets every week? Right now they're conducting over 900 active investigations into terrorism, with ten listed as high-priority. I'm afraid this hocus-pocus crap you're trying to peddle just doesn't make the cut." Looking at Warner, he taunted, "You wouldn't be inventing these warheads just to keep your job would you?"

Warner's face turned red. No one had ever openly challenged his integrity in such a blatant manner. "We consider these sources to be very reliable."

"Reliable?" smirked Bastardi. "You call those professional liars reliable?"

"Are you calling *me* a liar?" interrupted Friar, his jaw muscles tightening and his eyes narrowing.

Unconcerned, the President's National Security Adviser continued cleaning his fingernails. "Ah, Mr. Clarke. I understand you're the person telling everyone to duck and hide."

"I can assure you, there are *no* warheads," interjected Shymanski, trying to ease the tension. "I've checked with my Russian contacts and they've guaranteed me that *all* their nuclear devices have been fully accounted for."

"Oh, really?" queried Friar, shifting his attention towards Shymanski. During his tenure with the Agency he had encountered a lot of fourth-rate political hacks, but Shymanski was in a class all his own.

Avoiding eye contact, Shymanski said, "General Kiril, head of Russia's Strategic Rocket forces, told me personally that your General Zakharov was nothing but a lying, two-bit drug dealer. In fact, General Kiril said any talk about missing warheads was nothing more than a feeble attempt by Zakharov to cover up his heroin deals."

Friar looked at Bastardi. "Mr. National Security Adviser, I can personally guarantee you that within seventy-two hours, unless we locate a thermonuclear device hidden in downtown Manhattan, your boss is going to be blown right out of his cushy job as President of the United States."

"Enough of this goddamned bullshit!" Bastardi exploded. Glowering at Warner, he bellowed, "Is this man speaking for you?"

"Please, gentlemen, please," pleaded Vaughn who had been quietly listening to the arguments. "Let's keep the discussion civil." It secretly pleased him to see Bastardi jerked short by an outsider he couldn't control.

Shymanski raised his hand. "To show everyone how convinced I am there's no bomb, I've agreed to deliver a noontime address in

Manhattan on the thirty-first of October to the Board of Governors of the New York Stock Exchange. They've asked me to speak on the CIA's role in industrial espionage."

Friar looked at Shymanski and smiled. The Sandman had delivered on his promise. And, what's more, Shymanski, the poor dumb bastard, didn't have a clue. His was the worst case of hard-wired, congenital stupidity Friar had ever encountered.

Shymanski glanced at Bastardi with the wide-eyed look of a lap dog seeking approval, "I got the invitation two days ago. They insisted I be the one to speak. They wouldn't accept anyone else."

"Where's it going to be held?" Bastardi asked, mildly concerned.

"At the La Tour D'Or restaurant at the Bankers Trust Building on Wall Street."

Friar almost felt sorry for Shymanski. He was too incompetent to be held responsible for his own actions. Then Friar thought of Murphy, and gritted his teeth. If Bastardi's water boy happened to get caught up in the blast, it would be his own fault.

Peering across the table at Friar, Shymanski said, "I also had that man you claim to be a terrorist, Hashim, picked up by the FBI. They questioned him, but he doesn't know a thing. He's never heard of any organization called the Shaheeds."

"You did what?" Friar asked, incredulous. How could any one person screw things up so badly? Their best chance to locate the warheads, now locked up and protected by the FBI.

"I'm surprised you forgot about him," Shymanski chided. "The one person who was supposed to know where your mysterious warheads are located, and you ignored him? Not smart, not smart at all."

"I've heard enough," Vaughn stated, his mind set. Although new to the job, he realized that the final responsibility for gathering, analyzing, and disseminating the nation's intelligence rested with the director of the CIA. It was a duty he couldn't delegate or shirk. "I'm going to contact Nancy Lopez, the Director at the Nuclear Emergency Search Team and request that she launch a hunt for a nuclear warhead in Manhattan. If nothing else, it'll be a good training exercise."

Bastardi jumped to his feet, "But, there's no—"

Vaughn crossed his arms, "Bruce, the only way you're going to stop me is to have the President replace me. I'm also calling the director of the FBI."

MANHATTAN: 3:37P.M.

"I've been trying to reach you all day," Volodinsky said, his face drawn, his heart pounding like a jackhammer. Not feeling well, he had returned early from the opera, only to find Boyra sprawled across the blood-soaked bed, semiconscious and incoherent.

Dubov glared at Volodinsky. He was furious at him for having left Boyra alone. He bit his lip to keep his temper under control. It was enough that Boyra was still alive.

"Doctors Reis and Walker wanted immediately in OR seven," blared the speaker, two feet from Dubov's head. The antiseptic smell of St. Vincent Hospital's emergency room, and the stress had given him a migraine. Six feet away, a scuffle erupted between two drunks awaiting treatment for cuts and abrasions. A cop slammed down his coffee cup and rushed over.

Dubov pulled Volodinsky into the corridor next to the waiting room, where it was quieter. "Tell me what happened?"

"I don't know," Volodinsky replied, placing his hand against the wall for support. "It must've been a robbery attempt. They said Boyra was shot five times with a small caliber handgun. Three times in the chest, once in the jaw and once in the upper shoulder. Hotel security claims this type of attack has never happened before."

"Was anything stolen? Were there witnesses?"

"No. No one heard shots and there's nothing's missing. On the top of his head were two smudges of lipstick. He's been drifting in and out of consciousness ever since I found him."

A chill went down Dubov's spine. No noise and five shots. It must have been a professional hit. Someone lured Boyra into bed and shot him there. Whoever did it must know about them. But a professional assassin would have fired the last two slugs directly into his brain. Why only Boyra and not Volodinsky? "Where is he now?"

"In intensive care. They've got him hooked up to all those machines." Volodinsky shuddered. He hated hospitals. The sight of blood made him nauseous. "I had to leave. They said his condition was critical, that only family members could be with him."

The double door next to Volodinsky flew open, almost knocking him headlong down the corridor. An emergency room doctor and nurse dressed in bloodstained, green OR scrubs pushed a gurney towards the nearest operating room. An orderly followed closely behind, pulling a metal crash cart.

"Boyra's babbling," said Volodinsky.

"What do you mean, babbling?"

"He's delirious. Mumbling all sorts of things. Most of it in Russian."

Dubov's face grew dark, "What kind of *things*?"

"He's ranting about nuclear bombs and angels. He keeps repeating the same phrase over and over. 'Angel did it. *Volchy bilet, Volchy bilet.*'"

"*Volchy bilet*—the wolf's ticket," Dubov grunted. "He's drawn the wolf's ticket all right. He's finished and he knows it."

"Another thing, two detectives were asking questions."

Alarmed, Dubov glanced around, "Are they still here?"

"No. The doctors made them go. Before they left, they asked me what he was mumbling. I told them he was speaking Russian and I didn't know. They said they'd be back with an interpreter."

"We've got to shut him up," Dubov growled. "Have you got all the information you need—about the device?"

Sheepishly, Volodinsky whispered into Dubov's ear, "The protocol for arming the warhead is in his laptop. I don't know the password. If I can only get the password—that's all I need."

Dubov's turned red with rage. He had specifically ordered the two physicists to cross-train on *all* procedures. Between clinched teeth, he hissed, "Wait here. Don't talk to anyone."

"Dr. Boyra, it's me," Dubov whispered in the ear of the semi-comatose form strapped to the bed in the dimly lit intensive care unit. It had not been difficult to convince the distracted gatekeeper on the desk that he was Boyra's grief stricken brother.

Dubov shuddered as he looked at the IV tubes stuck in Boyra's arms and the breathing tube running down his throat. The smell of alcohol and sight of plasma bags brought back memories of Afghanistan. At least, here it was clean and sterile, not like that cow barn of a hospital on the outskirts of Moscow where he had been treated for his shoulder wound.

A gurgling sound rose from Boyra's throat. His eyes slowly opened. Feeble life signs beeped on the overhead EKG and EEG monitors. His body stirred slightly. The peaks and valleys on the screens swung in wider arches.

"Dr. Boyra, you're going to be all right. I talked with the doctors." There was no response. "I need the password for your computer. The entry code for the protocol program, what is it?"

Gazing down at the crumpled form, gauze-wrapped like an Egyptian mummy, wild thoughts coursed through Dubov's mind. What if the Manhattan warhead couldn't be activated? The only person who knew the complete firing sequence was stretched out in front of him and was slipping fast. One of the larger warheads would have to be substituted, but that would take time. Who had done this? Who knew where Boyra was staying? Dubov could feel the pressure rising in his chest—there was a faint sense of panic.

The mouth began to move, but no words came out. Dubov leaned closer.

"*Volchy bilet, Volchy bilet,*" came the faint sound. Then, in a louder voice, "Angel did this–thi—" The voice fell silent.

Dubov shook his head. It was hopeless. Boyra was hallucinating. Glancing through the glass door at the nurses' station, Dubov removed a small vial from his coat pocket. Unscrewing the 2ml dropper, he squeezed five squirts of undiluted potassium chloride into the top of the IV bag attached to Boyra's left arm. In the autopsy the chemical would leave no detectable residue. The cause of death would be attributed to cardiac arrest from shock and loss of blood.

Dubov stood back and looked down at the now peacefully resting form. The fluctuations on the monitors were slowing down, it would only be a matter of minutes. There was no rush now.

Dubov felt pity for the jovial little man whose breathing was coming in short gasps. He had always been so optimistic, so full of life. Dubov reached over and patted Boyra on his flabby, cold cheeks. "Sleep well, my little friend. May all your kasha be buttered in heaven."

Chapter 14

OCTOBER 29: WILLIAMSBURG: 10:09A.M.

A chill, autumn wind swept against Bosworth House in gusts, rattling the storm shutters. Inside, electricians and carpenters from Camp Peary strung wire and built shelves for additional phone lines, television sets, and computer terminals. The living room, now designated the War Room, was fitted with a foldout conference table, a row of TV monitors, and a detailed, wall-sized map of New York City and Long Island. The two front bedrooms had been converted into his and hers crash pads. From here on in, the vigil would be maintained around-the-clock. In the garden, the separate reliance building was now the communications center, complete with its own array of roof-mounted antennae and receiver dishes.

Entering the War Room from the garden, a windblown, but triumphant Marcie announced, "Laurence, I found Murphy's book."

"Where was it?"

"The Property section at Langley had it in a box along with his other personal effects. It was left behind in his Cairo hotel room, just like you figured. I got there in the nick of time. They were getting ready to send it down to Sarah."

On the cover of Etiene R. Fortier's, *Nostradamus: Prophecies for the Millennium*, was a full-face, color portrait of a somber Nostradamus.

"What does it say?" Friar asked, eager for anything that would place into context Murphy's use of the word Normans.

"Don't know yet. Page 93 is missing. Murphy must've torn it out and taken it with him in the helicopter. Professor Rowlson said he'll fax us a copy in an hour or so."

"Chop, chop, please. By the way, what's the word on Ellsworth going to New York for that induction ceremony?"

"He's being pigheaded as usual." To Marcie, the most grievous of all mortal sins was unbridled ego, especially unwarranted male ego. "Claims he's waited a lifetime for an invitation to join the Society of the Cincinnati and he's not about to let some rumor about terrorists ruin it for him now. He's convinced that if there was a real threat it would be on CNN." She shook her head, "Heck, I'd buy his plane ticket and take him to the airport if it weren't for Eloise and Atlee."

"How's Eloise taking it?"

"What do you expect? Eight and a half months pregnant and all tears. She even threatened to take Atlee and move in with Mom if he went. Of course, Mr. Ego knows it's just a bluff."

"Wouldn't hurt if she actually called his hand and left for a couple of days."

"That's exactly what I told her, but she doesn't want to upset *him*. Imagine that? She's afraid of upsetting Mr. Testosterone." Marcie laughed, "Bad thing is how ridiculous I'll look if it turns out there is no bomb."

"Want me to talk to him? It wouldn't hurt for him to get a second opinion." Friar grinned, "Especially from a reasonable male."

Ignoring Friar's comment, Marcie said, "Would you? Like I said, if it weren't for Eloise and Atlee—"

1:30P.M.

"Less than forty-eight hours," Warner needlessly reminded Friar and Kat as they gathered in the War Room for a situation report.

"How's the hunt coming?" asked Friar.

"Nothing so far," replied Kat. "They've only got two hundred NEST agents and a couple hundred FBI working the city." She shook her head. "New York's a big place."

Christ, thought Friar. Only four hundred when the FBI alone had over twelve hundred agents in the city. "I thought Vaughn was going to get them to pull out all the stops. What happened?"

"It's Bastardi," Kat replied, while sectioning off the wall map into twelve inch squares. "He and Shymanski are passing the word around

Washington the search is just an exercise and a waste of time. They're even pressuring the FBI to scale down below the two hundred."

"Any chance of convincing the Bureau's New York office to assign more agents on the qt?"

"I've already thought of that. I contacted Assistant Director Coyote earlier this morning. He said he had orders straight from Director Dolenski to keep the hunt small and low key. Seems Bastardi's afraid too much fuss might attract media attention and panic the public."

Bastardi again. Friar hadn't mentioned it to Warner, but he had called in a long-standing chit from Tony Fabrizio at the Directorate of Intelligence. On page two in this morning's edition of the President's Daily Brief, was a red-letter warning about New York. At least that would guarantee a permanent record of the DO and Warner's special task force having done their jobs. Friar smiled, Bastardi would stroke-out when he saw it. The Daily Brief was also Eyes Only to Vice President Hambright, Secretary of Defense Deathridge, and Secretary of State Hohlt. It was rumored President Morehead never read his copy, that he relied on Bastardi to keep him informed. Friar hoped today would be different.

Kat put the finishing touches on the wall map, sticking in brightly colored pins at different points denoting the known locations of NEST and FBI search teams. "When I told Coyote this was no drill he seemed very concerned. He plans to evacuate his whole office if he hasn't been notified by 0500 on the thirty-first that the warhead has been found." Reading between the lines, she was also confident he would assign another 200 to 300 agents to the operation on her own authority.

"Well," Warner concluded, "can't see there's much we can do at this point to help NEST." His feeling of powerlessness was overwhelming. "I hope they're checking out that refrigerator lead."

"They are," Kat assured him. "Hashim's picture is being flashed all over town, along with a cover story that should satisfy the media. This morning, the metropolitan edition of the *Times* ran a 'Have You Seen This Man' article on the front page of the second section. Several local TV stations are showing his picture hourly."

"What's their line?" asked Friar.

"They're saying that Hashim's infected with the Ebola Zaire filovirus and could be hot as hell. A ten thousand dollar reward is being offered to anyone who can prove they've had contact with him."

"That's too damn little," Friar grumbled. "It oughta be at least fifty thousand, maybe even a hundred." Of course, if it were up to Friar, Mossad would be interrogating Hashim now, instead of the FBI.

Kat nodded, "They're checking with every apartment building super in lower Manhattan on incoming household goods shipments since October 17. But, we don't even know for certain that Hashim was the person who made the delivery."

"Or," observed Friar, "that the refrigerator was placed in an apartment. It could be sitting in some out-of-the-way warehouse or appliance storage bin. Hell, it could still be in the van parked in a garage."

Friar held up a copy of Hashim's picture and studied the deep set, intense eyes. "Kat, I don't have to ask, but, I will. Any possibility of the FBI getting him to talk?"

Kat glanced at the defiant stare. "Negative on that score. He's a real pro."

"Where're they holding him?"

"At the Hoover building in Washington."

"Any chance you could get them to move him to your downtown New York office? It's at—"

"The Federal Plaza between Duane and Worth." She smiled. Why not? That would place him dead center in the expected target area. "I'll give it a try."

"Let's see how strong his nerves are." It was Friar's observation that professional terrorists made poor martyrs.

"Any luck on identifying the mutts with the fancy tattoos?" Warner asked.

"Affirmative," Kat replied. "Dorn sent out the artist's sketches over the Bureau's computer network. An informant in New Orleans recognized them as members of the Dolgochenskaya syndicate." Pulling a manila folder from her briefcase, she handed Friar and Warner copies of the sketches. The faces were generalized, but the tattoos were drawn in minute detail. "Sorry about the faces. Most of the witnesses only remembered the tattoos." Holding up the first sketch, she said, "Here we have Danya Petrov, a k a Danny Petty, a k a Short Cut. The next one belongs to Moriz Chapaev, a k a Mort Chapman, a k a Toonie. Both are ex-con émigrés from Moscow. They're hooked in with the stolen car market in New Orleans."

"Have you checked the sketches with Immigration?" asked Friar.

"Sure did. There was no match with recent mug shots from visa applications. Best we can tell, they slipped across the Mexican border near Matamoros sometime in June or early July. There's no record of their having been arrested in the US. We ran the descriptions by Interpol and our Moscow office. Interpol's got nothing and the Russians are stonewalling us."

Friar studied the sketches. Something about these two bottom feeders didn't fit. Why use such easily identified ex-cons in a complicated nuclear smuggling operation. "Where're they now?"

"Our New Orleans office had the NOPD issue an all-points, but no luck. They've disappeared."

Friar wasn't surprised. He didn't expect to find them alive. Their body markings were too distinctive. "Kat, what's the story on that syndicate—the Dolgochenskayas?"

"It's Russian, big, and has its US headquarters in Little Odessa. The New York office calls them the Dols."

"Little Odessa?" asked Warner.

"That's the Brighton Beach area next to Coney Island. So many Russians live there it's called Little Odessa. They deal mostly with stolen cars, prostitution, protection, and drugs."

"In other words, the usual low-level stuff," observed Friar. It would take a stretch of imagination to envision a run-of-the-mill syndicate like the Dols masterminding a complex, nuclear smuggling operation. "Kat, what's your opinion of them having the smarts for a project of this magnitude?"

"Quite frankly, unless I'm missing something major, I'd have to say, no way. But you never know." Her stint with the Bureau's Russian Organized Crime Squad had taught her to be wary of illusions. With the Russian syndicates, surface appearances were always suspect. In a country where the best and brightest gravitate to crime as the career of choice, the Russian organizatsiyas were capable of extremely sophisticated operations.

When Warner stepped out of the War Room to answer a phone call, Friar took Kat aside, "You were working on a DNA analysis for me."

"The Bureau's lab in Arlington couldn't read the saliva from the cigarette butts. The samples were too old and dry for standard nuclear testing procedures. They had to send them down to a forensic lab in North Carolina's Research Triangle for mitochondrial analysis. The results should be back by 1500 hours tomorrow."

"Let me know as soon as they come in."

"Can do." Kat walked over and raised the window overlooking the garden. She felt flushed and needed fresh air. Four days ago her appetite had disappeared completely and she hadn't gotten two hours continuous sleep since. Breathing deeply, she watched a pair of cardinals splashing in the bird bath. The tension was starting to give her headaches, but, to her surprise, was oddly exhilarating. A side effect, one she hadn't planned on and didn't want to acknowledge, was beginning to distract her. She was thinking more and more about Friar. It was temporary she had told herself. A brief infatuation tied in with the adrenaline rush from hunting real nuclear warheads.

Friar walked over and stood beside her. "What about those Ryder rental trucks? Were you able—"

There was a loud knock on the door. Marcie burst in, "Laurence! We've got page 93."

Taking the fax from Marcie's hand, he read, *The heaven will broil at five and forty degrees, / Fire approaches the great new city, / A large, widespread flame leaps high—* Glancing further down, he spoke aloud the part Marcie had circled in red, " 'This quatrain predicts the detonation of a nuclear warhead in an American city, most probably New York.' New York," he said, "that confirms it."

Marcie pointed to the lower right corner of the page, "Now read the sidebar, *When they want to have proof of the Normans.*"

Friar ran his finger to where she was pointing, " 'It may well be that the line refers not to France *but to a north Asian country—*' "

"That's what Murphy was trying to tell us."

"Yeah," Friar nodded. "His state sponsor is North Korea. That's why the sub picked up the warheads at Vladivostok. The Kilo belongs to Pyongyang, but how do we prove it?"

"Contact NOSIC," answered Kat. "They can find the owner. The Navy Ocean Surveillence Center in Maryland tracks and records all sub activity on the east coast. Have them look up their log for 16 October."

OCTOBER 30: NEW YORK: 1:30P.M.

With the sleeve of his shirt, Volodinsky mopped his brow. Glaring at the flickering computer screen, his tired eyes strained to pickup any detail that might hint at the password. Scrolling slowly, he painstakingly worked his way through the list of files: Ac=233, Au2&6, Br15, Bu23—gibberish, nothing but gibberish. It could be anything, a hidden word, a number, a phrase. A bead of sweat raced down the side of his cheek, dripping onto the keyboard. The stifling, over-heated air in the bedroom of apartment 2807, Skyview Plaza, was starting to blur his vision.

"For god's sake, Doctor, open a window," Dubov snapped, as he entered the room.

Volodinsky's knees creaked as he stood and walked stiff-legged to the blinds. Raising the window, he poked his sagging face into the blast of fresh air that came rushing in. The strong breeze cooled the patches of damp sweat on the back and armpits of his shirt. Flexing his cramped fingers, he walked around the room, flapping his arms like a crow, trying to work out the kinks from being perched for two hours in front of a hostile, uncooperative computer screen. Plopping back down in the wing-backed chair, he continued his search. It was Boyra's revenge.

Earlier that morning, Dubov had received the final go-ahead from the Phoenix Committee to proceed as planned. It had taken Petya and him more than an hour and a half to move the warhead to the roof and, using pulleys, lift it to the tower. To gain access to the building's freight elevator, it had been necessary to use the services of Quincy Totten, the building superintendent. Once or twice, Totten had shown a little too much interest in the strange, 275 pound metal cylinder being hoisted to the platform. But, he appeared to accept the explanation that it was merely replacement pollution equipment.

"I can't find it, Comrade," Volodinsky announced, his voice quivering. "I've tried everything. Dr. Boyra's birthday, his mother's name, the date we came to the US, his weight, the name of the mission, everything. We've *got* to postpone the project."

"Easy, Doctor, easy," Dubov said soothingly. "I think I've found the answer to our problem."

For the past forty-five minutes, Dubov had been busy searching the yellow pages and calling various computer service companies. Finally, Voitlander's Computer Services, Ltd. had given him the lead he needed. While it was against their policy, they assured him, to hack programs for unknown persons, they suggested he look in the Bulletin Board section of *The Village Voice* for ads offering assistance in retrieving lost files. On the back page of the October 24 edition, wedged between "Transvestite Fashion Boutique," and "Goddess Ball, Call Tammalyne," was "Captain Marvel, Caped Crusader of the Internet. Lost files located while you wait. No questions asked. Privacy guaranteed. Rock bottom prices. (212) 595-2528. Call after 3:00P.M."

There was a light knock on the bedroom door. Petya stepped in and whispered into Dubov's ear, "It's that janitor, Quincy Totten. He's in the kitchen asking to see you. Says it's important."

"What the hell does he want?" Dubov growled. "Okay, tell him I'll be there in a minute.

While he waited, Quincy Totten, the forty-five-year-old, three-times-divorced, frequent substance abuser, nervously eyed the gleaming white GE model 704E refrigerator. Trying to organize his muddled thoughts, he mumbled to himself, "Quincy, opportunities like this don't come along everyday. You got to be smart and take advantage." Maybe he ought to ask for twenty thousand dollars—or even twenty-five thousand. Heck, why not a whole forty thousand? That would be enough to get away from these darn New York winters for good. He had always wanted to go to California, hang out on crystal white beaches, and surf the waves with some of those real bitchin' "Baywatch" babes—just like on TV. He'd take his time in LA, snort a little coke, toke some high-grade Acapulco Gold. In a month or so, maybe work his way up the coastal highway to San Francisco. When his money ran out, he'd get a job in Napa Valley at one of those fancy wineries he had read about in that food magazine pulled from the trash last week.

"What do you want?" demanded Dubov. "You've been paid."

Startled, Totten recoiled. "Er, sir, I–er, that is—"

"No more money. Understand?" Irritated at the intrusion, Dubov turned to leave.

Totten braced himself. This was his golden opportunity. "There was two men, come by the office about an hour ago."

Dubov paused and looked back. "So?"

"FBI, th–they said they was FBI. Showed me their badges and everything. I said to myself, 'Quincy, them's federal agents. This looks *darn* serious.'"

Dubov stopped in his tracks. FBI? How did they—? Breathing deeply, he exhaled slowly, forcing himself to think. Walking to the front door of the apartment, he opened it and looked down the hall. Nothing.

Watching Dubov's reaction, Totten knew he was right. They *were* hiding something. "Them agents was looking for that A-rab who brung this refrigerator here. They said he's got some kind of killer virus and may be contagious. Can you imagine that? A killer virus." He forced a laugh, but his throat was dry and it sounded more like a cough. "They offered me ten thousand dollars if I could tell them anything about this feller."

"You didn't—"

"Hey, no way, man," insisted Totten, holding his hands up in front of him and shaking his head vigorously. "I didn't tell them federal guys nothing. I said, 'Quincy, don't be no darn fool. Keep your trap shut.'" Pointing to the refrigerator, he said, "Them guys said this here appliance might be contaminated with that killer virus. Said anybody that touches it will git it, and die a real painful death."

"Good man," Dubov answered, slapping Totten on the back. As the super watched wide-eyed, Dubov ran his hands over the top and down the sides of the refrigerator, then rubbed them on his face. "See, no virus."

Totten forced another hollow laugh, "I figured it was all malarkey. About that virus thing, I mean. I says to myself, 'Hey, Quincy, if it's worth ten thousand to them FBI guys, it's gonna be worth—' "

"A lot more to me," Dubov said, finishing the sentence. "You're a smart man Mr.—er?"

"Totten, Quincy Totten, with two T's. Totten, that's my father's name. My mother give it to me even though they was never married. The Quincy part comes from my uncle Quincy Ammadon. He used to own a bar down in Dallas before he disappeared. Yes, sir, I says, 'Quincy, this is your big chance.' "

"You were right, Mr. Totten. Those agents weren't after any virus." Holding his hand beside his mouth, Dubov whispered, "They think we're dealing in drugs. You know, the expensive stuff—cocaine, heroin." Throwing his hands up in mock disbelief, he winked at Totten.

Totten grinned broadly, jerking his head up and down to show he understood. He just knew it—the jackpot. He could tell all along there was something fishy about that pollution equipment story. And, that tower, that's where they stashed the drugs. "Of course, I know you fellers ain't selling no drugs," he said, with a mercenary gleam in his eye. He wanted his new boss to know he was street smart and could be trusted.

"What did you tell them?"

Totten leaned forward, "*Nothing*. Hey, Quincy Totten didn't fall off no garbage truck yesterday. No, siree. When they showed me the picture of that A-rab, I took my time and looked it over real careful like." Totten squinted and held the photo the agents had given him, close to his face. "All the while I knowed it was him. Then I said, 'I 'ain't seen nobody that looks like that.' That's exactly what I said— 'ain't seen nobody.' They left this here card along with this picture in case I chance to recollect a detail or two." Totten handed Special Agent Pollock's card to Dubov along with a five-by-seven, black and white photo of Hashim.

Dubov pulled Totten aside. "Would a hundred thousand be okay? You could be real useful to us. We need someone sharp to help keep the Feds off our back."

Totten couldn't believe his ears. A hundred thousand dollars! And, they wanted him to join the gang. Why, in a couple of months he could buy his own California winery. Reaching his hand forward, he said, "Heck, yes. Quincy Totten knows opportunity when he sees it.

That'll suit me just fine."

The two shook hands.

"Hold on for a second, Mr. Totten, let me consult with my associate. I need to see how much money we have on hand."

Totten waved him away, "Hey, don't you worry about that none. I don't need no money right now." He thought it important to show trust, after all, they were partners.

"Getting rid of those agents the way you did, you deserve a down payment. Of course, we don't keep a hundred thousand in cash just lying around."

"Heck no," Totten answered slyly. "There's too many crooks that would try to steal it."

After a brief discussion with Petya in the next room, the two Chechens returned to the kitchen where Totten was leaning against the refrigerator to demonstrate his faith in his new associates. While Dubov stood on his left, Petya boxed the super in from the right.

Totten shifted uneasily between the two, powerfully built, towering men.

Joking with Petya in Russian, Dubov placed a large, muscular arm around Totten's shoulders. Seeing the two men laughing, the building superintendent grinned and started to relax.

"There's twenty-five thousand in hundred dollar bills inside the icemaker. Help yourself, but leave the drugs." Dubov smiled broadly while shifting his hand to the point on Totten's neck where the third cervical vertebra joins the forth. "You get the rest of the money, first thing tomorrow morning."

Totten grinned and gave Dubov an approving thumbs-up. Reaching over, he opened the refrigerator door. He stared blankly at the empty box. There was no icemaker, no money, no drugs.

WILLIAMSBURG: 4:15P.M.

"Friar," Kat called softly, leading him into the pantry which had been converted into a small, standing room only, private conference nook. The six-by-ten windowless cubicle, which had been christened the Sidebar, contained no chairs or furniture, just a thick rug on the hardwood floor, a telephone attached to the wall and four inches of wrap-around sound insulation. A force field had been installed behind the insulation making it the most secure room at Bosworth House.

Closing the door, Kat said, "Washington has turned us down on moving Hashim to New York." Gazing into Friar's eyes, a powerful surge of emotion engulfed her.

"You okay?" he asked, noticing her flushed appearance.

"Me? I–I'm fine, but thanks." *Get a grip*, she told herself.

"What's their problem?"

Looking down at the notes in her hand, she said, "Hashim's got some hotshot lawyer representing him. His name's Frank Donatelli. He's filing motions, seeking writs, and habeas corpusing all over the place. I mean, that guy's a blizzard of paperwork. Last I heard, he was threatening to sue the Bureau for false arrest. Claims he's being discriminated against because he's an Arab. The Washington office is afraid to do anything, I mean *anything*."

"Damn," Friar muttered under his breath. The ease with which the legal system could be manipulated revolted him, but it was useless banging his head against that wall. "Any good news?"

Kat moved closer, invading the outer fringes of his body zone. Closer, on the pretext she might be overheard. "The DNA report came back on the cigarette stubs from Wanchese. There was a match on the filter-tip Camels. Guess who?"

Friar shook his head—

Without waiting for an answer, she said, "Your Russian informer, Alexander Dubov. Those were his cigarettes."

Friar looked puzzled, "*Dubov*? Are you sure?"

"Positive." Kat was pleased her statement had caught him by surprise. "We ran a second test. Figured the lab might have screwed up. It came back ditto. The DNA on all four Camel cigarette butts belongs to Dubov."

Friar stared at the floor. Dubov? *How could that be?* He was the informer. He had told them where to find Captain Wentworth and Hashim. If anyone other than Kat had said the match was Dubov's—Wentworth's Russian—he wouldn't have believed them. Did this mean Dubov controlled the warheads? What about Hashim, where did he fit in? Were the Shaheeds only a sideshow, one of the layers to be peeled away? Wentworth had said, "Russian—i.e. Dubov was the leader." The contradictions tumbled through Friar's mind. It was too much, he would have to sort them out later.

One thing for certain, it would be futile to arrest Dubov. He would only clam up tighter than Hashim. Maybe the Sandman's interrogation team could force him to talk, but that would take days and there were fewer than twenty hours left. Besides, Friar didn't even know where the Chechen was, he was still waiting for him to call.

Gently taking Kat's arm, Friar said, "The DNA report. Don't tell anyone else. Not yet, anyway. Okay?"

There was a lump in Kat's throat as she obediently nodded. There, she had done it again. Given in without a whimper. Why did she let Friar manipulate her so easily? It was the strain and lack of rest, she told herself, and he seemed to have all the answers. After a good night's sleep this obsession would disappear as quickly and illogically as it had begun. "Yeah, I'll bet," she softly murmured to herself.

"Oh, I almost forgot," Kat exclaimed. "Under hypnosis Wentworth remembered a sixth truck. A large, tan vehicle hidden in the bushes behind the loading shed."

"Any unusual markings?"

"He said it was plain, with North Carolina tags and a Raleigh license plate holder. He saw it when he went behind the shed to relieve himself. He didn't pay much attention to it at the time, just figured it belonged to the Russians or the Shaheeds."

A *sixth* truck. Five warheads and six vehicles. One that Wentworth wasn't supposed to see. "Kat, find out all you can about that truck. It's probably from a dealership in the Triangle area. We need to know who rented it, how far it was driven, when it was turned in—everything."

"Can do," she answered, noting the detached tone of his voice. He was oblivious. Her system was working overtime sending out pheromone, but his receptors were switched off.

Chapter 15

Friar picked up the pace as he hurried down the middle of DOG Street, toward the Robert Graves House. He glanced at his watch—5:38P.M. Where had the afternoon gone? Dodging to his left, he narrowly missed a group of German tourists headed towards the Williamsburg Inn. Late afternoon shadows jutted across the sign in front of Chowning's Tavern while the street lights flickered on in front of the Courthouse and Bruton Parish Church.

Without fanfare Tovi Hersch ushered Friar into the converted living room-command center. The plush, Williamsburg sofa and chairs had been replaced by six institutional, metal chairs with hard padded seats. The writing desk had disappeared. In its place were two functional, nondescript fold-up tables. Banks of communications equipment crowded the walls, hooked to an array of encryption devices by wires strung from eyebolts in the ceiling. The windows were covered with removable black-out shades.

"What's the news from New York?" the Sandman asked as he began hooking up TV monitors.

"Nothing, so far. NEST is doing all it can, but—" Friar shrugged, "They've only got 400 to 500 agents working the streets."

Tovi raised an eyebrow, "Why so few?"

"Cockpit trouble. Bastardi's trying to keep a lid on the search. He says he doesn't want things blown out of proportion. Claims there's no hard evidence nuclear warheads are actually in the country."

"No evidence?" snorted Tovi. He wasn't surprised. "It's the

Cassandra curse. You bust your hump collecting intelligence, and they don't believe you. People hear what they want to hear. You can chalk it up to plain old bureaucratic, lead-ass inertia."

"Speaking of Cassandra, it turns out our informer, Alexander Dubov, is the one who smuggled in the warheads."

Tovi stopped working on the equipment and sat down. "So, Dubov is playing both sides. That's interesting. Any idea what his game is?"

"I haven't put it together yet, but he's hell-bent on painting Iraq as the state sponsor. Also looks like he's setting up a rival syndicate to take the fall when the Administration starts seeking revenge. He was supposed to get back in touch with me on the twenty-seventh, but he's dropped out of sight." Friar quickly brought the Sandman up to date on his belief North Korea was the supplier of funds. It was against his instincts to share such sensitive information, but there was no other way. "I have a favor—"

"Ask."

Friar reached in his coat pocket and pulled out a computer print-out of Dubov's DNA map, along with a complete set of fingerprints. "I need more background on our Chechen. Anything you can find before he came to the US. Sleeping habits, service records, place of birth, sex preferences, phobias, you know the tune."

"I'll get our people on it right away. Shouldn't take long." Relaxing, Tovi reached into a cardboard box and withdrew two miniature bottles of cognac. "I've got good news. I think we may have cut off the head of the snake."

Friar perked up. "Really?"

Pouring the cognac into two Styrofoam cups, he said, "We located the trigger-man for the New York warhead. It was that Russian scientist, Dr. Danya Boyra, I mentioned a while back. He has been terminated." Offering a cup to Friar, he asked, "Care to celebrate?"

The possibility of short circuiting the enterprise by surgically removing the physicists needed to detonate the warheads had not occurred to Friar. It was their Achilles' heel. It would take months before Dubov could find replacements, and with the CIA and Mossad alerted, maybe forever. Then he asked, "You also got Dr. Volodinsky?"

"Volodinsky?"

"There's a *second* physicist. Dr. Fredek Volodinsky. Murphy gave us his name in his first report. I thought you knew."

Tovi was crushed. "No. My source said there was only one—Dr. Boyra." The perfect opportunity, gone. How could it have happened? Then he remembered, the Eunuch that Bunnie had mentioned. That was Volodinsky.

Commander Rhodes and Chief Koenraad sat in the back of the staff car, watching the street lights of Williamsburg click by. Rhodes studied the two silent escorts seated in the front and wondered if they were used to this kind of exciting cloak-and-dagger work. He envied them. It had only been forty-five minutes since he and Koenraad had been whisked from their cubicles at NOSIC and placed on board an unmarked helicopter at Andrews Air Force Base. For Rhodes, this hush-hush spy work was nirvana, the kind of James Bond sleuthing he had always dreamed of. The black helicopter with no running lights; the nondescript staff car with smoked windows; the polite deference from anonymous agents who spoke to each other in whispers.

Hurriedly ushered into the War Room at Bosworth House where Warner and Friar were waiting, Rhodes asked, "Can anyone tell us what this is all about?" All he had seen so far were copies of the special order from Admiral Orlando Simmons, Director of Naval Intelligence, assigning Koenraad and him to Task Force Red Bravo for the duration. They had also been directed to bring with them a copy of the log book for Koenraad's sector on 16 October.

"I'm afraid not, Commander," Warner replied. "Not yet, anyway. But, I can assure you this special op is absolutely critical to national security."

Friar looked the two men over carefully. Bright, professional navy, he liked what he saw. "During the evening of 16 October, a foreign, diesel sub delivered a highly classified cargo to a shrimp boat off the Outer Banks of North Carolina. We need to know the country of origin for that sub."

Koenraad's eyes brightened, "Yes sir, I remember the incident. Commander Rhodes and I discussed it at the time. I can check the log, but as I recall, we never did determine whose boat it was."

Friar frowned, "Was there anything unusual about that particular sub that might help us locate and identify it?"

"Aye, sir," answered Koenraad. Unlocking and opening the brief-case handcuffed to his wrist, he pulled out a copy of the log. "Let's see—" He turned the pages slowly until he found one flagged in red. "Here it is. A super-quiet, Kilo-class diesel. On 16 October at 1718 hours, it was located 113 nautical miles due-east of Morehead City, North Carolina, heading, north-northeast at twenty knots."

Rhodes asked, "Is that the one?"

Warner nodded.

Koenraad continued reading from the log, "At 2031 hours, Commander Rhodes and I fed the specifics on the sub's hull noise and propulsion system into the computer and asked for a match against all known Kilos. There was a negative response. At 2121 Commander Rhodes dispatched a SH-3D Sea King from the naval base at Norfolk for possible visual and sonar identification. Sometime between 2130 and 2135 hours target sub surfaced and ceased all forward movement. Radar contact by Sea King was made at 2225. At 2228 the Kilo reversed course, submerged, and headed due South. At 2238 dunking sonar was lowered into water. At 2245, readings were conducted and verification made as to class, dimensions, and speed. Precise propulsion system and hull noises were mapped for future reference. At 2318 hours Sea King completed its mission and headed back to base."

"Commander, do you think you can identify *that* sub again?" Friar asked.

"Affirmative, sir. We have her signature nailed to the mast with the ASQ-13B dunking sonar. Whoever owns it would have to replace the propulsion system and reconfigure the hull to avoid positive identification.

Warner looked pleased. "Commander Rhodes, Chief Koenraad, what I am about to tell you is *Top Secret*. Do you understand?"

"Aye, aye, sir," they replied in unison.

"It's our belief the sub in question is North Korean. It's imperative this be quickly confirmed or disproved. Is that possible?"

"Affirmative, sir. It shouldn't take long, provided the sub's stationed close to home base and is out there moving around." Rhodes crossed his fingers, hoping it wasn't in dry dock or tied up in a sub pen.

Third world countries like North Korea could not afford to operate their boats over extended periods. But, with a new Kilo, there would be sea trials and a strong urge to play with their new toy.

NEW YORK: 8:16P.M.

The cab slowed to a halt at the corner of Columbus and Seventy-fourth. "Near side, far side?" queried the driver.

"Far side," said Dubov.

As Volodinsky exited the cab, Dubov cautioned, "Doctor, be careful with that computer."

Volodinsky nodded, clutching the laptop close to his chest.

Across the street, a skinhead, two days out of rehab and cruising for quick money, spotted the computer. Fondling the switchblade stuffed in the pocket of his ratty, denim jacket, he sized-up the slightly built physicist and started crossing the street. Midway, he pulled up when he saw Dubov climb out of the cab. Turning to a much younger felon-in-training, he shook his head and slouched back into a corner fruit market to await easier prey.

At the top of the concrete stoop at 120 West Seventy-fourth, Dubov ran his finger down the list of names posted on an antique brass roster. Finding the name *Gerald Frankel*, he pushed the button.

"Yeah, who is it?" demanded the squeaky voice over the intercom.

"Smith, Donald Smith," Dubov replied.

"Third flight up. Apartment 3S, on the right."

When the buzzer sounded, Dubov pushed open the chipped, pea-green metal door and glanced down the long, narrow, dimly lit hall. On the left were two bicycles chained to a radiator pipe. At the end of the hall was a flight of steep, well-worn wooden stairs.

By the time they reached the third floor, Volodinsky's face was red and he was puffing. Dubov turned to the right and knocked on the door marked *Captain Marvel, Caped Crusader of the Internet*. The shadow of an eye passed over the peephole. In seconds, there were the sliding, metallic sounds of three, heavy-duty bolts being unlocked.

Frankel eyed Dubov and Volodinsky with the predatory curiosity of a street-smart, shell game hustler. "C'mon in, *Mr. Smith*," he scoffed. He liked working with stupid people. They were easy marks. He detested these virgin computer crooks, Internet illiterates who were greedy but too dumb or lazy to do their own hacking.

Dubov quickly glanced around the room, then turned his attention to Captain Marvel. In medical terms, the Caped Crusader was morbidly obese. A twenty-three-year-old, City College drop-out, Frankel had the pale, junk food complexion of a hairless, overfed sewer rat.

"So, Mr. Smith, you have a job for me?" Frankel hissed, slowly munching the last few bites of a day-old, pastrami sandwich. "Something on the Internet? A problem with your company's accounting system? Remote entry's my specialty, but it's going to cost you."

"No, nothing like th-that," Dubov replied hesitantly, imitating the nervous sincerity of a novice, white-collar thief. It was important to project a stereotype Frankel understood. "It's a small job. Nothing complicated. We just need a password for a computer program. That's all. My forgetful friend here, Dr. Jones, misplaced it."

"Sure he did," Frankel sneered, grabbing the laptop from Volodinsky and placing it on a chipped, vinyl-topped table in the middle of the cramped kitchen. Flipping open the top, he examined the machine. Bypassing the security system of this generations old IBM 386SX 40MB dinosaur was going to be a snap. Catching a glimpse of Dubov's reflection in the grimy kitchen window, his brow furrowed. Better not make it look too easy, or Mr. Smith might not want to pay up. A pigeon on the ledge outside the kitchen window cooed softly. Captain Marvel snorted at the thought of his two pigeons, waiting to be plucked.

"Gonna be real hard digging it out," Frankel said. "This is an advanced model. Yeah, it's gonna be real tough." Alternating between examining the laptop and jotting down numbers like a used car salesman, he said, "Tell you what I'll do. Five hundred bucks and the password's yours. Cash." Noticing that Dubov wasn't shocked, he immediately regretted not having demanded more.

"Four hundred, max," Dubov finally replied, aware that Frankel expected him to bargain.

"Five hundred, or I don't touch it," the Caped Crusader insisted, holding up his hands and sliding his chair away from the table.

"All right," Dubov replied. "An extra hundred if you do it in an hour."

"Two hundred and fifty extra if I do it in half an hour?" Frankel sniffed, his pencil-thin eyebrows rising expectantly.

Half an hour? The relief flashed across Dubov's face. "Agreed. Seven hundred and fifty, cash, if you find the password in half an hour."

Frankel smirked, exposing two rows of yellow, unbrushed teeth. Looking at his watch, he turned the computer on. The screen blinked to life. Bringing up the file manager, he asked, "If your friend here, uh, Dr. Jones, sees his password, will he remember it?"

"I'm not sure," Dubov replied.

"Humph," chuckled Frankel. This was going to be child's play.

Volodinsky leaned over Frankel's shoulder to watch as the hacker scrolled through the files. One by one, the file names appeared, and one by one Volodinsky said, "No."

Next, Frankel queried the file manager for unlisted files. Bringing them up sequentially he asked, "How about these?"

Volodinsky examined each one. Again, they were all meaningless numbers or letters.

As the seconds ticked by, Frankel's agitation grew. With only seven and a half minutes left to get the full seven hundred and fifty, he clicked the exit command. "Let's go back to the beginning. Watch carefully while I check the icons."

The icon menu appeared on the screen. Frankel grunted, "Recognize any of these?"

"No," Volodinsky replied.

At the end of the group Frankel stopped. "That's a strange one. I've never seen anything like that."

"What is it?" Dubov asked.

"A big dog's head."

"It's not a dog, it's a *wolf*," Volodinsky corrected.

"Okay, wolf—dog, same difference."

Wolf? It *was* a wolf. Dubov examined the icon. "The wolf's ticket. That's what Boyra was trying to tell us."

Frankel clicked the icon twice. The screen lighted up with the command, "Enter Password Now."

"Most excellent," Frankel muttered. The file had been encrypted using WordPerfect's password file lock. Reaching into a plastic case containing several computer discs, he selected one labeled WPPASS.

If that didn't work he would try HYPERZAP. In thirty seconds the letters *V-o-l-c-h-y b-i-l-e-t*, appeared on the screen.

"Is that it?" asked Frankel.

"Yeah. That's it," Dubov replied, crouching over Frankel's shoulder.

Frankel returned to the wolf's head icon, clicked twice, then typed in *Volchy bilet*. Black letters appeared against a red background. The head of a cartoon wolf appeared at the top of the screen. Below was headlined, *Firing Sequence: 100-Kiloton Nuclear Warhead, Model SS-N-23*.

Frankel gawked, "Firing sequence? What the hell is this? Are you guys *meshuga*? This is *really* going to cost you—"

Captain Marvel's words were cut short by the slicing force from the piano wire garrote looped around his neck. Blood gushed from the severed carotid arteries onto the computer keys as Dubov slammed his knee into the back of Frankel's neck, jerking the wire back until he heard a snap.

OCTOBER 31: NEW YORK: 9:47A.M.

Alphonse Sapp carefully examined each of the twenty-five photos taped to the wall. "Dat's the one," he exclaimed, pointing a scarred, misshapen finger at Hashim's picture. "Dat's the guy I seen. Now where's my ten grand?"

"Not so fast, Mr. Sapp," replied Nancy Lopez, Director of the Nuclear Emergency Search Team. He was the seventy-third person since midnight claiming to have spotted Hashim.

Still out of breath from having rushed down from field operations at the UN building, Lopez sat back in the cramped, institutional chair, waiting for her surging pulse to calm down. The fifty-five block, bone-rattling, pothole-dodging race down East River Drive to the tactical command center at Federal Plaza had consumed a valuable twenty-three minutes. The checklist in her hand was beginning to blur. Had she remembered to notify the meteorological unit to release the weather balloons for tracking the fallout pattern? Right—there was the check mark. George Thorn had taken care of it at 0430.

Scrutinizing Sapp closely, she studied the pupils of his eyes for signs of lying. She desperately needed an indication he was telling the truth. At least he had picked out the correct picture, but the newspapers and TV had been showing a similar one all over town for the past fifty-two hours. Holding a duplicate photo of Hashim twelve inches from Sapp's face, she asked, "You're telling me you delivered a large plastic container to an apartment in downtown Manhattan for this man? Say again the place and date."

"Dat's right." Sapp replied, indignant at having to repeat himself. "It was at da Skyview Plaza, North Tower; you know, da one over in Battery Park City." Looking at a series of barely legible notes scribbled on the back of an Aqueduct racing form, he continued, "Let's see. It was October 17, in da afternoon. Dat's right, da seventeenth. Hey, where was youse guys? I called yesterday morning. I told dem bozos everything. They said they'd get right back with me. Never heard from 'em again. I waited all day long for dat damn phone call. Had to tell my boss I was sick and miss work. I almost got fired. Took a cab over here dis morning to tell youse in person and git my money. All the way from Brooklyn. Youse owe me an extra twelve-fifty."

The cellular phone clipped to Lopez's belt began to vibrate. She flipped it open, "Lopez."

"Mike, here. You looking for me?"

"Have the vans picked up *any* radiation in the UN grid?"

"Negative. We got a false positive from a mobile X-ray machine, but that's all."

Lopez dropped her head. "Okay. Take one last swing around Grand Central, then scoot on down to the World Trade Center." They were rapidly running out of options. The radiation detector vans hadn't found a single, unusual burst of neutron or gamma radiation. Other than the vans, she was having to rely on a limited force of 135 two-person search teams to comb Manhattan's labyrinth of public, commercial, and apartment complexes. Each team carried a suitcase crammed with sodium iodide crystal detectors capable of detecting minute traces of gamma radiation. But the narrow streets and tall buildings made such locators virtually useless. It certainly would have been helpful to have had another 200 teams scouring the area. What was Washington thinking, that this was just a walk in the park?

Exhaling slowly, Lopez studied Alphonse Sapp. Watching him

fiddle with the dial of his portable Walkman, she wondered why command center had waited so long to tell her about him.

It was probably better she not know. The switchboard at NEST central had been swamped with hundreds of false sightings, sending NEST and FBI agents scurrying all over Manhattan, chasing shadows. In the confusion Alphonse Sapp had been lost, or more precisely, neatly tucked between the cracks. His call, logged in at 1045 hours, 30 October, had been shuffled to the bottom of the pile with the notation, "Priority 2, rpt a prob false. Skyview chkd & clrd: 1233 hrs, 30 Oct. Agts C. Pollock, G. Klimas tlkd w Quincy Totten, bldg super, N. Tower, Skyview Plaza. Super failed to ID photo of Hashim. Rptd no—repeat no deliveries of lg appliances to apts on 16, 17 or 18 Oct. No phys insp wrntd."

Lopez turned to Sapp. "October 17? You're sure?"

"Yep. I had a toothache dat morning. It kept me up all night. Right after I moved dat refrigerator, I went to the dentist and had an impacted tooth pulled. I ain't about to forget a pain like dat. It hurt like hell."

"Do you remember the apartment number?"

Sapp looked at his scribbling. "It was—let's see, uh, yeah, apartment 2807. That A-rab had dat refrigerator inside some funny looking blue plastic container." He held out his hand, "Now, where's my ten grand?"

"What shade of blue? Dark? Medium?"

"What shade? What does dat matter?" Sapp asked, testily. "Youse gonna pay me or not?"

"Please, Mr. Sapp. You'll *get* your money." He was close, *so* close to giving her the confirmation needed. Lopez could feel the frustration welling up in her throat. Rising to her feet, she started pacing back and forth, "Please, it's very important—what shade of blue?"

Sapp crossed his arms and stared glumly out the window. After a moment of prickly silence, he said, "Okay, okay, don't get all bent out of shape. It was light blue. Baby blue, like da sky."

Lopez quickly sat down, facing Sapp, "Good. Now, what about markings. Were there any numbers or letters on the container?"

Sapp scratched his head. "There was something—yeah, there was big, black numbers and letters on the side dat said 'GE refrigerator.'"

That's it, Lopez thought. He was legit. The reference to a baby blue plastic container, the black markings, GE refrigerator written on its side. His statements matched the FBI's poop sheet. It had to be the one. She glanced at her watch—1009. The report from Langley said the explosion was scheduled for the third call for Islamic prayer. That was 1227 hours. There was still time for a full scale search.

WILLIAMSBURG: 10:37A.M.

"You should've heard Bastardi," Warner said. "He threatened to have me *court-martialed*. He was so mad, he slammed the phone down, right in my ear. Said he knew I was the one who put that warning about New York in the President's Daily Brief. Wants me to report to his office first thing tomorrow morning. I think he's losing it."

The laughter that echoed off the walls of the War Room momentarily broke the tension and foreboding that hung over Bosworth House like a shroud.

In the reliance building's message center, Kat busied herself cross-checking the monitors connected by ground cables to the shock resistant video cameras installed on towers at Newark airport. The camera lenses were trained on mid and lower Manhattan and were capable of surviving the heat wave, shock front, and electromagnetic pulse of a one megaton explosion.

In the War Room, Marcie adjusted the reception from the five overhead TV monitors, each assigned a different network—CNN, CBS, NBC, ABC, and FOX News.

Friar opened and checked the secure, hard-wired phone lines set up with Langley and FBI headquarters in Washington. If and when the explosion occurred, it would be critical to have the insulated communications network up and running.

"I appreciate your letting me join you for the countdown," said Tovi. Friar had invited the Sandman over for the deathwatch. There was something comforting about being together at a time like this.

The door to the garden burst open. Kat rushed in. "Latest report from Nancy Lopez. They've got a hot lead at an apartment complex near the World Trade Center. She rates it a high probable."

"Excellent," replied Warner. "But if the warhead's not there, she'd better clear her teams out of Manhattan, pronto. They can helicopter over to the backup command center at Newark airport."

"She's not leaving," said Kat. "She's released anyone who wants to go, but so far, no takers."

Friar shook his head. There was a fine line between foolhardiness and bravery. Nothing required them to commit suicide. "What about the FBI?"

Exhausted from lack of sleep, Kat sat down in a chair. "Coyote passed word to his force at 5:30A.M., that there's a nuclear alert. Stay or leave, it's their option. Most left early this morning. The only ones staying behind are those involved with the search and some volunteer unmarrieds."

Unmarrieds. Kat repeated the word softly to herself. Singles like her were expendable. A wave of regret engulfed her, making her feel empty and alone. An inner voice reminded her that she was one of *those*, the sacrificial unmarrieds. There was no significant other to mourn if she disappeared in a flash of nuclear light.

Tovi lit his pipe, and watched the Play-of-the-Day, on CNN. It was a Hail Mary from mid-court that stripped the net just before the final buzzer. He wondered what prompted America's obsession with sports. It reminded him of the Roman Empire with its coliseums and gladiators. He glanced at a second monitor tuned to a morning soap opera. He shook his head. At least, there was no hint of unusual activity.

Turning to Friar, Tovi asked, "What's your guess on the number of victims joining the Nation of the Dead today?"

Friar stopped toying with the communications line. "Nation of the Dead? Haven't heard of that one."

"It's a morbid concept thought up by Gil Elliot, a Scotsman. He invented a fictitious nation made up of all those killed by their fellow creatures during our *civilized* twentieth century. It's an equal opportunity country. Membership's open to anyone slaughtered by wars, genocides, massacres, pogroms—whatever. Includes civilians as well as combatants. Most body counts don't bother with civilians, they're too inconsequential. He estimates membership at well over 100 million and climbing."

"One hundred million sounds low," replied Friar. "I saw an article by Rummel pegging the number killed by governments this century at 170 million. That's about the total population of Russia." Last night he had dreamed of Joanie and Kevin. Kevin was laughing and swinging that little red plastic sand bucket he had given him for his last birthday. It had been so vivid.

Looking out the window at the garden, Tovi said, "Killing. That's one thing we've certainly perfected." In his book, Elliot had discussed the evolution during the twentieth century of the capacity to destroy. He pointed out that with the development of thermonuclear warheads, mankind now has access to the total-death-machine.

"At least the nuclear option has kept us out of World War III."

"So far," Tovi replied. The 200-plus nuclear warheads in Israel's arsenal had certainly been instrumental in guaranteeing its survival. "If this warhead goes off, what's your best guess as to casualties?"

Friar walked over to the map of Manhattan hanging on the wall. He held a piece of clear acetate over lower Manhattan. There were two circles drawn on the sheet. One four inches in diameter, the other, eight. "Depends on which warhead they use. If it's the 100-kiloton from the cruise missile, I'd say anywhere from six hundred thousand to a million. If it's one of the larger nukes from the Satan-18, I'd guess 1.2 to 2 million."

Tovi studied the map. What if Dubov was planning on using all five warheads at once? Five cities—destroyed in the blink of an eye. That might force the US to unleash its total-death-machine, especially if they thought the Russians were involved.

"I hope they find it in time, "Marcie interjected. "Nancy Lopez said they have a good lead."

Friar bent over and kissed her tenderly on the forehead. He loved her for her unbounded optimism. She always saw the glass as half-full. Turning back to Tovi he said, "For the last twenty-four hours, Oppenheimer's quote at Trinity has been running through my mind. The one from the *Bhagavad-Gita,* 'Now I am become Death, the destroyer of worlds.'"

"Yeah, I know," Tovi replied. "This waiting has made me philosophical too. For me its the passage from Deuteronomy 30:19, 'I have set before you life and death, the blessing and the curse; therefore, choose life.' "

MANHATTAN: 11:12 AM

The *chop, chop, chop* from the twin rotor blades of the dark green Bell UH-1A Iroquois was the only sound heard on the roof of Skyview Plaza. Silently and with military precision, eight black-clad agents of the FBI's SWAT team, and six members of NEST, dressed in canary-yellow contamination suits, slid down landing ropes.

"*Quickdraw-two, Quickdraw-three, this is Quickdraw-one, report,*" ordered the terse, staccato voice.

"*Quickdraw-two, all ground entrances secure.*"

"*Quickdraw-three, roof secure.*"

"*Roger. There are no, repeat, no body images in target area. Begin advance. Rappellers stand by.*"

A battered, Ford van with TV News 27 painted on its side slowed to a halt at the corner of South End and Albany. Out of breath from his two-pack-a-day cigarette habit, Tom Bratlick climbed out and pinned a faded, ten-year-old photo ID to the lapel of his maroon sports jacket. Keeping an eye on the Huey hovering overhead and occasionally glancing at the black-garbed SWAT team guarding the entrance to the Skyview Plaza, he dropped his cigarette on the street and ground it into the concrete with the toe of his polished, Italian loafer. Reaching in his pocket, he withdrew a cheap, plastic comb and passed it lightly over his new, Astro-Man hairpiece. Examining his reflection in the van's side mirror, he adjusted his tie, and with his right index finger wrapped around a used, cotton handkerchief, rubbed the tobacco scum from his teeth. He wanted to look his best, in case his new squeeze at the station, Sheena Morgan, was watching.

Rapping loudly on the side of the van, Bratlick called to a police officer stringing yellow barrier-tape along a series of wooden saw-horses, "Say, Officer. What the hell's going on up there?" He had discovered long ago that if you had a TV camera and microphone, the cops would roll over on cue.

A ponytailed cameraman dressed in Levi's jeans and a faded Yankees sweatshirt, hopped out of the back of the van. Shifting the Channel-27 video-camera to his shoulder, he began panning the building, the policeman, Bratlick, and the helicopter.

Spotting the camera, the cop adjusted his cap and ambled over.

He held his head to the left so his good side was pointed towards the lens. In a loud voice he announced, "Hi, I'm Officer Deak. Jenci Deak. Those people—the ones you see up there, are making a movie." This was his first chance to practice the elocution lessons he had taken in acting class. "It is a made-for-TV action thriller called 'Manhattan Skyjack.'" Turning back towards Bratlick, he lowered his voice, "That's all they told me."

Bratlick stared at the helicopter circling the roof, then reached for another cigarette. "Nothing but a goddamned TV movie," he wheezed, motioning to the cameraman to stop filming. He wasn't going to waste footage advertising another station's movie. Besides, entertainment was Stew Axleworthy's beat and he wasn't about to do the grunt-work for that young, blond, curly haired snot. It all looked so real, the uniforms, the helicopter, the use of a major apartment building. Funny, he didn't see any movie or TV cameras. They must be on the roof or in the chopper. He wondered how the director had wrangled a city permit to fly so close to the roof of an occupied apartment building. Shaking his head, he mumbled, "Connections. Connections and payola."

"Shit, thought we had something there," Bratlick grumbled to the cameraman, who was leaning against the rear of the van. "Let's pack it up and get the hell out of here. May as well go over to City Hall and get a couple of shots of the fucking mayor handing out his Halloween treats."

"Quickdraw-three, in position."

"Enter, now!"

The door to apartment 2807 splintered into a hundred pieces as two muscular members of the FBI's SWAT team slammed a hand-held battering ram through the flimsy wooden frame. Four agents rushed into the apartment, submachine guns held tightly to their sides. Silence. The place was empty.

"This is Quickdraw-three. Target secure. Apartment empty."

From her command post on the top of the roof, Lopez swung the mouthpiece on her headset into position. "This is Granny-one. Granny-two, commence radiation check."

Two members of NEST's disabling team quickly moved into the apartment, waving probes from their portable Geiger counters from wall to wall. In the kitchen, beside the refrigerator, the dials began to flutter. There was a faint, telltale *click, click, click.* As the probes swept over the refrigerator, the chatter grew louder.

"This is Granny-two. Radiation readings in kitchen area light, but active around a refrigerator."

"This is Granny-one. Granny-two, commence object analysis."

Two members of NEST's diagnostic and assessment team wheeled in a portable X-ray machine strapped to a cart. A set of four wands were stationed around the perimeter of the refrigerator and the monitor switched on. Dark shadows from the refrigerator's interior appeared on the screen.

"Granny-one, this is Granny-two. Soft mass readings with elongated shadows inside refrigerator. Has consistency of meat with bone. Negative metal objects."

Lopez felt her pulse racing, and hoped no one noticed her shaking hands. In a steady voice she said, "This is Granny-one. Any wires, batteries, booby traps?"

"Negative. Only soft-mass images.

Soft mass? Nothing but *soft mass.* "Damn," Lopez muttered, scolding herself for having believed Alphonse Sapp. All this for a refrigerator full of groceries. Still, there were the radiation readings. "Granny-two, enter refrigerator for visual examination and radiation check."

A cart-mounted, liquid cutter was wheeled in. The high speed drill head, cooled by a steady stream of water, was capable of slicing through metal in seconds. Studying the monitor carefully, the team leader assessed the shaded contents one last time.

"Request permission for frontal opening."

"Affirmative," Lopez replied. If the radiation readings proved negative, she would sweep the building, then put the NEST team back working the streets. Maybe concentrate them in the Wall Street grid.

Grasping the refrigerator door handle with both hands, the team leader gave a hard tug. With little resistance, the door swung open. Out plopped the broken body of Quincy Totten.

Lopez could hear the team leader's sudden intake of breath. "Granny-two, are you all right?"

"Yeah. I'm okay. It's a goddamned body."

"Great," shouted Lopez, energized by the discovery. A body meant a murder, and a murder meant there was something to hide. "Check for radiation."

After dragging Totten's corpse from the refrigerator, the NEST team examined the empty refrigerator. "*This is Granny-two. There is no, repeat, no explosive device inside target. Traces of residual radiation are strong. Interior of target cut to house object of unusual configuration.*"

A feeling of elation swept over Lopez. The warhead *had* been there. "This is Granny-one. Teams Able, Baker, and Charlie form up and sweep the building." She looked at her watch—1137 hours. Fifty minutes until the third call for prayer. Where was that warhead? Maybe in the garage, basement, or parking—

"*Eagle-four to Granny-one.*" It was the Huey hovering overhead.

Lopez glanced up at the helicopter, two hundred feet away. "Come in Eagle-four."

"*I have a hot reading coming from the roof near you. Advise.*"

Lopez almost choked. "This is Granny-one. All NEST teams report to the roof on the double. We have a hit." Still watching the helicopter, she asked, "Eagle-four, have you pinpointed the exact location?"

"*Radiation appears to be coming from either the air conditioning duct, or that tower near you.*"

That's it, Lopez thought, looking up at the metal housing on top of the tower. She had been standing underneath the warhead the whole time. Checking the ladder leading to the platform, she saw wires under each rung. The ladder was mined, the C-4 would have to be airlifted to the top of he housing. "Granny-two, prepare a satchel charge. Eagle-four, lower a cable."

"*Affirmative. Cable being lowered.*"

Speaking rapidly into her headset, she ordered, "Granny-four, contact President Morehead. Request authorization to destroy the warhead in place with high explosives."

There was no time to dismantle the device. It would have to be blasted apart, before it could detonate as a nuclear explosion. The radioactive dust from the plutonium-239, uranium-235, and uranium-238 would kill hundreds, but better that than a million. "This

is Granny-one. All nonessential personnel clear the area at once."
Noting their hesitancy, she screamed, "I mean now, goddamnit!
Now!"

Lopez watched as Granny-two attached himself to the helicopter
cable and signaled to be lifted to the top of the tower. If anything
went wrong, it was a suicide mission. She felt a lump in her throat as
she watched the volunteers—*her* volunteers—functioning with the
precision of a finely jeweled Swiss clock.

"Granny-one, this is Granny-four."

"Go ahead, Granny-four."

*"Unable to reach the President. He's having lunch at the Congres-
sional Club. All communications are being channeled through Bruce
Bastardi. Estimate it will take ten to fifteen minutes to establish contact
with the President."*

Lopez blinked in disbelief. Bastardi had personally assured her
Morehead would be standing by. As head of NEST, her orders were
clear—do not blow up a live nuclear warhead in a populated area
without the President's *personal* authorization. Staring at her watch—
1158—she waited. Intelligence had said the estimated deadline for
detonation was 1227 hours. Estimated? What the hell did that mean?
What if they were wrong? From the left front pocket of her jacket,
she removed the rosary her grandmother had given her at her chris-
tening. It was a sterling silver cross with onyx beads. Clutching it
firmly in her right hand, she held it over her heart. "Holy Mary,
Mother of God, pray for us now at the hour of our deaths."

Chapter 16

OCTOBER 31: MANHATTAN: 12:00 NOON

"Visibility eight miles, ceiling unlimited," droned Chad Dalrymple, WNZT's discontented weatherman. Two years at the station providing background color by cracking jokes about potholes and rained-out picnics was starting to wear thin. In two months he hoped to graduate to a more lucrative, visible slot on the morning news team. "Grandpa Moses," as he liked to refer to James Moses Wilberforce, 3d, was about to be downsized. The fact Wilberforce was a womanizing alcoholic had less to do with his imminent departure than the station's subbasement ratings. Poor ratings meant that a career had to be sacrificed on the altar of profitability, and the suits had decided that Wilberforce, with his high salary and failing health, was the one.

Scuttlebutt had it the station was looking for an Asian female as a replacement, but that would mean an unbalanced team of three women and only one man. To enhance his ethnic profile, Dalrymple had paid fifteen hundred dollars to Gotham Genealogy, Ltd. to find and authenticate a Cherokee ancestor on his maternal side. He also had that crushed knee from last year's skiing accident. Next week he would start wearing a removable leg brace and limping whenever eyes were watching. With any luck, his disabled Native-American would trump plain Asian female. He had thought about changing his middle name to Keetoowah, but didn't want to appear *too* obvious.

On the advice of his voice coach, Dalrymple had decided to lower his delivery half an octave to add more authority. Today was the first test of his new, improved timbre. "Temperature's a brisk forty-four degrees with a wind chill of thirty-six." Still too high. Lowering his chin and relaxing his vocal chords, he tried again, "Breeze is out of the southwest at four miles an hour with occasional gusts from eight to ten. Scattered clouds are forecast for late afternoon with only a ten percent chance of early evening precipitation. All in all, a fairly nice Halloween forecast for you ghosts and goblins out there in the spooky world of W-N-Z-T." There, that was better. Dalrymple sat back and gazed lovingly, appreciatively at his image on the monitor. He was pleased at the way the camera picked up the rich, navy-blue of his new Barneys blazer. He frowned as an ad for discount airline coupons began to roll across the screen, blocking his face. During the station break, he would have a friendly chat with the editor in the control booth.

At Fraunces Tavern on Pearl and Broad, an unusually heavy lunch time crowd, lured out of their apartments and hotel rooms by the cool, sunny weather, lined up for reservations. In the Paul Revere ballroom a red, white, and blue banner headlined "Society of the Cincinnati Welcomes New Members." The room projected a genial atmosphere of inherited money, mixed with quiet hubris. In front of an empty place at the Charleston table, sat a card for David Ellsworth Pellingham III. The idle chatter from complacent sponsors and appreciative, fawning inductees gradually subsided as the master of ceremonies gaveled the meeting to order. The Cincinnati prided itself with starting on time.

Up and down Wall Street, assorted movers and shakers from the financial world poured out of their concrete and steel warrens, and hurried down William Street toward Delmonico's, Sloppy Louie's, or Sweets for one more, two hour, three martini lunch. International wheeler-dealers, from mega-priced suites at the World Trade Center escorted petrodollar sheiks, pliable government officials, and Colombian drug-money launderers to power lunches at the immaculately terraced Windows on the World.

In Battery Park, Rachel Levy pushed her Peg Perego stroller along the pitted sidewalk. Daniel, her nine-month-old son, outfitted in an orange and black Halloween clown costume from FAO Schwarz, cooed at the soft, white clouds drifting overhead. For Rachel, the outing was a welcome escape from her claustrophobic, exorbitantly priced apartment at Golden Vistas. She shuddered at the chill wind sweeping in from the Hudson River. It reminded her there weren't many pleasant days left before winter imprisoned her in her cramped, two-bedroom, single-bath high-rise.

On the southern tip of the island, a group of well-behaved seventh graders from Newark's St. Christopher's Academy scrambled aboard the Statue of Liberty Ferry. The special Halloween outing, sponsored by St. Christopher's PTA, was a well-earned reward for their having completed essays in the state wide competition, "What Liberty Means To Me."

In the alley beside the Guang Ho Vietnamese restaurant on Fulton Street, a pack of ravenous rats clawed through the overflowing garbage cans stacked haphazardly against the building. When the cold weather struck, they, and the other twenty-eight million rodents in the City, would have to seek shelter in the warm sewers and neighboring apartment and office buildings.

At the exclusive La Tour D'Or restaurant on top of Bankers Trust, 16 Wall Street, Oscar Shymanski nervously reviewed the cue cards for his keynote address. It had been quite a coup, receiving this last minute invitation to address the Board of Directors of the New York Stock Exchange. While he understood very little about the CIA's role in industrial espionage, his administrative assistant, Adriana Casale, had prepared a reasonably interesting twenty minute slide presentation. All he had to do was read the captions. Too bad Bruce Bastardi wouldn't be here to hear it.

Shymanski took a sip of chardonnay to steady his nerves. There it was again—the light-headedness, the sweaty palms, the hyperventilation. He hoped his fear of public speaking didn't make his voice quiver. It wasn't exactly a phobia, he assured himself, but a normal reaction to crowds. In fact, he had read in last Friday's *Wall Street Journal* that the average executive was more terrified of public speaking than of dying. He would manage. It was simply a matter of positive thinking, practice, and Prozac. Thank goodness he had rehearsed the presentation five times—twice in that hotel room with Adriana, and three times in front of a mirror. He looked at his watch. 12:02:30. It would be over soon.

Nancy Lopez paced the roof at Skyview Plaza. Where the hell was President Morehead? With all the electronic hardware in the world at his disposal it was unforgivable that he was not available. At least she could start the evacuation of Skyview Plaza. "Quickdraw-one, this is Granny-one. Pull the building's fire alarm."

Lopez could see Granny-two standing on top of the metal housing, waiting to set the timer on the four pound charge of C-4. If they didn't act soon, it would be too late. Checking her watch—12:03:25 —she decided, *That's it!* No more waiting. She would blow the warhead.

"Granny-two, this is Granny-one. Set the timer for fifteen minutes." That should give him enough time to re-hook the helicopter cable and make his get away. She watched while the Huey hovered protectively overhead, ready to pull them to safety.

12:03:57P.M.

As programmed, the firing circuit of the 100 kiloton nuclear warhead closed with a faintly audible, electrical *click*. The thermonuclear fission-fusion detonation had begun. The first electrons reaching the chemical explosive, wrapped evenly around the fission trigger, initiated a blast forcing the perfectly shaped, spherical pit of plutonium-239, to implode into its critical mass. At the same time, the neutron initiator at the base of the warhead sent a burst of neutrons hurtling into the condensed Pu-239, triggering an uncontrolled, fission chain reaction.

In less than a millionth of a second, the fission of the plutonium-239, boosted by the fusion of the deuterium-tritium gas at the core of the fission trigger, generated temperatures exceeding 20 million degrees Fahrenheit. This unearthly temperature produced X-rays powerful enough to compress the warhead's main fusion pit located twelve inches from the fission trigger. The fusion pit consisted of an outer layer of uranium-238 encircling a thicker, inner layer of lithium deuteride which, in turn, enclosed a core of uranium-235. As the layer of U-238 and the core of U-235 reached critical mass, they joined with the Pu-239 in a chain reaction, forcing the fusion of the lithium deuteride. In the millionths of a second it took the fusion of the lithium deuteride to combine with the fission of the U-238, U-235, and Pu-239, the resulting thermonuclear explosion set in motion a doomsday scenario blasting open the jaws of hell.

At the instant of explosion, a burst of deadly gamma rays and neutrons raced out from the disintegrating tower at the speed of light. This wave of initial radiation delivered a fatal dose of at least 1,000 roentgens equivalent man to anyone caught in the open within a mile of Skyview Plaza. Passengers in cars exiting the Holland Tunnel were bombarded with over 1,000 rem. In Battery Park, Rachel Levy and Daniel, only six-tenths of a mile from ground zero, glowed in a purplish haze of gamma-iodized light as they were saturated with 28,000 rem. Pedestrians, street vendors, and tourists as far away as Chinatown's Columbus Park were shot through with a lethal 1,500 rem. But, slow, painful death from radiation poisoning was not their fate. Within seconds, the heat and blast waves would arrive.

Simultaneously with the initial nuclear radiation, gamma rays racing out from the point of detonation collided with the surrounding air, generating an electromagnetic pulse, or EMP, of tens of thousands of volts of energy. This electrical surge knocked out all communication satellites over lower Manhattan and totally destroyed the power grids of Manhattan, Queens, Brooklyn, and Jersey City. The computer networks of the New York and American stock exchanges were instantly obliterated, as were all the local data storage systems for what, two seconds before, had been the financial center of the world.

As the fission-fusion reaction burned itself out in a fraction of a second, the released energy forged an expanding fireball. Within a tenth of a second, the fireball had grown to 500 feet in diameter, totally engulfing the Skyview Plaza apartment complex. In three and a half seconds the fireball reached its maximum width of 3,700 feet. This suffocating, crushing, broiling, destructive envelope of fire, nuclear radiation, wind, and shock trailed closely behind the heat and blast waves, swallowing the World Financial Center, the Federal Office Building, the World Trade Center, Trinity Church, the American Stock Exchange, Battery Park City, St. Paul's Chapel, the New

York Telephone Building, and the Equitable Building. The life force of all organic matter within this churning circle of energy was instantly snuffed out by temperatures exceeding 1,000 calories per square centimeter.

During the expansion of the fireball, a first, then second pulse of intense light and heat shot outward. The first thermal pulse lasted less than a tenth of a second and produced a flash of ultraviolet radiation blinding pilot Jack Gimbel and co-pilot Randy West as they made their final approach to Newark airport, nine miles away. Sightless, American Airlines flight 407, with 193 passengers and a crew of nine, veered to the right, cartwheeling into the tarmac and disappearing in a ball of flame.

The second thermal pulse, containing 35 percent of the warhead's total energy, sent out an incinerating heat wave lasting three and a half seconds. Anyone caught in the open within a mile from the point of detonation either carbonized in a puff of smoke, or was reduced to a seared bundle of black char as their internal organs boiled away. The temperature on the Statue of Liberty Ferry, still at the dock eight-tenths of a mile from Skyview Plaza, reached 97 calories per square centimeter. No one was alive by the time the burning, melting ferry disappeared into the steaming, hissing bay.

Helga Svenbjorn, an assistant superior court clerk, stood on the steps of the Jersey City County Court House, two and three-tenths miles from ground zero. It was her first day on the job and she was admiring the Manhattan skyline. The initial flash of light streaked through the lenses of her eyeballs, searing the retina and paralyzing the optic nerves. As the exposed skin on her face and arms began to bubble and steam from the three and a half second heat wave, the blast wave struck, ripping the flesh from her head and arms until it hung down like melted wax. The trial brief in her hands burst into flames.

With the formation of the fireball, the blast wave—containing over half the energy from the thermonuclear explosion—pushed ahead at supersonic speeds. This shock front of compressed air pulverized the World Financial Center and the American Express building into radioactive dust with an overpressure exceeding 225 pounds per square inch. The World Trade Center exploded into ash when it was struck by an overpressure of 200 psi.

All buildings and structures within a half mile of Skyview Plaza, were crushed and ground into radioactive waste. This concrete and molten-metal detritus was swept forward by trailing winds exceeding 1,000 miles an hour.

On Fulton Street, startled by the initial flash, the rats rose in unison and stared at the explosion. In eight-tenths of a second the heat wave struck, carbonizing their bloated bodies and turning their flashing white teeth into powdered ash.

At La Tour D'Or, four-tenths of a mile from ground zero and across the street from the New York Stock Exchange, Oscar Shymanski was standing by a picture window jotting down his final notes. When the heat wave arrived with 500 calories per square centimeter of energy, the eyelets of his Gucci loafers and the gold frame reading glasses balanced on the bridge of what had been his nose, glowed white-hot, then melted. A quarter of a second later the blast wave struck with an overpressure of 50 psi. The radioactive dust from the steel reinforced concrete building and Shymanski's carbonized remains joined the raging storm being blown towards the East River at 1200 mph.

At City Hall, the overpressure measured 20 psi. The walls of the historic 1811 structure crumbled like a sand castle before a tidal wave of 498 mph winds racing in behind the shock front. The trailing winds extinguished the flames leaping from the charred bodies of Mayor Simon Morrow and the twelve aldermen lined up on the steps of City Hall for a photo-op with Albrecht Braun, the Bürgermeister of Hamburg.

On Centre Street, the Chanel 27 news van exploded from the heat and blast waves before Tom Bratlick's bubbling hand could reach the door handle. The winds picked up the remnants, hurling them against the collapsing Municipal Building.

At the Federal Reserve Bank, eight-tenths of a mile from ground zero, an overpressure of 12 psi surrounded the building for 1.1 seconds, crushing it from the top and all sides. The mountain of gold housed deep within its bowels, was instantly entombed under a hundred tons of radioactive dust and melted steel.

The first tunnel to go was the Brooklyn Battery Tunnel. With the entrance only three-tenths of a mile from the Skyview Plaza, the heat wave and shock front caused the tunnel to explode like a giant shotgun. As the blast wave of 190 psi rolled through the tunnel at 1600 mph, gas tanks detonated scattering flaming vehicles and burning bodies out the Brooklyn end like projectiles from a Roman candle. Two seconds later the shock front struck the Manhattan entrance to the Holland Tunnel. Exploding cars and tumbling bodies shot out the Twelfth and Fourteenth Street exits in Jersey City, slamming against concrete abutments and metal light posts. On the Brooklyn and Manhattan bridges, cars and trucks were hurled like toy vehicles over the guardrails into the East River.

When the first thermal pulse streaked through Greenwich Village, grad student, Stephen J. Morehead, Jr., was seated at a study table at NYU's Bobst Library. He was busy making final preparations for the oral defense of his doctoral dissertation, "The Moral Mandates of a Just Society." Two secret service agents, assigned to guard the President's son, sat four tables away.

Stephen was immediately blinded by the light as the heat wave from the second thermal pulse engulfed Washington Square. Instinctively he grabbed for the only hard copy of his prized dissertation, knocking over a row of carefully stacked research books. Seconds later, the blast wave smashed into the library with an overpressure of 4.6 psi, followed by drag force winds of 140 mph. The splintering glass from the windows of the central, twelve-story atrium, hurled millions of razor-sharp shards through the building's interior at 245 feet per second. Stephen's torso stiffened, then flashed brilliant red as the glass fragments shredded his body. Racing in through the broken window frames, the shock front crushed the library floors and walls with a force exceeding 60 tons per 100 square meters. Stephen's limp corpse, sucked from the building by the trailing winds, skidded to a stop a hundred feet away, buried under tons of scorched books, library shelves, and rubble.

The sunshine in Washington Square was instantly blotted out by the swirling, churning radioactive dust. The only light came from the fires of shattered buildings, smashed vehicles, and exploding gas mains. Thirty-seven seconds later an afterwind measuring 115 mph came roaring back in the opposite direction, rushing towards the fireball which was now rising over Manhattan at 300 feet per second. The pulsating, orange-red-yellow-blue fireball was forming its signature tombstone—a mushroom shaped cloud.

WILLIAMSBURG: 1:17P.M.

One by one, the TV screens at Bosworth House blinked back to life as the major news channels activated emergency power systems. Only CBS was still out, its main broadcasting station and relay satellites, victims of the electromagnetic pulse. Mobile CNN units were already broadcasting from Union City, New Jersey, and JFK airport, their cameras focusing on the inferno billowing up from lower Manhattan. With filters and long range lenses, the camera crews tried to penetrate the pall of dust, debris, and smoke, but all that could be seen were fingers of fire shooting skyward through the thick, dirty columns of ash and soot. An NBC helicopter at Newark airport was preparing to lift off, ignoring the tower's warning of radioactive contamination in the dust clouds. On TV, chaotic scenes kept shifting back and forth from Washington to New York as frantic news editors tried to determine what had happened.

"Has the magnitude of the blast been determined?" Friar asked.

"NEST estimates the strength at between 98 and 104 kilotons," replied Kat, who was listening to the excited voices jabbering away over her head set.

"Any estimate on casualties?"

"Not yet."

"What about Nancy Lopez?" asked Warner, already knowing the answer.

Kat lowered her head. There was no chance anyone near Skyview Plaza had made it. Only a few sporadic signals from NEST teams stationed in Central Park and above, were still being picked up.

"Where's Tovi Hersch?" asked Warner.

"He left right after the explosion," Friar said. "Had to get back and report to Tel Aviv."

"Vaughn's on the line," Marcie said, handing the phone to Warner.

"Bryan, you were right. We should've gone over Bastardi's head, straight to Morehead. No excuse for not having launched a full scale search, none at all. There's going to be hell to pay."

It wasn't hard for Warner to imagine the confusion in Washington. "What I recommend is that we—"

"You wouldn't believe the turmoil. Washington's a madhouse. There're crazy people everywhere, running around yelling and screaming at each other. Morehead's ordered defense to go to DefCon 2. The White House thinks the Russians may be involved, that this could be the start of a major attack."

"There's no danger of that," Warner assured him, worried about an overreaction. Defense Condition 2—one step away from total war. All 7,250 operational strategic nuclear weapons in America's arsenal, armed and ready to fly. But, what were their targets? Russia? Iraq? The only other time the US had ever gone to DefCon 2 was October 24, 1962, at the height of the Cuban missile crisis.

"Easy for you to say. Try telling that to the White House or the press."

"What's Congress's position?"

"Don't know. Most politicians are abandoning ship and getting out of town. They're afraid Washington might be next. Morehead's on Air Force One circling somewhere over the Atlantic. I'm at Langley, trying to convene an emergency meeting of the National Security Council."

"The NSC? That's Bastardi's organization."

"Can't be helped. It has the people we need—The President, the Vice President, the Secretaries of State and Defense, along with the Chairman of the Joint Chiefs. By the way, I'm moving my base of operations down to Camp Peary. I'll try to get the meeting held there. I want you and Clarke to attend. You know more about what's going on than anyone. I'll let you know when and where."

As soon as Vaughn hung up, Marcie waved her arms to get everyone's attention. On all the TV screens was a special broadcast, "Live from the White House." The program began with a close-up of President Morehead, hair neatly combed, facial muscles relaxed, calmly sitting at his desk looking directly into the camera. While the "Star-Spangled Banner" filled the soundtrack, an unruffled Morehead opened a folder containing a neatly typed message. Friar, Warner, Kat, and Marcie watched as the camera lens zoomed back, giving a full view of the Oval Office. Standing behind the President was Vice President Ambrose Hambright, Secretary of State Eileen Hohlt, and Bruce Bastardi. With the camera still at a comfortable distance, the President began to speak. An excited, elevated voice, assured the public that the situation—although not fully known at this time—was definitely under control. He promised that the guilty parties would be swiftly apprehended and brought to justice.

"The video part is prerecorded," observed Friar. "He's transmitting from Air Force One but they're using a canned tape. Watch his lips, they're not synchronized with the words."

While Morehead continued to talk, an emergency bulletin flashed across the bottom of the CNN screen. Vice President Hambright's helicopter had just collided with a Huey carrying his security detail. It was not known if there were any survivors.

"Morehead's going to have a hard time explaining that one," Marcie said, watching the picture of a healthy, smiling Hambright standing behind the President.

Friar chuckled at the absurdity. The backlash would serve them right for dishing out such amateurishly prepared propaganda. "We've got better things to do than watch this farce." It was obvious, Morehead didn't have a clue as to what had happened.

"What about New York?" asked Warner.

"Forget New York," said Friar. "That's history. We've got to concentrate on finding the other four warheads."

When the President's special broadcast was cut off in mid-sentence, pictures of the devastation again filled the screens. On ABC, a mobile news crew at Bellevue Hospital was interviewing hordes of burned and wounded victims jamming First Avenue from East Twenty-sixth to East Thirtieth Streets. Emergency triage teams were shown trying to separate the living from the soon-to-be dead.

Friar signaled Kat to join him in the Sidebar. When the door was shut he said, "It's time for the Bureau to pull in members of the Dolgochenskaya syndicate."

"But, they're not the ones—"

"Yeah, I know, but we need to smoke Dubov out into the open. Make him think we've swallowed his story. Right now, he's our best lead for locating the rest of the warheads."

"Maybe we'll find those two tattooed mutts," Kat said hopefully.

"Maybe."

There was a knock on the door. It was Marcie. "Tovi's on the line." She frowned as she noticed Kat standing close to Friar, casually resting her hand on his arm.

"Patch him through," Friar said, pulling his cell phone from its belt holster.

"*Can you come over?*"

"Be right there."

1:37 PM

Tovi stood by a window in the Robert Graves House, looking at the empty streets below. DOG street was deserted except for a tabby cat toying with its mouse-prey. The shock of events had sent the tourists scurrying inside to gape, dumbfounded, at the death throes of lower Manhattan being played out on TV. It wouldn't be long before they came flocking back into the sunshine, seeking the communal therapy of being surrounded by healthy, complete humans—not those twisted, burned freaks in New York. They would want assurances this nightmare couldn't happen to them. He had seen it all before in Tel Aviv on June 5, 1967, at the outbreak of the Six Day War, and again on October 6, 1973, at the start of the Yom Kippur War.

Friar knocked, then entered.

Without turning, Tovi said, "You know, the US is never going to be the same." Fortress America had been irrevocably violated and the trauma would change the national psyche. Two centuries of isolation and invulnerability, gone in a nuclear nanosecond.

Friar poured himself a cup of tea and took a seat. "So far, no one's claimed responsibility."

"They will, soon enough. I imagine it'll be the Shaheeds who'll stick their necks out first. Be careful what you believe. It's Mossad's theory the militants are merely pawns." Tovi closed the blinds and took a seat beside Friar. Watching Friar closely for signs of stress, he was pleased to see there were none.

Waving a hand at the monitors tuned to CNN and NBC, Tovi said, "I hope you don't mind. It's really the best way of keeping up." Watching the chaos was hypnotic and surreal.

Pictures of burned, bloated bodies being dragged from the Hudson River with grappling hooks filled the screen on CNN. On NBC a reporter was interviewing a physicist who was pointing to an aerial view of the mushroom cloud which had risen to 40,000 feet. The radioactive mass was drifting, slowly, northeastwardly up the I-95 corridor, over the coast of Long Island and up the Connecticut shore line. The physicist spoke of rem and expected lethal doses from early fallout for Mt. Vernon, New Rochelle, Glen Cove, Stamford, Norwalk. In a dry, funeral monotone he discussed wind velocities and absorption rates.

Offering Friar some sugar for his tea, Tovi said, "Of course, it's important for Washington to keep its wits. They're not used to this kind of disaster. There's going to be tremendous pressure from the public to strike back—" his words broke off as he remembered how hard it had been for the Israelis during the Gulf War. Hit after hit from Iraq's SCUD missiles, and unable to counterattack.

Friar held the cup to his nose and breathed in the refreshing fragrance. "I've got a puzzle. The FBI traced the four Ryder rental trucks at Wanchese to an agency in Greensboro, North Carolina. All four were rented under the name of Hadi Riyami. This Riyami is a very visible member of the Shaheeds who used a personal credit card for payment. What does that tell you?"

Tovi lit his pipe. "The credit card was in Riyami's name?"

"That's right."

"It's too obvious—a false trail."

"That's my opinion also. Someone wanted us to find the four trucks." Friar held up four fingers on his left hand. "Four Ryder rental trucks. All decoys." He stuck out his thumb. "A van holding the 100-kiloton warhead heads for New York." He folded his hand. "There was a sixth vehicle."

"A truck?"

"A large one hidden behind the shed. Five warheads—six vehicles."

Tovi shifted to the edge of his chair. "That means the remaining warheads could still be together."

Friar nodded, "Placed on that sixth truck." It made sense. Keeping all four in one location would make it easier to hide and protect them. All Dubov would have to do is threaten to use the others. That would be enough.

Tovi walked over to the fax machine and retrieved a packet of papers. "This just came for you. It's a preliminary background report on Dubov."

Friar thumbed through the short report: Profile of Vakid Khadji Sayid, a k a Alexander Dubov. Spring 1982 drafted into Russian army. September 1984 sent to Afghanistan to fight mujahedeen. Seriously wounded by rocket attack on outskirts of Kabul 23 December. Shipped to military hospital, Moscow, to recuperate. January 1985 took army IQ test while at hospital. Scored highest in command. Recruited by *Glavnoye Razevedyaltelnoye*, Russian military intelligence February 1985. Trained at GRU's Andropov Red Banner Institute March-September 1985. Sent back to Kabul until released from active service May 1987. Moved to Moscow and joined Chechen crime syndicate June 1987. August 1988 enrolled by syndicate as student at University of Swansea, Wales. Spring 1992 graduated *cum laude*, English Literature. Fall 1992 sent to private camp outside Moscow run by ex-KGB for advanced training. Spring 1993 moved to the US.

"Excellent," Friar said.

"Never lose sight of the fact that he is a Chechen," Tovi warned. He recalled Mossad's dismal experience in trying to recruit Chechen agents. "He would rather cut your throat than spit. Never turn your back on him. Chechens are dangerous and cruel people to anyone they consider an enemy. They have a very different view of heaven than you."

"What's their motivation in all this? Money?"

"I've wondered that myself. What they've done seems awfully risky for a few million dollars."

"Maybe it's more than a few million."

"One important personality quirk to remember," Tovi said. "Chechens tend to underrate their opponents. They find it difficult to attribute intelligence to anyone not a Chechen. That can be a serious flaw."

A bright flash lighted the screen on NBC as a fuel tank near Greenwich Village exploded. A wall of flame leaped 400 feet into the sky. A tense voice announced, "It's an inferno—temperatures on the lower end of the island are 1200 degrees and *rising.*" There was a pause, "This just in. A firestorm has engulfed the financial district."

A message scrolled across the bottom of the screen—*Vice President Hambright confirmed dead.*

Chapter 17

After extensive arm-twisting and coaxing, Director Vaughn arranged for the National Security Council to meet at Camp Peary, the CIA's Virginia Farm operation. As expected, Bastardi had objected, but Secretary of State Eileen Hohlt and Secretary of Defense Klaus Deathridge overruled him. Located on the York River, five miles north of Williamsburg, Camp Peary was considered close enough to Washington for emergency meetings with Congress, yet secure and far enough from the media circus to allow the Council to meet undisturbed.

Called to explain what they knew about events leading up to New York, Friar and Warner waited in the anteroom of the small training building known as the Theater. Warner paced back and forth while Friar sat on a parson's bench, his back leaning against the gray, cinder block wall.

Before leaving Bosworth house, Marcie had informed them that Stephen, President Morehead's only child, was among the missing—and presumed dead. Reports from confidential White House sources said the President was taking it hard, depressed almost to the point of immobility.

While they waited, Friar watched the continuing horror show on a wall-mounted television. Images of people with blackened skin, hair burned away, disfigured so badly it was difficult to tell front from back, paraded across the screen. Reruns from a remote camera in Union Square showed solemn lines of walking dead, stumbling aimlessly about, arms held in front of them like zombies.

Since the explosion, the implementation of the government's nuclear National Emergency Contingency Plan—Victor Twelve— had not gone well. In less than twenty-four hours, Washington had degenerated into a dysfunctional mass of conflicting reports and media hysteria. Most top ranking federal officials, having classified themselves critical to national security, had abandoned their plush Capitol Hill offices and headed for higher ground.

The door to the conference room swung open. A spit-and-polish Marine Colonel, with a nametag reading "Dekker," entered the anteroom. "Mr. Warner, Mr. Clarke. They're ready."

Friar and Warner walked through a gray security door, past a humming metal detector, into a twenty-five-by-thirty foot, brightly lit, wood paneled conference room. On the far wall was a six-by-eight foot aerial photo of the I-95 corridor from Newark airport to Boston. Posted in each corner of the room were secret service agents with MP5 submachine guns slung under their arms and earphones plugged into their robotic ears.

Taking a chair at the small table facing the Council, Friar glanced at the members of the NSC, seated behind an elevated, semi-circular table. At the center was President Morehead, hands shaking so violently he could barely hold a glass of water. To his right was Bastardi, whispering into the President's ear and pointing to two red circles on the wall map. To Morehead's left sat Vaughn. Next to him was Secretary of State Eileen Miggins Hohlt, the high-energy Texan from Houston who would have been nominated for the Vice President's slot had there not been a bitter floor fight over the gender issue. To Bastardi's right sat Secretary of Defense Klaus Deathridge, holder of the Medal of Honor and no-nonsense hawk from Atlanta. He had been placed on Morehead's team to placate the hard-liners and counter the President's history of having dodged service in Vietnam by teaching high school geography in California. Absent was General Paul F. Eckel, the hard-charging Chairman of the Joint Chiefs of Staff.

Friar noted that the head table was mounted on a hastily rigged dais, elevated twelve inches above Warner's and his chairs. This infantile attempt at superiority was definitely a Bastardi touch.

As titular head of the NSC, Bastardi gaveled the meeting to order.

Glaring at Warner and Friar, he immediately demanded, "Why the hell weren't we warned there was a nuclear warhead in the US? Where was the Directorate of Operations when all this was going on?"

Friar smiled. Such posturing by the one person most responsible for the New York fiasco took real balls. Bastardi was grasping at straws to avoid blame, and it showed.

"The DO can't be faulted on this one," interjected Vaughn. He had been expecting hard questioning, but not an attack this blatant. "For the past several days, Mr. Warner and Mr. Clarke have been trying to warn anyone who would listen that New York was in danger. As I recall, the alert was even placed in the President's October 30 Daily Brief—"

"We won't go into that now," snapped Bastardi.

Feigning surprise, Friar said, "Mr. Bastardi, I'm amazed Oscar Shymanski didn't keep you better informed."

The National Security Adviser glared at Friar, the hatred seething from every pore. He had just attended a brief memorial service for his protégé at the almost empty Washington National Cathedral, and had promised himself to personally see that whoever was responsible for Oscar's death, paid a high price.

President Morehead turned and stared dully at Bastardi. His tired, sunken eyes blinked open. Was it possible that Stephen's death—that the New York devastation—could have been prevented? Fumbling with a small, engraved silver snuff box, he withdrew two light blue, oval pills, and popped them into his mouth. Washing the tablets down with a quick drink of water, he spilled a few drops on his sleeve.

Friar watched Morehead's ritual in disbelief. Two 10mg doses of Valium. He shook his head. Just what the country needed, a Chief Executive Officer and Commander in Chief strung out on drugs.

Eileen Hohlt looked up from her report. "Mr. Warner, would you give us your assessment of what's behind the New York disaster?"

For the next twenty minutes Warner briefed the Council on Murphy's mission to Cairo, the Shaheeds, Wentworth's confession, Friar's trip to Iguaçu, the suspected tie-in with a Russian syndicate, and the evidence that an additional four warheads were somewhere in the country. What he didn't disclose, because Friar had not told him, was the extent of Dubov's involvement.

Peering over the top of a pair of wire-rimmed glasses, Secretary of Defense Deathridge asked, "So, Mr. Warner, what's your conclusion as to why New York was attacked without warning?"

"It's our opinion New York is only part of a much larger plot involving blackmail. We'll know more when someone comes forward with a list of demands."

"Demands have already been made," admitted Hohlt.

Friar looked at Warner in surprise. Why hadn't they been told?

Vaughn said, "Less than an hour ago, the White House received a set of ultimatums from Sheik Gamal Jibril. He claims to be the leader of the militant Islamic group you mentioned, the Shaheeds. At 10:30 this morning, the FBI raided their headquarters in Jersey City. The Sheik was captured along with seven of his followers. They were shredding files and burning evidence when they were arrested. Interestingly enough, their building was severely damaged by the explosion. The Sheik claims full responsibility for what happened and threatens to use the other four warheads unless his conditions are met."

Mulling over Vaughn's comments, Friar was more convinced than ever the Shaheeds were merely a sideshow. Had they known about the explosion beforehand they would surely have moved their headquarters well before the thirty-first.

"I don't see how we can possibly comply with that list," said Hohlt.

"I don't see how we can refuse," countered Bastardi.

"May we see the list?" asked Warner.

Vaughn withdrew a sheet of light blue stationery from an Eyes Only NSC folder. He held it up for Morehead's permission before showing it to Warner and Friar.

Morehead nodded weakly. His glazed expression testified to the difficulty he was having following the conversation.

"There are three requirements," said Vaughn. "The first is that the United States turn over the oil fields in Kuwait and Saudi Arabia to the Supreme Islamic Council, an organization to be formed by the Shaheeds."

"I would like to point out once again," exclaimed Hohlt, her voice level and determined, "those oil fields are not ours to give."

"Not to mention the economic, political, and military consequences of transferring one-third of the world's oil supply to a bunch of terrorists," chimed in Vaughn.

"Then, goddammit, we'll just have to make them ours," snorted Bastardi.

Friar looked at Bastardi, then Morehead. He had heard Bastardi dictated foreign policy, but this was unbelievable. Was Morehead that far gone?

Vaughn continued reading from the sheet, "The second demand is that Mecca be placed under the control of the Supreme Islamic Council. It is to be managed by the Shaheeds for the benefit of all true believers of Islam."

"That's totally out of the question," declared Deathridge. "The Islamic world would never tolerate our interfering with Mecca. Can you imagine—a *billion* Muslims on a jihad against us, the Great Satan? That would be like trying to order the Pope to hand over the Vatican to the IRA."

Vaughn cleared his throat, "The last requirement is that the US renounce its support for the 'illegal' state of Israel and the 'criminal' government of Egypt."

"Impossible," said Hohlt, shaking her head vigorously.

Deathridge added, "Those demands are nothing short of a declaration of World War III. Do they think we're going to rip the world apart just to please them?"

"What choice do we have?" asked Bastardi. "They've got a nuclear gun pointed at our heads. It would be political suicide for the President to allow another American city to be bombed."

The door to the conference room swung open. General Eckel strode in, whispered a few words to Morehead, handed him a note, then took his seat.

Barely glancing at the message, Morehead passed it to Bastardi.

Bastardi read the note aloud. "General Eckel informs us we are now ready—if the President so decides—to launch a retaliatory nuclear strike against Iraq. Multiple ICBMs have been programmed to knockout Hussein's palace command centers in Baghdad, Baiji, and Basra; Iraq's biological and chemical plants in Mosul, Tikrit, Iskandariyah, and Arbil; and the ballistic missile sites at Al Ramadi,

Salman Pak, Kirkuk, and Al Kut."

Eckel added, "By 1600 hours, Washington time, the guided missile destroyers *McCain* and *Callaghan* will be in position to complete the mission with cruise missiles."

"But Iraq had nothing to do with New York," Friar protested.

This was the opening for which Bastardi had been waiting. A chance to attack Warner's and Friar's credibility in front of the Security Council. "Yes, *Iraq*, Mr. Clarke. But, I guess you didn't know. How could we possibly expect the DO to know anything?" Glancing at Morehead, he continued, "In the raid on the Shaheeds' headquarters, coded instructions were found from Iraq ordering the destruction of Manhattan. They were personally authorized by Saddam Hussein. I would call that a smoking gun, wouldn't you?"

"Can't be," Friar asserted, trying to halt Bastardi's momentum. It was critical to keep the Security Council from acting before all the facts were in. A knee-jerk nuclear strike was exactly what Dubov had anticipated. The confusion would create the chaos needed to achieve his goals.

"I agree with Mr. Clarke. We must go slowly," Hohlt cautioned. "A nuclear response should only be used as a last—"

"Last? Last *what*, Miss Secretary?" Bastardi hissed, stabbing his finger at Hohlt. He frequently referred to the Secretary of State as "Miss Secretary." The insult enraged and distracted her. "I say bullshit! Hit the bastards now—*hard!* Before they can kill another million Americans."

Morehead held up his hand for silence. After mustering his strength, he said, "Mr. Clarke, what makes you so certain the Iraqis are not responsible? What about that—that directive to destroy Manhattan the FBI found?"

"Plus the list of serial numbers for the warheads we found at the militants' headquarters—the ones the goddamned Russians now admit are missing," added Bastardi.

Friar had to talk fast. "Mr. President, we've received highly reliable intelligence from Israel's Mossad and A'man that Iraq is *not* involved. That directive the FBI found is probably a forgery, planted by someone wanting us to attack Iraq. We have strong evidence another country is behind the bombing of New York. In fact, Iraq doesn't even own a submarine."

"Submarine?" asked Morehead.

"Yes, sir," replied Warner. "The warheads were delivered to a shrimp trawler off the North Carolina coast by submarine. It was an advanced Russian export diesel. We believe it belongs to the actual state sponsor."

"We've also got to consider we haven't received any demands from Iraq since the explosion," observed Deathridge. "God knows, Hussein would be jerking our chain hard by now if he had his hands on another four nuclear warheads inside the US."

Friar was relieved to have Hohlt's and Deathridge's support, but he couldn't ease up as long as Bastardi had the inside track to a weakened Morehead. "Mr. President, it's our opinion neither Iraq nor the Shaheeds control the remaining warheads. We see *no* danger of another explosion before the actual blackmailers come to the surface."

"Are you trying to say those goddamned Shaheeds aren't involved?" snarled Bastardi.

"Only that they're not in charge. They're being used as decoys," Friar replied, struggling to keep his temper under control.

"Mr. Clarke, how certain are you this operation is not just the first of a series of unannounced nuclear strikes against more American cities?" asked Deathridge.

"The warhead used in New York was the smallest of the five, a 100-kiloton device from a Russian SS-N-23 Skiff cruise missile. Had they wanted to kill more people, they would have used one of the larger 750-kiloton warheads."

"Mr. Warner, you claim Iraq is not the state sponsor," Bastardi huffed. "You tell us it's some other rogue state, an unknown third party. Since you are privy to so much inside information, could you possibly—*possibly* share your little secret with the National Security Council?"

"We'd prefer not to say at this time," responded Warner, his voice taut, but firm. "We're working on confirmation and will let you know as soon as we have proof."

Bastardi jumped to his feet, "There's no way—"

"Thank you, Mr. Warner, Mr. Clarke," Morehead said. "You gentlemen are excused."

When Warner and Friar reached the anteroom, Friar sat down on the parson's bench to collect his thoughts. Dubov's strategy was working. The Administration was groping in the dark and didn't know who the enemy was or how to respond. The Shaheeds and Iraqis were being targeted for retaliation and the demands from Sheik Jibril were so outrageous, that anything that followed would appear reasonable.

"Looks to me like Morehead's just about gone," said Friar.

Warner nodded, "Eileen Hohlt doesn't think he'll last much longer. Dr. Kernodle, his personal physician, is going to commit him to Walter Reed if he doesn't improve."

"Why doesn't the Doc go ahead and do it? I'd say he's already over the edge."

"Bastardi's blocking it. He's telling everyone Morehead's fine." Noticing Friar's puzzled look, Warner said, "Think about it. If Morehead can't handle his job, who's next in line?"

Friar played the scenario out in his mind. Of course—that was it. With Vice President Hambright dead, succession to the presidency would shift to Carl Jonas, Speaker of the House and a Republican. As Morehead's chief critic and leading member of the opposition, there would be changes, plenty of changes. Bastardi would be the first to go.

Friar's cellular phone began to vibrate. Fishing it out of his pocket, he flipped it on. It was Kat.

"*How'd it go?*"

"Don't ask. I'll tell you all about it when I get back to Williamsburg."

"*I'm not in Williamsburg. I'm at Walter Reed. Hashim's been murdered.*"

WALTER REED HOSPITAL, WASHINGTON

"Accession number?" mumbled the skinny, ruddy-complexioned morgue assistant named, Joe Speed. He sat hunched over a dark green metal desk, his hand resting on a paper wrapper holding the half-eaten remnants of a MacDonald's cheeseburger. A dab of ketchup clung to the hairs of his untrimmed Fu Manchu beard. Speed made no attempt to hide his irritation at the interruption. His lips curled down as he studied Friar and Kat. They definitely looked like more paper work.

"Number 1Nov.A236," Kat said, tapping her heel impatiently on the cold, concrete floor.

Speed slowly pushed the sandwich to the side and began methodically thumbing through the entry log. "That's a John Doe checked into the hospital by the FBI at 7:33P.M. last night. Died sometime after midnight. Body was brought here at 4:30 this morning."

Friar reached over and rapped on Speed's clipboard with his pen. "Where's the medical examiner?"

"Cain't you see? He ain't here," Speed replied, brushing a few crumbs from his soiled lab coat and turning his attention back to the unfinished burger.

Stepping forward, Friar leaned over the corner of the desk and with a powerful right hand grabbed the collar of the morgue assistant's lab coat. Lifting the startled man out of his chair, Friar snarled, "I suggest you go find him. Pronto." He was in no mood to be jerked around by some bottom-rung flunky like Speed.

When Friar let go, Speed recoiled so violently his chair rammed into a metal filing cabinet, almost knocking over a skull with a cigarette wedged between its grinning teeth. "Uh, yes, sir. You must want to see Dr. Van Gelder. He's in the cafeteria."

It only took ten minutes to locate the short, stocky forensic pathologist who wasted no time escorting Friar and Kat into the refrigerated autopsy room where Hashim's body was stored. The room reeked of disinfectant and the sickly-sweet odor of burned flesh. There were thirty to forty bodies stacked against the rear wall with a single sheet of plastic draped over the collected mass. Additional cadavers were piled on each of the six autopsy tables.

Waving his hand nonchalantly at the corpses, Van Gelder muttered, "My visiting New Yorkers. All the morgues on the east coast are crammed with bodies. They've even got 'em stacked in refrigerated boxcars and restaurant food freezers. Some of the politicians and military brass were sent down here. At least, the ones still recognizable."

Along the west wall of the brightly lit, tile covered laboratory was a row of thirty-six stainless steel drawers, stacked four high and recessed into the wall. Speed quickly located Drawer 1Nov.A236. Pulling out the sliding, stainless steel rack, he checked the toe tag, then flipped back the sheet and stepped aside.

"Sorry for the chilly temperature," Van Gelder said, drawing his lab coat tightly around his thick neck. "Got to keep all this meat from over-cooking." Checking Hashim's tag, he asked, "Why so much interest in this particular one?"

Kat hesitated, "He was an important witness." She was surprised Washington hadn't informed Walter Reed how special Hashim was. But, by the time Van Gelder became involved, it didn't make much difference.

"Any idea what killed him?" asked Friar, gazing down at Hashim's cold, gray face.

"Chart," the pathologist said, jutting his right hand towards Speed and snapping his fingers. After studying the report, he grunted, "Damn lot of stats for being in the hospital less than half a day. First three pager I've seen. You wouldn't think they'd bother, what with all that New York traffic flowing in."

"Cause of death?" Friar repeated.

"It would only be a guess. At least, until I've completed my examination." Van Gelder turned his face towards Friar, "You wouldn't settle for a partial?"

"Sorry, Doc, we need the whole nine yards."

"Afraid you'd say that." Studying the chart, Van Gelder said, "Preliminary report from upstairs says it happened all of a sudden. Yesterday, the picture of health, then—*whammo*! Let's see. Admitted to emergency at 7:33P.M. Nausea, acute gastroenteritis with severe stomach cramps. 8:46, respiration became labored. Rushed into intensive at 9:03 and hooked-up to life support. Delirium, coma. At 2:45 this AM, brain function ceased. 4:00—all life support removed. Respiration and heartbeat flat-lined immediately. Brought here at 4:30."

"Poisoned?" ask Friar.

Van Gelder raised his bifocals to the top of his head. "Could be. Must've gotten hold of some of our cafeteria food. Won't know for certain until toxicology does their bit."

Friar looked down at Hashim's expressionless face. Somehow,

Dubov had gotten to him. "Doc, I know you're overworked. But could you please put a push on this one?"

"May as well," replied Van Gelder, casting a weary glance at the pile of corpses on the floor. "I don't think any of my New Yorkers are going anywhere."

NOVEMBER 2: LANGLEY

It took Friar an extra twenty minutes to clear the added security at Langley. Marcie had arranged with NOSIC for an update on the search for the missing sub, and had chosen CIA headquarters as the safest place to evade Bastardi's network of informers. In addition to Commander Rhodes, she had assembled Cho Jong Tae, a representative from NSPA, South Korea's National Security Planning Agency, and Colonel Peter W. Houck, General Eckel's personal intelligence adviser from the Defense Intelligence Agency.

Marcie met Friar at the building entrance and led him to a small, secure conference room on the second floor. The sparse furnishings were limited to a round conference table, five wooden chairs, and an overhead projector.

When Friar entered the room, Commander Rhodes jumped to his feet. "I'm afraid it's only me today, sir. Chief Koenraad's in bed with the flu." This was Rhodes's first visit to Langley and he was excited.

Across the table stood an athletic, forty-something, officer from South Korean intelligence. Stanford educated, he had coal black hair and was dressed in a conservative, blue pinstriped business suit.

"Pleased to meet you, Mr. Clarke. My name is Cho Jong Tae. Please, call me Johnny."

"Still raking the rocks, Johnny?" Friar asked. Back in September 1996 he had accompanied a squad of South Korean soldiers on their evening patrol to rake the gravel along the seashore at Kangnung. He returned with them next morning to help check for footprints from infiltrators.

"Every night," Cho replied with a grin.

Beside Cho stood Houck, a ramrod straight, forty-four-year-old, bird Colonel, with a boot-camp crewcut, steel rimmed glasses and the confident handshake of a professional at ease under pressure.

"It's a real pleasure, Mr. Clarke. You've got quite a following among the old hands at the DIA."

Marcie closed the door. "Gentlemen, please be seated. Commander Rhodes, it's your show."

Rhodes began by positioning a transparency of the Korean peninsula on the base of the overhead projector. Fidgeting with the laser pointer, he said, "I hate to admit it but we've been unable locate the target sub. At first, we thought it would be easy. We've got such a good profile of her acoustical signature in our computer. Unfortunately, she hasn't moved. Most likely, the boat's in dry dock."

"You've checked the whole area?" asked Friar.

Rhodes switched on the projector. "Yes, sir. For the last couple of days we've been monitoring every cubic meter of ocean to the west, south and east of the Korean peninsula. In the Yellow Sea, it's knee-deep shallow between North Korea and China. They couldn't hide a beer can in there without us spotting it. The NRO positioned a satellite over their sub-base at Pipa-got. We picked up a couple of old Whiskey-class boats, a Romeo, and several Shark-class midget subs, but no Kilo."

"What about their east coast bases?" asked Cho, pointing to Mayang-do and Cha-ho.

"There's a satellite monitoring both those pens. We even sent in an unmanned stealth surveillance drone for a closer recon of Mayang-do. Still no luck." Pointing to a deep ocean ridge not far off the eastern coast, Rhodes added, "There are a lot of places along here for a sub to hide. You can see where the Sea of Japan drops off sharply about ninety nautical miles from the coast. Plenty of good gullies and trenches. But, even an upgraded Kilo can't go down more than 300 to 350 meters."

"What's your opinion, Johnny?" Friar asked.

Cho studied the map projected on the screen. "It's my guess the Kilo's holed-up at either Mayang-do or Cha-ho. Both have advanced, underground facilities. If I had to pick one over the other, I'd say it's at Mayang-do. That's where they keep their newest equipment."

"Is there any way of forcing it to move?" asked Colonel Houck.

Friar perked up. "Johnny, what if NSPA were to put out word you're trying to locate Pyongyang's Kilo? Let it be known that Mayang-do and Cha-ho have been targeted for a special op. Maybe leak information to a double agent that you're going to sabotage the Kilo in retaliation for Pyongyang's having landed that commando team near Kangnung. Heck, it wouldn't hurt to actually let them find a set of plans and a couple of anti-sub mines."

"That's awfully provocative," observed Marcie, worried that such an aggressive deception might trigger a military response.

Friar had momentarily forgotten Marcie was in the room. He had long known she was too sensitive for field operations. "I'm afraid we don't have a choice. We're out of time."

Colonel Houck nodded, "General Eckel needs to know ASAP how North Korea fits in."

"I like the idea," said Cho. "It wouldn't take much to scare Pyongyang into moving the Kilo. They're paranoid anyway. By leaking information to the right people—it just might work."

Rising to his feet, Cho said, "Mr. Clarke, I must speak to you and Colonel Houck, in private. It's a matter of extreme urgency." Looking apologetically at Marcie and Commander Rhodes, he said, "It's not that I don't trust—"

"I understand," said Marcie, gathering her charts and notebook, and heading for the door.

After Marcie and Rhodes had left the room, Cho pulled the door closed. "My superiors wish me to convey to the appropriate American officials information of *great* concern." He hesitated, as if having second thoughts.

"Please go on," Friar encouraged.

After a brief pause, Cho said, "Two days ago, a high ranking North Korean official secretly working for Seoul was killed trying to cross the border at Chorwan."

Friar waited patiently, not wanting to pressure Cho.

"This source, whom we called 'Peacock,' was a deep-cover asset in Kim Jong Il's government. His real name—Park Doo Ryol—was known to only two people at NSPA. He was ordered to contact Seoul only in case of a pending crisis."

A sleeper, thought Friar. "Do you know what caused him to break cover?"

Cho shook his head. "He was killed before he could deliver his message. For safety reasons he had been supplied with only limited communications equipment. He had a single transmitter hidden in a TV set, programmed to send a prearranged signal when he was coming over. Three days ago the signal was activated. Yesterday, he and Chun Song Woo, one of Pyongyang's leading trade ministers, tried to cross at Chorwan. Both were detained at the border—we assume by the military. They made a run for it in Park's car. They were shot and killed before they could reach our outpost."

"And you have no idea what he wanted to tell you?" asked Houck.

"There was a firefight over the bodies. Fortunately, Park had almost reached our outpost. We recovered the corpses, along with the car and their personal belongings. At the autopsy we found a scrap of paper in Park's stomach with a reference to 12:00 noon, November 7. Nothing more."

"Too much of a coincidence not to be tied in with the warheads," Friar observed.

Lowering his voice, Cho said, "We fear the worst. It's our belief November 7 signals the deadline for a military coup against Kim Jong Il's government, or possibly an invasion of the South."

"I will inform General Eckel at once," said Colonel Houck.

WILLIAMSBURG

The midday sun warmed the garden at Bosworth House to a comfortable sixty degrees. A slight, southerly breeze brought the smell of freshly spread hay drifting in from the horse pastures across the street at Bassett Hall. Kat leaned back and closed her eyes, letting the sunlight wash across her face. She enjoyed eating lunch in the solitude of the picnic table. It was her private retreat from the unreal world inside the War Room. Here, among the boxwoods, birds, and squirrels, she could temporarily forget Manhattan and the grotesque images crowding the TV screens. Listening to a sparrow splashing in the bird bath, she relaxed and tried to think of only pleasant memories.

Recently, she had found herself preoccupied with thoughts of mortality, and marriage—or, at least establishing a stable relationship. Just last week she had removed the refrigerator magnet, the one Angela had given her for her twenty-ninth birthday, right after she broke up with Marshall. It had been one of those inside sister-jokes—funny, but cutting. On the magnet was a picture of a harried housewife holding two screaming babies. It was captioned, "All the women moaning about not finding husbands have obviously never had one." Now she found the quip slightly depressing. Maybe it was watching Marcie and Friar together. Maybe it was Manhattan. Maybe it was the wrinkles.

During this morning's ritual she had noticed the first signs of crow's feet in the bathroom mirror. Little, silent folds at the corners of her eyes, reminding her that her body was changing. Sure, the lighting had been bad, but still—she had attempted to laugh off the evidence of aging, but the reminder wouldn't go away. She thought of Marshall and tried to remember why they had broken up. He wanted to move to Annapolis, and she had opted to stay in Arlington. Two head-strong people, too stubborn and career minded to compromise. They had kept dating for awhile, but eventually the distance proved too inconvenient. If only she had a second chance—then she remembered. Last Christmas, Christy, Marshall's sister, had said he was becoming serious about Heidi Hogshire, a Sweet Briar debutante from Northern Virginia's horsey set. What kind of name was that—Hogshire?

Kat watched a second sparrow join the fun in the bird bath. She threw them a few crumbs. Life was slipping away. The old lies and excuses weren't working anymore. Her career wasn't filling the void. Strange, how empty it all seemed when you finally reached your goals. After this operation was over she would take some time off and go to Longboat Key to visit her parents. They didn't meddle, and watching the ocean helped place life's disappointments in perspective. At thirty-two, her options were still open, but the door was closing.

Kat stood, stretched, and strolled the few steps to the rear entrance of Bosworth House. Friar would be here any minute. Removing the Colombian Supremo coffee beans from the freezer, she ground enough for a fresh pot. The beans were expensive, but they were his favorite.

He had called earlier that morning, but only to remind her to bring in the fumigators. They had swept for bugs, but if someone at the National Security Agency were in cahoots with Bastardi, you could never be sure. Big Daddy had listening devices even the CIA had never heard of. Kat perched on a kitchen stool and waited.

Friar entered carrying a box, gift wrapped in a slick, coated orange paper and tied with a large white bow. "Don't want anything but good news today," he kidded, parking the box beside a TV monitor.

She smiled. Her news was not only good, it was outstanding. It pleased her to be able to provide him with what he wanted. Unfortunately, information was all he ever asked for. Friar followed her into the Sidebar where she unrolled a large map of North Carolina and taped it to the wall.

"The Bureau's traced the sixth truck," she said, watching for a reaction. "The leasing company is the Pendleton Ford Truck Agency in Cary. Their records show a twenty-four-foot maxi-van and a Komatsu forklift were sent out on a four day rental from noon October 15, until 10:00A.M., October 19." She wasn't disappointed. His eyes lit up like those of a kid with a new toy.

"You think that's our truck?"

"We passed a pile of sketches by Pendleton's manager. It took him twenty minutes, but he finally selected a drawing of one of the two Chechens who was with Dubov at the Rusty Dog Tavern. He identified him as the person renting the truck. We had sketches made with and without beards and tattoos."

"And, he picked a sketch with a clean face."

"Hey, you peeked," she kidded, bumping playfully against him. "It was a cash transaction. The manager said he remembered it, since most rentals are charged to credit cards. Our Chechen had to pony-up a two thousand dollar deposit. He did it with postal money orders. The name shown on his Illinois drivers license was 'Stephan Arnold.' "

"Bogus?"

"As phony as a sad undertaker at a $20,000 funeral. We checked with Illinois. Stephan Arnold was real enough, but he died of stomach cancer in Florida two years ago. Our renter just assumed his identity and got a new license issued."

"At least the truck's been found," Friar said, pleased his yin and yang were coming back into balance.

"The manager let us store the vehicle and forklift at a warehouse in Raleigh. Pendleton sent the truck out on a couple of short rentals after the eighteenth, but the forklift hasn't been used since. There's a lot of interesting mud on the forklift's tires. The lab's going over both items in detail."

"Make sure a forensic geologist analyzes that mud."

"You haven't guessed the really *good* news," Kat said, moving closer.

"Dubov left a map in the truck's glove compartment with a big X marking the spot where he hid the warheads?"

"Not quite, but almost. Our truck was involved in a fender-bender in Boone on October 17."

Friar beamed at the news. This was the break they needed. "Did you get an accident report?"

"You mean this report?" Kat said, waving the paper under his nose.

It was all there. October 17, collision in Boone, NC, between a yellow, Nissan 300ZX, vanity tag "1GDMAN," and a Ford rental truck, NC license plate, AB-786. The truck was headed south on US221. Place of accident, the Blowing Rock Road intersection. Name of truck driver, Stephan Arnold. Reporting officer, Rufus C. Clapp.

"Where's officer Clapp?" Friar asked. The policeman would be another loose end Dubov would try to tie up if he thought anyone was closing in.

"We took him into protective custody. He didn't want to go at first. Changed his mind when he found out the people in the truck were tied in with the New York bombing. The cover story with his department is that he's going to California to visit an ailing father. Only Boone's police chief knows we've got him, but he doesn't know why."

"Did you show Dubov's picture to Clapp?"

"He picked him out of a stack of twelve. He also recognized the sketch of the driver. It was the same person identified by Pendleton's manager."

Once again Friar was impressed with Kat's attention to detail. He wondered if he had been that good when he was thirty-two. "And the mileage report?"

"Right here," Kat replied, handing him a copy of the rental agreement. It showed the total number of miles driven at 774.

Stepping over to the map taped to the wall, Friar measured the distances from Cary to Wanchese to Boone, back to Cary. Seven hundred fourteen miles. "Looks like they made a sixty mile loop out of Boone." Using a compass, he drew an arc south of Boone with a radius of thirty highway miles. The line cut through Lenoir, Spruce Pine, Buladean, and Hampton. "Unless they took a lot of side trips or backtracked to throw us off, their destination should be somewhere along this line."

Friar reviewed his notes for the past few days. Finding Dubov was now top priority. "Kat, check with Dorn. If he hasn't heard from our Chechen, have him put out an APB. But don't let them pick him up. We just want to know where he is."

"Will do," Kat replied. She had already made inquiries. A sighting had come in last night from the Bureau's New York Russian Organized Crime squad. Dubov had been spotted at Brighton beach, checking on the damage from the explosion. She planned on personally finding him with the aid of an informer working for the Russian language newspaper, *Novoye Russkoye Slovo*. That way, there would be no danger of Dorn mucking things up, and, it would impress Friar.

"I've got a special present for you," Friar said, retrieving the gift box from the War Room.

Grinning, Kat carefully removed the orange wrapping paper, folding it and laying it aside. The box was an expensive, dimpled white, sweater box. She raised the lid. Inside was what looked like a padded, baby blue ski vest.

Friar removed the vest from the box and held it against her trim torso. "It's designer kevlar, level III. This stuff will stop a .44 Magnum slug weighing 240 grains." His voice turned serious, "From now on, I want you to wear it whenever you're in the field."

"Thanks. I think," she replied, touched that he was concerned, but disappointed it wasn't something more personal. At least it showed he cared. Maybe not as much as he should, but it was step one.

Turning back to the map, Friar pointed to the thirty mile arc radiating out from Boone. "We need to get as many NEST and FBI people working this area as we can. Someone might remember seeing three large Chechens and a truck." For the first time, he felt good about their chances of finding the warheads.

Chapter 18

NOVEMBER 3: SPRUCE PINE, NORTH CAROLINA

The slanted, asphalt parking lot at the Mt. Zion Baptist Church made a hazardous landing pad for Friar's JetRanger helicopter, but it was the only open space available. At the far corner, beside a 100-year-old cemetery full of worn granite tombstones, Jason Dorn waited patiently in his Chevy Blazer.

While the pilot concentrated on maneuvering the helicopter between two sprawling oak trees and a set of low strung power lines, Friar peered out the Plexiglas windows, searching for Kat. The churchyard was empty, except for Dorn. Friar had tried to reach her by cell phone over an hour ago, but there was no response. It wasn't like Kat to be out of touch. She had called last night at 6:30, excited about a discovery by John Perlin, a forensic geologist with the Bureau's Materials Analysis Unit. It had something to do with the mud wedged between the forklift's tire treads. She said she would explain everything at the meeting this morning with Perlin at the Museum of North Carolina Minerals.

Exiting the helicopter, Friar trotted over to the Blazer. "Jason, have you seen Kat Mills?"

Shaking his head, Dorn said, "Maybe she's at the museum."

A dull sensation in the pit of Friar's stomach told him she was in trouble.

It was a short, six mile drive from Spruce Pine to the rustic, gray granite building at milepost 331 on the Blue Ridge Parkway. The National Park Service building, with its massive stone chimney and cedar shingled roof, was nestled quietly off the main road in a thicket of Fraser fir and poplar trees. Riley Quick, the burly, thirty-nine-year-old director met them at the entrance. Quick wore a black-and-red checkered flannel shirt, faded Levi's jeans, and a constant smile.

"Is Ms. Mills here?" Friar asked.

"Nope," Quick replied. "Last contact I had with her was yesterday afternoon when she called to set up this meeting."

Skipping the usual museum tour, Quick ushered Friar and Dorn into his private office, where Perlin was already waiting. Of medium build, slightly balding, and soft-spoken, Perlin was well known within the closeknit world of forensic geologists for his sharp eye for detail and encyclopedic knowledge of rocks and minerals.

Using an Estwing rock chisel as a pointer, Quick motioned toward a relief map of western North Carolina fixed to the wall. "Like I was telling Mr. Perlin, North Carolina's a real mother lode of gemstones and minerals. In the Spruce Pine area we've got plenty of mica, feldspar, tungsten, kaolin, and some of the sexier stones like rubies, emeralds, garnets, amethysts, and sapphires." It was his abbreviated Chamber of Commerce pitch.

By the time Quick had finished his Mother Nature spiel, Perlin had his stereomicroscope set up and the illuminator switched on. Taking a petri dish from his briefcase, he carefully centered a container of washed minerals in the middle of the stage plate.

Addressing Quick, Perlin said, "These samples came from the tires of the forklift. We're hoping you can help us locate their point of origin."

"What's the composition?" asked Quick, pulling out copies of the US Geological Survey maps for Watauga, Mitchell, and Avery counties and spreading them on the rough-hewn table that served as his desk.

Looking through the eyepieces of the stereomicroscope, Perlin said, "Magnetite, apatite, amphibole, calcite, and hornblende."

"Any unusual feldspar?"

Perlin swirled the sample in the dish, "Several traces of oligoclase. It fluoresced blue on the edges when I flamed it earlier this morning. It's my guess these minerals came from an excavation of magnetite ore surrounded by some sort of a granite-gneiss host."

Quick sprinkled a sample of the ore on the stage plate of his own stereomicroscope. "Yep, it's Cranberry granite-gneiss all right. There's the albite, biotite, and epidote."

"Any magnetite mining operations around here?" asked Perlin.

"There's an old Civil War iron mine over in Avery county, right off US 19E. Used to be known as the Cranberry Iron Works. It's on Birchfield Road, half a mile up Yellow Mountain." Quick took the Avery county map, ran off a photocopy and drew a large, red X pinpointing the location. "That immediate area has magnetite as the primary ore-zone material with foliated clinopyroxene in the border area. The host rock is cataclastic Cranberry gneiss, same as in this sample."

"Is the mine still in operation?" asked Friar.

"Nope. Closed in 1930." Quick rummaged through his files. "Here's a copy of State Bulletin 42, Plate 10. It's a 1979 geological survey of the mine showing the collapse pit, and the adit with all the slopes and drifts."

It was noon by the time Dorn and Friar reached Finlay's General Mercantile in Minneapolis, North Carolina. A call had come in from FBI Special Agent Karl Jaeger that an employee at Finlay's had recognized Dubov's photo.

The store fronted on US Highway 19E with parking spaces on both sides and in the rear. It wasn't one of the numerous cutesy, mountain-chic knock-offs dotting NC 105 from Boone to Linville, but a real working general store with cast iron skillets, hard rock candy, and three sizes of Ace rat traps. It also featured a large front porch which served as home base to several of Minneapolis' porch sitters and mountain philosophers. From the rocking chairs strategically placed at both corners, there was a commanding view of US 19E as it entered town from the north and exited due south. It was from this vantage point that Big Ed Hazelwood had spotted Dubov's truck on October 18.

"Yep, that's him all right," Big Ed said, holding Dubov's photo close to the light. Passing the picture over to his son, he asked, "Ain't that the feller we seen from Chicago, Little Ed?"

"Shore is, Pa," Little Ed replied, vigorously nodding his head.

"What'd they do?" asked Big Ed, his eyes narrowing. "I could tell they was up to no good when I first seen that big one with the scar acrost his face. You don't get no scar like that dunkin' for apples at the church social. No, siree. And he weren't very friendly neither." Big Ed cast an all knowing glance at Little Ed. This promised to be a good story for the men's fellowship group at the Wooden Cross Holiness Church outing on Sunday. Hobnobbing with the FBI would top Zeke Blanchard's old, worn-out yarn about how his prize bull had tried to service that mule.

"You saw them at the Cranberry mine?" asked Friar.

"That's right. Back on the eighteenth. Me and Little Ed here got a call from Miss Odelia—that's my wife—we live up on Birchfield Road in the white clapboard house. Anyhow, she called to tell me there was this here oversized truck chugging up the mountain. I figgered it was the one we'd just seen passing by the mercantile. So, me and Little Ed here, we took off and went to check it out. Nothing goes on around Yellow Mountain we don't know about."

"How many men were in the truck?"

"There was three fellers. Big, mean looking guys. By the time we got there, they'd been hauling things around on one of them forklifts. Claimed they was moving generators and safety equipment." Big Ed studied Friar's face for confirmation. Maybe it was drugs. That would be something, a big city drug operation, right here in Avery county.

"Have you seen the one with the scar since the eighteenth?" If the warheads were in the mine, chances were good Dubov was nearby.

"Let me think. The eighteenth? That was two weeks and three—naw, two days ago. Nope. Ain't laid eyes on him or give it much mind since then. He promised to stop by and tell me what they was up to, next time he come to Yellow Mountain." Big Ed reached into his coveralls and pulled out a wrinkled pouch of Red Man chewing tobacco. After offering it around, he extracted a wad and slipped it into the corner of his mouth. "My cousin Wilfred Zayner over in Boone was the one that rented 'em that mine. He said they was crazy folks."

"Why crazy?" asked Friar.

"Dag-blamed mine's full of water. Wilfred said anybody who'd rent it didn't know bull-turkey about liabilities. Said that mine was what them lawyers call an attractive nuisance. You know, some neighborhood kid sneaks in there and breaks his neck or drowns in all that water. They gonna get sued for a million dollars."

"Did Wilfred tell them about the water?"

"Shore did. Why, he's a deacon at the church. He wouldn't hide nothing like that. Heck, Wilfred said they acted like they was *glad* it was dangerous and flooded."

Friar put his hand on Big Ed's shoulder. "I'm going to need your help."

"Is it cocaine?" whispered Big Ed, eyes glinting in anticipation.

Friar winked, "Can't say. It's a government secret."

"I knew it, just knew it," Big Ed said, rubbing his hands together. "Can I git me one of them badges? One like Mr. Dorn's got?" He knew Harold Smith and Oaky Sizemore would be jealous as all gitout if he showed up at the church social with a government badge hidden in his billfold. Or maybe he'd just hook it inside his coat and kinda show it around like, to special friends. "And another one for Little Ed?"

"I'll see what I can do," Friar promised. "Until then you'll have to be special secret agents." Friar handed Big Ed a cellular phone with his number preprogrammed. "Those men are killers. If you see the fellow with the scar, don't do anything. Just call me on this phone. Punch in number one."

As their Chevy Blazer approached the large, dark green communications van hidden in a cove at Beech Bottom, Friar and Dorn could see and hear an argument in progress.

"I don't give a good damn," drawled the taller of the two men, standing by a Jeep Cherokee marked, Sheriff, Avery County. The husky, broad shouldered lawman stood six-feet-six and wore the Smoky Bear hat of a marine boot camp DI. He had closely cropped rust brown hair, a pug nose and held his head erect with the authority of someone used to being obeyed. "You outsiders think you can just waltz in here anytime you feel like it, and tell us locals when and where to take a whiz."

Dorn immediately recognized the shorter of the two men, the one dressed in a coat and tie. Whispering to Friar, he said, "That's Mark Hastey, Assistant Director at NEST. I asked him to meet us here."

Hastey, his face flushed, stepped over to the Blazer. A lean, wiry, no nonsense, professional from New Hampshire, he knew he was out of his element in the backwoods of Avery County. "Jason, would you *please* explain to Sheriff Maynard that we're not here to tell him how to run his county?"

Dorn glanced at the hulking sheriff, climbed out of the Blazer, took a step forward, stopped and turned back towards Friar. "How about a hand? You speak the language."

Friar tried to hide his amusement at two senior FBI and NEST officials, chasing nuclear warheads, stopped cold by a local sheriff protecting his turf. It was obvious Hastey hadn't confided in Sheriff Maynard why they were here. The solution was simple, the Sheriff would have to be told about the warheads and the hell with his lack of security clearance.

It only took Friar ten minutes to bring Maynard up to speed. The Sheriff was a quick study and understood instantly.

Grabbing Hastey's hand, the Sheriff said, "For Christ's sake, son, why didn't you tell me you were chasing the bastards that nuked New York. Hell, I thought you were just another Washington asshole down here trying to tell me how to cook my grits. Call me Charlie. If there's anything I can do—"

"Sheriff, are you familiar with the old Cranberry iron mine on Yellow Mountain?" Friar asked, unfolding a copy of the geological survey Quick had given him and spreading it across the hood of the blazer.

"I know that mine like the back of my hand," Maynard answered, studying the map. "When I was young and stupid, I used to lead spelunking dives in some of the slopes dropping off the main shaft. Several go down a couple hundred yards or more. They follow the veins of magnetite back into the mountain." Tracing the main shaft on the map with his hand, Maynard added, "All the slopes below 3,150 feet are flooded. Takes real guts to strap on your scuba gear and disappear into one of those holes."

"Is the main shaft flooded?" That's where Friar suspected Dubov had hidden the warheads. The surrounding rock would mask the telltale signs of radiation and block the prying eyes of any observation satellites.

"It's flooded back towards the end. The footing's pretty tricky in there. Roof's caved in at several spots." Drawing three X's on the map with a black felt-tip pen, Maynard pinpointed the known danger points.

"Have you been inside lately?"

"Yup. Had to go in six months ago and drag out Bill McPhee's twelve-year-old boy and Walt Irving's kid. Those two rug-rats were in pretty deep when their flashlights went out. Lucky I found them when I did. They could've lost their way and drowned in all that water." He shook his head, "Nothing you can do to keep kids out. You can nail up boards, post signs, it doesn't mean a thing." Shaking his head, he chuckled, "Can't say I really blame 'em. I was the same way when I was that age."

Friar took an instant liking to Sheriff Maynard. In spite of his good-ole-boy ruse and rough edges, he was razor sharp and knew the terrain. In these mountains one Maynard was worth a hundred NEST and FBI agents.

Friar turned to Hastey, "Are your people ready?"

"We've got Alpha team standing by at Banner Elk with a backup in Asheville. I didn't want to bring them up and spook the target."

"What about your attack force? Who's going to provide the muscle?"

"We've got several choices," said Hastey. "We can use an FBI SWAT team from Charlotte, the Delta Force at Ft. Bragg, or a SEAL team from Norfolk."

"You probably ought to wait until you see what you're up against before making that decision."

"I agree," said Hastey.

"But, before we go jumping in, we need to make certain those warheads are in there. Any suggestions?" The element of surprise was crucial. A premature raid would only drive Dubov and the warheads deeper into hiding.

"We could use the dogs," said Hastey.

"What kind you got?" asked Maynard, casually adjusting the holster of his S&W .44 combat magnum.

"German Shepherds. They're specially trained to search buildings and caves. Shouldn't take them long to check it out. We've got infrared video cameras to attach to their heads and radiation monitors for their backs. Problem's going to be getting them past the entrance."

"That's easy," said Maynard. "There's a hidden opening to the main shaft through the collapse pit. It's not on the maps. It hooks into the second slope 'bout half way down. Right now it's boarded up, but you could break through in a couple of minutes. That's how those kids snuck in."

"How far's the collapse pit from the main entrance?" asked Friar.

"Clear around the south side of the hill. Two, maybe three hundred yards. It's hidden by a big dump of worked ore."

Maynard walked over to his Jeep Cherokee and pulled a topographical map of Yellow Mountain from a pile of charts wedged behind the driver's seat. Placing the topo beside the geological survey, he said, "I'd suggest you enter the collapse pit from the left. You could circle around the mountain on Roaring Creek Road, sneak up using a dry creek bed and you're right there."

Studying the topo, Friar said, "We'll need to set up a command post. One that's got a good view of the entrance."

"Best place for that's going to be over on Pizzle Knob. It's across the valley, maybe a quarter of a mile away. You can see the mine entrance and the collapse pit from there."

Friar nodded. As soon as he got back to Williamsburg he would contact the National Reconnaissance Office and have them position a thermographic satellite over Yellow Mountain. Once that was in place, anyone moving in or out could be spotted.

"I'll get the dogs and work them in after dark," said Hastey.

NOVEMBER 4: WILLIAMSBURG

Hastey's call came in at 7:11A.M. The dogs had failed to locate the warheads. However, there was minor residual radioactivity in a stack of four, empty shell halves lying fifty feet inside the main shaft. Entering through slope two, the German Shepherds had managed to slip in unnoticed and prowl the mine for over an hour. The videos from the cameras showed what looked like tire tracks from the forklift leading deep into the interior, but the light had been bad and

Hastey couldn't be sure. There were no signs of recent excavations or evidence the warheads had been buried. The best news was the mine was lightly guarded. The cameras had picked up images from only two men. Friar told Hastey to wait for further instructions.

After hanging up, Friar went over Hastey's report again and again, looking for missed clues, searching for explanations. The warheads could easily have been moved to a second location, but unless Dubov suspected someone knew about the mine, why take the risk?

Friar was becoming increasingly concerned about Kat. She had last been seen at the Camp Peary airport trying to hitch a ride to the FBI's emergency field station at Dyker Beach Park in Brooklyn. From there, she had simply disappeared. He had asked Dorn to start a search, but with all the turmoil in New York, she was low priority.

Warner arrived at Bosworth House at 10:08A.M. After a brief discussion, he agreed their best bet was to focus the search on the Cranberry mine area. It would be intense, but low key in order not to alert the Chechens.

Marcie arrived at 10:30, joining them in the War Room. A heavy fog had forced her to drive down from Langley. Friar poured her a mug of strong, hot Earl Grey tea, then closed the door.

Cupping the mug in both hands, she sipped the tea, letting the hot vapor drift into her clogged sinuses. She was glad Kat wasn't there. During the past few days, every time she saw Laurence, Kat was at his elbow. She hadn't mentioned it to Laurence for fear of looking like an overly possessive, neurotic wife. At least Laurence didn't seem to be romantically interested in Kat. If he were, she could tell. She would wait, and trust him.

Placing the mug on the table, Marcie said, "The ruse worked. I had a meeting this morning at Langley with Commander Rhodes. NOSIC traced the mystery sub to the base at Mayang-do and made positive identification. The boat is definitely North Korean."

Turning to Warner, Friar said, "That's the confirmation we need."

"I'll contact the Security Council. They'll need to know."

"Has anyone seen Kat?" Friar asked. "I was supposed to meet her at the mineral museum yesterday morning. She didn't show."

Marcie opened her mouth, but simply shook her head.

There was a rapid knock on the door. Amy Schmidt from the

communication center stuck her head in, "Mr. Clarke, there's a call for you. It's a Mr. Dubov."

Friar reached for the room phone, "Put it in here." Flipping on the record and locate switch, he motioned for Marcie and Warner to listen in on extensions.

"Mr. Clarke? This is Alexander Dubov. You remember me, we met—" The identification light blinked on. The number was 504-529-5333, registered to the Royal Orleans Hotel in New Orleans.

"Ah, yes, Mr. Dubov. I'm glad you called. What can I do for you?"

"No, Mr. Clarke, it's what I can do for you. Actually, I believe I can be of service. I have a couple of presents. Special gifts of particular interest."

Games, Friar thought. He must be feeling confident. "Okay, where can we meet?"

"You'll have to come to New Orleans. Your presents are too heavy to carry." There was a pause as he conferred with someone in the background. *"Let's say, 10:00 tomorrow morning, in Jackson Square in front of Old Hickory's statue. Oh, and please come alone."* The line went dead.

Marcie lowered her headset, "Don't go, it's a trap."

It pleased him when she showed such concern. "I've got to find out what he's up to. He's the key to locating the rest of the warheads." Walking over to where she was sitting, he sat down beside her. "If it'll make you feel better, I'll take Joe Don along as backup."

CAMP PEARY

The emergency meeting of the Security Council was delayed fifteen minutes while Bastardi had his staff check with NOSIC to verify that the Wanchese sub was indeed North Korean. The delay was a deliberate challenge to Warner's and Friar's credibility. While they waited, Morehead sat slumped in a chair at the head of the conference table, his head in his hands, his eyes closed. A worried Dr. Donald R. Kernodle hovered in the background, ready to step in if needed.

Seated with Friar and Warner at the small, cramped witness table were Stirling Phillips, chief negotiator for the North Korean Geneva Nuclear Accord, and Johnny Cho, from South Korean Intelligence. Warner had asked them to be present to personally answer questions about Pyongyang's involvement.

When he was ready, Bastardi whispered into Morehead's ear. The President slowly opened his eyes and made a halfhearted attempt to sit up. Without speaking he motioned for Bastardi to begin.

With a nod towards the President, and without waiting for Bastardi, Vaughn announced, "With the help of the NRO and the DIA, we've confirmed that the sub in question belongs to North Korea."

"Even so," interjected Bastardi, irritated at Vaughn's having spoken first, "that doesn't prove North Korea was behind the bombing of New York. They could've simply been providing a delivery service for the Iraqis. Nothing more."

General Eckel, Chairman of the Joint Chiefs, leveled his gaze at Warner, "It seems to me we're faced with three questions. First, who's responsible for New York? Second, where the hell are the other four warheads? And third, what's North Korea up to? I'd like to hear what the DO has to say on that score."

"Mr. Warner no longer works for the Directorate of Operations," huffed Bastardi.

Eckel twisted in his chair and glared at the National Security Adviser. "Goddammit, man, I was directing those questions to Mr. Warner, not you. I want *him* to answer."

There was silence. Bastardi's face turned beet red while he shuffled through the pile of papers lying in a pile in front of him. The Chairman of the Joint Chiefs had just earned top billing on his well known enemies list.

Warner stood to give his reply. Standing made the blood flow and helped him concentrate. It also put him eye-level with Bastardi. "It's still too early to identify all the participants, but we're convinced North Korea provided the funds to buy the warheads. It's my opinion—and that of Mr. Clarke, Mr. Phillips, and Mr. Cho—that North Korea controls the four missing nuclear devices and intends to use them to prevent the United States from interfering with its planned invasion of the South."

A murmur rose from all the council members, except General Eckel, who had been forewarned by Colonel Houck. Even Bastardi seemed surprised.

"What about that group calling themselves the Shaheeds of the

Islamic Ummah? And the directive from Iraq ordering them to bomb New York?" asked Secretary of State Hohlt.

"It's our analysis the directive is a fake, a clever piece of disinformation fabricated to shift the blame to Iraq. We also believe the Shaheeds are decoys. We don't think the militants ever controlled the operation, or that Iraq was in any way part of the conspiracy."

"If that's true, it means we can scrap those outrageous demands," said Hohlt.

Directing his attention towards Warner, Bastardi sniffed, "But, what if you're wrong, Mr. Warner? What if the Shaheeds *do* have their fingers on the triggers? You yourself admit the New York nuke was delivered to Manhattan by that terrorist Hashim. Plus, you've failed to mention the Russian syndicate. Are they merely decoys too?"

Warner referred the question to Friar. It had been agreed between them that Friar would do the professional equivocating. It was important Bastardi not know about Dubov, and Warner made a poor liar. In fact, as Friar had noted repeatedly, Warner was lousy at it. In a business based on the ability to shade black and white until it turned gray, honesty was often a serious character flaw.

Friar stood and addressed the Council, "There's definitely a Russian syndicate involved. We've seen evidence it's the Dolgochenskaya clan, the ones the FBI calls the Dols. However, we won't know for certain until the Bureau has finished its investigation." Quickly sitting down, he winked at Warner. It was important to keep Bastardi from asking too many questions. The less he knew and tried to interfere, the better.

Deathridge said, "Mr. Warner, assuming that what you say is true. That this whole nightmare is part of a plot by Pyongyang to invade the South. How much time do we have?"

"South Korean Intelligence thinks the invasion will be launched at noon, November 7. Whether that's Pyongyang time or Washington time, we don't know.

Another murmur rippled through the Council. That was fewer than three days away.

"You think North Korea destroyed New York for that?" sneered Bastardi.

"That's precisely what we think," said Warner.

"Mr. Phillips, do you concur with these conclusions?" asked Hohlt.

Stirling Phillips rose to his feet. "I most certainly do. North Korea is a country in its death throes. The population is starving and the economy is in shambles. It appears that certain army generals have determined that to survive, they have to seize control in Pyongyang and blitzkrieg the South with an invasion. If they're successful, they think they can take over South Korea's wealth and resources. Standing in their way are 37,000 American troops stationed along the DMZ and the threat of full-scale war with the US. If they can blackmail us into stepping aside, the military believes its 1.2 million man army will be able to reach the end of the peninsula before they can be stopped. Once in place, they'll be able to secure their position by deploying five primitive atomic bombs we believe are now in their possession. If we don't interfere, there's a high probability they can make it."

General Eckel nodded, "I agree. I don't have to remind the Council that from the standpoint of numbers, North Korea's army is almost as large as ours. In addition, with 10,000 guns, they have the highest concentration of artillery in the world. In a recent computer simulation we found that a surprise attack by the North could envelope Seoul in six to eight days, and, that's with the US being fully committed."

"Mr. Cho, what's Seoul's position?" asked Deathridge.

"I can only speak for the NSPA," replied Cho as he rose to his feet. "We are *very* concerned." Turning to General Eckel, he bowed respectfully, "I would hope the South Korean army could hold out for longer than a few days. We have excellent equipment, and 630,000 well-trained, highly motivated soldiers." Turning back to Deathridge, he continued, "But, for long term survival, we are heavily dependent on continuing US military support."

"Are there indications the North is preparing an attack?" quizzed Hohlt.

Cho unrolled a large map of North and South Korea and taped it to the wall. Stepping back, he used a ruler to point to the DMZ straddling the thirty-eighth parallel. "During the past two weeks there has been a substantial increase in military activity north of the DMZ. Forth Corps and the 820th Armored have moved into position in the Munsan Valley." Pointing eastward along the DMZ, he said, "From Wonsan they've brought the Ninth Mechanized forward to the Chowan Valley. They've also shifted I Corps and Fifth Corps closer to the DMZ."

Withdrawing eight eleven-by-fourteen aerial photos from a canvas carrying case, Warner passed them around the table. "Recent NRO satellite photos show a transfer of over 110 bombers, MIG-17s, and IL-28 fighters to bases close to the border."

Cho continued, "In July, several of Pyongyang's senior generals were ousted by a small group of young, hard-liners. They're desperate, foolhardy men with no memories of the earlier war. We believe they may have already staged a coup against Kim Jong Il's government. In the past two weeks there has been a marked increase in military propaganda calling for the immediate liberation of the South."

The President propped himself up on his elbows. "General Eckel, what's the status of our forces in the region?"

Thanks to the early warning from Colonel Houck, the general was ready. "Mr. President, we're well underway with preparations to defend Seoul. The Navy, Air Force, and Army are implementing the guidelines laid out in war plan 5027-92."

"Can we stop them?" asked Deathridge.

"Right now, we only have 37,000 combat troops on the ground. In three weeks we'll have a additional 400,000."

"Three weeks is too long, General, too long," mumbled Morehead.

"Mr. President, we're shuttling troops and matériel as fast as we can. In two days the aircraft carrier *Independence* and the guided missile cruiser *Bunker Hill* will be within striking distance. In five days the Ninth Marine Brigade will be at In-Pohang and by 14 November, we'll have the Army Heavy Brigade Afloat ashore at Inchon. I've also ordered the 82nd and 101st Airborne Divisions to move out. They'll be in Chojon, with full combat gear, in four days."

"What about the Naval forces in Hawaii?" asked the Secretary of Defense.

"I've notified the *Frederick* and *Paul Hamilton* to get under way. That'll give us another amphibious assault ship and guided missile destroyer.

"And the Air Force?"

"I've put the bases in Japan, Alaska, and Guam on full alert and ordered them to stand by. If North Korea tries anything, we can hit them when they pour over the DMZ. Enormous firepower can be concentrated on the killing zones they'll have to cross to reach Seoul. In addition, the B-52 bombers from Guam can carpet bomb the DMZ on twelve hours notice."

"But that won't stop them, will it, General?" snorted Bastardi. "My analysts tell me the North has over twenty tunnels dug under the DMZ that can funnel in 50,000 troops per hour. Your planes can't do jack-shit to those tunnels."

Mustering his strength, Morehead declared, "I don't want them reaching Seoul, General. I want them stopped at the DMZ."

"Sir, the only way we can do that is by using the nuclear option."

"If they're responsible for New York, I don't think world opinion would be against it," said Deathridge. "We also have to factor in the possibility that Pyongyang might use their Rodong missiles to launch chemical warheads against Seoul."

"And against Japan," said Hohlt. "What was it that North Korean defector, Hwang Jang Yop, said about scorching Japan?"

"He claimed that Pyongyang has enough nuclear and chemical warheads to scorch Japan if the US interferes when they attack the South," replied Deathridge.

Hohlt leaned forward, "Mr. Cho, is Hwang's threat valid?"

"It's very difficult to tell. Mr. Hwang was Pyongyang's chief of propaganda, not defense. We know Pyongyang has a chemical weapons capability, but we don't think their Scud-based Rodong missiles can handle any nuclear weapons they may have developed."

"I still say there's no proof North Korea is involved," Bastardi protested. "We can't rely on the word of these two ex-CIA—"

"President Morehead," interjected Hohlt. "Aren't we getting a little ahead of ourselves? All this talk about using military force to stop an invasion. What about the four remaining warheads?"

Morehead leaned forward, knocking over his water glass. The heavy sedation was wearing off. His eyes blazing with hate, he said, "General Eckel, I *order* you to prepare to use nuclear weapons."

Chapter 19

NOVEMBER 5: NEW ORLEANS

A blanket of heavy morning fog rolled in from the Mississippi River, gliding gently across the French Quarter levee and settling over Jackson Square. The visibility in the Vieux Carre was reduced to less than two hundred feet. Friar knew that if he waited a couple of hours, the fog would burn off, but he didn't have a couple of hours.

From the second floor apartment window in the Pontalba Building, he scanned the square with his binoculars. It was almost deserted. Since the New York explosion, the tourist trade in New Orleans had slowed to a trickle. Across the square, in front of Hebért's Tile and Praline Shop on St. Peter Street, two burly figures huddled in the doorway, the thick mist obscuring their features. A pair of newlyweds, oblivious to the eyes watching their every move, strolled through the square, past Jackson's statue, towards the nearly empty Cafe Du Monde.

Friar glanced at his watch—9:50 A.M. Still no sign of Dubov.

"You're gonna be pretty much on your own out there, Hoss," Joe Don said, adjusting the body mike attached to Friar's kevlar vest.

The vest made his jacket bulge and would be uncomfortably warm in the high humidity, but it might stop a slug in the back.

"Try to keep tabs on where I'm going. If anything happens, don't rush in. Just report back to Warner." *And to Marcie,* Friar wanted to add. He frowned as he thought of how little he knew about Dubov and his organization, but, there was no choice, he had to play the Chechen's game. With NEST batting zero, Dubov was their only lead.

Feeling like a duck in a shooting gallery, Friar zipped up his bright yellow nylon jacket, nodded to Joe Don, and headed down the flight of oil soaked wooden stairs leading to St. Ann Street. Crossing the street, he entered the heavy wrought iron gates encircling the square.

"Mr. Clarke," called a shabbily dressed man sitting on a park bench near the statue. There was a black plastic garbage bag on his lap and an earphone attached to his right ear. It was Dubov, his hair dyed gray and his face covered with a four-day stubble. He was wearing a ratty, New Orleans' Saints baseball cap, baggy, army-surplus pants, and a faded denim shirt. After checking to see if Friar was being followed, he signaled to the figures on St. Peter Street. Nodding in the direction of St. Louis Cathedral, he said, "Let's take a stroll."

Without talking, they left the square via the Cathedral gate, then headed northeast along Chartres Street. On reaching Ursulines, Friar noticed a face peering down at them through a grimy, second floor apartment window. He hoped Joe Don hadn't gotten antsy and was staying well back. Turning right on Ursulines, they walked half a block to a store front with a large, glass window lettered, "Guidry Brothers' Fish House." The window had been freshly painted on the inside, blocking the visibility from the street. A hand printed sign— Closed for Renovation—dangled from the door handle. Dubov knocked three times, then twice. The heavy, wooden door creaked open.

When Friar stepped inside, the strong, cool odor of days-old fish stung his nose. The main room was dimly lit and spacious. The only sound came from the rattle of an unbalanced wall fan. Wooden crates of iced speckled trout and redfish were stacked in the far corner. On the left, between two large, empty refrigerated display cases, was a thick, metal door leading to a walk-in cooler. On the right, a shaft of light streaked out from under a door leading to a small office. In front of the door, two husky guards, built like Olympic weight lifters, stood watch. They were dressed in the full length white coats and plastic aprons of fish merchants, but they carried AKS-74 submachine guns.

"I'm glad you could make it," Dubov said in a relaxed voice, while peeling off his hobo attire. "Please excuse the security measures, but we're in danger of attack from goons working for the Dols."

"You said you had something for me." Friar said, surveying the room, searching for an emergency escape route.

"All in good time, Mr. Clarke. You won't be disappointed." Walking over to the office door, Dubov spoke in hushed tones to the guards. The blinds on the office windows were tightly drawn, making it impossible to see in. "I've taken the liberty of ordering beignets and coffee. I hope you like the New Orleans French roast with chicory."

Opening the office door, Dubov beckoned for Friar to enter.

Not knowing if he would leave alive, Friar braced himself, then stepped across the threshold. In the center of the cramped space was a yellow and white checkered tablecloth draped over a large wooden fish crate set up as a table. Across the table sat a lone figure, perched on a stool, eyes wide with fright. It was Kat, pale but unharmed.

"Laurence!" she shouted, jumping to her feet, and rushing over. She hugged him, burying her face in his shoulder.

He held her while she shook uncontrollably.

"I see you two know each other," Dubov said, grinning slyly.

"I thought they were going to kill me," she exclaimed, tears of relief streaming down her face.

Dubov poured three cups of French coffee. "Sit down, please. Enjoy the refreshments, they're getting cold." Placing two beignets on each of three plates, he sprinkled the still warm dough with powdered sugar. "We found Miss Mills at Brighton Beach, kidnapped by thugs from the Dols. An informant told us she was there, asking questions about *me*." His face hardened, "It was fortunate we arrived in time. Those *swinya* are brutal. They would have enjoyed raping her, cutting her into little pieces, and grinding up her body in a commercial garbage disposal."

Friar looked at Kat who nodded it was all true. Then he glanced at Dubov who pretended to be absorbed with his beignets. To Friar, who believed in personal accountability, the Chechen's action rated a gold star to be filed away in his private record book of rewards and punishments to be meted out on judgment day. He didn't care about the motive, only that Kat was unharmed and well.

"I'm sorry, Laurence," she said. "I was only trying to help." She hoped he didn't mind her calling him Laurence, like Marcie did.

"You're not wearing your vest," he admonished.

She lowered her eyes. How could she tell him she thought the thick kevlar made her look overweight. He would think she was vain and unprofessional.

Friar held up Kat's hand, and looked at Dubov, "Present number one?"

"Number one."

"And, number two?" Friar was no longer concerned the Chechen intended them harm—at least not today. Dubov had not even bothered to pat him down for weapons, and the ritual being played out was much too elaborate for a prelude to murder.

Dubov rested his hands on the checkered tablecloth. "Please listen carefully. Take notes if you like." From a cardboard box on the corner of the table he produced notepads and pens. "As you will recall, at our first meeting I told you nuclear warheads were being smuggled into the US."

"I remember."

"I provided you with information on Iraq and the Dols. I even gave you the name of Hashim, the terrorist behind the plan to blow up New York. I gave you his address." Feigning disappointment, he shrugged, "What more could I have done?"

Friar was impressed with the performance. "The FBI arrested Hashim, but he refused to talk."

Dubov shook his head. "Refused to talk! You had him in your grasp, and he *refused* to talk?" Dubov rolled his eyes, "How can you be so weak?"

A bell went off in Friar's head. Tovi had warned him that Chechens despised weakness. Maybe it would lead to overconfidence.

Dubov pushed the beignets aside. "What happened to Manhattan was a tragedy. In Chechnya we have great sympathy for America. We too have suffered much."

Eating his beignet, Friar managed to grunt and nod appreciatively.

Satisfied with Friar's reaction, Dubov continued, "When we saw the extent of the damage to New York, we decided to help. We didn't want to see another American city destroyed. We know how the Dols operate and are not bashful about obtaining information."

"Are you offering to help us locate the warheads?"

"Better than that, Mr. Clarke, we have already done so. All four nuclear devices have been captured and are in our possession."

Friar blinked in disbelief. "Fine. Just tell me where to pick them up."

Dubov shook his head. "If only it were that simple."

"Okay, Mr. Dubov. What's your price?"

With an expansive wave of his hand, Dubov replied, "If it were up to us, we would just hand them over. Unfortunately, that's not possible. During the past few years, the world has grown more complicated. In our war for independence, Chechnya was attacked by Moscow without mercy. Grozny, Shali, Vedeno—totally destroyed. Much worse than New York. But, we won. Now, we need money to rebuild. A committee of patriots has been formed to oversee the transition. The organization is called the Phoenix Committee."

Friar jotted down the name. So, that was his master plan. Chechnya had decided to play footsie with Pyongyang in exchange for a few billion when the Russians granted them autonomy and left.

Dubov continued, "We Chechens know the West looks on us as Muslim outcasts. Neither Europe nor the US has offered financial aid. Everyone is too busy stroking the fur of the Russian Bear and feeding him honey. So, we have been forced to look elsewhere for support."

Chechnya's pact with the devil was beginning to make sense. Lay a false trail of misinformation and set up Iraq, the Shaheeds, and Dols to take the fall. If Washington ever did unravel the knot, it would be too late. All of Korea would be under the control of Pyongyang, and Chechnya would be hiding behind Russia's nuclear umbrella.

"I believe your government will find the requests of our partner to be *very* reasonable. Especially when compared to the specter of four more American cities destroyed." Dubov's voice now took on the cutting edge of an order. "You must remember, the remaining warheads are large ones, not small devices like the 100-kiloton bomb the Iraqis used in New York."

"I understand. What are your instructions?"

"At midnight tonight, Washington time, a call will be placed to the President of the United States. It will come from Pyongyang in the name of 'The True Revolutionary Government For a Unified Korea.'" Dubov was puzzled by how calmly Friar took the news of North Korea's involvement.

Friar rested his pen on his notepad. "One small detail, Mr. Dubov. How do we know you're not bluffing, that you actually have the warheads?"

Dubov chuckled, "Whatever happened to trust?" Rising from his seat, he said, "That's a reasonable question, Mr. Clarke. Please follow me. The proof is in the next room." Leading Friar and Kat into the main room, he walked over to the heavy, metal door to the walk-in cooler. Flipping on the light, he pulled open the door. Inside, hanging from meat hooks, were four frozen bodies. Beside the trussed-up corpses of the Shaheed's driver and young martyr were the two missing, heavily tattooed members of the Dolgochenskaya syndicate.

Kat gasped, leaned forward, and vomited. Friar quickly pulled her away.

Dubov pushed the heavy door closed. "As I said, it was not easy. We lost a lot of good men in the fight to take the warheads. What you saw was just a sample." Dubov led them back into the office and sat down. Handing Kat a glass of water, he said, "I'm sorry I had to expose Ms. Mills to such a sight, but you wanted proof."

"I'm afraid that's not good enough," Friar said, bluntly. "Four dead bodies don't prove a thing."

"What more do you need?"

"Perhaps if a neutral party were to verify—"

"And tell you where the warheads are? No, I don't think so. What if I were to give you a sample? Would that suffice?"

Friar eyed him skeptically. "A sample? You mean a warhead?"

"Why, yes, Mr. Clarke. That's exactly what I mean."

"Of course—"

"Then here you are," said Dubov, removing the cloth from the box they had been using for a table. Inside the fish crate was a 550-kiloton, thermonuclear warhead.

3:55 P.M.
The Vieux Carre was empty except for teams of NEST and FBI

agents scurrying around inserting probes of gamma sniffing, sodium iodide crystal detectors into every hole bigger than a praline patty. From the Mississippi River to Esplanade Avenue to North Rampart Street to Canal Street, every foot, every inch was being inspected as a possible hiding place for the remaining three warheads.

At the southeastern edge of Washington Artillery Park, where the levee holds the Mississippi River in check, Mark Hastey and Friar stood on top of the concrete retaining wall. From their elevated vantage point, Hastey could supervise the search while overseeing the loading of the warhead onto a barge tied up at Governor Nichols Street Wharf. Earlier, he had made the decision to float the nuke down river before dismantling it.

"It's one of the older models," said Hastey. "Must've come straight out of a Russian Satan missile."

"Yeah," Friar grunted as he watched the NEST specialists, dressed in yellow containment suits, gingerly maneuvering the warhead into position on the barge. "Any danger of that thing going off?"

"No, it wasn't armed," Hastey replied. "Kinda weird though. There was a 'How To' computer disc taped to the base of the neutron initiator. We played it out on the computer in the command truck. It was all there. The protocol for bypassing the permissive action links, the internal wiring diagrams, the voltage requirements for triggering the initial chemical explosion—everything. Of course, you'd have to know how to tie it together to arm it."

Friar grimaced. It was Dubov's way of letting them know he held the keys for detonating the remaining warheads. Friar wondered where the Chechen was now. In all the hubbub, he had quietly slipped out the back door of the fish house with his bodyguards and disappeared.

Hastey watched the muddy waters of the Mississippi lapping against the sides of the barge, holding it fast against the dock. It wouldn't do to have the warhead fall overboard, not at this stage. "The serial number on the housing matches one from your Cairo list. That pretty well confirms there are three more out there somewhere."

"Reckon it does," replied Friar, distracted by the shambles made of his theory that all the warheads were together. Glancing west he noticed a marine diving bell resting on Dock 3. It was tethered to an overhead gantry, its spiderlike arm hovering protectively overhead. A sense of *déjà vu* flashed through his mind.

Watching the gantry, he mentally sorted through the turmoil of recent events. If the warheads weren't at the Cranberry iron mine, maybe the large truck had been the decoy and the smaller ones the real carriers. New Orleans certainly made it look that way. Pulling a small notebook from his jacket pocket, he turned to the transcript of the last meeting with Dubov at the Watergate Hotel. On page seven was the comment, "The warheads were smuggled ashore in Wanchese, where they were *loaded onto trucks and driven to their destinations.*" But, if that was so, why were Dubov's men still at the mine? Turning to Hastey, he asked, "Any word from the other NEST teams?"

"Nothing so far. We've got people in Chicago, Dallas, and San Francisco—the cities where the remaining three rental trucks were turned in." Hastey shook his head, "That's a big area. Too bad they weren't at Yellow Mountain."

"All we know for certain is the dogs didn't find them. I still think there's a good chance they're somewhere in the vicinity."

"Might not hurt to check the mine with a couple of FLIR units."

"FLIR? What's that?"

"Forward-looking infrared scanners. One of our newest toys. The units can pick up temperature changes as small as .18 degrees Celsius. We've got two rigged for canine use."

Friar's interest perked up. Infrared that sensitive could tell if *anything* inside the main shaft had been recently moved or disturbed. "Let's give it a try. Can you send the dogs in tonight?"

Once again, the diving bell perched on the wharf caught Friar's attention. "Mark, have you got a copy of the video the dogs made of the mine?"

"Not here, it's at Camp Peary. We can call and have them beam it to us by satellite. Give me twenty minutes."

Sitting in front of the computer in NEST's command van, Friar moved his chair closer to the screen, "Stop, back up a couple of frames.

The video operator rewound five seconds of tape.

"There—freeze it—*there*." Friar studied the murky view of several dark objects stacked against the wall of the mine.

Squinting at the images, Hastey said, "I don't see anything, just a couple of empty shells."

"That's it. Empty shells. Count them."

"Hard to tell without computer enhancement. But, it looks like—four. Yeah, four shell halves."

"Exactly," Friar pointed out. "There are *only* four. That means the other three warheads are still in their original containers." It was so obvious. The mud on the tires of the forklift; the comment by Big Ed Hazlewood that the renters seemed pleased the mine was flooded; Wentworth's description of the pods; and the fact the shells were designed for underwater use. He wished Kat were here to go over Wentworth's description of the pods. He would check with her as soon as the doctors at Charity Hospital in New Orleans said she was okay.

Gotcha now, Dubov, Friar thought.

NOVEMBER 6: WILLIAMSBURG

Friar relaxed and leaned back in the fourteen-foot, two-person raft, watching the muted colors of the Flaming Gorge Canyon drift by. It was their second float trip in two days down the Green River. Still daydreaming, he watched as Marcie hooked another rainbow trout. When it jumped clear of the water, he could see it was a monster—twenty-six inches, easy. It was her second big fish in less than thirty minutes. While he helped her net the trout and remove the barbless hook, he peeked at the fly she was using. It was a Gold-Ribbed Hare's Ear. When they stopped on the riverbank for lunch, he would switch his Woolly Bugger for a—there it was again. That noise that sounded like tin cans being scraped over concrete. Gradually, the grating turned into a series of rings. Finally, it stopped. He rolled over and went back to sleep.

"Laurence, wake up, it's for you," Marcie said, gently tugging on his shoulder. "It's Mark Hastey."

Still groggy, Friar reached for the phone. Gradually, his dream-state receded and he remembered he was at the Williamsburg Inn. Dragging himself into a sitting position, he eyed the bedside clock. 5:12A.M. "Okay, Mark, whatcha got?"

Hastey spoke rapidly, "*The dogs found something. The infrared picked* up tire tracks leading from the entrance back to a wooden barrier in front of slope four. When we enhanced the images we could tell the barrier had been removed and put back. There were fresh boards mixed in with the old and some of the nails are new."

"Hold on." Swinging his legs around until they hit the floor, he whispered to Marcie, "Coffee, please. Industrial strength."

Thumbing through the black notebook he had placed on the night stand before collapsing into bed, he reached the special op section. "Contact Commander Frank Ferrier at Joint Special Operations Command, MacDill Air Force base in Tampa. He's expecting your call. His number is 813-227-5634. He's got SEAL Team Six standing by in Norfolk. When they get there, have them check slope four."

"I've got some bad news. One of the dogs is missing. His video went dead at the end of the search. He was probably picked up by a laser beam near the entrance. If they see how he's rigged—"

"Damn," Friar muttered. Now they would have to assume the element of surprise was gone. With any luck, the Chechens still didn't know about the hidden entrance in slope two. One thing for certain, the Chechens would contact Dubov. "Any unusual radio traffic?"

"Affirmative. They've got a CHIRP transmitter. It went crazy right after the video blacked out. It's operating on an alternating time slope. We're using a spot jammer, but we keep lagging behind."

Friar bowed his head. He should've had NSA drop a temporary communications blackout over the mine. Now it was too late.

"Let me know what the SEALs find." Friar hung up the phone. If the warheads were still in the mine, NEST would have to act fast.

The phone rang again. Friar grabbed the receiver, "Yeah, Mark?"

"Friar, it's me, Tovi. Need to see you right away."

ROBERT GRAVES HOUSE: 6:15A.M.

Perched on a round, wooden stool with a swivel top, the Sandman was wide awake. "I hear you caused quite a stir down in New Orleans," he said, handing the still groggy Friar a mug of strong, instant coffee. "So, we scratch one warhead off the list."

"Three more to go," Friar said, sipping the bitter brew.

"Sorry to have to call you so early." The corners of Tovi's mouth turned up in an impish grin. An insomniac and morning person, he enjoyed waking sleepers. "I have information I thought you might need. We got the second one."

"The second what?"

"Not what—who," Tovi answered, smugly.

"Okay, you've got the second who." Friar arched an eyebrow, "Anyone I know?"

"Volodinsky."

Friar's face brightened. Even with a computer disk of instructions, Dubov wouldn't be able to arm the warheads without an expert's help. "Is he dead?"

"Better than that," Tovi replied. "He's alive and talking. We have him tucked safely away."

Friar was wide awake. "How?"

"Actually, it was quite easy. We asked our friends at GCHQ in central London to enter 'Fredek, Ekaterina, and Dasha' into their Flintlock Dictionary at Morwenstow in Cornwall. It's all part of NSA's ECHELON system."

Friar nodded, he was familiar with ECHELON and the way it screened all international communications for listed keywords.

Tovi continued, "Mossad's behavioral science unit combed the archives and asked around. It took several days but they finally formed a working profile of Volodinsky." Pulling a black leather notebook from his briefcase, Tovi opened it to a section marked by a paper clip. "The good doctor is methodical, dependable, and impotent. His wife's name is Ekaterina—which means pure. I can assure you, she's anything but pure. It seems his weak point is his concern for his mother, Dasha, who's dying from leukemia. The wife and mother live together in a cheap, walk-up flat in Moscow. Our Fredek is a good son. He calls home regularly."

Friar was surprised to see what looked like genuine sympathy on the Sandman's face.

"Yesterday, we were notified by our friend in London that all three words appeared thirty-six hours ago in the same phone call from the US to Moscow. The signal was channeled through the Intelsats monitored by NSA's satellite dishes at Morwenstow. Our friend gave us the phone number and street address of the point of origin. It was a phone booth in Boone, North Carolina. We immediately stationed a lookout across the street and waited. This morning at 1:10 A.M., the good doctor showed up to call home."

"Has he—?"

"We've questioned him *extensively*," Tovi replied in a somber tone. "He broke easily. He tells us there are definitely three more nuclear devices in the US, although he's only seen one."

"Did he say where?"

Tovi referred to his notebook. "On 18 October he flew from Newark to the Greensboro-High Point airport, where he met a Chechen named Dima. He was driven to Boone, blindfolded, then taken by truck to a dilapidated building in the country. He estimated the trip from Boone took approximately an hour and a half." Tovi spread a map on the table with a circle radiating out from the center of Boone. Inside the area was Yellow Mountain and the Cranberry iron mine.

"Did he describe the building?"

"Only to say it had a creaky wooden floor, a high ceiling and shuttered windows. It was late at night and there weren't many reference points."

Friar knew better than to ask where Mossad was holding the physicist.

From his briefcase, Tovi removed a large sheet of paper with a hand drawn schematic diagram of the warhead along with a series of rough, hastily penciled sketches and numbers. He pushed it over to Friar. "Here's the bad part, the reason I dragged you away from your charming bride at this hour. The Chechens had Volodinsky arm a 750-kiloton warhead."

Friar studied the diagram and notations. The figures and lines were jagged and smeared, a sign they had been produced under extreme duress. There were letters and numbers marking contact points, electrical lines, input-output voltages, and two cutaway views of the container holding the warhead. "Did he say how it was wired?"

"It's rigged to be detonated by a timer or remotely."

Friar grimaced, "Remotely. I hope not by radio waves."

"No. They understand that would be too risky. It was hard wired to a remote switch connected to the warhead by 600 meters of wire. The firing mechanism is soldered to the inner shell. After Volodinsky armed the warhead, they placed it back inside the outer casing. He was instructed to make certain the connections were waterproof. Does that make sense?"

"You bet it does."

"I asked him how to disarm it. He said you would have to neutralize the firing mechanism between the two shells. But, tell your people to be careful, he was slow giving me the answer."

Tovi stood and walked around the room, checking to see that the doors and windows were shut and the blinds tightly drawn. Pulling up a chair, he sat down facing Friar. "I've received authorization from Tel Aviv to share a *top secret* report with you. This information is for your eyes only. The source can never be revealed. *Not ever*. Do you understand?" The Sandman's face was hard and cold.

Friar nodded agreement.

Tovi placed his briefcase on the table, took a knife from his pocket and slit open the stitching holding the false bottom in place. Inside a narrow, hidden compartment was a plain, dark brown envelope. He handed it to Friar.

Friar opened the envelope and removed a seven page report. The innocuous cover sheet read, "Private banking records, Account Number A277." The next five pages were lists of itemized banking transactions for A277 from the Gesandschaftbank, 23 Boulevard Royale, Luxembourg. There were names, debits, credits, transaction notations, dates, and telephone numbers. Two names appearing with great frequency were the governments of Kuwait and Saudi Arabia. The last page was titled, "Confidential Identity, Account A277." At the top, was a color photo of a smiling, relaxed Bruce E. Bastardi. Beside the photo was the handwritten notation, "National Security Adviser, USA." Below Bastardi's picture was a smaller photo of an unsmiling, worried Oscar Shymanski. Beside his name was the comment, "courier."

Friar thumbed through the report again and again. Mossad had caught Bastardi with his paws in the cookie jar.

Tovi leaned back in his chair, "Seems your friend has been skimming kick-backs for the last two years on sales of military hardware to Kuwait and Saudi Arabia. This report shows he has piled up a nest egg of over $11.25 million."

"How did you—?"

Tovi grinned mischievously. He didn't mind sharing this piece of tradecraft with Friar. "Actually, we were just lucky. It was a combination of facial thermography and Van Eck monitoring that tripped him up. Last year, we installed a thermographic monitoring system at the entrance to the bank. One of the bank managers works for us. The system measures 65,000 temperature points on a person's face and can scan twenty faces a second. You can't fool it by using a disguise or with plastic surgery. Shymanski and Bastardi were identified as soon as they showed up and checked in as account A277. We were fortunate their profiles were already in the computer's memory. We logged them in last year when they attended a Mideast conference in Jordan."

"And Van Eck monitoring?"

"With Van Eck you can remotely read the low levels of electromagnetic radiation emitted by any computer. We have parallel hardware in an office building across the street that can duplicate images on the banks monitors. It's all very cutting edge."

Friar now understood why Bastardi was so eager to blame Iraq for the New York bombing. It would have meant massive arms sales to Kuwait and Saudi Arabia that would have generated handsome profits for account A277. Mossad's report would be helpful, very helpful. Blackmail was a dirty game, but one Bastardi understood.

CAMP PEARY: 8:15 A.M.

Kat waited in the theater's anteroom in case the Security Council decided to question her. At least, that's the reason she gave Friar for being there. The streaks of red in her eyes testified to the continuing emotional trauma of her ordeal. Whenever she thought of Brighton Beach, waves of panic gripped her. The phantoms only disappeared when Friar was near. The psychiatrist at Charity Hospital had explained it was Survivor's Syndrome. She said it would diminish over time.

Friar and Warner took their usual seats. They were surprised at the deterioration in Morehead's condition since the last NSC meeting two days ago. The hounding by the press had been relentless and his depression had only grown worse.

The President's face was pale and drawn, his skin almost transparent, his eyes glazed. He no longer sat at the head of the table. That position had been taken over by Bastardi as head of the Council. The President, slouched in a wheelchair with a lap robe drawn up to his waist, was parked on Bastardi's left. Dr. Kernodle, Morehead's personal physician, sat at his side, watching for further signs of stress. All pretenses about his state of health had been dropped.

Secretary of State Hohlt passed around copies of a two-page report titled, *North Korean Ultimatum*. "Last night, at 11:48P.M., we received a call from someone referring to themselves as 'The True Revolutionary Government For a Unified Korea.' The caller faxed us a set of demands addressed to 'United States War Maniacs.' I guess that's us."

A ripple of laughter echoed off the paneled walls.

As the Council members read the report, Secretary of Defense Deathridge said, "I see they list the next three targets as San Francisco, Chicago, and Dallas."

"They don't exactly call them targets," replied Hohlt. "Their wording is more ambiguous. They say, 'Do not interfere with our plans for the Grand Unification. To make that mistake would bring lifetimes of shame and irreparable damage to Chicago, San Francescor and Dallas.' They even misspell San Francisco."

"To me, that's a *direct* nuclear threat," declared Deathridge.

Vaughn tapped his pen on the rim of his water glass. "I would like to comment."

"Please do," replied Hohlt.

"Early this morning, South Korean intelligence notified us there has been an attempted coup against Kim Jong Il's government. It was led by Generals Han Young Hwan and Roh Jang Hae on behalf of the so-called *Inmungun*, or People's Army. We don't know how successful the coup has been. This list of demands is from the coup leaders, not Kim Jong Il's government."

"Where's Kim now?" asked Deathridge.

"NSPA believes he's under house arrest in Pyongyang," replied Vaughn. "Last night, President Lee's office in Seoul received a frantic call for help from someone claiming to be acting on Kim's behalf. Contact was broken off before the source could be identified or an answer given."

Waving the list of demands in the air, the Chairman of the Joint Chiefs said, "These bastards are ordering us to clear our 37,000 troops out of the country by noon on the seventh, Washington time. I can tell you this, if we cave in to that crap, we may as well kiss the Korean peninsula, and our influence in Asia, goodbye."

"Who's this other group, the ones calling themselves 'The Phoenix Committee'?" Deathridge asked, holding up the second page of the report.

"Mr. Clarke can answer that," replied Vaughn.

Friar stood while gathering his thoughts. It was time to bring the Council in on Dubov's involvement, at least part way. "It's a Chechen nationalist organization in Grozny. It's operating in league with the crime syndicate controlling the three remaining warheads. It was the Chechens who gave us the New Orleans warhead. It's my opinion—"

"What the hell are you talking about?" snarled Bastardi. "First you say the Iraqis control the weapons. Then you tell us it's the militant Islamics, then North Korea, now it's the goddamned Chechens. I thought the FBI said the crime syndicate involved is called the Dolgo—something or other." Glancing around the table he asked, "Does anyone know what's going on?" Stabbing a finger at Warner and Friar, he said, "I'd certainly take the FBI's word over that of these two jerks."

Friar patiently waited for Bastardi to finish his tirade. He wasn't going to be goaded into making a mistake. When the room was silent, he continued, "The Chechens claim to have captured the warheads from the Dols. They blame them for the Manhattan explosion. It's my—"

There was a commotion as Dr. Kernodle jumped to his feet and grabbed the President who had slumped forward.

After conferring with the President's physician, Bastardi called a one hour recess, then helped wheel the unconscious Morehead out of the conference room to a waiting ambulance.

Chapter 20

While waiting in the theater anteroom, Friar's cell phone began to beep. It was Hastey at Yellow Mountain. "*We've hit pay dirt. A recon team of SEALs found a submerged container in slope four. It has wires leading back to the entrance and the line's hot. This has got to be the live warhead.*"

Friar tapped Warner on the shoulder, "They've found it." Turning back to the phone, he asked, "So slope two's still open?"

"*The Chechens haven't figured it out yet.*"

"What about the other two warheads?"

"*Haven't had time to look. Right now we're concentrating on the nuke in slope four. It's submerged in thirty feet of water.*"

"Did you get the schematic I faxed?"

"*It's right here. Damn good thing you sent it. We're working on a plan to float the container to the surface. It can't be moved far. If the circuit's broken, its gonna explode.*"

"I'm coming down as soon as I finish here."

10:05 AM

When the meeting of the Security Council resumed, Friar was surprised at how washed-out Bastardi appeared. The old swagger and arrogance was gone. That could mean only one thing—the President's health had taken a turn for the worse.

Bastardi gaveled the meeting to order. "Dr. Kernodle has taken the President to Walter Reed for a last minute checkup before his flight to Geneva this evening."

Hohlt's head jerked up from the notes she was taking. Glancing around the table at the other Council members, she could see the looks of disbelief.

Ignoring the stares, Bastardi explained, "The UN Security Council called an emergency meeting in Switzerland to discuss the New York bombing. The President felt he had to go."

"Geneva?" blurted Hohlt. "I haven't been notified of any—"

"The President's put me in charge of the Security Council while he's gone. He's asked me to head up the search for the three remaining warheads."

Hohlt winced at the thought of Bastardi taking over. Something was wrong, terribly wrong. The President was unconscious when he left an hour ago and was certainly in no condition to fly to Geneva.

Sensing Bastardi was lying, General Eckel turned to Hohlt, "As Chairman of the Joint Chiefs, I demand an official determination by Congress as to who's in charge. If the President's incapacitated, I have a right to know. It's my understanding—"

"*I* am acting for the President," Bastardi said acidly, his eyes raking the room. "The President is *not* disabled, only temporarily exhausted. He's been under a lot of stress lately. The trip to Geneva on Air Force One will do him good. Dr. Kernodle has ordered that he not be disturbed. If you have any questions, I'll pass them along. The President has issued written orders—"

"Bullshit," growled Eckel through clenched teeth. "Words on a piece of paper don't mean a goddamned thing to me. I'm not taking orders from a pipsqueak like you. I demand to see Morehead. I only answer to the Commander in Chief. If he's not available, I'll go to Congress."

"Where's Dr. Kernodle?" asked Hohlt. "I want to personally hear what he has to say."

"He's with the President and unavailable," snapped Bastardi.

Hohlt glared at the National Security Adviser. As soon as the meeting was over, she planned to contact Carl Jonas, Speaker of the House, and convince him to call an emergency meeting of Congress to handle the situation.

Holding up his hands in a plea for cooperation, Director Vaughn said, "Please, ladies, gentlemen, please. Mr. Clarke has just received a call from NEST. They've located another warhead in the mountains of North Carolina. NEST thinks the other two may be nearby."

For the next fifteen minutes Friar briefed the Council on the status of NEST's operation at the Cranberry iron mine. The amount of interest Bastardi showed in the details worried him.

"So what's our next step?" asked Secretary of Defense Deathridge, looking around the room for consensus. "With the deadline less than twenty-seven hours away, we can't wait to start making preparations."

"Question is, in which direction?" said General Eckel. "Do we cave in like a whipped dog and abandon Seoul, or do we hit Pyongyang hard, with a preemptive nuclear strike?" This face-to-face encounter with asymmetrical warfare frustrated Eckel. At the Army War College, he had studied the concept of facing a threat against which there was no effective counterattack, but that had all been theory. Now, the reality of having to respond militarily to an ill-defined group of blackmailers and terrorists was overwhelming.

With a black, felt-tipped marker, Hohlt listed both options on a sheet of white cardboard and taped it to the wall. It was the President's call and she didn't even know where he was or his condition. "I recommend we prepare for both courses of action. The final decision can be postponed until midnight. Mr. Clarke, how sure are you that all three warheads are in that mine?"

Friar crossed his fingers. "I give it a fifty-fifty chance. We should know for certain by early this evening."

"Everything depends on the answer to that question," she said. "If just one American city is in danger of being destroyed, we'll have to comply with their demands. But if we can locate all three warheads by midnight—"

"If the warheads are in that mine, I say we blow them up right there," said Bastardi. "I'm sure the President would agree." Seeing no immediate opposition, he added, "New York would still be in one piece if NEST had followed my orders and blown up that warhead when they had the chance."

"That order was not yours to give," scoffed Hohlt. "Or have you forgotten that you're not President?"

Bastardi fumed in silence while jotting himself a reminder to have

Morehead sign an order replacing Hohlt as Secretary of State.

"It would be better to deactivate the warheads in place," said Deathridge. "We don't want to risk turning western North Carolina into an American Chernobyl."

"That's a decision best left to NEST—and the President," said Vaughn.

"Don't worry," Bastardi assured the Council. "I can speak for the President and I'm going down to North Carolina to personally supervise the operation."

This was the type of power play Friar had anticipated. Bastardi was running scared. When the dust settled and the public found his fingerprints all over the New York debacle, they would demand his head on a pike. His only chance at political survival was to cover his tracks before Morehead could be declared mentally incompetent and removed from office. Friar braced himself—Bastardi had to be stopped and he was the only one who could do it.

Rising to his feet, Friar said, "Mr. Bastardi, we appreciate your offering to help, but task force Red Bravo and NEST can handle the situation at Yellow Mountain." Pulling a small, black notebook from his coat pocket, he flipped to the page marked by a yellow Post-it note. "We could use your assistance in tracing the payments for the warheads. We believe some of the funds went into a secret account at the Gesandschaftbank, in Luxembourg. The records show over $11 million deposited into a numbered account—A277. I believe you're familiar with that bank?"

Bastardi went pale. "That's—the CIA h-had better not be spying on American citizens. I–I, er have no—" He collapsed back into his chair, unable to speak.

The room fell silent. The Council members looked at Bastardi, then Friar, then each other. They had never seen the National Security Adviser at a complete loss for words.

"No comment?" asked Friar. Sitting back down, he caught Warner's attention and nodded towards the door. He would have to move fast. It wouldn't take Bastardi long to recover.

Excusing themselves, Friar and Warner quickly left the Council room.

Grabbing Kat on the way out, Friar said. "I need your help." He was pleased she seemed to have recovered.

"Anything."

"I want you to act as my liaison with General Eckel. He's one of the good guys. Stay with him and keep me informed."

WILLIAMSBURG: 10:45A.M.

It only took Friar ten minutes to reach Bosworth House. Marcie was on the telephone and Joe Don was pulling on a set of rust brown, mechanic's coveralls over his regular clothes.

On the kitchen table was an innocuous, black, cigar-box sized container with a magnetic clamp on the back and a telescoping antenna attached to its side.

"Okay, Hoss, I've got the gizmo. Where's the target?"

"It's a red Range Rover in the motor pool at Peary. The government tag is NSA-1." A wry smile crossed Friar's face It was just like Bastardi to use a high profile, foreign luxury car, complete with tell-tale vanity tag, as his mobile communications center. Once the ARS-4 locator was clamped to the Range Rover's muffler system, the vehicle could be located anywhere in the world by means of signals bounced off the Global Positioning Satellite.

Hanging up the phone, Marcie said, "That was Eileen Hohlt. She wants you to know President Morehead is still in Washington. He's locked up under guard in the psychiatric wing at Walter Reed. Supposedly he's there for his own protection. She tried to contact Dr. Kernodle, but he's missing. Bastardi is the only one who has access."

PIZZLE KNOB, NORTH CAROLINA: 1:14P.M.

It took the modified Cobra helicopter one hour and fifty-four minutes, running at top speed, to ferry Friar the 332 air-miles to the landing pad at Pizzle Knob.

"Glad you could make it," Hastey said. "SEAL Team Six is moving into position now. There's a NEST team going in with them."

"Can they hear us?" asked Friar, pointing to the microphone hanging from the overhead beam.

"Nope. They're on their own, but, we can hear them. I only get involved if there's an emergency."

From the camouflaged command post just below the crest of Pizzle

Knob, Mark Hastey had a clear view of the entrance to the Cranberry iron mine, a quarter of a mile across Roaring Creek Valley. The electronic nerve center, constructed around a fifteen-by-thirty-five-by-nine-foot weathered gray wooden frame, was nestled under a large outcropping of granite. The exterior was draped with gray camouflage netting interwoven with brown strips of cloth and dusted with leaves and twigs.

"You can see three life forms near the mine," Hastey said, pointing to a cluster of red thermal images appearing on a wall-mounted TV screen. One person was in the storage building closest to the hillside, the other two were standing just inside the entrance to the mine. "We think there's another person in the main shaft, but the infrared can't penetrate the rock."

"Any unusual activity?" asked Friar, peering at the mine through the lens of a tripod-mounted observation telescope.

"This morning at 1117 hours, right after I talked with you on the phone, someone slipped in. They came in from the east. We didn't pick them up on the monitor until they were a couple hundred yards from the entrance."

Dubov, Friar thought.

The overhead speaker rattled to life. *"Cracker-one, this is Baby Duck-four. We're entering slope two. Over."* Hastey moved to the table in the center of the room and leaned over a large map of the mine. A NEST operator pushed seven blue squares on the map into the short slope marked 2.

"That's SEAL Team Six," Hastey said.

"Affirmative, this is Cracker-one, standing by," replied a soft, firm feminine voice.

"That's Jillian Margot-Li," Hastey said, proudly. "She's one of ours and the best in the business. This is her operation." Secretly, he was pleased there was a live warhead inside the mine, that this was not just another empty drill. It had been difficult maintaining the high morale required of NEST personnel when all they had to respond to were dry runs and rumors.

The NEST map operator shifted six yellow squares to the acetate overlay of slope two.

"What's your plan?" Friar asked.

"Jill wants to examine the container. She thinks there's a good chance the warhead can be deactivated in place. The SEAL team's going to float it to the surface by pumping carbon dioxide between the hulls. If they can remove the outer shell and freeze the detonator with liquid nitrogen, that should do it."

"What about blowing it up right where it is with HE?"

"That's our back-up plan, but the container's only fifteen meters from the rim of the collapse pit. Perlin's doing a computer analysis to see how much C-4 it would take to do the job and not rupture the side of the mountain. We don't want to contaminate the area with radioactive waste."

"Baby Ducks now entering main shaft. Defensive positions established. Proceeding along shaft to slope four."

"Affirmative. ZZZZZZZZ—"

The NEST technician twirled the dials on his radio, trying to filter out the static. Someone was blocking the transmission. Nothing worked. Communications from the mine were now only a stream of crackling, garbled noises.

Hastey glared at the equipment. "That can't be. This gear's supposed to be jam proof."

Friar frowned at the implication. Dubov couldn't have equipment that sophisticated. It had to be the work of National Security Agency. That meant Bastardi was making his move.

There was a rattling on the door of the command center. An FBI agent entered, escorting a grinning Big Ed Hazlewood. "Caught this man snooping around the motor pool."

Big Ed was decked out in a pair of tree-bark camouflage coveralls and was carrying a rusty, 10-gauge Ithaca shotgun. On seeing Friar, he snapped to attention and saluted, hitting the bill of his cap with his hand. "Special Secret Agent Hazlewood, reporting, sir."

Hastey muffled a laugh as Friar walked over to Big Ed, returned the salute and commanded, "Report, Special Agent Hazlewood."

"That feller with the scar. He come by the house this morning around 10:00–no, it was just after that. I'd have to say it was about 10:10 A.M., 'cause Miss Odelia's favorite TV program, "Hollywood Queens," had already started. Anyhow, he wanted to know what was going on up at the mine. I said, 'Ain't nothing I know of.' I don't think he believed me. He looked real mad. Even slammed the door when he left."

WILLIAMSBURG: 1:28 P.M.

Marcie sat at the kitchen table at Bosworth House, doodling on the calico cat notepad Laurence had given her for her birthday. She shook her head—why had Warner been arrested? That phone call from the President to FBI Director Dolenski was bound to have been arranged by Bastardi. Why else would Morehead have gotten personally involved? It didn't make sense. Stan Watkins, the Attorney General, had always been the White House's contact with the Bureau, never Morehead himself. And, arrested—on what grounds? "In the interests of national security"? What a crock. At first, Dolenski had thought it was a practical joke, that someone was impersonating the President's voice. But the speech pattern, shaky and strained, had been computer verified. It was just one more bit of evidence Morehead's grasp on reality was spinning out of control. Marcie put her head in her hands. What else did Bastardi have in mind? Whatever it was, it didn't bode well for Laurence.

Marcie jumped at the sound of the front doorbell. Quickly and silently, she moved to the bedroom window and peeked through the curtains. She sighed with relief at the dark green uniform, the crewcut hair, and the steel-rimmed glasses. There was no mistaking that profile. It was Colonel Houck, General Eckel's personal intelligence adviser. Opening the door, she let him in, glancing behind his back at the beige, Plymouth Voyager minivan that had been parked across the street since 8:00 A.M. *It's just a tourist's car*, she assured herself.

"I have an urgent message from General Eckel for Mr. Clarke," Houck apologized, as though his visit might be an imposition. "With the communications blackout, you're the only one who can still get through."

Marcie nodded and led the Colonel into the War Room. "I spoke with Laurence thirty minutes ago." She was glad Friar had taken the precaution of running an insulated land-line from the radio tower on top of Beech Mountain to the command center. "This blackout, it's not the military's is it?"

"I don't think so," Houck replied, though he wasn't certain. There were so many services involved, and so many conflicting orders being issued, it was impossible to tell who was doing what. "And I'm pretty sure it doesn't belong to the NRO." After a pause, he said, "It's probably the work of National Security Agency. Mr. Bastardi has connections there."

Marcie led the Colonel into the Sidebar and turned on the force field. Now that Big Daddy might be an eavesdropper, no place was safe. When the power surge kicked in, there was an unusual blip in the lights she hadn't noticed before.

Houck spoke slowly and precisely, "Tell Mr. Clarke that a battery of three cruise missiles at Pope Air Force Base in Fayetteville and two on board the guided missile destroyer *Justin Kildare* in Norfolk, have been placed under Mr. Bastardi's direct control." Houck cleared his throat, "General Eckel believes he plans to use the missiles to try to destroy the nuclear warheads at Yellow Mountain as soon as they've been located."

Marcie breathed hard, "The cruise missiles—they're not nuclear?"

"No, thank God," Houck replied. "Mr. Bastardi tried to gain access to a low yield, one kiloton missile, but couldn't obtain clearance. Not even with the President's written authorization and a personal phone call."

Noticing Marcie's flushed expression, he said, "I'm sorry, Mrs. Clarke. There's nothing General Eckel could do. The commanding officer at Pope and the captain of the *Justin Kildare* received verbal orders directly from the President." Shifting uneasily on his feet, he said, "The President's voice was—"

"Computer verified," she said, finishing the sentence.

Houck opened his brief case and pulled out a small, cinnamon-colored container, the size and shape of a cigarette pack. Attached to its side was a small antenna. "We did learn that the missiles are programmed to home in on the coded radio waves emitted by this transmitter. It's an exact duplicate of the one being used by Mr. Bastardi."

"He's using a homing device? Why not just program the missiles with the coordinates of the mine's entrance?"

"Cruise missiles aren't that accurate. Working off the Global Positioning Satellite, plus or minus fifty feet is the best they can do. And, there's no telling where the warheads will be by the time the missiles arrive. At 550 miles an hour, it'll take them at least twenty-five to thirty minutes to reach the target after launch."

"Couldn't you simply jam the cruise missiles' homing signal?"

"We're working on it," Houck said reassuringly. "Tom Reich at the NRO thinks he can have a Boeing RC-135U in place over Yellow Mountain by 1900 hours. But that's over five hours away. In the meantime, we'd better hustle this duplicate down to Mr. Clarke and hope it works."

Marcie reached for the wall phone and dialed 3. Amy Schmidt answered on the first ring.

"Amy, find Joe Don. It's urgent."

There was a second blip of the overhead lights in the Sidebar. Across the street from Bosworth House, the motor of the Plymouth Voyager purred to life. A delicate feminine hand, with meticulously manicured nails, flipped on the toggle switch to the Ultrastar 23 GHz microwave transmitter. A single .8 second burst was all it took to send the message: *Eyes only: B. Bastardi: General Eckel has taken the bait. He believes the cruise missile guidance system is programmed for homing transmitter.* The minivan slowly eased into the flow of traffic.

WASHINGTON: THE CAPITOL: 2:10 P.M.

Kat placed her teacup and saucer on the corner of the highly polished, Newport mahogany table and settled back in the plush, upholstered wing chair. The flashbacks of Brighton Beach only bothered her now when she tried to sleep. She was glad to have a chance to help Friar. Thinking of him helped keep the anxiety and apparitions at bay.

With a tinge of jealousy and admiration she surveyed the elegant suite, tastefully decorated with select pieces of eighteenth century, Queen Anne furniture and late 1700s English pewter antiques. The spacious perk, located on the second floor of the Capitol building, belonged to Carl Jonas, Speaker of the House, Republican, and chief adversary of the Morehead Administration.

The scion and only heir to a wealthy James River plantation family, Jonas had used his wealth from an early age to gain political power and social influence inside the Beltway. His soft-spoken, bourbon-laced, southern gentleman demeanor masked an all-consuming political ambition which would have led to a nomination for the Presidency had it not been for his rather untidy divorce from Caroline. Caroline Byrd Jonas, née Carter, was a scorned southern belle with a will of steel, who had gouged out her pound of flesh during the divorce proceedings by using depositions, interrogatories and requests for documents as politically lethal weapons. By threatening to disclose some rather nasty skeletons dangling in the family closet, and by hinting at several beyond-the-pale business deals involving prostitutes, Las Vegas side-trips, and corporate slush funds, she had successfully torpedoed Jonas's chances of ever being elected to the White House.

"Mr. Speaker," Eileen Hohlt said, her voice strained with emotion, "we need your help." As Secretary of State for a Democratic President, she felt like a turncoat, talking with the ranking Republican in the House about the possibility of removing her boss from office. It wasn't her fault the GOP controlled both the House and Senate, but it made what she had to do all the more difficult.

"Paul filled me in on what's been going on," replied Jonas with a cursory nod towards General Eckel. He and the General were long-time duck hunting buddies who had grown up skinny-dipping together in the James River. They even shared a common ancestor, General Rufus Adolphus Dolan, who had been shot through the chest by a Yankee ramrod at the siege of Petersburg during the waning days of what Jonas referred to as "the First War of Northern Aggression."

"As I understand it, Mrs. Hohlt, you want *me* to call an emergency session of Congress to inquire into the President's health?"

"That's correct. It's our opinion the President has suffered a mental breakdown and is *temporarily* incapable of fulfilling the duties of office." She emphasized the "temporarily" more out of a sense of loyalty than any conviction Morehead would ever recover. She braced herself for what she was about to say. "In light of Vice President Hambright's death, that puts you next in line for succession to the Presidency."

"I understand," Jonas replied, lowering his head to show the proper degree of humility.

Ever since the bombing of New York and Hambright's death, Jonas had been anticipating such a call. The rumors about Morehead's illness had made the rounds, and the secret service had already assigned a team of agents for Jonas's around-the-clock protection. He was determined to approach the crisis with a positive attitude, but the whole affair infuriated him. From what General Eckel had told him about North Korea's involvement, it had all been so unnecessary. First, the destruction of Manhattan, now, the US being held hostage—all because of an outdated commitment to protect South Korea from an invasion by the North. He had argued for years that America had no vital interests at stake in Korea, North or South. With a population twice the size of the North's and a gross domestic product eighteen times larger, it had been Jonas's unwavering position that Seoul could damn well take care of itself. But his warnings had gone unheeded. Too many powerful, vested interests wanted to retain the status quo.

"Goddamnit, Carl, we've got a nut case out there running the Administration using Morehead's name," Eckel groused. "The only way we're going to stop him is for you to take over. No telling what that shit-merchant's going to do next."

"By 'nut case' I assume you're referring to the President's chief chamberlain, Bruce Bastardi?" Jonas bore several scars from run-ins with the National Security Adviser and nothing would please him more than terminating Bastardi's swilling at the public trough. The Speaker glanced to his right at David T. Goslin IV, who was furiously scribbling notes on a yellow legal pad. Goslin, one of the country's leading authorities on Constitutional Law, and a letterhead name at the prestigious Richmond firm of Goslin Lewis Horvath and Smythe, had been called in to advise Jonas on how to navigate the hazards of the Constitutional maze.

"You're goddamned right I mean Bastardi," Eckel replied, hotly. "He's got Morehead stashed away somewhere at Walter Reed, and won't let anyone near him. That sonafabitch is manipulating the President like a two-dollar puppet. Morehead signs whatever he puts in front of him." Eckel wagged his finger in Jonas's face. "Carl, the last thing that little prick did was have the President order five cruise missiles transferred to his personal command. Hell, for all we know, he may be pointing those things at us right now."

Jonas laughed a deep belly laugh, his jowls bouncing up and down. Removing his glasses and wiping them with an embroidered linen handkerchief, he said, "Paul, I don't think things are all that serious." Turning to Goslin, he asked, "Counselor, what's your opinion of the succession issue?"

Goslin stopped writing. "Mr. Speaker, we're in uncharted territory. I dislike using the term crisis, but I think we're confronted with a genuine Constitutional crisis." Opening his briefcase, he withdrew several copies of the Constitution which he passed around. "On page 7, Section 3 of the Twenty-fifth Amendment states that the President can *voluntarily* step aside by sending the President pro tempore of the Senate and the Speaker of the House a *written* declaration that he is unable to discharge the powers and duties of his office."

Hohlt shook her head. "There's no chance that's going to happen. Bastardi would block it even if Morehead were willing. He's got the President totally incommunicado."

Goslin nodded, then continued, "Section 4, specifies that the President can be temporarily replaced by the Vice President, if the Vice President *and* a majority of the principal officers of the executive departments, or *such other body* as Congress may by law provide, transmit to the President pro tem of the Senate and the Speaker their written declaration that the President is unable to discharge the powers and duties of his office."

"Hell, we don't have a Vice President," noted Jonas.

"Correct," responded Goslin. "That's part of the problem. It's pretty clear to me that without a Vice President, the Twenty-fifth Amendment doesn't cover the situation at hand. As you will note, the language in Section 4 is conjunctive not disjunctive. It calls for 'a declaration by the Vice President *and* a body appointed by Congress.' If it had used *or* instead of *and*—"

"Counselor, would you cut the legal crap and talk in plain English?"

Goslin blushed. "As I read it, Mr. Speaker, there is *no* Constitutional provision providing for succession under the conditions we're facing. What we've got is a missing President who *appears*—and I have to underscore the word *appears*—to be incapacitated by stress.

No recognized medical authority has declared him incompetent, so we can't say for certain. In order to replace him without his written consent—or countermand his orders, whatever they might be—you're going to have to prove to both houses of Congress, and the Supreme Court, that he's *non compos mentis*, and get them to act on it. That means at least a statement from his personal physician that he's unable to fulfill his duties and a general consensus by Congress that he should be removed."

With a mother-of-pearl-handled cigar cutter Jonas snipped the end off a Macanudo Jamaican cigar. "That could take several days, Counselor. Isn't there some other way? What about that secret plan for the transfer of power drawn up back in 1996 by the Working Group on Presidential Disability?"

"I haven't seen the actual provisions of that agreement, but as I understand it, it's nothing more than a contract between the President, the Vice President, and perhaps four or five officers of the Executive Branch stating what they'll do if the President becomes disabled. That type of document's not worth much, especially if someone with legal standing challenges it—and they would. No written contract can override the provisions of the Constitution."

"So what the hell *can* we do?" Jonas demanded, his voice edgy with frustration. "We can't just sit on our heinies while the country is blown apart, city by city."

Goslin thumbed through his copy of the Constitution. "My suggestion is for you to call an emergency session of Congress and put it to a vote. You'd better get a two-thirds majority from both the House and the Senate. Then run it by the Supreme Court for final approval."

"Two-thirds? Hell, most members of Congress aren't even in town. It'll take days to get a quorum." It disgusted Jonas the way so many politicians had bailed out of Washington immediately after the explosion.

"We've only got hours, not days," Hohlt reminded them.

General Eckel tossed his copy of the Constitution back to Goslin. "Carl, there's no telling how all this is going to shake out, but I can't just stand around shoveling shit against the tide while North Korea invades the South. As Chairman of the Joint Chiefs, I've got a duty to prepare my troops for combat. I'm depending on you to get the green light from Congress and I need it *now*. If I don't have the go-ahead by 2400 hours—"

"I understand," replied Jonas, reaching for his private, Congressional telephone directory.

General Eckel stood up. "I think you ought to know, I'm sending Miss Mills down to North Carolina with twenty-four, hand-picked members of Delta Force with orders to keep Bastardi from fucking-up NEST's operation. I've put the Commander under her direct orders. He has clearance to shoot-to-kill. If there's a showdown, there may be serious repercussions."

"You think Bastardi's going to take it that far?"

"You're damn right I do. He's got cruise missiles at his command and a burr up his ass. He's also placed a communications blackout over the whole search area. Ms. Mills is the only one who knows who's who down there. She's FBI, but I've ordered her to report to me."

Jonas nodded, then turned to Hohlt, "Eileen, as Secretary of State, do you agree?"

"I most certainly do."

"Okay, Paul, go ahead. I'll grant you whatever authority I have. I'm going to call Senator Harness and try to get Congress moving."

Kat gazed at the distant rays of sunlight flooding the top of the Washington monument. It was a good sign. She wondered if she would live to see it again.

Chapter 21

NOVEMBER 6: GRANDFATHER MOUNTAIN: 4:02P.M.
Joe Don rolled up the sleeves of his new deputy sheriff's shirt and slanted his Smoky Bear hat forward until the rim sat two fingers off the bridge of his nose. The shirt was a size too small, but it was the best Sheriff Maynard could do on such short notice. Slipping on a pair of World War II aviator sunglasses, Joe Don grabbed the overhead hand-bar as the Jeep Cherokee rounded the corner and rumbled into the visitors' parking lot on top of Grandfather Mountain.

Straight ahead, at the far end of the lot, was Bastardi's red Range Rover, just as the ARS-4 locator had indicated it would be. Flown in by military transport to the Elk River airport, the vehicle was being guarded by four sentries, dressed in woodland-camouflage battle fatigues, Kevlar fragmentation vests, Ft. Lewis Go-Devil boots, and combat crewmen's helmets. Joe Don scanned their uniforms for insignia and unit markings. There were none. They were contract mercenaries.

Dressed in khaki chinos and a dark red windbreaker, Bastardi stood at the western edge of the lot. A baseball cap embroidered with the presidential seal, shaded his eyes from the afternoon sun as he peered in the direction of the Cranberry iron mine. A thick valley haze obscured the view of Yellow Mountain, six and a half miles away.

"Just leave this to me," Maynard said, edging the Jeep towards the Range Rover.

A guard, brandishing a 9mm Colt submachine gun, stepped forward and held up his hand.

Maynard brought the Jeep to a gradual stop, rolled down his window and shouted, "Son, you gonna have to move that vehicle. It's blocking a major fire lane." Maynard winked at Joe Don and motioned for him to follow. Holding a clipboard, he opened the door of the Cherokee, leisurely climbed down, squared his shoulders, and sauntered over towards the Range Rover.

Bastardi ran up, waving his arms, "Move on Sheriff. This is none of your business. It's a federal matter."

Pulling himself up to his full six-foot-six height, Maynard centered his sunglasses and glared down at Bastardi. In a slow, mountain drawl he said, "Son, while you're in Avery County, you're standing on my gravel. It's going to take more firepower than you're showing here to run me off my own mountain."

Bastardi backed up a step. He didn't have time to argue. "I'm sorry, Sheriff, I didn't mean to—"

"Jasper," Maynard yelled to Joe Don, "Go back there and take down that license number. We're gonna have to check this mess out." Walking to the front of the Range Rover, Maynard jotted a few notes on his clipboard. "Mighty fancy car you've got here for a government vehicle. Now, why don't you just take your time and tell me all about this here federal matter and why it ain't none of my business."

While Bastardi sputtered an explanation, Joe Don walked to the rear of the Range Rover. He ran his hand with the transmitter under the bumper until he felt the strong tug of magnet against metal. Standing up, he nodded to Sheriff Maynard.

With a big ham of a hand, Maynard clapped Bastardi on the back. "Why didn't you tell me you were a personal friend of the President's?" Tucking his clipboard under his arm, he said, "Tell you what we're gonna do. Jasper and me are going to run everybody off the top of this mountain so you can have it all to yourself. Then, we're going to go down to the bottom and set up a roadblock so you won't be disturbed."

Waving to Joe Don, Maynard led the way back to the Jeep. In a whisper he said, "We don't want any of our paying tourists getting hurt when those cruise missiles come tumbling in."

CRANBERRY IRON MINE: 4:15P.M.

Bubbles hissed from the oblong container rising slowly from the depths of slope four. Two green lights clamped to its side, glared out from the water, like a pair of malevolent eyes. Jill Margot-Li watched while a member of SEAL Team Six surfaced beside the pod, pushing it through the murky liquid to the edge of the slope. The bright light from Margot-Li's hand-held lamp glistened off the wet sides, outlining the umbilical hose used to pump carbon dioxide into the space between the two hulls. A set of double electrical wires trailed ominously behind the container. Margot-Li pointed to the wires and wagged her head.

Using hand signals, she motioned for the pod to be gently pulled from the water and placed on the slippery, muddy floor. Looking at her watch, she noted they had been in the mine two hours and eighteen minutes. It had taken longer than planned. Whispering into her throat mike, she said, "Baby Duck-four, this is Cracker-one. Begin the search for the remaining two containers." Shielded by the Cranberry gneiss from NSA's jamming transmitters, their communications system continued to function inside the mine.

"*Affirmative,*" came the instant reply. "*Baby Ducks-two and five, search slopes six and seven, Ducks-one and six, take slopes three and five.*"

Margot-Li removed a radiation detector from her shoulder pack. Passing the extender probe, with its two Geiger-Müller tube detectors, around the outside of the container, she checked for traces of alpha, beta, X-ray, and gamma radiation. The shell was intact, the readings were minimal. She signaled for the members of the NEST team to remove their bulky containment suits.

Carefully examining the hole in the shell where the wires entered the outer hull, Margot-Li shook her head. Soldered shut. The outer shell couldn't be removed without the danger of jerking the wires out of the initiator, risking a nuclear explosion. They would have to displace the carbon dioxide with liquid nitrogen and hope that worked. She ordered a canister of nitrogen brought forward.

It bothered Margot-Li that she wouldn't be able to visually examine the initiator's wiring. She would have to rely on Volodinsky's primitive, hand-drawn diagrams. But, if the electrical triggering mechanism could be completely covered with nitrogen, that should do the trick. At minus 210 degrees Celsius, the colorless, odorless substance was only 62 degrees short of absolute zero. A temperature that cold would freeze the gates of hell. But what if there was a back-up detonation system present, one not dependent on electricity?

Thump, thump, thump. The hollow sounds of automatic weapons' fire echoed down the shaft. Margot-Li's heart stopped as slugs ricocheted off the rock walls. She wasn't worried about herself, but if just one bullet hit the canister of nitrogen—or severed the wires leading to the initiator—

"Cracker-one, this is Baby Duck-four. There's a Duck down."

PIZZLE KNOB: 4:35P.M.

Friar and Hastey could hear the faint, muffled sounds of gunfire rolling across the valley floor.

"They've been discovered," Friar said, scanning the mine entrance with his binoculars."

"Maybe we ought to launch the attack," Hastey said.

As quickly as it had started, the gunfire stopped.

"Let's hold off a little longer. We don't want to panic them into detonating the warhead." Friar knew Dubov would not hesitate to destroy them all if he thought it was necessary.

"Damn this blackout," Hastey said, exasperated at not knowing what was going on inside the mine. Swiveling the head of the spotter scope from the collapse pit to the mine entrance, he noticed a shadow moving across the pilings on the right side of the timbered door frame. A lone figure emerged, waving a stick with a white handkerchief tied to the end. "Friar, look," Hastey said. "It's one of the Chechens. They're giving up."

Friar moved behind the telescope. Flipping the magnification from 50X to 100X, he adjusted the focus. No mistaking that face, that scar, it was Dubov. "Nope. Not a chance," he grunted. "Probably just wants to talk. I'm going down."

As Friar started out the side entrance of the command center, he stopped. The possibility of Dubov pushing the button was too great. "If your team hasn't disarmed the warhead by the time you hook up, better have Margot-Li blow it with C-4. I'll distract the Chechens."

Hastey hesitated, then nodded. Operations protocol required him to secure the President's personal authorization before using high explosives to destroy a live warhead in a populated area. But with the communications blackout, and the President out of reach, it would have to be a personal judgment call. He had listened dozens of times to the recorded conversations between Nancy Lopez and Washington just before the New York explosion. He wasn't going to let that happen here.

Friar jumped into one of the Fast Attack Vehicles in the command center's motor pool located on the back side of Pizzle Knob. The low-slung, dark olive dune buggy had been specially modified with solid tires for negotiating the rugged, rocky terrain around Cranberry mine. It took eight minutes to cover the quarter-mile distance to the mine's entrance. As he approached, he could see Dubov standing in the shadows. The only sound came from the crunch of gravel under the FAV's tires.

Holding his arms away from his body, Dubov stepped into the fading afternoon light. Dressed in a pair of chocolate brown pants with matching shirt, his face was creased with dark furrows. It was the first time Friar had seen the Chechen looking drawn and haggard.

"Ah, Mr. Clarke. I knew this had to be your handiwork. In New Orleans—I could tell you were hiding something." Pausing, he forced a faint smile, "Your finding a second entrance to the mine was quite unexpected."

Without taking his eyes off Dubov, Friar climbed out of the FAV and walked over. "You haven't got a chance. You're completely surrounded. Hand over the warheads now, and I promise safe passage to Chechnya for you and your men."

Dubov listened with detached amusement. "Cigarette?" Removing a pack of Camel filter-tips from his shirt pocket, he shook one out and placed it loosely between his lips.

Friar watched as he withdrew the silver matchbox with "Jean-Louis" stamped on its face in gold foil.

Dubov lit up, then slowly inhaled. Returning the box to his pocket, he rested his left hand against an outcropping of granite. "I'm afraid it's not quite that simple. The warhead is not mine to give." Waving in the direction of the mine, he added, "What happens to us is of no importance. Our work is not yet finished."

Friar dissected Dubov's comment. He had said—*warhead*—spoken in the singular. If there was only one warhead in the mine, where were the other two? Had the comment been a slip or carefully planned? The Chechen's air of resignation bothered him. He had seen it before in a suicide after he had made his decision to kill himself.

Stalling for time, Friar asked, "Tell me, Mr. Dubov, why detonate the warhead in New York without warning? Does Chechnya want nuclear war with the US?"

Dubov took another drag on his cigarette, "As I've said, New York was not our doing."

"I remember your saying that, but tell me anyway."

Dubov flicked the ash from his cigarette, "Does the date April 21, 1996, have any meaning for you?"

Friar mulled over the question. "No, I'm afraid not."

Dubov's eyes narrowed, "Dudayev? Have you ever heard the name Jokhar Dudayev?"

So, that's it, Friar thought. Dudayev, the President of Chechnya was killed in 1996 by an air-to-surface missile fired from a Russian Sukhoi Su-25 jet. "That was Yeltsin's decision. The US wasn't involved in Dudayev's death."

Dubov scoffed, "Don't be so naive, Mr. Clarke. You're much too intelligent to believe your own propaganda. It was an American Vortex spy satellite that picked up the signals from Dudayev's portable phone and transmitted the coordinates to the waiting Russian warplane. Killing our President was an act of war." He shrugged, "However, as you say, the US was not responsible."

Friar had heard rumors of NSA's involvement in the assassination. It was Morehead's way of helping Yeltsin win re-election against his Communist rival, Gennady Zyuganov. Bastardi had guaranteed the President there would be no repercussions.

Glancing at his watch, Dubov stubbed out his cigarette. "Enough small talk. You have exactly twenty minutes to clear your people from the mine."

"Twenty minutes isn't enough. I'll need at least thirty, maybe thirty-five."

"All right, all right," Dubov snapped. "Thirty-five minutes."

"And after we're out?"

"I am staying here until my mission is finished. If you follow instructions, the warhead will be defused and handed over on November the fifteenth." Reading Friar's expression he said, "No more tricks, Mr. Clarke. Think of how much damage a 750-kiloton warhead can do. And, there are still two more."

Friar climbed into the FAV and headed back to Pizzle Knob. He hadn't seen any trip wires or unusual defensive positions guarding the mine's entrance. It worried him that Dubov had agreed so readily to the extension of time.

5:15 P.M.

Joe Don was at the command center, still dressed in the dark brown uniform of an Avery County sheriff. That was the second time in less than fifteen minutes Friar had seen the same uniform. Dubov had also been wearing a dark brown shirt with an oversized collar and military press. That was how he had slipped past the perimeter guards and entered the mine.

Joe Don unfolded his wiry frame from a metal chair. "Hastey's down in the collapse pit. Marcie called ten minutes ago. She said it's urgent."

Reaching for the handset of the still functioning land line, Friar dialed 0. After three short rings, Marcie answered, *"Laurence, thank goodness it's you. Tovi Hersch tried to send you a message, but couldn't get through."*

Friar could tell from the rapid way she spoke, she was upset. It wasn't like her to get rattled.

"He said whatever you do, don't use explosives inside the mine. He's on his way down there now to explain. I wrangled a Cobra helicopter for him from Peary. I hope that was all right."

"It was fine, you did just fine." No explosives? What could that mean? Hastey had to be stopped from using the C-4.

"Another thing. Warner's been arrested." After pausing to catch her breath, she continued, *"And Bastardi's somewhere in your area. Joe Don has the details."*

"Bastardi?" The muscles in Friar's jaw tightened. What the hell was he up to? And what was the story with Warner?

Marcie quickly told him about the cruise missiles. After hanging up, Joe Don filled him in on Bastardi's location and how the duplicate homing device had been placed under the Range Rover.

Friar sifted through the new information, trying to fit the pieces together. Bastardi's game plan was starting to take form. Drop enough cruise missiles on Friar's head to shut him up permanently, then discredit Warner with lies and innuendoes. In a month or so, after the political dust had settled, he could manufacture enough evidence to show that he, Bastardi, had been the one who had found and destroyed the warheads. In all the confusion, it just might work.

There was a loud knock on the door. Without waiting for an answer, the Sandman rushed in. Waving to Friar, he asked, "Have you talked with Marcie?"

"Five minutes ago."

Pulling a sheet of engineering tracing cloth from a manila envelope, Tovi said, "That Russian physicist didn't tell us everything—at least not at first. Take a look at this." He pointed at a new cross-sectional drawing of the triggering mechanism. Built into the housing was a round, metallic object shaped like a miniature meat thermometer. The top was attached to a spring loaded plunger screwed into position against the warhead's chemical primer.

"What's it mean?" Friar asked.

"It's a concussion trigger. The electrical initiator can be bypassed and the warhead detonated with a change in as little as 5 psi in the surrounding atmospheric pressure."

"That's not much pressure," said Joe Don. "A grenade exploding nearby would set it off."

Friar studied the diagram. "What happens if the electrical initiator is frozen?"

"That won't stop the concussion trigger," Tovi replied. "It's mechanical, not electrical."

"What else did he tell you?"

The Sandman shook his head, "He stroked out during interrogation. He was dead before we could bring him around. A card in his wallet warned of diabetes and high blood pressure. I guess that's what got him."

"I have to find Hastey," Friar said, racing for the door. "Joe Don, you and Tovi stay here in case I miss him."

When Friar reached the motor pool he saw Jason Dorn standing beside two beefy agents dressed in navy blue jackets with FBI stenciled on the back in large, white letters. One of the men, with the name "Sugar" printed over his front pocket, towered six-feet-five and had the scarred face and bull neck of a pro-football lineman. The other, named "Lightfoot," was ten inches shorter and had the protruding browridge and darting eyes of a mountain gorilla. Swinging into the driver's seat of the nearest FAV, Friar called to Dorn, "Jump in. I'll brief you on the way."

Dorn slid into the passenger's seat. "I hate to do this, Friar" he exclaimed, "but you're under arrest." Reaching over, he jerked the keys from the ignition. "You have the right to remain silent—"

While Friar's head was turned, the football lineman leaned over the driver's door and snapped a handcuff on Friar's left wrist.

"Hey!" Friar shouted, jerking his arm backwards, striking Sugar in the jaw.

Wide-eyed, Dorn stopped his Miranda spiel. "Sorry, Friar. Orders straight from the top." Climbing out of the vehicle, he motioned for Friar to follow.

Yanking hard, Friar ripped the handcuffs from Sugar's grip. Without warning, Lightfoot's heavy fist smashed down on the back of Friar's neck, knocking him unconscious.

Dorn cringed when he saw Friar's limp body, slumped against the steering wheel. Reaching over, he felt the back of his head and neck. Nothing seemed broken. Dorn shook his head. That call from FBI Assistant Director Shaman ordering Friar's arrest had to be a gigantic screw-up. They were both on the same team. Why hadn't Friar simply gone along? A phone call here, a contact there and it would have been taken care of.

Lightfoot and Sugar dragged Friar's unconscious body from the vehicle. Grabbing him under the arms, they began lugging him up the path towards the command center. Dorn started to follow, but stopped at the sound of an approaching helicopter. Looking over his shoulder, he saw a lone aircraft nearing the landing pad. Seeing the FBI markings on its side, he turned and started walking towards the tarmac. It must be the federal marshals Washington had promised as backup.

When the JetRanger III touched down, a single, slight figure jumped out the far side. It was Kat. "What was that all about?" she demanded. "Where's Friar?"

"He's under arrest, orders from the President." Seeing the fire in her eyes, Dorn said, "Look, Kat, there was nothing I could do. In a couple of days, we'll get this whole mishmash straightened out." He started to leave.

"Jason!"

Dorn stopped and looked back. Kat was standing twenty feet away, crouched in a combat stance. Pointing at him was the open end of a 9mm Beretta.

"I want him released—*now*," she ordered, surprised at the calmness of her own voice. "Jason, I said *now*." She cocked the hammer. If Dorn didn't call off his goons, or if anything had happened to Friar—

Wham. A single shot rang out from sixty feet away. It came from the direction of the command center. Kat's body slammed backwards, crashing down on the tarmac. The round had struck her squarely in the chest. Standing on the hill, Lightfoot flashed a savage, self-satisfied smirk. It had only taken one shot. Lowering the smoking 10mm Smith and Wesson, he started walking towards the prostrate figure.

Whump. A second shot echoed off the hillside. Lightfoot pitched forward, facedown onto the gravel walkway. Dorn looked up at a grim-faced Joe Don, still holding the .44 magnum in both hands. Beside him, eyes flashing with anger, stood the Sandman. Behind him, knees wobbling, was Friar.

Joe Don raced forward, grabbed Dorn's handcuffs, and roughly shackled his arms behind his back. Tovi walked over to Lightfoot and kicked the Smith and Wesson out of reach. With the toe of his shoe, he examined the gaping hole in the agent's right shoulder.

Friar stumbled down to the landing pad where Kat lay, her body crumpled into a fetal position.

In the background, the faint, staccato sound of helicopter blades echoed down the valley.

Two black, Sikorsky Night Hawk helicopters, with no markings or running lights, slipped over the crest of Cane Creek Mountain. The lead aircraft circled once, then hovered thirty feet off the ground, at the far corner of the landing area. The backwash from the twin 1,560 shp motors churned up gravel and dust, choking Friar and sending bits of debris into his throat, ears, and eyes. The side doors of both helicopters popped open and twenty-four dark figures slid down nylon landing ropes. They were wearing black jump suits, Spectra composite helmets, tactical assault vests, black combat boots and had Heckler & Koch submachine guns strapped to their chests. It was Kat's Delta Force.

Friar kneeled over Kat, covering her head with his jacket to keep the dust out of her face. As the helicopters rose and moved away, he gently rolled her over. She was unconscious. Gingerly, he examined the midsection of her jacket. All he saw was an ugly black hole in the maroon fabric and a tuft of baby blue kevlar, peeking through the void. A lump rose in his throat. She was wearing the body armor he had given her in Williamsburg. "Good girl," he mumbled, "Good girl."

Friar felt someone shaking his shoulder.

"Colonel Crosby Hamblin reporting, sir." It was the Delta Force commander, fully alert and all business. "Orders from General Eckel. I'm to report to a Ms. Kathryn Mills." Looking down, he asked "Is that her? Is she hurt?"

Kat's eyes flickered open. Through the haze she saw Friar's face. "I—what happened?"

"Don't move. You may be injured," Friar said, gently brushing the dust from her face.

"Are you Ms. Mills?" Colonel Hamblin asked.

It was all coming back. "You're the Delta—"

"Affirmative," the Colonel said, leaning over and saluting. He wasn't sure how to report to an injured female civilian, especially one lying on a landing zone with a jacket wrapped around her head.

When she tried to raise up on her left elbow, a sharp pain shot through her rib cage, making her gasp.

Friar eased her back down. "Don't move. You may have a couple of broken ribs. Got to get you to a doctor before they puncture something."

Kat reluctantly nodded. She didn't want to leave but knew she would only be in the way. A feeling of accomplishment swept over her. When the crisis had come, she had stood her ground and hadn't flinched. She motioned for Colonel Hamblin to draw near. "You're to take your orders directly from—from Mr. Clarke here. No one else. Understood?" She squeezed Friar's hand and closed her eyes while the pain wracked her upper body.

"Affirmative," replied Hamblin, saluting again. Forming his men on the edge of the landing pad, he ordered the unit medic to attend to Kat.

After injecting her with morphine, the medic immobilized her on a wide board which he placed on a canvas stretcher.

Friar helped carry Kat to the waiting helicopter that would fly her to a hospital in Asheville. After she was safely on board, he returned to where Joe Don and Tovi were standing beside the wounded agent.

Frothy, red bubbles were rising from the hole in Lightfoot's back. The Delta medic quickly and efficiently stemmed the flow of blood. The labored breathing produced a wheezing-sucking sound. Good, thought Friar, the slug had punctured a lung. He couldn't resist hoping the son of a bitch died. After the wound was stabilized, Friar directed the medic to place Lightfoot on a stretcher and put him in the helicopter with Kat.

Calling Tovi over, Friar said, "How about going with Kat to make sure she's taken care of." It was more an order than a request. There was no need for Tovi to stay and risk being killed. He wasn't needed and Friar wanted a witness to tell Marcie and Warner what had happened.

Tovi started to object, but stopped. He saw the detached, far away look in Friar's eyes, and understood—he probably wasn't going to make it. Patting Friar on the shoulder, he turned, and without saying goodbye, walked silently towards the waiting helicopter.

Kat watched Friar through the open door of the Sikorsky as the helicopter lifted off and headed south. She felt a warm glow as the morphine coursed through her system, blocking the pain.

When the helicopter was out of sight, Friar turned his attention to Dorn, whose hands were shackled behind his back. The dejected agent's shoulders were slumped forward and his eyes were closed.

Friar couldn't help feeling sorry for him. Caught in the middle, he had only been doing what he thought was best.

Rubbing the back of his throbbing neck, Friar lifted his watch to his eyes. "I've got to find Hastey."

Joe Don took him by the elbow, "Hoss, you'd better let me go. You're in no condition to find anybody."

5:45P.M.

Dubov's thirty-five minute deadline was up. Friar sat down on a chair in the command center and placed a towel soaked in cold water on the back of his neck. The flow of events was now beyond his control. He wondered—how do you prepare for a thermonuclear explosion? If Dubov didn't detonate the warhead with his remote electrical switch, NEST would do it for him when they tried to destroy the device with C-4. At least Kat and Tovi were safe. By now, their helicopter was beyond the reach of the shock waves. There was only one base left to touch. He picked up the phone and dialed 0.

"*Is that you Laurence?*" It was Marcie.

"It's me—" His voice choked in mid-sentence. He couldn't speak. Marcie instantly understood. She began to talk, to tell him how much she loved him. He listened without hearing the words. He had always liked the soothing sound of her Tidewater accent. He gazed out the window at the clouds over Grandfather Mountain. They were shifting from pastel blues, to reds, to golden orange, just as they had on the first night of their honeymoon in Montana. His life floated before his eyes, a flood of images of Marcie and their happy times together. He hoped one day she would move into her colonial house in Williamsburg, and occasionally think of him.

There was the faint crunch of boots on gravel as footsteps raced up the path towards the command center. The door burst open. It was Joe Don and Hastey.

"It worked," Hastey yelled triumphantly. "We froze the electrical hookup with nitrogen."

"And the C-4?" asked Friar, still holding the phone receiver in his left hand.

"Didn't have to use it. That's not all. The SEALs found the other two containers under fifty feet of water in slopes six and seven."

Friar turned back to the phone, "Marcie, everything's okay. They've found *all* the warheads. Notify General Eckel. I'll call back as soon as we've secured the mine. And, Marcie—thanks."

"We're laying insulated phone lines now," Hastey said, pointing to two SEALs spooling wire up the hill.

"Good," said Friar. "It's time to move. Let's hit 'em before they figure out what happened."

Friar, Hastey, and Joe Don huddled around the map of the mine while Colonel Hamblin called the signals. From here on in, it was his show.

"Joe Don, you guard the entrance to the collapse pit. Mr. Hastey, you stay with the SEALs and secure the warheads. Delta Force will attack from the front and work its way back down the shaft to you. Mr. Clarke, you come with me."

"What about communications?" asked Hastey.

"We'll have to use hand signals until we're inside," Colonel Hamblin replied. "Remember, *no* concussion grenades or explosives—just small arms."

"You might want to have the SEALs put that warhead back underwater," Joe Don advised. "If there's an explosion, it'll help protect the detonator from the pressure."

"Good idea," Hamblin said. "Let's go."

In twelve minutes, Delta Force was in position near the mine's entrance. It was 6:10P.M. and already dark.

"You'd better stick with me, sir," Hamblin whispered. "After you've done your negotiating bit, we'll take over. Don't want to lose you in the cross-fire." Friar knew it was the Colonel's polite way of telling him to stay the hell out of the way and let the professionals handle the attack.

Friar gave a thumbs up and crawled up to the boulder where he had last seen Dubov. With an electronic megaphone, he called out, "Dubov, this is Clarke." He waited. "You're surrounded. Have your men come out one by one with their hands over their heads."

The lights inside the mine went dead. A burst of machine gun fire raked the entrance, chipping rocks off the boulder over Friar's head.

Using an infrared flashlight, Colonel Hamblin signaled the leader of Team Able to begin the attack. Six Delta members rapidly crawled to the entrance. Using a carbon dioxide fire extinguisher they sprayed the opening, highlighting the beams of red light from laser tripwires crisscrossing the passageway. With the mist still hanging in the air, two Deltas crawled under the laser beams while the remaining members fired a covering volley into the mine. The bullets could be heard ricocheting down the shaft.

The Deltas swiftly located and neutralized the Semtec charges connected to the tripwires. Six members of Team Baker raced forward, leapfrogging Team Able. When they were in position, they fired illumination rounds into the mine's interior, creating shadows that darted along the wet granite walls.

Within minutes, the two Delta Force teams had worked their way deep into the interior of the main shaft. When a Chechen lunged for a detonator wired to a second charge of Semtec, his body was riddled by two, three-round bursts.

"This is Big Boy-two, entrance secure."

"Affirmative," replied Hamblin. "This is Big Boy-one, proceed to link up with SEAL team."

"Affirmative. Advancing now."

Friar and Hamblin zigzagged into the mine, stopping at the first outcropping of rock. Friar was close enough now to use the direction finder to see if he could locate the matchbox transmitter inside Dubov's shirt pocket. He flipped on the switch. A signal came in loud and clear. Using triangulation he pinpointed the source. The Chechen was hiding thirty-five feet down the main shaft, behind a stack of empty shells close to the right wall. In the confusion, the Delta teams must have swept past him.

Friar whispered to Hamblin. "I'll go to the right, you take the left."

"Affirmative."

Friar and Hamblin rushed the stack simultaneously, almost colliding on the other side. There was no one there. Taped to the back of the top shell was a scribbled note and the matchbox.

Friar ripped the note from the shell. It read, "I tried to send us both over the River Styx. Maybe next time."

Colonel Hamblin raced back to the entrance. Stationing two Deltas as guards, he turned to Friar, "He may still be inside the mine."

Hamblin barked into his mike, "This is Big Boy-one, status report."

"*Big Boy-two. One Chechen captured, two killed. One SEAL down and stripped.*"

"Stripped?"

"*Affirmative. His suit is gone.*"

Chapter 22

NOVEMBER 6: CRANBERRY IRON MINE: 6:27P.M.

Friar worked his way over the sharp outcroppings of granite leading from the mine entrance to the collapse pit. In the dark he could barely make out the profile of Joe Don, crouching among the boulders, poised to intercept any Chechens trying to escape. The barrel of his snub-nosed MP5 machine gun poked out from the recesses in the rock.

"Has anyone left the mine?" Friar shouted.

"Only that wounded SEAL," Joe Don replied, keeping his eyes trained on the entrance to the collapse pit. "I offered to get him a medic, but he said he could make it on his own. I told him to take the Hummer."

"How long ago was that?"

"Ten—maybe twelve minutes. Why?" Joe Don could tell something was wrong. Now that he thought back, it was odd the SEAL *wasn't* limping. From what Joe Don could see, it was a gut wound. It was also strange that he still wore his face mask. Joe Don remembered his own reaction in Vietnam when they were gassing the tunnels outside the perimeter wire. The moment the hot shrapnel tore into his shoulder, he had immediately ripped off his face mask.

"It was Dubov," Friar replied, peering down the now empty road. The dust from the Humvee's oversized tires had long since settled back into the hills.

"Coming out!" a voice called from within the collapse pit. It was a SEAL leading a captured Chechen.

Seeing the mine was under control, Friar motioned Joe Don over. "Hustle up to the command center and phone Marcie. Have her notify General Eckel we've secured the mine. I'm going in."

Picking his way over the rocks leading to the narrow entrance of slope two, Friar braced himself, then stepped into the dark, wet tunnel. A borderline claustrophobic, he dreaded having to squeeze between the cold, granite walls. To help keep a sense of panic from paralyzing his legs, he stared straight ahead and concentrated on the warheads. In places, his shoulders struck both sides of the tunnel at the same time, forcing him to turn sideways in order to slide between the rock. Twice he had to crawl on his hands and knees to keep from banging his head on low, overhanging granite. He breathed a sigh of relief when the path widened, and he could see lights and hear the muffled voices of Mark Hastey, Colonel Hamblin, and Jill Margot-Li.

As he approached, Margot-Li was saying, "I suggest we bring in a SuperTransport and fly it out. Maybe take it to an oil rig where we can defuse it."

"I agree," replied Hastey. "Too risky to work on it here."

"What about the other two?" asked Margot-Li.

"Let's airlift them down to Amarillo for processing." At the Department of Energy's Pantex plant in Texas, the two unarmed warheads could be disassembled under laboratory conditions. It would be a simple procedure. First, the electronic brains would be removed, then the physics packages taken to Zone Twelve where the nuclear pits could be separated from their HE wrappings. If there was a slip-up and the high explosives accidentally detonated, the blast-proof walls and dirt roof of the bunker-style gravel gerties would contain the explosion.

Using the newly installed land line, Hastey called the command center, "Bring up the forklifts."

While they were waiting, Friar explained the threat posed by Bastardi's cruise missiles. Even in the dim light, he could see the disbelief etched across their faces. They had risked their lives to capture a hot, 750-kiloton warhead—now they were in danger of being carbonized by the President's National Security Adviser? It didn't make sense.

Hastey shifted uneasily on his feet. In a hoarse voice, he said, "The sooner we get these things out of here, the better. We've got a couple of amtracs standing by. We could load them up and be gone in an hour."

Friar looked down the shaft at the live warhead. Puffs of nitrogen billowed from its side, making the container appear as if it were breathing. He thought of Bastardi perched on top of Grandfather Mountain—waiting. That's exactly what he expected and wanted them to do. Move the warheads into the open where they would be vulnerable to his cruise missiles.

Friar said, "Mark, why don't you leave the nukes where they are for now. What if you were to reconnect the four empty shell halves, load them on the forklifts, then parade them around outside?"

Hastey immediately understood. "Yeah, that oughta work. From a distance, they would look like the real thing." After directing Margot-Li to assemble the NEST team, he said, "While we're at it, we'll start searching for the homing transmitter."

Friar turned to Hamblin, "Colonel, have your men search the area in front of the mine. Let me know if you find anything or anybody out of place." He wasn't sure exactly what or who he was looking for, but he had a hunch there were parts of Bastardi's plan he still hadn't figured out.

The pupils of Friar's eyes quickly adjusted to the dull, red glow of the operational night lights in the command center. Against the far wall, Joe Don sat perched on a stool. Beside him, handcuffed by his left wrist to a support post, was a disheartened Jason Dorn.

Dorn stammered, "Friar, I—I'm sorry for the misunderstanding. Joe Don explained everything."

Friar pulled up a chair, and sat down facing the bewildered agent. "Okay, tell me precisely what your instructions were."

With his free hand, Dorn held out a portable radio transmitter. It was NSA designed, complete with Marconi analog scrambler. "I should've given this to you sooner. It's got a rolling code and low level frequency that can penetrate the blackout."

Friar took the transmitter and tossed it over to Joe Don. "Better check it out."

Using a Phillips screwdriver, Joe Don quickly removed the back cover. Inside, wedged between two nine-volt batteries, was the cruise missile homing device, wired to the antenna.

Dorn blushed, "I didn't know. They told me to use the radio to broadcast an all clear as soon as the warheads were in the open."

"Who told you?"

"Written orders signed by Robert Shaman, the Bureau's Assistant Director in Washington. He's a friend of Mr. Bastardi's. I called the Director's office to double check. The orders were confirmed. I was directed to follow the instructions of Special Agents Sugar and Lightfoot."

Friar grimaced, "Those two goons?"

Dorn glanced meekly at the floor. "I know, I know. It's not standard procedure, but since New York—nothing's the same."

"Sounds like one big cluster-fuck to me," said Joe Don.

Without looking up, Dorn said, "Sugar told me I had to arrest you. I refused—at first. Then, he threatened to arrest *me* for disobeying a direct order." Dorn tugged weakly on his handcuffed wrist. "Don't you see? That would have ruined my career. I decided to go along and help straighten things out when I got here."

In a calm voice, Friar asked, "Where did they tell you to place the homing transmitter?"

Dorn's eyes widened, "I swear, Friar, I didn't know it was a homing transmitter. All Sugar told me to do was stay with the warheads and wait for a helicopter pickup. He insisted I keep you handcuffed to my left arm so you couldn't escape."

Friar snorted at the sheer brashness of Bastardi's plan. Send Dorn on a suicide mission to shackle the troublemaker and keep him beside the uranium and plutonium until the missiles arrived. Reaching over, he unlocked the handcuff. "Jason, I need your help. It's going to be dangerous—"

"Whatever, Friar, just name it."

Looking out the window, across the valley floor, Friar could see the headlights of the forklifts bumping along the gravel road, gingerly carrying the empty containers away from the mine. He smiled. Behind the forklifts, dressed in their canary-yellow containment suits and carrying flashlights, trooped several members of the NEST team.

In turn, they were followed by four Humvees topped with halogen search lights, all focusing their beams on the two reassembled containers. Hastey was staging his own Hollywood spectacular just for Bastardi's benefit.

Friar put his hand on Dorn's shoulder. "Go to the motor pool and get agent Sugar. He's locked in the back of the prisoner transport van. Drive him down to the forklifts and put him on display. Bastardi will think it's me. As soon as you get there, use the transmitter to send the all clear, just like they told you."

Jumping from his chair, and heading for the door at a trot, Dorn called over his shoulder, "You won't regret this."

When Dorn was out of sight, Joe Don walked over, "Hoss, you think you can trust that man, after what he's done?"

"He's a little slow, but once he gets the picture, he's okay." Using binoculars, Friar continued to follow the progress of Hastey's parade. When they were four hundred yards from the mine, the forklift operators stopped and parked the containers on a slight rise. Five minutes later Dorn drove up, walked to the rear of the van and pulled Sugar out.

Friar turned to Joe Don. "Turn the radio on. Any frequency."

"Roger." Joe Don leaned over and flipped the toggle switch. There was the low crackle of static.

Friar watched as Dorn raised the transmitter to his ear. "Let me know when there's a change."

Wham! The door to the command center burst open. Colonel Hamblin and a member of Delta Force lumbered in, dragging a trussed-up figure wearing woodland-camouflage battle fatigues. Roughly forcing the man into a chair, Hamblin handed Friar a sniper's rifle with silencer, outfitted with what appeared to be an oversized telescopic sight.

"Found him hiding behind an outcropping of rock down along Stagger Weed Creek, about 300 meters from the mine. He had a clear line of sight to the containers. Refuses to give us his unit or say why he was there."

Joe Don stepped over and took the 7.62mm M21 sniper's rifle. After examining the Kevlar-graphite stock, the custom trigger mechanism, and the hand-fitted silencer, he concentrated his attention on the oversized sights. Taking the rifle, he signaled Friar to follow him outside.

When they had gone fifty feet, Joe Don said, "Our friend in there's wearing the same outfit as Bastardi's crew on Grandfather Mountain. What's got me really interested is this modified scope." Using a flashlight, he showed the elongated housing to Friar.

Friar studied the scope. "Other than being kinda large, what's so special about it?"

Joe Don ran his hand lovingly over the flat-black metal outer casing, caressing the finely crafted features. "This ain't no ordinary piece of hardware, Hoss. It's a modified AN/PAQ-4 laser aiming light. I thought I recognized it." Joe Don removed the plastic, front lens cap and twisted the dial to On. Pointing the rifle and scope at a granite boulder thirty feet away, he asked, "See that big dot of light?"

Friar squinted into the darkness. "Nope, I don't see a thing."

Joe Don chuckled. "That's 'cause it's infrared. You gotta be wearing your night eyes to see it. It uses a gallium aluminum arsenide laser diode to project the light."

Friar glanced at his watch and turned back towards the command center. "That's interesting Joe Don, but we've gotta get—"

Joe Don grabbed his arm. "Hold on there, Hoss. You ain't catching my drift. I used a device like this down in Colombia a couple of years back to take out a whole series of drug labs."

Friar stopped in his tracks. "What are you telling me?"

"Just this. The rifle part of this gizmo ain't nothing more than an aiming platform for the laser. You paint the target with the infrared, and—"

Friar's heart skipped a beat. The laser was a homing device for the cruise missiles. Bastardi had switched from using a radio transmitter to a laser guidance system. All a sniper had to do was mark the target with the infrared beam and the cruise missiles would lock in on the reflection.

"Let's get moving," Friar yelled, racing back up the hill to the command center. Spotting Colonel Hamblin, he shouted, "Have your men search for more snipers. If you have to, shoot to kill."

Checking the communications terminal, Joe Don called out, "Hey, Hoss. The static's stopped. I can hear the Asheville radio station loud and clear. The blackout is lifted."

Friar flashed an okay. The clock was running, the missiles were on the way. "Colonel, I need to borrow one of your Night Hawks for a short run."

"They're fueled and ready to fly," replied Hamblin, who always kept the engines of his helicopters running during field operations. "Wait and I'll go clear it with the pilot."

"Don't have to. You can call from here."

The rotor blades of the Sikorsky were churning up dust by the time Friar and Joe Don scrambled aboard. Joe Don swung into the navigator's seat while Friar crawled into the cabin. Pulling on a flight helmet and flipping down the boom mike, Friar said, "Patch me through to Hastey."

"*Is that you, Friar?*"

"You bet. Get ready, the missiles are coming. We're going to Grandfather Mountain to try to shortstop them. Kill the lights around the mine entrance and see if the SEALs and Deltas can rig a makeshift blast door."

"*What about our decoys?*"

"Move them a couple hundred yards further away from the mine. Get Dorn and the rest of your people out of there." Friar didn't want the containers moved out of sight. It might tempt a sniper to aim his laser at the mine entrance as the next best available target.

"*You still think there's a danger?*" Hastey asked. "*We've got the homing device and we're going to fly it to the top of Pumpkin Patch Mountain.*"

"They're using a backup laser system. Bastardi's got spotters in the bushes with infrared scopes to guide the missiles in."

"*I can screen the mine with smoke.*"

"Good. Go ahead and put down a layer at the entrance. But keep the containers visible in case any missiles get through."

The Night Hawk leveled off at 200 feet, dipped its nose in a southeasterly direction and slowly moved down the valley between Buck Hill and Big Elk Mountain. Using the aircraft's forward-looking infrared, the pilot navigated the rugged terrain.

Skimming over Chestnut Knob, the helicopter narrowly missed a row of tall, red spruce. Joe Don instinctively jerked his legs up. "*Close,*

Hoss, close," he mumbled into the headset. Using a topo map, he directed the pilot to follow Licklog Road to Big Plumtree Creek, then easterly toward Snakeden Mountain.

"*Clarke, can you hear me?*" boomed a voice over Friar's headset.

"Affirmative," Friar replied. "Please identify."

"*This is General Eckel. I don't have time for codes so I'm broadcasting in the open.*"

"Go ahead, General."

"*Two squadrons of F-104 Starfighters shot down both of that sonofabitch's cruise missiles from Norfolk. But two out of the three from Pope Air Base escaped and are headed your way. Estimated time of arrival in your area is approximately eight minutes. Good luck.*"

Friar set the timer on his watch. Glancing at the map, he estimated it would take three minutes for the Night Hawk to reach Grandfather Mountain. There wouldn't be time to land. Joe Don would have to aim the laser directly from the helicopter.

Rounding Sassafras Knob, the aircraft headed north, up Gragg Prong Creek. In the distance, Friar could see the blinking lights of the US weather station on top of Grandfather Mountain. The surge of power from the twin GE-700 turboshafts rattled his whole body as the pilot gunned the engines for altitude.

With a roar, the helicopter swept up the pitch black side of the mountain, clearing the crest. A rush of exhilaration swept over Friar as he looked down on the dark shape of Bastardi's Range Rover. Beside the vehicle was a table covered with maps and charts. Flashlights winked on and off as figures scurried around, trying to get a fix on the intruder.

"*We need to get within 400 meters of the target for this laser to work,*" Joe Don said.

A high-pitched voice called out over the all-channels frequency, "*Ground to helicopter. This is Mr. Bruce Bastardi, the President's National Security Adviser. You're in restricted airspace. Identify yourself or be shot down.*"

Bringing the Night Hawk around for another pass, the pilot said, "*I can take them out with a couple of Hellfire missiles.*"

"Negative," replied Friar. Explaining to Congress would be easier if Bastardi's own weapons were the source of his destruction.

"*This is your last chance,*" screamed the shrill voice.

Joe Don removed his flight helmet and climbed out of the navigator's seat, back into the cabin with Friar. A blast of cold air rushed in as he slid open the side door facing the parking lot. Removing the lens cover from the laser aiming light, he pointed the sniper's rifle towards the hood of the Range Rover.

Shouting above the whine of the engines, Joe Don said, "Hold her steady, west of the target." When the cruise missiles came crashing in at 500 miles per hour, he didn't want to be in their line of flight.

"*Incoming,*" yelled the pilot.

The radar warning light on the instrument panel flashed a brilliant red. Lurching violently upwards and sideways, the Night Hawk took emergency evasive maneuvers. Joe Don fell backwards against the cabin rigging, almost knocking the rifle from his grip.

Reaching up, the pilot jerked the M130 chaff dispenser, sending streams of reflective, decoying aluminum shooting away from the aircraft. Next, he stabbed his thumb on the button activating the ALQ-144 ultraviolet and infrared jammer.

Whoosh. A thirty-five pound POST Stinger missile shot past the helicopter at mach 1.

"Level off," Joe Don yelled, scrambling back to his feet. The laser would have to be held on the Range Rover until the cruise missiles' guidance systems picked up the reflection and locked on target. The helicopter came back around and leveled off. Ignoring the small arms fire, Joe Don wrapped one arm around three shrouds of netting and steadied his aim.

Peering eastward into the night sky, Friar caught a glimpse of a small cylindrical object racing low across the horizon. A small flame sputtered from its tail. As it cleared the crest of Globe Mountain it disappeared behind Wilson's ridge. Friar's heart sank. The cruise missile was headed towards Yellow Mountain.

"Paint it now Joe Don, *now!*" he yelled.

Joe Don braced himself against the open door and switched on the laser. An infrared dot the size of a quarter reflected off the hood of the Range Rover. Skimming the tree line of Big Rough Knob, the twenty-one foot Tomahawk cruise missile slowed, then gently swung in a ninety degree arc, heading straight towards Grandfather Mountain. Before Friar could utter a sound, the missile climbed up over Big Lost Cove Ridge and plunged its 2,650 pound payload squarely into the Range Rover's engine block.

The shock from the explosion buffeted the helicopter, causing the rivets in the fuselage to groan and creak. "That's from Murphy," Friar schouted into the noise and destruction.

Before the Night Hawk could fully recover, a second cruise missile tapped out its own version of *Götterdämmerung* on the disintegrating remnants of Bastardi's command center.

"That one's for me."

WASHINGTON: THE CAPITOL

It was almost midnight by the time the tires of the JetRanger touched down on the concrete landing pad beside the Capitol. It had taken an extra forty-five minutes to swing by Camp Peary and pick up Marcie, but Friar was in no hurry. For him, the battle was over.

Without fanfare, Colonel Houck escorted them through the swarms of media and TV cameras camped on the Capitol steps, past the stone-faced sentries guarding the building entrance, straight into the offices of Carl Jonas, the newly appointed President of the US. Inside, crowded around a microwave radio receiver were Bryan Warner, General Eckel, and Jonas. Friar was pleased to see Warner was safe.

"Well now, well now—" Jonas said, rushing over. "That was quite a show Mr. Clarke, quite a show."

In an unusual display of affection, Warner embraced Friar and kissed Marcie on both cheeks.

"Good work, Clarke," Eckel boomed. "That dick-head got what he deserved. Blown up by his own goddamned missiles. Ha! How the hell did you pull that off?"

Friar winked, "With a bit of luck and your help, General." Even within this closely knit group, the less said, the better. There were certain to be the obligatory Congressional hearings with full media coverage, inevitable misquotes and accusations. Changing the subject, he asked, "What's happening with North Korea?"

Walking over to the radio, Eckel said, "The reports are coming in now. At 2147 hours, we took out General Hwan's headquarters at Ongjin with a surgical nuclear strike. The guided missile cruiser *Chosin* nailed them with a 200 kiloton Tomahawk. Satellite photos show the base was totally destroyed. We also knocked out the sub-pen at Pipa-got and most of General Ryol's Rodong missiles stationed along the DMZ. It couldn't have gone better."

"It's our guess the threat of invasion is over," Jonas chimed in.

Eckel nodded. Now that the conflict had been ratcheted up to nuclear, North Korea was out of its league. "If they attempt to cross the DMZ, we'll blast a ten mile wide dead-zone from the Yellow Sea to the Sea of Japan." This was the kind of showdown the General liked. The objective was to win and the nuclear arsenal was open. The *Chosin* alone held another ten, nuclear-tipped cruise missiles.

The special operations phone rang. "*General Eckel, Colonel Hugin here. We've just received word that forces loyal to Kim Jong Il have retaken Pyongyang and crushed the revolt. They're asking for a cease-fire. We're waiting for confirmation.*"

"What do the satellites show?" asked Eckel.

"*North Korean troops and equipment pulling back from the DMZ, sir.*"

"Tell General Dornmeyer to cease firing but stay engaged. It may be a ruse. Don't let them pull an end run."

With Warner in tow, Jonas led Friar and Marcie into the next room and closed the door. Lowering his voice, he said, "Mr. Clarke, there are a couple of problems we need to straighten out before the media circus descends."

Sensing a shift in mood, Friar braced himself.

"I've checked with Senator Harness and Secretary of State Hohlt. They both agree we should keep a tight lid on this Bastardi thing."

"Meaning?"

Glancing at Warner for support, Jonas said, "With all that's gone wrong during the past few days, we don't feel it would be in the national interest to undermine the public's confidence any further in the Morehead administration. If word leaked out that his National Security Adviser had tried to—" Shaking his head, he mumbled, "Well, you know what I mean. It just wouldn't look good. Heaven knows, after what's happened to New York, the peoples' faith in

Washington has sunk lower than whale shit."

Studying Friar closely for a reaction, Jonas continued, "The official story's going to be that Bastardi was killed in an accident. Struck down in the line of duty by a missile straying off course. We'll hold a state funeral over at the National Cathedral in a couple of days. A religious pageant will help calm the public. We'll probably have to bury the son of a bitch at Arlington, with full honors. I guess I'll be expected to deliver the eulogy."

Friar arched an eyebrow, "Mr. President, you mentioned a couple of problems?"

Stepping aside, Jonas said, "I'll let Mr. Warner take over from here."

Placing his hand on Friar's shoulder, Warner said, "I explained to Senator Harness, Secretary Hohlt, and President Jonas that there's substantial evidence a nationalist organization in Chechnya was involved. They've decided it's best to focus the blame for New York on the North Korean generals and that militant Islamic splinter group, the Shaheeds."

"And that Russian mob, the Dols syndicate," Jonas added.

"But, the Dols weren't—"

Jonas raised his hand, "Yeah, I know. But we've got to consider the implications."

"We don't want to drag the Russian government into this mess," said Warner.

"I believe there's enough evidence to convince Congress and the public it was the Dols who did it. We've got statements from the FSB and MVD swearing they were the ones who brokered the transaction. Also, we've got those bodies with the tattoos and the testimony of the witnesses at that bar in Manteo."

It was clear to Friar that a political decision had been made and he was being told to keep his mouth shut and stay out of it.

Gazing out the window at the Washington Monument, Jonas said, "In the next few weeks, Congress will start holding hearings. They'll be looking for scapegoats and trying to fix blame. If they found a smoking gun in Grozny, it wouldn't take much to whip up public sentiment demanding nuclear retaliation against Chechnya. Since Moscow still considers Chechnya part of Russia, that's all it would take to start World War III. We don't want Armageddon, Mr. Clarke."

"I understand," Friar said. "The Chechens weren't responsible."

"Good," said Jonas, patting Friar on the back. "We'll say they were working with us to help locate the warheads, just like they claim."

Friar winked at Marcie and took her hand. How Jonas and his spin-meisters doctored events for public consumption was no concern of his. He would leave the dissembling and equivocating to the politicians.

Pleased at Friar's cooperation, Jonas relaxed. "Mr. Clarke, I've been directed by Congress to form an emergency administration. I hope you'll consider acting as my National Security Adviser." Nodding towards Warner, he continued, "You come highly recommended by the new Director of the CIA."

Friar answered without hesitation, "Thanks for the honor, Mr. President, but I'll take a pass."

"Think about it, Friar," Warner pleaded. "You could help restructure the country's entire intelligence system."

"Bryan, you know how I am with committees. Group-think and kissing Congressional butt just isn't my style. I'll leave that battle to you and the President." Friar had no intention of spending the next few years shuffling between the Capitol and White House massaging overblown egos while trying to reinvent the intelligence wheel. As always, it would be the entrenched vested interests pitted against a few honest reformers, and he wasn't confident there were enough Bryan Warners to make a difference. Gently pulling Marcie towards the door, he said, "If we have your permission, Mr. President, we'll head back to Williamsburg. It's getting late."

NOVEMBER 7: WILLIAMSBURG

The rattle of the bedside phone pulled Friar from an all too colorful nightmare. He and Murphy were on top of Grandfather Mountain, chained to the bumper of a woodland-camouflaged Range Rover. Hovering overhead in a bright red helicopter was Bastardi, his skull-like face wrapped in a checkered turban, and fixed in a permanent grin. The thumb of his right hand was poised over the launch button of a cruise missile with a nuclear payload.

Friar lay there for a moment, breathing hard and staring at the pitch black ceiling. The phone rang a second time. Through leaden eyelids he squinted at the digital clock-radio—6:33A.M. Who could be calling at this hour? Before collapsing into bed at the Williamsburg Inn he had left strict instructions with the front desk to block *all* calls. Fumbling for the phone, his hand hit the water glass, spilling cold water into his only pair of shoes.

"Friar. Is that you?" asked the sprightly, familiar voice.

"Dammit, Tovi," Friar whispered, trying not to wake Marcie. "We're trying to get some sleep. Can't it wait?"

"I'm afraid not," came the brisk, pleased reply. *"Fifteen minutes? Here at my place? I'll have the coffee on."*

By the time Friar reached the rear door of the Graves House, the morning sun had begun its journey down the glistening frost on the cedar shingled roof. When he reached for the brass handle, the door popped open, almost knocking him off balance. A workman dressed in gray coveralls trudged past, cradling a Sony TV monitor in his tight-fisted grip.

Friar peered down the hallway leading to the Sandman's suite. "Tovi?"

A head of silver-blond hair poked out the door, "Glad you could make it. Grab some coffee and let's take a stroll."

Friar poured himself a mug of the witch's brew that passed for coffee to the Sandman. It was instant, bitter, and strong, but it was hot. In the background, he could hear directions being shouted to the workers in Hebrew.

After grunting a final set of instructions, Tovi pulled on a wool-lined, corduroy jacket and briskly escorted Friar out the front door. Turning right, they strolled down DOG street towards the old Capitol building.

Without the usual diversionary chatter, the Sandman said, "You've only got two hours left."

"For what?"

The reply came with sledgehammer directness. "To eliminate that Chechen, Dubov."

In the jumble of events, Friar had almost forgotten about Dubov. "Where is he?"

"On a nonstop to Rome. Alitalia flight 004 out of Miami. He's traveling with a Ukrainian passport."

"How do you know it's him?"

"Thumb print identification. It's all that extra security they've added at the airports. We got it off his ticket."

"And, you can, uh—"

"Terminate him?" Tovi asked. "One of the male flight attendants is a Mossad operative. In forty-five minutes, they'll be passing around the hot towels. There's a special one for your Chechen. It's soaked with DMSO and ricin."

Friar closed his eyes as he pictured Dubov reaching for the soothing, scented cloth. The flight attendant would be offering the poisoned towel with a pair of plastic tongs. When Dubov wiped his face and neck, the dimethyl sulfoxide solvent would quickly transport the odorless, tasteless, highly toxic ricin through the pores of his skin, straight into his bloodstream. He would be dead from systemic failure within five minutes. At the autopsy, there would be no trace of poison. The protein based toxin, distilled from the common castor bean *Ricinus communis*, would have broken down and been absorbed by the Chechen's blood. Friar hesitated, "Maybe, we should try to—"

"Kidnap him?" Tovi shook his head. "I don't recommend that. Too difficult. And, if we tried to get the Italians to arrest and detain him—well, you know their system. Within twenty-four hours—*poof*, he's gone." Tovi sipped his coffee, "It's your call."

Friar turned his face into the cold breeze sweeping in from the York River and thought of Dubov and what he had done. By Chechen standards, he was not a terrorist but a good soldier. Now, the war was over and the Chechens and Korean generals had lost. According to Jonas, Dubov and the Chechens were officially our allies. Friar wondered what Dubov would do if the roles were reversed? Probably, snuff him out without a second thought. However, this decision was Friar's and would be made using his rules. To kill Dubov now would be nothing but murder, an execution, plain and simple. Friar recalled how the Chechen had saved Kat's life at Brighton Beach. By doing that, he had saved his own.

"Let him go," Friar said, quietly but firmly.

Tovi cocked his head to the side, "Are you sure? We may not get a second chance. Once he gets to Rome, that's it."

"I'm sure." It wasn't hard to rationalize the decision. Dubov was an important messenger. Alive, he would confirm to the North Korean generals and the Phoenix Committee that all was lost. Dead, they might fatally misjudge the situation.

"Good," Tovi said, continuing his stroll towards the Capitol.

They walked the last few steps to the outer edges of the massive brick wall without saying a word. Checking his watch, Tovi said, "We'd better head back. I've got to return to Tel Aviv and brief the Prime Minister."

They returned to the Graves House in silence. On reaching the front door, Tovi pulled Friar aside. With a sparkle in his eye, he asked, "One more thing. How are you with numerology?"

Friar chuckled softly. One last game. "Numbers and I don't mix."

"I thought not," Tovi replied, his face beaming. Handing Friar a matchbook from the King's Arms Tavern he said, "Here's your lucky number. It's inside the front cover."

Friar flipped open the matchbook. The notation read—SP-407Z002.

"It's the key to General Zakharov's private account at the Banque Luxembourgeoise. That's where he stashed the $2 million Washington paid him while he was in Cairo. Before he boarded that helicopter, he transferred the funds from the Bonhote & Cie in Neuchatel to Luxembourg. It's all untraceable. Just show up with this number and the password, 'Natasha,' and you'll have unlimited access."

Friar tried to protest, "Tovi, I can't take—"

Tovi frowned. "I'm not doing this for you, Friar. It's for me. This money doesn't belong to Washington. It was General Zakharov's. He earned it, but his whole family was wiped out on that helicopter." He shrugged, "If $2 million showed up in my bank account, Mossad would have my head. I need to close the book between us. Consider it a gift from Murphy."

Friar nodded and took the matchbook. It would be an insult to refuse such a generous gesture. He would figure out later what to do with the money. "Tell me, Tovi. What are your plans for the future?"

The Sandman paused and gazed at the mist rising from the pasture in front of Bruton Parish Church. "When I get back, I'm going to work in the vineyards. My twin brother and I own a small winery in Hadera. To me there's nothing that compares to the feeling you get when you come home in the evening from the fields, covered in clean dirt and honest sweat."

"No more smoke and mirrors?"

"No more Mossad, no more politicians, no more angst. This is the end of that part of my life. When I started, I was young—a true believer. Then Lillehammer, Lebanon, the Iran-Iraq war, the *Intifadah.* I woke up one morning and realized that parts of the Israeli experiment had gone terribly wrong and that I was, in some way, accountable."

Friar lowered his head. He had experienced much the same erosion of faith at the CIA.

Standing in the sun, Tovi continued, "When my twin brother and I reached eighteen we came to a fork in the road. He chose to become a doctor, I decided to join the military, then Mossad. We both believed we could contribute, that we would make a difference. Frankly, until this trip, I had concluded that my life's work had been an illusion." He clapped Friar on the back. "Now, I can return home, hold my head up and look my brother in the eye."

NOVEMBER 21: HILLSBOROUGH

It didn't take Friar long after returning home to metamorphose back into the uncomplicated life of a country squire. Slowly, and with patience, Marcie helped him overcome the nightmares. Last night, he dreamed of fly-fishing on the Snake River in Wyoming. Marcie was there, decked out in her rust red neoprene waders and L.L. Bean fishing vest. Joe Don was the guide, complete with slouch hat, wooden dory, and unlimited fish stories.

At 10:30A.M., a director from the LaRoche & Cie in Basel, Switzerland, stopped by for a visit. He needed Friar's signature on a trust document. Murphy's short position in XMI puts had exploded into an inheritance of $956,000, for his daughter Sarah. Murphy would have been pleased.

At noon, while Friar was putting the finishing touches on his Pyle's Massacre lecture series, Marcie handed him a powder blue envelope with a Florida postmark. There was a USA Love stamp in the upper right hand corner. No name appeared on the return address, just the scribbled notation, "Box 313, Longboat Key, FL." He immediately recognized Kat's handwriting. He had tried to contact her several times in the past couple of weeks, but no luck. Dorn had checked with Human Resources and learned she had been discharged from the hospital in Asheville on the morning of the seventh. Her injuries were limited to two broken ribs and a sprained wrist. On her return to Washington she had immediately signed out for extended medical leave, then disappeared. No one knew where.

Friar slipped the single sheet of notepaper from the envelope. There was a photograph of a smiling couple attached by a paper clip.

> Dear Friar,
>
> Sorry I haven't had the common decency to call and check on you. I saw Warner at the Hoover building on the eighth and got a complete rundown on all the action at Grandfather Mountain. It must have been exciting. Please forgive my seeming lack of attention, but I've had to sort through some rather heavy mental clutter. Life doesn't always deal you the cards you want.
>
> Enclosed is a picture of me with an old boyfriend, Marshall Watson. You would like Marshall. He's a civil war buff and still hears the guns. We're trying to glue the pieces of a broken relationship back together. It's been five years, but maybe we've both matured enough to make it work this time.
>
> I've spent most of my leave fishing for red snapper in Sarasota Bay and reflecting. Director Dolenski offered me a two year assignment in Paris, working with Interpol. If things don't work out with Marshall, I think I'll take it.
>
> On my way back to Washington, I want to stop by and say hello. Hope that's okay. Thanks for everything. Give my regards to Marcie.
>
> Love always,
> Kat

Friar handed the note and photograph to Marcie who folded it and slipped it back in the envelope.

Friar heard the throaty roar of the Mazda MX-5 Miata as it pulled into the driveway in front of the house. Taking the short cut through the garage he arrived in time to see Joe Don hopping out of the metallic blue, two-seater. Marcie was already admiring the new toy.

"Sporty ragtop," Friar said, running his fingers along its sleek side.

"It's my new plaything, Hoss," Joe Don replied, winking at Marcie. "Not too expensive and attracts women like bees to honey."

Friar led Joe Don through the garage, out to the patio. Handing him a beer, he said, "I've got one last favor to ask."

"Fine by me. As soon as I take care of whatever it is you want, I'm heading to Jackson Hole."

"Vacation?" asked Marcie.

"Nope. I'm finally going to pitch it in. No more gunslinging for the government. My reflexes aren't what they used to be. Thought I'd put a down payment on this sports car and go West. Maybe rent a raft and hire out as a fishing guide. Wouldn't mind doing some mountain climbing and learning to ski."

"What about that ranch you always wanted?" asked Friar.

"The dream's still there, Hoss," Joe Don replied, sipping his beer. "But, like the song says, 'I owe my soul to the company store.'"

"I've got something for you," Friar said, handing Joe Don the matchbook from the King's Arms Tavern. "A little Cajun lagniappe for your new life."

Joe Don took the matchbook, turned it over, then offered it back. "Thanks, but I gave up puffing those coffin nails ten years ago."

"It's part of that special favor I mentioned," Friar said. With his thumb, he flipped open the matchbook and showed Joe Don the coded number to General Zakharov's $2 million bank account. He explained the proposition. Joe Don was to fly to Luxembourg, gain access to the General's account, transfer $500,000 to Jamila, Mukhtar's widow, then keep the rest for his ranch in the Tetons.

"Damn, Hoss—Marcie. I don't know what to say."

THANKSGIVING DAY

An engraved invitation for Thanksgiving dinner at the White House lay on the kitchen table. President Jonas had even offered to send a helicopter down to Hillsborough to pick them up. There was to be a full day of activities in Washington on this Day of Remembrance for all those killed and wounded in the explosion. A noontime gathering was planned on the Mall with speeches and prayers. A special evening concert was scheduled at Kennedy Center with proceeds to go to aid the survivors. But Friar and Marcie had declined. Turkey Day was going to be a private celebration. There was only one invited guest—the memory of Murphy.

As the evening sun began to fade, Marcie handed Friar a brandy snifter of Courvoisier V.S.O.P. and curled up beside him on the newly upholstered couch. Yesterday they had visited the Cary Forge and purchased a fireback with a fox's head in the center. This would be its first test. A twelve pound turkey, with oyster dressing, and a pumpkin pie waited in the oven. An extra chair was set at the dinner table in honor of Murphy.

The phone rang.

"Don't answer," Friar pleaded.

"It won't take a second. It could be Ellsworth. I hope Eloise isn't having problems."

Covering the receiver, she said, "It's him. Ellsworth." Her eyes lit up as she held the receiver to her ear. Turning to Friar, she whispered, "Twins, a boy and a girl. Eloise is fine."

Marcie handed the phone to Friar. "Ellsworth wants to speak to you."

"*Friar? Eloise and I have a favor to ask.*"

While Friar listened, a broad grin crept across his face. "Marcie and I would be honored."

Hanging up, he settled back down beside Marcie.

"They want us to be godparents. They're naming the twins Marcie and Laurence."

Glossary of Intelligence Acronyms, Titles, and Definitions

Al Mukhabarat: Iraqi General Intelligence.

A'man: *Agaf Mode'In.* Israeli Military intelligence. Responsible for collecting information on enemy forces. Similar the US's DIA and NSA.

BKA: The *Bundeskriminalamt.* Germany's internal police force. Similar to the FBI.

BND: The *Bundesnachrichtendienst.* German foreign intelligence service. Similar to the CIA.

Boomer: US Navy nickname for SSBN nuclear-powered, ballistic missile submarines. The US currently has operational, 18 Ohio-class SSBNs carrying 432 Trident missiles with 3,456 nuclear warheads.

CIA: The Central Intelligence Agency is headquartered in Langley, Virginia, and is charged with conducting foreign intelligence operations for the US. The CIA has no operational authority within the US, no power to arrest and cannot place anyone in the US under surveillance. Of the country's total intelligence budget of $26.6 billion, the CIA gets approximately $3 billion.

Cobbler: A person who produces forged passports.

CTC: The CIA's CounterTerrorism Center is headed by an official from the FBI and is responsible for preventing terrorists acts against America's interests and American nationals on a worldwide basis.

DIA: The US Defense Intelligence Agency. Coordinates intelligence activities for the military services and functions as the intelligence agency for the Secretary of Defense and Joint Chiefs of Staff. Ten billion dollars of the annual intelligence budget goes to the DIA.

DCI: The Director of Central Intelligence. The chief officer of the CIA responsible for co-coordinating all intelligence activities for the US. There are over sixteen different government agencies involved in gathering intelligence. The DCI serves as the chief adviser to the President on intelligence matters.

DO: The Directorate of Operations. The branch of the CIA responsible for the clandestine collection of foreign intelligence, for conducting covert operations and for recruiting and managing the Agency's human intelligence resources(HUMINT). Known within the CIA as the DO it is also called the clandestine service, the spy shop and the black side of the house. The **DDO**, Deputy Director for Operations, heads this section.

Dying from Measles: CIA term for terminating a foreign agent and making it appear that death was from natural causes.

ECHELON: A global system of satellites and listening posts designed and operated by NSA to intercept and filter all communications (e-mail, fax, telephone, radio) for keywords listed in its several dictionaries.

Estikhabarat: Iraq's Military Intelligence.

FSB: The Russian Federal Security Service. The major successor organization to the KGB. Responsible for fighting organized crime, conducting counterintelligence activities and providing security for all branches of the government and armed forces.

Fumigate: To check for listening devices (bugs).

GCHQ: Government Communications Headquarters in Britain.

One of NSA's listening posts in its ECHELON network.

GRU: *Glavnoye Razevedyaltelnoye Upravlenie.* Russia's military intelligence. Similar in operation to the US's DIA.

HATZAV: Hebrew for Quarry. The Open Sources Unit of Arabic speaking agents in Israel's military intelligence (A'man) used to infiltrate hard targets in the Mideast like Iraq, Syria, Iran and Libya.

Honey trap: Use of sex to trap an individual for blackmail purposes.

HUMINT: Intelligence obtained from a human source.

MEGAHUT: A secret NSA and FBI activity specializing in the placement of clandestine listening devices in the homes and businesses of foreign nationals living in the US.

Mossad: *Ha'Mossad Le'Mode'In U'le'Tafkidim Meyuchadim.* The best known of Israels three main intelligence services. Responsible for conducting foreign intelligence operations. Similar to the CIA.

MVD: *Ministerstvo Vnutrennikh Del.* The Russian Interior Ministry. Responsible for maintaining internal security. Similar in operation to the FBI.

NRO: The National Reconnaissance Office. A super-secret agency that builds and operates America's spy satellites. Reports to the Department of Defense and is jointly managed by the CIA. The NRO receives $6 billion of the Country's intelligence budget.

NSA: National Security Agency. The ears of the US intelligence community, responsible for conducting electronic eavesdropping on a world wide basis and for breaking foreign codes. Also known as Big Daddy. Has an annual budget of $4 billion and reports to the Department of Defense and the DCI.

NSC: The National Security Council advises the President on all issues concerning national security. The NSC develops guidelines for conducting the country's foreign intelligence and counterintelligence policies. Permanent members are the President, the Vice President, the Secretary of Defense, the Secretary of

State and the National Security Adviser who heads the NSC. The DCI and the Chairman of the Joint Chiefs of Staff serve in advisory roles.

NSPA: South Korea's National Security Planning Agency. Formerly the KCIA (Korean Central Intelligence Agency). Responsible for conducting foreign intelligence.

Savama: Iranian foreign intelligence service.

SDECE: The *Service de Documentation Extérieure et de Contre-Espionnage*. The French foreign intelligence service.

Shin Bet: *Sherut ha-Bitachon ha-Klali*. Responsible for counterintelligence and internal security in Israel. Similar to the FBI.

Sleeper: An agent placed in a foreign country with orders to blend in with normal life and carry out no espionage until activated by a special event or ordered to do so.

SPETSNAZ: *Chasti Spetsial'nogo Naznacheniya*. Russian special forces trained for sabotage, assassinations, surveillance and kidnappings.

SSBN: Nuclear-powered ballistic missile submarine.

About the Author

John S. Powell was born in 1938 in Burlington, North Carolina, and grew up in Elon College, North Carolina. He is a graduate of the Virginia Military Institute (BA), Tulane University (MBA), and Duke University (JD). During the Vietnam conflict he served two years in the US Army Artillery as the officer responsible for conducting preliminary investigations for all general and special courts-martial and board actions for the Fourth Army area. In his career as a businessman, he was president of Carolina Biological Supply Co., a co-founder and executive vice president of Biomedical Reference Laboratories, and president of Nova Scientific Corporation.

Currently, he lives in Hawfields, North Carolina, where he is at work on his next novel, *The Fourth Horseman*. It is the second in a trilogy on the dangers facing the US from nuclear, biological, and chemical weapons of mass destruction.

WAR BREAKER
JIM DeFELICE

"A book that grabs you hard and won't let go!"
—Den Ing, Bestselling Author of
The Ransom of Black Stealth One

Two nations always on the verge of deadly conflict, Pakistan and India are heading toward a bloody war. And when the fighting begins, Russia and China are certain to enter the battle on opposite sides.

The Pakistanis have a secret weapon courtesy of the CIA: upgraded and modified B-50s. Armed with nuclear warheads, the planes can be launched as war breakers to stem the tide of an otherwise unstoppable invasion.

The CIA has to get the B-50s back. But the only man who can pull off the mission is Michael O'Connell—an embittered operative who was kicked out of the agency for knowing too much about the unsanctioned delivery of the bombers. And if O'Connell fails, nobody can save the world from utter annihilation.

_4043-3 $6.99 US/$7.99 CAN

R. KARL LARGENT

RED WIND

When a military jet goes down off the California coast, killing the Secretary of the Air Force, it is a tragedy. When another jet crashes with the Undersecretary of State on board, it becomes cause for investigation. When a member of the State Department is found shot in the back of the head, his top-secret files missing, it becomes a national crisis. The frantic President turns to Commander T. C. Bogner, the only man he can trust to uncover the mole and pull the country back from the brink before the delicate balance of power is blown away in a red wind.

___4361-0 $5.99 US/$6.99 CAN

Dorchester Publishing Co., Inc.
P.O. Box 6640
Wayne, PA 19087-8640

Please add $1.75 for shipping and handling for the first book and $.50 for each book thereafter. NY, NYC, and PA residents, please add appropriate sales tax. No cash, stamps, or C.O.D.s. All orders shipped within 6 weeks via postal service book rate. Canadian orders require $2.00 extra postage and must be paid in U.S. dollars through a U.S. banking facility.

Name_____
Address_____
City_____State_____Zip_____
I have enclosed $_____ in payment for the checked book(s).
Payment <u>must</u> accompany all orders. ❏ Please send a free catalog.